CHASING THE SU

CHASING THE SUN

———

Natalia Sylvester

NEW HARVEST
HOUGHTON MIFFLIN HARCOURT
BOSTON   NEW YORK
2014

Library of Congress Cataloging-in-Publication Data
Sylvester, Natalia.
Chasing the sun : a novel / Natalia Sylvester.
pages cm
ISBN 978-0-544-26217-1 (hardback)
1. Husband and wife—Fiction. 2. Kidnapping victims—Peru—Lima—Fiction.
3. Terrorists—Peru—Lima—Fiction. 4. Peru—Lima—Fiction. I. Title.
PQ8498.429.Y57C43 2014
863'.7—dc23
2013045021

Printed in the United States of America
DOC 10 9 8 7 6 5 4 3 2 1

To Eric, for insisting

PART ONE

Lima, Peru
1992

1

———

H E I S A L W A Y S thinking of the last words he said to her—*thank you, see you at dinner*, rarely a simple *I love you*—as if they were status reports to a colleague, a quick memo to see where they stand. Andres always speaks last; Marabela has never cared for last words because her power lies in silences. When he calls to say he'll be home late from work, he waits several seconds for her to respond. In that time, he tries to guess what she'll say next, his thoughts teetering from hope to dread, and when she finally speaks, her words land flatly in the middle.

"You promised you'd be home for dinner. We haven't sat down together in weeks. Can't work wait?"

He tries explaining why it can't. Andres is already on his way to meet with the president of one of the largest canned food manufacturers in the country, hoping to convince him to switch the printing of his labels to his company. The meeting is about more than business; it's about setting a good example for his son. "Even if I could reschedule, I've already picked up Ignacio from school. You know how much it means to me that he come along." He wonders if Marabela still remembers (if she even still cares about) the stories Andres used to tell her of how he started shadowing his father when he was only nine. Ignacio is already sixteen, and today will be the first time he sees his father in action. It's time he learned about business, responsibility, and confidence—things he won't absorb sitting in a classroom.

Marabela sighs in that half-resigned way she always does when she knows there's no arguing with him. "Fine, but why does it have to take so long? Just finish early and come home."

"I left a few reports on my desk. I'll need to go back for them after the meeting." His company's projected earnings for the next several months will need to be adjusted if he lands this new client, and the exercise will help demonstrate to his son that hard work adds up. "It shouldn't take more than half an hour."

"It's just that I don't like asking the girls to work late. They have their *novela* at eight. It's the least I can do." Marabela sounds hesitant.

Andres scoffs. It's ridiculous that his household schedule is dictated by a soap opera. Is *La Perricholi* really more important than his and his family's time together? "You ask more of me than you do our own help," he says.

"*Por favor*, Andres." She sounds tired, always so tired, of arguing with him. "Don't make me seem like the unreasonable one when I'm just trying to be fair. They shouldn't have to work late just because you do."

He can sense the conversation going nowhere—just more hurtful words and no solutions. As usual, he's overcome by an urge to take it all back and start over. "What if you pick up the papers for me? Could you do that?"

"Right now? I wasn't even planning on going downtown. I was just on my way out to the pharmacy to get Carla's medication, but your office is completely out of my way."

Picking up medication for the maid is going completely out of the way, too, he thinks. "But I'd be home for dinner. Isn't that what you want?"

The line goes silent as she considers.

"Only if you promise you'll be home for dinner on time."

"I'll do everything I can."

She doesn't agree or disagree. She simply hangs up.

For months now, they've moved past good-byes, but the conversation leaves him feeling unsettled. He thinks about calling her back and saying forget about the papers, but perhaps he's making a big deal out of nothing. Marabela often runs errands downtown. Why should a man have to be so careful with his wife that he can't ask for a simple favor? Would she really leave him over a stack of forgotten papers, over a tie that needs straightening? Lately he has tried not to be needy, but the truth is, a husband has needs. Every marriage does, especially theirs, yet they've gone months, maybe years, ignoring this simple fact.

The driver turns a sharp left and Ignacio gets pushed against his father in the backseat. They can already see the factory up ahead, its perimeter enclosed by a thick sky-blue wall. The security guard at the entrance asks to see their national identification cards, jotting down their names and license plate number before letting them in. As the gate rattles open and they pass under the factory sign, Andres points to the long, stocky building up ahead.

"Manuel Orozco started out canning just *olluco*, precut in strips and chunks," Andres tells his son. He remembers what the packaging looked like years ago, with its red and white stripes and several of the root vegetables in the center, as if someone just wrapped the Peruvian flag around a can and slapped a picture of its contents on the front. The design hasn't changed much, and the printing quality is atrocious. "They do all sorts of fruits and vegetables now. Peaches and peas and *choclo*. But the *olluco* is what they're known for, and they really need a label that'll bring out its bright yellow color to catch people's eyes."

"Is that what they called you for?" Ignacio asks.

He adjusts his tie and grins. "Well, it's what I called them for."

They're greeted by Manuel and his wife at the front steps of the factory, then led through its heart, full of rows and rows of workers in hairnets and aprons filling an endless line of naked cans with food. A small conference room upstairs overlooks the machines and assembly lines, and once inside, Andres can see his son is mesmerized by their perpetual motion. He hands him his suitcase, hoping to redirect his attention to the client.

"Never too young to start learning to be more like his father, right?" Manuel says.

"Hopefully not too much. I suspect he's gotten most of his best qualities from his mother."

Manuel's wife laughs and asks how Marabela is doing. The women know each other from a mutual acquaintance, and when the couples last ran into each other at a dinner party, Andres seized the opportunity to set up this meeting. From the way Lara spoke about the company, he could tell Manuel's wife was the one he'd need to convince, despite her lack of an official job title. He'd hoped Marabela would come with him today to help make a good impression.

"She's so sorry she couldn't make it. She was really looking forward to seeing you again," he says.

"Tell her I said hello and that I hope she feels better," Lara says.

The meeting goes better than expected. Manuel tells them all about the history of his company and what they're planning on doing next. He asks if Andres's company has ever handled this quantity of canned food products, and Andres jokes that lucky for Manuel, they've had plenty of practice on smaller competitors. He has Ignacio hand out printing samples from his suitcase, and the vibrant colors and glossy finish seem to impress them. Lara runs her fingers over the paper, which pleases Andres immensely. It's meant to be touched to be fully appreciated; his ink never runs.

On their way back to the car Andres bets his son that Manuel will call soon, possibly in the next week or two, but Ignacio seems more interested in Lara.

"Why did she think Mom doesn't feel well?"

"It's nothing. It was just easier to tell them that than say your mother wasn't interested in coming."

"Why would she come?"

He sighs, unsure how to explain the less concrete aspects of business. "Sometimes those kinds of things help the situation along. A man like Manuel wants to know the person he's about to do business with shares his values. That he's a good husband, a family guy. That he can be trusted."

Marabela tired of this early on in his career, saying it made her feel like she was showing off their marriage for profit. Andres hopes his son won't ask for further explanation, but he only nods and says, "Can't really blame her for not being interested."

❖ ❖ ❖

The ride home is slow and quiet. It is nearly seven and traffic still swells with people anxious to get home, to be one day closer to the weekend. Unwilling to let their tardiness or his son's attitude ruin his good mood, Andres settles comfortably into the backseat of his Town Car, feet stretched before him so that his pants reveal his thin black socks. Ignacio sits by the opposite window, staring at passing cars and street vendors. Through the tint of the glass, the city looks grayer than usual, the horizon obscured by thick smog ahead of them and tall, jagged desert dunes covered in makeshift homes to the north and east of them. The only sound in the car is the low hum of the engine and the whistle of the air conditioner. Ignacio won't stop fidgeting with the buttons on the door, and when they come to a red light, his fingers get away from him and the glass starts lowering.

"*Señor, tres paquetes de galletas por un sol.*" A young boy, no older than thirteen, pokes his head through the window. Ignacio shakes his head and starts rolling up the window when his father leans forward to stop him.

"Not so fast. You already got his hopes up. Don't toy with the kid." He leans over and shouts, "*¡Dos paquetes!* Go ahead, pay him." He nudges his son.

"But you're the one who—" With a stern look from his father, Ignacio stops protesting and fishes two coins out of his pocket. He takes the packets of cookies from the boy and hands one to his father. As they drive away, Ignacio turns the cookies over in his hands, the thin plastic crinkling between his fingers. The wafers and their creamy centers are all crumbled together, having been carried up and down the street in the little boy's bag for God knows how many months. "You know I'm not going to eat these," Ignacio says.

"That's not the point. He's a hardworking boy. You have to give him credit for jumping at an opportunity," Andres says. He tries to ignore how his son shakes his head, looking at his father out of the corner of his eye. Andres slaps him softly on the elbow and smiles. "Next time you need air . . ." He raises his voice so the driver can hear him: "Jorge! The sunroof."

Without turning to look at him, Jorge pushes the sunroof button, and Andres lights a cigarette, exhaling toward the sky. They leave the busy intersection behind.

He leans forward to the center console between the front seats, which used to be an armrest until Andres had a car phone installed. He is the first of his friends to have one, and lately he's been using it at every opportunity; it comes in handy when he needs to fill an awkward silence or ignore troubling thoughts of work and home. Now, he picks up the heavy brick from its base and dials the house, anxious to know if Marabela ever passed by the office. Yes, Consuelo says, Marabela left soon after they spoke but has yet to return.

By Andres's calculations, Marabela should have been home at least an hour ago from running his errand. Strange—Marabela is never late. She has a schedule written out for each day. Her charity meetings, lunches with friends, salon appointments, and even the kids' activities are planned to the minute.

He puts out his barely smoked cigarette and quickly lights another to keep his hands occupied.

Of course, Marabela was late once before.

Four months ago, he came home to find the kids eating alone, their faces blank and bewildered when he'd asked after their mother's whereabouts. He remembers how quiet the house felt that night, as if maybe she was just sleeping, or sick, instead of gone. The kids read in their bedrooms all evening and brushed their teeth with the bathroom door closed, and, after Marabela still hadn't come home in time to tuck Cynthia in and kiss Ignacio good night, they poked their heads into Andres's bedroom and announced they were going to bed. He couldn't tell if they were checking on him or checking for her.

Hours later, Marabela finally called to say that she was leaving him. It was a short conversation, with little explanation and too many silences in which she was probably trying to spare his feelings. At least she was being truthful, he'd thought back then. He, on the other hand, had been burdened with lies, making up stories to the kids about her visiting a friend who'd suddenly fallen very ill. If Marabela hadn't changed her mind and come home after three long days, he might've had to tell Cynthia and Ignacio the truth. He's not sure he could've forgiven her then.

Andres wonders if he'll get a similar call tonight, if they haven't moved past this at all but only masked it, poorly, for the past several months. As they turn off Avenida Benavides into his neighborhood, he's flooded with uncertainty. He imagines the kids' muted movements as they get ready for school, the maids' extra care setting dishes on the table and refilling his drink. If Marabela's left him again, he's not sure he can bear another day of convincing everyone she'll be back, least of all himself.

❖ ❖ ❖

When they finally reach the house, Andres holds his breath as the wooden-paneled door to his driveway tilts open to reveal an empty spot where Marabela's car is typically parked. They wait for the door to close behind them before Jorge gets out and opens the passenger doors. Like most upper-class homes in Lima, the Jimenezes' residence, even their front yard and garage, is completely enclosed by cement walls and locked gates that clear the first floor of the home. Anyone passing along the sidewalk would have to call in through an intercom by the Spanish-style door, and only then, once they're buzzed in and have walked down the thin terra-cotta-tiled pathway that winds through the yard, lush with palms, fruit trees, and scattered orchids, would they reach the entrance to his home.

They walk through the garage into the kitchen, and he instructs Ignacio to take his suitcase up to his office. Andres walks through the dining room, where the table's already been set, and into the living room, where Carla is dusting off the wooden furniture, half expecting to find Marabela reading a book or sifting through shopping bags. Ignacio disappears up the stairs while Andres checks the mail piled up next to the telephone in the corner of the room. There's just enough sunlight left to illuminate the dust Carla's sweeping off the cabinets, coffee table, and chest of drawers. It seems that's all the poor girl ever does, but the furniture, covered almost entirely in hand-carved swirls of leaves, flowers, and berries, creates the most intricate pockets of dust Andres has ever seen.

He clears his throat and Carla stops what she's doing to say hello and ask if he needs anything. Something strong, he thinks.

"Just have Consuelo bring me a pisco sour upstairs," he says. Consuelo, who's been working with them for nearly two decades, knows exactly how Andres likes his pisco sours, and Andres isn't sure he feels comfortable asking her fifteen-year-old niece to make him a cocktail.

He trudges up to his office, throwing his tie over the back of his chair, but otherwise doesn't know what to do when he gets there. Andres had anticipated having the papers he'd asked Marabela to pick up, and without them there isn't much he can do but wait. Already his son has locked himself in his room, having scampered off quietly like a rabbit.

He phones his secretary, Edith, to ask if Marabela came by the office.

"No, sir, and I haven't left my desk, even for a minute." Edith, a middle-aged divorcée who has never had a job before this one, is always eager to please.

"Thank you, Edith. I'm sorry you had to stay so late, please go ahead and get home. In fact, come in a couple of hours late tomorrow. I'll take care of the papers in the morning."

Now he is truly worried. Ever since Marabela left, he has been careful not to ask anything of her. Not for a section of the paper in the morning. Not for a kiss good night in the evening. He has not even asked her for a quick glance to check if he's shaved his sideburns evenly. If she's left him again, he'll have no one to blame but himself. He should have stuck to what was working for them — ask nothing and expect no problems in return.

What strikes him now is that he should've seen this coming a second time. He searches their bedroom for signs he might have missed, but her belongings are intact. The luggage is filled with smaller baggage and winter clothes as usual. Her toothbrush and French soaps are still in their place by the sink, always within reach of her right hand and then her left. Her favorite purses are arranged by color and size along the top shelf of the closet. Perhaps most shocking of all, her camera is still tucked among her bras and underwear in the top drawer, in a padded case so large it makes the clothes look like an afterthought.

Still, the presence of Marabela's possessions does nothing to convince him she hasn't left. The first year Andres's company started seeing a profit, he'd tried to indulge her with jewelry and expensive European shoes, but she'd insisted that she could give it all up in a day; it mattered only that the family was together, healthy, and happy. Now he's afraid only half that statement remains true.

Consuelo walks by quietly with his drink, on her way to his office, then takes a few steps back toward the bedroom. She hesitates to come in.

"What is it?" Andres says.

"Your drink. And dinner is ready. Would you prefer I wait—"

"No, no. I'm sure the kids are hungry by now. Marabela will probably just have coffee and toast later this evening." He pictures his wife dipping her folded slice of buttered bread into her coffee with milk, as she'd done when they were newlyweds. Back then, they'd had a smaller kitchen and sat so close together her elbows would gently jab at him if she so much as stirred her drink. These days, he mostly watches Marabela from across the head of the table, marveling at how she holds the cup as if it weighs nothing at all. Watches how she wipes both corners of her mouth every few bites, how she turns away on the rare occasion that she accidentally slurps.

Andres glances at the clock and feels his nerves settling into his stomach. He hears the soft clatter of serving dishes downstairs as Carla brings the food to the table, and he pictures Marabela's chair empty, like a jacket missing a button.

❖ ❖ ❖

"How was school today?" he asks when he reaches the table. The kids are still in their uniforms—Cynthia in a navy-blue jumper with a white collared shirt underneath, and Ignacio in gray pants and a black sweater that displays his school emblem on the right side of his chest—so it seems like an appropriate way to start a dinner conversation. It's the kind of question he's heard Marabela ask for years, except she usually adds specifics like teachers' names and homework assignments.

Both the kids have a mouthful of food, and they know better than to answer immediately. Andres begins answering his own question to fill the silence. "Well, Ignacio and I had a great meeting with a new client today. He finally got a chance to see what it is your father does," he tells Cynthia. He sometimes wonders if she understands his work at all, or if at eight, she's still too young to grasp it. "Maybe next time you can come with me. I was just about your age when I started visiting my father at work."

"Will I get a sticker?"

"A sticker?"

"Mom says you make stickers," Cynthia says, pointing to the Inca Kola on the table, its yellow-and-blue label wrapping neatly around the bottle of golden soda.

Andres laughs. "It's something like that. 'Stickers' is a very simple way of putting it, though. Son, why don't you explain to your sister what we do? Tell her about today?"

Ignacio chews his food slowly, staring at his father with a hint of suspicion in his eyes. "He's going to create labels for cans of peas and corn, or something like that. Mom can explain more to you later. Where is she?" he says, turning to his father at the last question.

"She had too much to take care of downtown. She called to say she'll be home late tonight."

Ignacio sits up. "But before ten, right?"

"Of course," Andres says, his mind already racing for an excuse in case Marabela doesn't come home before curfew. It's the third time in six years that the government has implemented a citywide curfew, but Andres knows his son was too young to remember the first two. This time, Ignacio's well aware. He's taken an interest in scanning the papers for any mentions of the Shining Path, pounding his fists and mumbling obscenities under his breath when he learns of another car bomb or fire that the guerrilla group has unleashed. When President Fujimori declared no traffic would be allowed between ten at night and five in the morning, Ignacio yelled, "*¡Bien hecho!*" at the television screen, as if he'd just seen his favorite soccer team score a goal. Andres isn't so worried about the bombs—they're always happening to other people, to police stations in slums and near government buildings—as he is about knowing his son will stay up, head glued to the window, waiting for Marabela's car to show. The boy is more like his father than he'd care to admit.

"You know how busy she gets when these charity galas are approaching. She mentioned that if she didn't get done in time, she'd stay overnight at one of the committee members' houses so they can work through the night." He tries to make it sound like this is the most normal thing in the world, like Marabela's done this countless times before. His son looks like he's about to protest until Andres glances at Cynthia and back in a silent plea.

"Yeah, that makes sense," Ignacio says, with a light sarcasm only Andres catches.

DAY 2

In the morning, Andres's instinct is to roll onto Marabela's side of the bed and search for her with his touch. Even after months of sleeping in separate beds, it's a habit he hasn't been able to break in this half-awake, half-asleep state. She has always been the anchor that bridged his dreams with his reality, and it's not until he opens his eyes and focuses on the folded bed against the wall, still untouched since yesterday, that he gets reacquainted with the present. *She didn't even call*, he thinks, though he's unsure it would've made this less painful. Again, he tries to think of what he'll say to the children when they ask for their mother. Again, he imagines they won't believe him.

Andres tries to get up, but he's not ready to face this day. He has little hope left, but even a shred of optimism is enough in this quiet moment before the day starts, so he lies still and listens for the sound of Marabela's car in the driveway. Minutes pass in silence, and he resigns himself to the nagging suspicion that he's always had her on borrowed time. The clues seem obvious in retrospect. From the beginning, he and Marabela have never even looked like they belonged together. She is all contrasts: her lips soft but her cheekbones sharp, her height negligible but her presence difficult to ignore. Lush, dark lashes frame her gaze, giving it a piercing intensity.

When Andres looks at his children, all he sees is Marabela. Her features are so prominent they easily overpower his. Hints of Andres—Cynthia's upper lip, thin as a crescent moon; Ignacio's freckles, only noticeable in the summer—are quickly glazed over as strangers swoon over Cynthia's long, curly lashes and Ignacio's heavy brows. They pause to look at Marabela, as if comparing a photo to its painting, and then they look blankly at Andres, shocked to learn that he is their father.

Andres knows he is not an unattractive man; enough women have tried (and failed) over the years to prove it to him. But there are moments when he wonders if his appeal is only an illusion created by wealth and confidence. Maybe he's like a piece of furniture that arrives in boxes, nothing but unimpressive parts until someone puts them together. So he tries to look put-together. A buttoned-up suit hides his growing waist. A well-groomed beard traces his chin and connects to his mustache, hiding the round edges along his neck.

There has never been any hiding from Marabela. He may have been younger and his body much firmer when they first met at the university, but even then Andres knew she saw through him—every insecurity and white lie to impress her exposed. He often joked that he had to become a better man to win her over, something he used to thank her for regularly. But it's been years since either of them cracked a smile at this quip, and Marabela always says that things are funniest when they have hints of truth to them. Perhaps, he thinks, they're also saddest when that truth has faded.

Enough putting off the inevitable. Andres puts on a robe and heads to the kitchen. As he walks down the stairs, he decides he'll catch up on work from home today. He'll wait by the phone like a teenager, and when Marabela calls, he'll promise to do it right this time, go anywhere she wants on vacation, just the two of them. He can already hear the pleading in his voice, useless. If Marabela's made up her mind, there's little he can do to change it.

"Where's Mami?" Cynthia asks the instant she sees him. Andres merely kisses her on the forehead and squeezes Ignacio's shoulder with one hand. His son leans over a bowl of cereal, reading a paperback sci-fi novel that is so thick he can't hold it up with one hand. He mumbles good morning without even looking up.

"How did you sleep?" Andres asks them. If he's to pretend this is just another morning, better to keep the conversation small and meaningless.

Ignacio shrugs.

"Where's Mami?" Cynthia asks again.

"Your mother had an early appointment this morning. She told me to give you a kiss and make sure you ate all your breakfast."

This seems to satisfy Cynthia, who crams such a large spoonful of cereal into her mouth that pieces of it fall out as she chews.

"*Cuidado*," Andres says. He wipes her mouth, once on each corner of her lips, and tells her to take smaller bites. When she barely scoops two flakes and a raisin onto her spoon, Andres can't help but laugh. This must be what Marabela meant when she told him, not even three nights ago, that Cynthia's been taking things to a literal extreme as of late.

"I told her to stop running in the house and she practically slowed to a crawl," Marabela said. She was rubbing lotion onto her arms and elbows, part of her evening ritual before bed. "If I tell her not to slouch, she stands up rigid as a board. The other day I reminded her it's rude to sing at the dinner table, and the next day I caught her telling the same thing to her dolls as she served them tea. It's the weirdest kind of quiet rebellion. I can't tell if she's mocking me or trying to make me happy."

"From the smile on your face, I'm guessing it's the latter," Andres said.

"She gets smarter and sharper every day."

They'd left it at that and gone to bed their separate ways, Andres trying hard not to move much in the foldout bed (the temporary bed, as he called it) because it made too much noise. Despite their new living arrangement, the one thing that hasn't changed is their late-night talks about the children, and for that, Andres is grateful. He can't imagine feeling like much of a father without Marabela.

"What's so funny?" Cynthia says now, her spoon still hanging in the air.

"Nothing. It's just . . . you'll never finish your breakfast like that."

"*Apúrate*, Cynthi," Ignacio says. "We'll be late for school. Jorge's already outside."

Andres leans back in his chair and looks through the kitchen. The door to the garage is open and through it he can see Jorge wiping the car down and checking the tire pressure, keeping busy as he waits for them.

"Brush your teeth first," Andres says, trying his best to channel Marabela's authority and confidence without sounding like he's imitating her. For a moment he swears he sees a flicker of confusion on Cynthia's face, as if he were speaking to her in a foreign language, but then Ignacio taps her on the back and she seems to understand again. They return a few minutes later to kiss him good-bye, their breath cold with mint. The kiss is a habit, a quick check for keys on one's way out the door, but Andres finds himself already missing them as they go.

After breakfast and back at his desk, he notices the mail has arrived early. At the very top of the pile is a blank envelope with only his first name, written in all capital letters on the back. It looks odd and bare next to the other envelopes that have been stamped and scribbled on. He opens it, thinking it's probably a note from a neighbor complaining about noise or wanting to borrow some tools, but before he's even unfolded the thin sheet of paper, he recognizes Marabela's penmanship. The hurried curves of the letters are hers, but there is something different about them, as if she wrote them on a train or a bus. The note is short:

> *Querido* Andres,
> I'm being held by three men who say they'll keep me safe as long as you cooperate. They say that means no cops and no media. They say they'll call when they're ready to talk to you. Kiss our children for me and tell them not to worry. Keep me in your thoughts as I will be keeping you in mine.
> Marabela

Andres reads the letter three, four times, until he realizes that what he sees in her handwriting is fear, the trembling of the pen. He reads it until he can hear her whispering the words in his mind, in that same low voice she used when she told him they'd become the most disappointing versions of themselves, just before her last disappearance. He memorizes the letter. Suddenly, he wishes Marabela had actually left him instead of being taken.

He thinks again of the last words he said to her, turned into a promise.

I'll do everything I can.

❖ ❖ ❖

Andres has never dreaded something and hoped for it at the same time. If the phone rings, and Marabela really has been kidnapped, he will know that this is real. In this moment when he has never felt more incapable and ill equipped, her life depends entirely on his careful handling of this phone call.

All he knows is that he has to do something. He rushes to the stairs and calls down to the maids. There is some commotion in the kitchen, followed by the sound of their heels tapping against the living room tile as they rush to the bottom of the stairs. Consuelo wipes her hands on a washcloth that hangs by her waist as she looks up at him. Carla looks to Consuelo.

"No one answers the phone today. Under any circumstances. I'll pick it up when it rings, got it?"

They both nod. Curiosity spreads across their faces but they don't dare ask for an explanation.

"Please bring me a drink in my office," Andres says to Consuelo. She nods but keeps her eyes on him just a second too long, as if trying to search his face for clues about Marabela. He's not comfortable enough with Consuelo to try communicating without words, with some silent language she and Marabela seem to share. Ever since Andres can remember, the maids were thought of as employees, not confidantes. Since Marabela never grew up with maids, she was ignorant to the natural hierarchy; they share an odd bond, developed over the seventeen years Consuelo's worked for them, that he's never fully understood. Only Marabela can tell the girls the food is too salty in one breath and ask about their families in the next. He knows she collects Ignacio's old clothes in plastic bags and sends them home with Consuelo for her grandson. She also listens to their stories—how Consuelo once owned a restaurant with her husband, how the great earthquake of 1970 shook its walls so hard they were left with nothing but dust—and retells them to Andres at night. Marabela is the one who asks how the maids are doing and genuinely wants to know. He catches himself envying them sometimes, how they can hold her full attention, even if just for a few seconds, while he'll often talk to her for minutes and wonder if she's listening. Two days ago, when Carla mentioned she had a toothache, Marabela ordered her medication from the pharmacy. She was supposed to pick it up after her quick stop at Andres's office yesterday. She was planning on taking Carla to the dentist next week.

He keeps himself busy reading reports and contracts from work, rereading entire paragraphs three or four times because his mind is elsewhere. An hour goes by before the phone rings. Until now,

Andres has never noticed how the sound disrupts the entire house. His fingers rest on the receiver while he lets it ring once more, and it sends a vibration up his arm. When he speaks, the words scrape against his throat.

"Hello," he says, with an exaggerated authority in his voice.

"You were expecting us by now, Señor Jimenez. This is a good start." The man sounds chipper, excited even; his words are light but Andres can feel their meaning in his chest. Gripping the phone, he brings his forehead to the edge of the desk, staring at the ground like a drunkard who's trying to keep balanced.

"I want to talk to her," Andres says.

"I didn't call to take your demands."

"You can't possibly expect to make any if you can't prove that she's safe," Andres says, each word confirming a new fear as he speaks. He's surprised by the steadiness of his voice, his ability to reason with such madness. Perhaps the panic will come later, but for now he tries to stay strong.

The man chuckles, and then it sounds like he dropped the phone or like he stuck it in a dryer, because for seconds all Andres hears is rustling and faraway voices. He hears a faint noise, a weak version of Marabela's voice. It takes a moment for the recognition to sink in.

"Andres?" Marabela repeats his name for the third time.

"*Mi amor.*" He hasn't called her that in years. "How are you?" A stupid question, followed by silence. "Are you hurt?"

"No." He can hear her tears, her fear, her anger, and her desperation all mixed into that one word. Her breath trembles through the phone line like static. "I'm not, but—"

"That's enough," the man says. He is so confident and calm. "This can all be very simple if you want it to be. That means keep quiet. No police or media. We'll need your cooperation, Señor Jimenez, *¿entiendes?*"

"*Está bien,*" he says, though things are far from fine. "What do you want?"

The man speaks slowly and clearly to get his point across. He is not even done saying the number before Andres knows it is more than he has, more than he can imagine making in a year, especially in American dollars.

"You must have the wrong impression of me. I don't have a million dollars. I don't have that kind of money."

"Then you better start thinking of ways to get it."

"There must be another way," Andres says, tossing numbers around in his head. He tries to think of one that is close and in the least bit feasible, but it's only a fraction of what the man is asking. He tries to tell the man that the sum is impossible, but the line has already gone dead, monotone. The last thing the man said is that he'll call again.

It takes Andres a few moments to hang up the phone, and when he does he hears the clink of an ice cube in a glass. Consuelo stands at the threshold of his office, her foot in the air as she tries to step backward. He signals for her to come in with one hand, watches as she lowers the glass and sets it on a coaster, how the gold liquid trembles in her grasp.

"How long were you there?" he asks.

"Long enough," she says, her voice heavy.

He shakes his head. "It all happened so damn fast," he says. "Well, now you know that this time, she hasn't disappeared by choice." He waits for her to answer, though he knows she won't say anything; Consuelo, who consoles the family with her quiet servitude, has always been discreet. Even now, she makes her face unreadable and pretends not to know what he's talking about—not about the kidnapping, not about Marabela's leaving. Andres catches a quiver in Consuelo's throat before she lowers her head, and he remembers how busy she kept the last time Marabela left, rushing at every chance to go to the market, never serving dinner even a minute late, as if she were incapable of holding still. He'd thought she'd work herself to exhaustion.

"I haven't told the kids yet. I need this news to never leave our house. Carla and Jorge will figure it out soon enough so I'll be rely-ing on you to make sure it doesn't get out."

"Of course. I'll talk to them today. If there's anything else you need . . ."

"Just shut the door, please."

Outside, the sounds of horns scream back and forth at one an-other as cars try to squeeze through spaces that aren't big enough. Even in his neighborhood, there's no escaping the city noise; quiet is relative. Andres takes a sip of his drink and looks out the window. These are the same streets where he used to play soccer as a child, where he let his dog run free without a leash. Now everyone seems to be rushing by, looking straight ahead at no one in particular and everyone in the same glance.

He stares at the desk, at papers from work scattered across the surface, some folded, others highlighted, others perfectly clean. Had they really been so important? He pictures them scattered across the city, like a path of bread crumbs to wherever Marabela is being kept. The coldness of the glass in his hand turns his fingertips numb, and the condensation has made it so slippery that it simply falls from his grip. The sound of the glass shattering startles him, but only enough to make his neck tense and his nose constrict with one quick breath. His hand still hangs in the air, holding a glass that isn't there.

The captors will bark orders, but they are still waiting on him to make the next move. He tries thinking of it like this to muster up some courage, yet he knows he is the only one with everything to lose. They have Marabela. Worst of all, this is a game to them, prac-tically the country's unofficial sport.

The kidnappings started slowly. He first started hearing about them from colleagues who'd had too many drinks at the end of a long workday. Leaning too close to him with whisky warming their breath, they'd whisper about executives sending their children over-seas, how the men were making plans to follow suit. They'd shake their heads at the scratched-up Toyotas friends had bought in exchange for their beautiful Mercedes-Benzes, trying to conceal their wealth. It was all gossip back then, talk of terrible things that had happened to other people. Andres and his friends were not like the executives being targeted, the ones who ran international, billion-dollar corporations. Their companies were successful within limits, within their country, where they'd foolishly felt safe until recently.

Now the kidnappings have trickled down, from the extremely to the moderately wealthy—to the family of a prominent surgeon and the owner of the telephone company, to the heir of the country's smallest airline. Each family that pays adds to the collective bank that aspiring criminals feel entitled to.

Andres feels utterly sideswiped. Ever since the Shining Path guerrillas and the Túpac Amaru Revolutionary Movement began inching closer to the capital, all his attention has been misplaced in their terror, in car bombs detonated outside the government palace, in arson, in assassination attempts on the president of the electoral council. Both groups claim their war is on the government, but every day they attack more civilians. What Andres can't understand is how quickly civil unrest can become normal, how instead of finding a solution, people adapt. Things have been this way for so long that the general unease has become common. It is like a stovetop left unattended—everyone feels the heat but they've chosen to protect themselves rather than get close enough to shut it off. Why risk getting burned?

In the nearly two years since the new president was elected, his promises of a crackdown on terrorism have turned as brittle as cracking paint. Tired from sleepless nights in the darkness of terrorists' blackouts, Lima's spirit has aged decades in only twenty months; the city is now the perfect incubator for a thriving business in kidnapping. While the majority of the country's police force focuses on controlling armed uprisings and terrorism, smaller crimes are overlooked. Who has time to track down a missing mother of two when terrorist groups are detonating bombs at multiple embassies and gunning down the former minister of defense?

Except the kidnappings are not small crimes at all. They are deep and personal, they target everyone, even random men riding in taxis who get held up and taken to an ATM, where they are forced to empty out their accounts and, with it, their hopes for a new home or health care for a sick child. Each class has its own set of criminals. Some plan months ahead of time for millions in ransom, others inject a lifetime of fear into their victims with a quick hour that yields a couple grand.

Andres suspects this won't be the case with Marabela. He wants to think that her captors are just desperate fools acting on impulse, that perhaps they won't be able to carry through on their threat to bleed him dry of every penny he has and then some. He tries to hang on to this thought, even as the sound of the captor's voice echoes in his mind.

✦ ✦ ✦

He spends the rest of the day inundated by numbers, calculating his life's worth. Calls to the bank and his financial managers leave him feeling less than hopeful, and he becomes so focused on retracing each conversation and leafing through accounts that he barely notices when the kids come home from school. Andres catches Cynthia scampering through the hall out of the corner of his eye. Soon an unusual sense of calm settles over the house, and he can hear the faint whispers of his daughter, playing in her bedroom. She likes to give tea parties or make-believe lectures to her dolls; or so Marabela has told him. He gets up and walks toward her room, until he is standing at the doorway unnoticed, watching her tiny fingers wrap themselves around miniature plastic teacups, the ones with rose petals similar to the set Marabela inherited from her great-grandmother. She is at an age where she still enjoys dolls but feels she should be growing out of them. She stops when she notices she has an audience in her father and sets the dolls down on the floor behind her bed, trying to push them out of sight. Again, he recognizes the look of confusion on her face. Is he really such an odd sight in their home?

Andres smiles but says nothing. He can feel the back of his neck tingling and the tears coming to his eyes. Cynthia lives in another world, in a roomful of pink wooden furniture and white eyelet curtains, her only worries her doll's high fever and whether she can stay up late. He wants to keep her there, protected, but when he steps inside, he feels like he has carried all his horrors into the room with him.

"Hi, sweetie. That looks like fun."

Cynthia smiles and shrugs her shoulders.

"Will you pour me some?" he says, pointing at a cup.

She does, careful not to spill any of the invisible fluid on his clothes. For minutes they sip on their tea, not saying a word. Andres tries to stay engaged, but his mind is somewhere else, wondering if he should tell his daughter that her mother is in danger, wondering if she is even capable of processing the concept, half hoping she isn't. His eyes wander across her room to the pink-and-green plastic purse hanging from her doorknob.

"What's in there?" he asks, grasping at any chance to change the subject of his thoughts.

Cynthia stands up and walks to the door, her feet pointing slightly inward with each step. The purse is no larger than a book, but she opens it with two hands and glances inside as if looking through a window.

"My hairbrush and some gum," she says matter-of-factly.

Andres sets his cup down, but it teeters on the round rim of the plate and tips over. Cynthia drops her purse to grab a napkin and clean up the invisible mess on the table.

"What's wrong, Papi?"

He looks down at her brown eyes, her long lashes that curl back far enough to touch her eyelids. "Nothing, sweetie."

⬧ ⬧ ⬧

It used to be that when Andres couldn't fall asleep, he'd ask Marabela to tell him a story. They'd lie in bed—him with his back to her, her fingernails tracing loops and lines against his skin—while she told him about the village she'd visited when she was eighteen, the summer before they'd met. She'd gone along with eight other volunteers, traveling by bus, by train, then foot, uphill, to help build a school for eighty-five families. She spent only three months there but the experience stayed with her. Marabela's stories always went back to that summer; her memory of it was like a bottomless valley, full of life, and she'd always find a fresh experience to pluck out of it. The characters and the narrative changed while their stories of hardship did not. As he began to fall asleep, Andres tried to hold on to her words and the pictures they conjured, and images of the little town would slip into his dreams.

She told him, "The little girl was only four but she'd wake up every day at dawn and walk three miles uphill to collect water for her family. By the time she'd walk back, the sun would be shining so bright her cheeks would turn pink. She was so proud of how strong she was."

Andres listened and dreamed about the little girl. Each time she tried to wipe the tears from her cheeks or the sweat from her forehead, she'd scrape herself and cry even more. One day she nearly lost her grip on her bucket as she pulled it out of the well, and in a panic she reached too far for it and fell inside. The warm water soothed her, softening her limbs and nurturing her cracked body until she began growing into a tree.

The next night, Marabela would start again. "On our way into town the first thing I remember seeing was a woman peeing on the side of the dirt road. It took me a few seconds to realize what she was doing because she was wearing a long black skirt with all these layers underneath, and as she bunched them up close to her chest they created a bundle of reds and blues and oranges. I was so distracted, trying to figure out what it was. I thought it was a baby at first, then maybe flowers, and then I realized she was squatting and there was a thin stream of urine slivering down the road. I tried not to stare at her but when she caught my eye she didn't seem to mind. I guess it was nothing out of the ordinary for her. Not really meant to be a private moment."

Andres listened and dreamed Marabela was a bouquet of flowers: her long legs, the stems; the features of her face, each a rose. He was trying to keep them bundled together as he walked down a dirt road, but the wind kept pushing against him, peeling petals off Marabela's face so she now had only one eyebrow and was missing a patch of hair. She started to cry tears that dripped one by one like pearls sprinkled on the bouquet, until he noticed a black ribbon on the side of the road and managed to tie her stems together. The next second he had the bouquet in his hands and was giving it to her. She untied the ribbon and wrapped it in a bow around her hair, and then she took the bouquet in both hands, brought it to her face to breathe in its scent, and tossed it into the air, letting the wind carry it onto the road behind them as it turned into a river.

Tonight Andres can't sleep, so he tries to think of the school she built, tries to piece it together from the snippets of stories he can scrape off the bottom of his memories. It was a tiny house, she'd said, with a roof that slanted slightly to the east so that rain could slide off. They'd painted it white and its main door blue. Inside, the floors were just cement. To the back of the room there was a sink that was actually a large basin because there were no pipes, and next to that a door split horizontally across the middle so it could double as a window. If you stepped outside, you were only ten yards from the outhouse. They had placed the windows in the front of the room closer to the ground, for the younger children, and as you made your way to the back they grew taller and taller.

Andres lies in bed with his eyes forced shut, trying so hard to fall asleep that his eyelids start to feel sticky, like they're sucking on his dry eyes. He pictures the little house on top of a hill and he pictures a younger Marabela walking through the door, but when she steps inside it's empty and dark and someone neither one of them can see is pushing her to the center of the room, to the floor that they could never afford to tile. The cement is scraping her knees and palms as she tries to crawl away. In an instant Andres realizes he's dreaming but he's not yet in control enough to make it stop. Marabela's hands are leaving bloody prints as she moves across the floor and tries grasping at the walls, and the hand marks start multiplying in every color all around the room, looking almost like children's artwork except that the hands are too large, the fingers too desperate, to be innocent. Andres wants to do something but he isn't even in the room. He has never been there and he doesn't know where it is or how to get there, and the more he tries to recall if Marabela ever gave him directions the farther away he feels. He watches the little house pull away from him and tries not to leave her there, alone and trapped, but the house is getting smaller and her screams are getting louder, and though he can't figure out where either of them is, all he knows is that their pain is being held somewhere deep inside of them in the same exact place.

2

DAY 3

IN THE LAST two days Ignacio has asked about his mother only twice, a fact that both relieves and astounds Andres. He doesn't want to keep telling the same lie, and he senses that likewise, Ignacio doesn't want to hear it. Now that she's been gone more than a day he's had to change his story. Marabela is on a last-minute search for a venue for a weekend fund-raiser she's planning with friends. They're dead set on having the event near Huancayo, which is about a five-hour drive to the east.

"You know how particular the ladies are," Andres says. "Who knows how long it will take to find a place equally rustic and luxurious."

His son rolls his eyes and laughs in the way men do when they complain about women. If he only knew what Andres was really thinking, maybe they could share this burden. Instead Andres is completely alone, and, worse, he must keep his pain invisible. Every time the phone rings he must walk calmly to the next room to answer it, wishing his senses could run ahead of his body. He must pretend this is just a casual conversation, that his wife's life isn't hanging on the other line.

None of this is made easier by the fact that it's the weekend; all this extra time only slows its passing. He tries to read the paper in the family room upstairs, sprawled across the couch while Cynthia doodles outside all the lines in her coloring book. Andres rarely spends time here. He's used to seeing Marabela's wet photographs hanging from a line of twine by the windows, but it seems she didn't get around to starting a new roll this week. The couch cushions do little to support his back, and he readjusts his position every few minutes to keep it from aching. Through the wall of Ignacio's bedroom, he can hear the staccato bass of his music. This, combined with the sound of the newspaper pages turning, of Cynthia's crayons scratching against paper, feels like it could drive him mad, make him scream out for silence.

He turns onto his side and reaches over to Cynthia's book. "What are you coloring?"

She sets down her crayon and cups her chin in her hand, sighing as she shakes her head at the pictures. He knows he's seen this gesture before, in Marabela when she reads the morning paper. "Nothing. It's stupid."

"That's not true. Here, let me see." When he flips through the book, he can see she took great care with the first few drawings. There are sweeping mountain landscapes with two-toned skies, colors Cynthia blended with her fingers so that the marks of the crayons are barely visible. He flips to a picture of a woman weaving a rug, the threads stretched tight over a wooden loom. Rather than fill the rug in with one color, Cynthia created a bold, multicolored symmetrical pattern. "These are beautiful," Andres says, flipping back to the current page, which is full of dark, sharp scratches that seem to have no purpose other than to wear the crayon out. "You didn't like this one?"

"It's not that, it's just . . . I'm bored with it."

"Why don't you get some blank paper and draw something new? It can be whatever you want."

She seems to like this idea and runs to her room to get a pad of paper. "Here," she says, ripping a sheet out for Andres. "You pick a word and we'll both draw whatever it makes us think of. Then we'll see what we came up with. But you can't peek, okay?"

He smiles, amused. "Where did you come up with this?"

"It's a game Mami and I play sometimes. Pick a word. Point to a random one in the paper."

He does, but all he keeps landing on are words like *conspiracy* and *threats* and *capture*. The paper is flipped to a story about a group of army officers arrested for allegedly plotting to assassinate the president. He quickly scans it and finally lands on a word he's satisfied with.

"Leaders."

With her elbow over her paper, Cynthia begins drawing, hurriedly switching colors as she sets one crayon down for another. Andres takes an orange one but doesn't know where to start. He's never been able to draw more than stick figures, so he makes a line across his paper, where he sets a rectangular box with a microphone coming out of it. Two men stand behind it, and all in front of them, a crowd of round heads looks up to them, listening.

"Time's up! Let me see." Cynthia trades sheets with him and giggles when she sees his attempt. "We didn't think of the same thing at all," she says.

And it's true. Hers is a simple depiction of four people, fully outlined with clothes and hair. There's a girl with brown hair, who's the smallest, and a boy just slightly bigger than her, who looks like a mini version of the man who stands in front of them. He holds hands with a woman in a red dress and long black hair parted in the middle. They're all in a line, and it's clear they're going somewhere, that the two children are following.

"It's not very good. I did it in, like, twenty seconds," she says.

"I love it. Can I keep it?"

She nods. Andres lies back on the couch and Cynthia sits on the floor against it, her pad flipped to a new page. He rubs her head and feels the softness of her hair. He prays that God will help him be strong for her, but all he feels is his chest tightening and the air thinning around him.

The only thing that saves him is the sound of Consuelo's voice. He startles, not realizing she'd come upstairs.

"The food's ready," she says. It's early afternoon and for the first time in his life Andres finds himself starving but lacking an appetite—his body isn't in agreement with his mind. On weekends, they eat the largest meal of the day around lunchtime instead of waiting till the evening when he's home from work, so he tries to prepare himself for the sight of all the food he's not ready to stomach. Consuelo and Carla have prepared the kids' favorite dish, *tallarines verdes.* It's spaghetti with a basil, spinach, and garlic sauce, a Peruvian-style pesto, served with a thin fried steak. Not exactly a choice for the most refined palates, Andres thinks, but at least it's good comfort food for the kids.

Cynthia gives a quiet gasp when she sees her plate. In a loud whisper she thanks Consuelo, who's already halfway to the kitchen. She uses both hands to twirl the spaghetti onto her fork, then nods approvingly as she chews.

"*¿Te gusta?*" Andres asks.

"Mm-hmm. Don't you like it?"

He looks down at his untouched plate and picks up his fork, but before he can use it the phone rings. Andres sets it down and stands up slowly. "Go ahead and eat without me. I'll be right back." The nearest phone is in the kitchen, where Carla and Consuelo have just sat down to eat next to the refrigerator on a table set for two. Andres reaches over them and nods at Consuelo, who instantly gets the hint. The women exit the kitchen, leaving their half-eaten meal behind.

"Hello?"

"Andres? How are you?"

Any trepidation he felt over speaking to the kidnappers is quickly replaced by a different kind of panic. Andres recognizes the voice right away, but he can't place the name. She's a friend of Marabela's, the vice president of a charity she does work for, and the two frequently meet to discuss the next gala's theme and colors. The woman is calling because Marabela has missed two meetings, something she's never done before.

"It's just so unlike her not to call," the woman says, as if this is a great tragedy. "Is she okay? We're all so worried."

Although he'd known this moment would come, Andres struggles to come up with a plausible answer. He's already used Marabela's charity work to manufacture a lie, but he's not prepared to face her friends from the organization with another. The line fills with static and the sound of the woman's breathing.

"She had to go to Miami. It was a family emergency," Andres says. He adds that extra detail hoping she won't ask more questions out of respect.

"Family emergency? I didn't know Marabela had family in the States."

"She doesn't, but it's complicated."

"Oh. *Qué pena*. Do you know when she'll be back?"

"No."

She waits for him to elaborate and the silence makes him uneasy. "Do you want to leave a message?" he adds.

"Tell her the gala's on the sixteenth of the month, and that we need her," she says. "It's important."

The desperation in her voice agitates him. Andres knows she let it slip out purposely, just to drive home her point. He resents her assumption that he's not taking this seriously. *If you only knew*, he thinks, but he politely agrees to deliver the message and hangs up before she can say good-bye.

Almost instantly, the phone rings again.

"*Carajo*," he whispers, yanking the phone off its receiver. "Hello."

It only takes a small moment of rustling silence for him to realize it's not Marabela's friend. Andres feels his stomach sink and, with it, his voice.

"Hello?" he says again. This time the word feels more like a question.

"Señor Jimenez. Have you given more thought to our offer?"

Today the man on the line sounds younger. Andres wonders how many men are involved in his wife's kidnapping, which of them is in charge of doing what. If one is tasked with feeding her and keeping an eye on her, he hopes it's this one. This one sounds weak; maybe Marabela can manipulate him.

"I told you, I'll do everything I can, but even half a million will be impossible. There's no way I can come up with that much money."

"Nobody wants this to take that long."

"Of course not," Andres says in his calmest voice, hoping he can set an example for both men to be reasonable.

"Well, how much do you have right now, then, in dollars?"

The question takes Andres by surprise. Is the man mocking him? Like in any negotiation, he's uncomfortable stating a number first. Name a price that's too high, and the offer's off the table. Name a price too low and risk no one doing business with you. But as much as he tries, Andres can't think of this as a business deal. What kind of man puts a price on his wife's life?

"Are you there, Señor Jimenez? If this is too difficult for you we can just wait. Weeks, months, it's your call."

"No, no. I can bring one hundred thousand. Where?"

"Make it one-fifty and we won't drag this out."

"That's more than my life's savings."

"Do you want this done soon or not?"

"Yes, but this is the best I can do right now." He does the numbers in his head, imagines all those years he's been saving for an emergency he thought would never come. A new roof, a bad year at

the company . . . those were the kind of crises he was capable of fore-
seeing.

The line goes silent. He can tell the man has cupped the receiver
because all he hears are muffled voices.

"One-twenty, with jewelry, watches, any valuables added in. We'll
count it all once we have it and send her home."

"Okay. Yes." He exhales into the phone, unaware that he was holding his breath in the first place. "Where do I go and when?"

They give him a location and a time, mere hours from now.

"That's not possible. I need to get the money out of the bank and
they won't be open until Monday."

The man spits out half-words, trying to argue though they both
know this problem is out of their control. "Fine. *Lunes, pues*." He
gives him a new time and reminds him to come alone. "She won't be
released unless everything has gone as planned. Better make sure it
all goes smoothly, Señor Jimenez. Don't go cheap on the extras," the
man says, and when he hangs up, Andres swears he can hear several
giggles.

He stands by the phone a few more seconds, half expecting it to
ring again. When it doesn't, he lets out a breath so deep it feels like
he's been holding it in for days. *This will all be over soon*, he thinks, but
the relief he expected never comes. The phone call has left him feeling unsettled. How can he trust the promises of a criminal? There
will be time to thank God and the heavens when Marabela is home
safe. For now, there is plenty of hell left to survive.

DAY 5

On Monday morning, Andres raids his and Marabela's jewelry boxes
and stuffs the inside pockets of his jacket with his grandfather's gold
watch, Marabela's tennis bracelet and necklace, and a pair of solitaire
diamond earrings that dangle from a thin gold chain. Out of habit,

he locks the now near-empty metal jewelry boxes and tucks them back in their hiding places beneath the bathroom sink. The remaining jewelry is mostly worthless, simple handcrafted silver pieces that cost no more than fifteen soles at any *artesanal*. The weight of his jacket pockets tell him he's giving the captors enough, but Andres knows this isn't true. He's holding back and he's ashamed for even considering it. Quickly, like a criminal, Andres reopens the bathroom cabinets and pulls out Marabela's jewelry once again. This is the most painful item of all, a pair of earrings that once belonged to his mother. They're antiques, two brilliant sapphires atop a small string of river pearls. As he holds them up and they dance between his unsteady fingers, he mourns never seeing them frame Marabela's delicate face and long neck. His mother gave Andres the earrings years before he met Marabela, always intending for them to go to the woman he would marry. After he and Marabela eloped, Lorena had warned Andres that he was giving them to the wrong person. What would his mother say now, seeing him give the earrings to a criminal?

Andres tucks them away with the other jewels and accepts the fact that his mother was right about one thing: Marabela will never wear them.

❖ ❖ ❖

There are so many questions he forgot to ask and now it's too late. Andres has already left his house and given Jorge the day off, and any chance he has of talking to the kidnappers vanished the moment he hung up the phone. Andres backs out of the driveway just as Jorge makes his exit. His driveway is a long, thin stretch of pavement not wide enough for two cars to park side by side. He wishes he had taken the time last night, like Jorge normally does, to back the car into the garage so he wouldn't have to drive in reverse. His nerves are making it difficult for him to navigate while looking over his shoulder.

Anyone following the swerving path of his vehicle might question Andres's sobriety.

He reaches the street just as Jorge turns the corner and disappears, and for a moment Andres wishes he could run after him and switch places. For the past fifteen years, his driver has shown up every weekday morning at six thirty. He is never late. He parks his rusty Volkswagen Beetle on the side of the street and walks up to the front door, where Consuelo hands him the keys to Andres's latest toy—first the red BMW coupe, then the black '81 Mercedes-Benz, and, most recently, the navy-blue Jaguar—so he can warm up the engine and get the air-conditioning going. Sometimes, depending on the order in which Andres's and Marabela's cars are parked, Jorge takes both keys and rearranges the cars himself, as if they were a pair of cards he doesn't want to lose track of while they get shuffled into a deck.

All those years of driving Andres from place to place, tagging along for the minutiae of his daily life, and Jorge has never once compared his shaky, unreliable engine with Andres's flawless ride. Today Andres wonders what kind of life Jorge is going home to. He has never given much thought to what happens to Jorge after he drives away every evening in his own car. His driver is a private man, and over the years they've gotten to know each other only in the quiet bubble of his vehicle, where they talk about things like traffic and politics on the radio. He's learned about Jorge's character from how he drives; he's the kind of man who keeps calm when someone cuts him off, who doesn't hesitate to swerve into a faster lane if he sees a fleeting opportunity. If Jorge could take the wheel today, and Andres his usual spot in the backseat, he would say nothing about Andres going to the bank and emptying out an entire savings account, but his silence would be a welcome comfort, a reminder that Andres is not completely alone.

Now Andres feel disoriented behind the wheel of his own car. His palms start sweating on the steering wheel as he looks for a parking spot close to the bank, which isn't even open for business yet. Andres would rather wait and be the first one through the door than risk being late for the drop. In the meantime, he goes through the mental list in his mind to make sure everything is in place. He wrote the address on two different sheets of paper, one tucked into his shirt, the other in his pant pockets. His bag is a canvas duffel with a zipper and no pockets, just as the kidnappers specified. It is dark and inconspicuous—no loud logos or distinctive characteristics. His deadline is three hours from now, more than enough time to get out of his car and run to his destination if traffic or some act of God tries to interfere. All that's left is the money.

The bank manager greets him as he always does, insisting that he personally attend to Andres's needs instead of the tellers behind the glass. He is one of their biggest customers, after all, which unfortunately warrants some extra attention that Andres would rather do without today. Juan Miguel asks how the family is doing, how work is going, and what Andres thinks about the bombs that went off at a nearby Japanese restaurant a few days back. Andres resists the urge to say he hasn't been keeping up with the news unless it's kidnapping related, and even if he had an opinion he has no time to chat about it.

"Terrible, just terrible. This needs to stop soon," he says as he takes a seat at Juan Miguel's desk.

"What they need are more of those bomb-sniffing dogs. At least animals can't be bought, unless the terrorists start investing in dog treats." Juan Miguel giggles to himself as he waits for his computer to turn on. "So, what can I do for you?"

Finally, they can get this over with. Still, the words do not come easily. "I need to withdraw the funds in my savings account. In American dollars."

"Of course," Juan Miguel says. He has the kind of relaxed look that people give when they're trying hard not to react. He doesn't blink, doesn't smile or frown. It's like the muscles in his face have gone numb. When he asks to see Andres's identification, he makes a crack about rules and process, then quickly excuses himself. Ten minutes later he comes back with a green leather bag and slides it over the desk to Andres, keeping his eyes on his own paperwork at all times. Andres recognizes this act well; it's the same kind of nonchalance he feigns when waiting for a client to respond to his company's fees and proposals. Everyone tries to be casual about money because any other reaction would reveal we can be bought, we all have a price.

Andres inspects the bag's contents. It has such a large zipper it practically crunches open. Inside are twelve stacks, each maybe one inch thick, of hundred-dollar bills and a paper envelope with a couple thousand and change.

"*¿Eso es todo?*" Andres asks.

"You're welcome to count it if you'd like. I can offer you a more private space if you'd be more comfortable."

"No, it's not that. I just didn't expect so much to amount to so little, that's all."

"Yes, well, they're American." Another joke only he laughs at. Andres has been less than amused by the continually shrinking value of his country's currency.

The two men sign a few papers and wish each other a good day. With every step out of the bank, Andres picks up his pace. He's never felt desperation quite like this. He feels vulnerable and exposed, like he's just stepped out of the shower and been hit by cold air. He imagines that every person walking by knows what he's up to (how could they possibly not, when it consumes him so completely?), and he both longs for and fears the recognition. Then there's the guilt, the violation. He's taken out this money but it's really being stolen from him with his own hands.

He feels guilty for even considering the size of the payout. All that matters is Marabela. Despite their recent ups and downs, she is worth the world and more.

❖ ❖ ❖

Everything about this feels wrong, and it gets worse when he gets to the drop point. Only now does Andres realize why the drop-off address sounded familiar: it's a bus stop a couple of blocks from Ignacio's school, both a statement and a threat: *We have our eyes on you. We know where your family works and plays.*

His instructions are simple, the transaction quick enough that he won't have time to look around and catch a glimpse of his enemy. Andres has been instructed to wait at the stop and leave the bag tucked under the bench in a way that it isn't obvious to passersby. When the next bus arrives, he will get on it and stay for the next hour before getting off and boarding another bus that will take him back to his car.

"Don't try turning around to get a look. We'll know if you do," they said.

He assumes there will be someone on the bus, keeping an eye on him to make sure he doesn't try to be a hero or call the police.

It's actually a sunny day, a rarity this time of year, when the sky is so gray everything loses its shadows. Once he's parked, he takes off his sweater and lets it hang over his forearm in an effort to cover up the bag of cash. The wind pushes against the back of his neck, almost as if it's hurrying him along but reassuring him at the same time. It's the only part of his body that feels slightly at peace, and as he approaches the bus stop he tries to tap into that small sense of calm, willing it to multiply and cover him like a warm blanket.

There is a small group of people gathered at the stop, making it easy for him to blend in. They don't all stand under the cement threshold because the air is too cold under its shadow. An older woman leans against the streetlight, encircled by half a dozen or so plastic bags of groceries, surrounding her like a fort. A few feet away, a teenager sits on the curb, bobbing his head to his Walkman. Andres tries to hear everything, see everything, but the more alert he is, the more everything blurs together. All around him cars beep their horns in short, persistent bursts as they try to pass one another. The sounds multiply until they're practically in harmony, a cacophony of desperation. Andres squeezes onto the edge of the bench and rests his back against a picture of a man selling insurance. The faded ads that paper the shelter are covered in spray paint, tired messages of consumerism smothered with protests against capitalism.

He places Marabela's ransom beneath his legs, looking around and half expecting to catch somebody watching him. But to the others he is only a small piece of the scenery, lost in the background. Moving slowly so as not to call any attention to himself, he pushes the bag under the bench with his legs. He pretends to tie his shoe, letting his sweater fall to the floor and just over the duffel.

"Are you okay?" The man next to him puts a shaky hand on his shoulder, looking concerned.

Andres has stared just a few seconds too long at the package, his head almost tucked between his knees. His hands still clutch at the bag, unwilling to listen to his mind and let its contents go. He must look sick, like he's having a hard time breathing, and then he realizes he is.

"I just got a little dizzy. Thank you." He sits up straight and inches his thigh away from the man's leg. Andres has never had the need or desire to ride the city buses. They remind him of unsafe canisters stuffed with the wrong kind of people; under the circumstances he has more reason than ever to mistrust everyone he encounters.

The bus arrives, billowing out a gasp of warm exhaust. The old man places his hand on Andres's shoulder and pushes down on him for balance as he stands up.

"Take care," he tells him.

The crowd lines up, waiting for the bus to empty, but Andres remains seated. He wants to be the last to board so no one can tell him he forgot it, or, worse, take it for themselves. By the time Andres gets on, the driver is impatient. He steers the bus away from the curb while Andres walks down the aisle, swaying side to side, his gaze forced on the ground. He knows if he looks up he'll be tempted to look out the window to see if his bag is still there.

Andres is used to tasks being marked with some sort of punctuation at the end: a handshake, a door closing at the end of the day, a signature on a contract. He has only climbed aboard a bus. After the excruciating buildup to this moment, it feels like he hasn't done enough.

Over the course of several blocks, Andres's adrenaline calms and his mind starts to clear. He watches as ice-cream vendors push their carts on yellow tricycles down the narrow sidewalks along the street. When the traffic stops at a red light, the rush of pedestrians squeezing through the small spaces between cars makes him cringe. No one pays attention to the street signs indicating when and where to cross; everyone, whether on foot or in cars, seems to push one another along. He scrutinizes each passing face until he can no longer keep track of them. The thought that any one of them could penetrate his life so deeply makes his stomach harden.

Finally his hour passes. Andres gets off the bus on a tree-lined residential street corner where several houses have been partially converted to nail salons and general stores. He crosses the street and boards the bus heading in the opposite direction. When he arrives back at his starting point, Andres checks the bottom of the bench. The bag is gone, but its absence brings no relief. He makes his way back to his car, feeling less in control than he's ever felt in his life. It's almost two thirty, and across the street children are running out from behind the green gates of his son's school.

Andres decides he'll wait by the school entrance for Ignacio; he could use the company on his drive home. At first, Ignacio walks right past, then takes a step back.

"What happened? Is everything okay?"

"Everything's fine. I didn't go in to work today, so I gave Jorge the day off. I thought I'd come by to pick you up."

"Okay," Ignacio says, unconvinced. They get into the car and Andres makes his way toward Cynthia's school, just a few miles away. "What's really going on, Dad? You're acting weird."

"I'm sorry that you find my wanting to spend time with you strange," Andres says, trying to make his voice light and cheerful.

"Whatever. Take this right," Ignacio says.

"What? Why?"

"If you keep going straight you'll hit too much traffic and keep Cynthia waiting. This is the back road Jorge takes."

Andres follows his son's directions until they reach the back of Cynthia's school. It's a tall three-story building with the classroom windows tilted open. As they pull up to the front, Andres lets the car idle. Girls of all ages rush out the main door, pouring onto the street in clusters. The smallest ones walk hand in hand with an older sister, or, like Cynthia, stay behind the main gate waiting for their ride.

He scans the crowd for his daughter, but before Andres can spot her, Ignacio climbs out of the car. "I'll go get her," he says.

In the brief moment that the car door opens and closes, Andres hears the sounds of the students' voices come and go. Their collective rejoicing at being free from school hits him like a quick breeze and leaves him cold. He can barely breathe as he sees his children walk toward the car, Ignacio with his arm wrapped around Cynthia's shoulders. When he smiles at them he can feel his lips start to quiver.

"*Hola, mi linda*. Surprised to see me?" he manages to say.

Cynthia giggles as she squirms out of her backpack and nods. "Did Jorge go to get Mom?"

Andres can feel her eyes on him through the rearview mirror. "I gave Jorge the day off and your mother is still on her trip. She's very busy but she misses you both and sends you kisses. She'll be home soon," he adds. He remembers the last lines she wrote to him in her letter and struggles to keep his focus on the road, his mind flooded with images of what she must be going through in this moment. To not even know whether she's alive or dead, safe or hurting . . . the possibilities are almost suffocating. And yet, here they are, driving home from school on a Monday afternoon—Ignacio scanning the radio stations and Cynthia staring out the window—as if . . . nothing. He has never felt so lonely.

"Can you believe this?" Ignacio says. He turns up the volume and a reporter's voice comes through quick and urgent, like a sportscaster watching his soccer team lose. An explosion has gone off at the Jorge Chávez International Airport, wounding five airline workers. Andres switches the station, taking the next left to avoid the panic-induced traffic near the airport.

When they get home, he tells Ignacio to go inside and help the maids set up lunch.

"Aren't you hungry?" Ignacio asks.

Andres shakes his head and decides that he will not eat until Marabela comes home. He sits on the trunk of his car with the garage door open and watches the driveway. Watches how the sun makes it appear moist, how the shadows glide across its surface as the sun sets, how the streets start to clear with the coming night, and then finally, when the sky turns black and moonless, Andres waits for the motion-activated driveway light to flicker on. It never does.

DAY 6

It's now dawn. Somehow, the sun has crawled halfway across the sky and still Marabela has not arrived with it. Everyone else sleeps, but Andres is so hungry his stomach seems to wrap itself around his spine. He pictures what Marabela must look like now. Is she even with them? Did they release her in a location so remote that she'll never find her way home? Did they toss her aside, thinking she's worthless to them now that they have their money?

He has done everything they asked and they have given him nothing in return. The last fourteen hours have been a silent torture. He tries not to think of all the things he should've done—asked to speak with her first, at the very least; arranged to pick her up from wherever they left her—because he needs to be strong for her despite his feelings of incompetence. He envies Ignacio's and Cynthia's dreams, their minds capable of thoughts that have nothing to do with death, blood, or broken promises.

Andres paces the house quietly and steps into the bathroom in the upstairs hallway to splash cold water on his face. When he comes out and turns off the light behind him, his eyes struggle to adapt, so he feels his way through the darkness, running his fingertips against the wall. Its rough texture gives way to a sleek, cold door barely the width of a linen closet. Instinctively, he pulls his hand away, but then he leans into it, his ear pressed against the metal surface, wishing he could hear Marabela's breath or gentle movements on the other side. The darkroom is Marabela's sanctuary, but to Andres it is another place she goes where he cannot follow. Even now, when her absence is a bleeding wound, he feels like an intruder at the threshold of her space.

He returns downstairs and sits on the living room couch that faces the front door. If Marabela were here, she'd yell at him to put on a shirt, remind him that the white couches are for guests only, and ask why hasn't he shaved in four days. Doesn't he realize he looks like a bum?

This normally irritates him, but today he would welcome her harshest words. He would welcome her coming home just so she could pack her bags and leave him of her own free will. Anything but the thought of Marabela being held somewhere, thinking that he is not coming to her rescue.

As sunlight enters the house, Andres stares out the window at the potted plants on the patio. Last night they were soaked in raindrops; this morning, the moisture has gone. He searches for any bit of hope inside of him, but it, too, has evaporated. Tears come in its place, bringing a reluctant sleep. When he wakes it is because someone is shaking his shoulder, gently coaxing him to get off the fancy couches.

"These are for guests," a sweet voice says.

When he opens his eyes, Andres sees a small figure just inches from his face.

"Off the couch," Cynthia says, in her very best impersonation of her mother.

❖ ❖ ❖

Because everything good in his life has come when he least expected it, Andres tries his best not to think of Marabela. There have been so many things worth waiting for—the acceptance letter from college, the day he met Marabela, even Ignacio's birth, which came six long days after his due date. None of these things happened in the exact moment when he was wishing for them. Still, Andres can't will his attention to focus on anything but his wife, and for this reason he wonders if he's already doomed.

He drags his feet across the living room and starts climbing the stairs, stubbing his toe on a step his body should have memorized by now. As the pain settles in, it spreads from his foot all the way up his thigh, and he has to lean against the wall for balance. He focuses on his breathing so as not to yell.

The phone rings in the exact moment he can barely move.

He pushes the pain aside, separates his mind from his body to get to the phone. When he hears the voice on the other end he barks out, "Where is she?!"

The man mumbles a question Andres doesn't understand, his tone confused.

"I've been waiting almost twenty-four hours. You said she'd be home by now. What did you do to her?"

"She's right here, Señor Jimenez. She's not going anywhere until we've agreed on the proper payment."

"What? What are you talking about? I gave you everything I have. I did everything you asked. I even went back after the hour passed and I know you took the money because it wasn't there any-more. I did my part, now it's time for you to do yours."

"*Para de joder.* How could we have picked up the ransom when we haven't even agreed on an amount?"

"You said one-twenty and all the jewelry in the house. Haven't you counted it yet? It's more than you wanted. The watch alone was my great-grandfather's."

"I would never agree to such a stupid deal. You should know bet-ter than that," the man says, an undercurrent of laughter in his voice. "Whoever you spoke with wasn't me. I go a couple of days without calling and already you've allowed yourself to be taken by some im-postor hoping to make quick cash."

It can't be true. Andres would rather believe that this man is cruel enough to go back on his word and pretend that they're starting from nothing than believe he was had by a stranger who had never seen Marabela in his life. "You're lying."

"Why would I lie?"

Now he can see everything he did wrong, clear as daybreak after the fog. The different voice, the rush to agree to an amount so much smaller than the one originally demanded. How could he be so stu-pid? The warning signs all fit together like puzzle pieces, though he knows he couldn't have seen them coming. How was he supposed to distinguish one uneasy feeling from another?

"That quick money was everything I had."

"You'll come up with more. You'd be amazed how resourceful people can be when they absolutely have to."

The man is so confident. That should have been the first sign. When Andres thought he could control the situation with the last caller, he let his ego get in the way of his judgment.

"Please let me talk to her," he says.

He waits—he always waits—minutes and centuries until he hears Marabela's voice.

"Andres, they're telling me you're not coming."

"You know that's not true."

"They say we don't have the money, but I know we do. Just give them what they want."

"I will, Marabela, I promise."

She doesn't answer. They've already taken the phone away, and the man is back on the line, serious now.

"Don't do anything stupid before we call next time," he says.

He hangs up and Andres listens to the dial tone. It is empty, just like he is.

3

ANDRES TRIES NOT to think about where Marabela might be right now, about what they might be doing to her, but despite his best efforts, his thoughts have already carved a path to the darkest corners of his mind. This path is so well traveled by now that to think of anything more productive is a struggle, an effort in waking his mind and convincing it to trudge past its sorrows. Andres rips a sheet of paper from a spiral notebook, jots down the ransom, and stabs it into the corkboard that hangs behind his desk with a red pin. *There, I've done something*, he thinks. It is a fruitless action but an action nonetheless. When the frayed side of the sheet twitches from the fan's circulated air, Andres rips the paper from the corkboard and crumples it up. In almost the same motion he lifts the phone and dials.

He hasn't called this number in two years, but his fingers know the motions across the keypad by heart. He's had a long-running joke with Marabela that when he and his mother finally speak, it will be a life-and-death situation. Marabela has never really laughed at his hypotheticals, and he finally understands why.

"Hello, Mother," he says, and just like that he feels like a child again.

Though she doesn't respond right away, he can hear her catching her breath. He imagines his mother in her pearls and heels, one hand on the long, ornate wooden table where the phone rests, with just her fingertips grazing the surface as if to show she can hold herself up. Perhaps she reaches for the cold glass of wine that's always nearby, likely preparing ammunition for what she's about to say next.

"*Hola, hijo*. I guess we both knew you'd call eventually. It's just that I hoped for this moment for years until I realized you probably would only call if your life depended on it. I can't imagine you picked up the phone with good news."

"I'm sorry to call like this."

"I'm sorry you had to. What is it?"

Andres finds he can't just spit it out, not like the kidnappers did. There has to be a way to share this news with some humanity, but by its very nature, he knows this is impossible. Instead, he says, "Marabela's been taken. Somewhere between the gala committee's offices and my building, I think. The kidnappers called a few days ago demanding a ransom."

As he waits for his mother's response, he's struck with an unfamiliar longing to be with her. It makes no sense at all; at best, Lorena will be indifferent to news of Marabela's suffering. At worst, she'll be pleased.

"What is it . . . ? What do you hope I will say? I can't say I'm surprised. These things happen all the time, to people we all know."

"I want you to say that you'll help me."

"Andres. What have they told you so far? Is she hurt?"

"I don't know. I don't think so. But the money is too much. It's all too much."

"The ransom, you mean."

He wants to say he meant the pain, the guilt, but he just nods as if she can see him. "Can you help us?"

"She wouldn't want my help, and frankly I'm not exactly inclined to give it to her. You don't remember what she did with the last favor we gave her?" Lorena says.

"Not this again. Not now."

"It seems Marabela finally got her wish. She always wanted to be in the middle of the action, didn't she?"

"Mother, that's cruel."

Lorena says nothing, which is the closest she'll ever come to an apology. Then, instead of changing the subject, she restarts the conversation as if nothing ever happened. "I don't know what I could possibly do. Although you could bring the children here. They would be much safer, and they're long overdue for a visit, don't you think?"

"She's your grandchildren's mother," Andres says. "They need their mother."

"They need a good mother," she replies.

"Let's not make this an argument about something we'll never agree on."

"Then let's say what this is really about. You want my money because you don't want to let go of yours."

"Do you think I like admitting that I don't have it?"

"I think you can't admit to yourself that you do have it."

He takes his drink, already warm, and finishes it.

"Life is hard work and sacrifice," Lorena says. "That's what your father would have said."

"Christ."

"Hard work and sacrifice," she says again. "You've done the work. Now sacrifice."

"Mother—"

"I can give you a name."

"A what?"

"A consultant. He helps people through these kinds of situations. So you have a better chance for a good outcome," Lorena says, lowering her voice to a near whisper that Andres recognizes. His mother, ever the problem solver, has never been capable of helping him out of trouble without first getting in a good reprimand.

He scoffs. "Right. I've heard of these kinds of people. Men I pay to help me pay to get my wife back."

"Not just pay. They help you negotiate so you don't do anything stupid out of desperation."

Andres feels his face grow warm, his cheeks and forehead flooding with anger and shame over the failed ransom drop. It's just like Lorena to hit a nerve that she doesn't even know exists.

"And if all goes well, you get her back, Andres. That's what counts. *¿Me entiendes?*"

It's the second time someone's asked him that today. "How do you know about him?"

"Guillermo helped the Duarez family when Elena was captured. They say they owe everything to him."

"Elena." He says her name as if he is only just remembering it, as if he hasn't been carrying it around for years, thinking that he should at least call and ask how she's doing.

❖ ❖ ❖

He'd read about Elena's release in the papers. If he'd been aware of the kidnapping while she was missing, he would've visited her family, offered to bring them dinner at their home, or at least sat awkwardly in her parents' living room, staring at the family portrait that he and Elena might have been part of, together, in another lifetime.

Instead, he learned about her kidnapping after it was over. Andres remembers it vividly, right down to the taste of the coffee he was sipping when he got into an elevator, pressed the button, and caught the back-page headline: "Kidnapped Daughter of Newspaper Owner Released after 37 Days." The article explained that the family hadn't disclosed the kidnapping to the public sooner in order to ensure Elena's safety. Andres experienced fear and relief, desperation and gratitude, all in the time it took to get from the first floor to the fourth. When the doors dinged open, as if to say, *Time's up,*

Andres decided he would process the news later. Later, when calling Elena didn't frighten him. Later, when the sound of her name didn't make Marabela clench her jaw so tightly he could hear her teeth click.

❖ ❖ ❖

When Elena and Andres were children, born just four months apart, their parents would leave them with the *empleadas* while the mothers went to their gatherings together and the fathers went to work. The men were cofounders of *El Tribunal de Lima*—a small newspaper that had grown into one of the city's larger dailies by the time Andres and Elena were in school.

To make up for the fact that he was always at work, Andres's father let him spend entire days at his office. The first time Rolando took him to work, Andres took a notebook and a pencil with him, thinking that working alongside his father meant he'd be a journalist. Instead, they went from sales meeting to sales meeting, where Andres was encouraged to take notes on his father's pitching style. Fifteen minutes into the first meeting, the men were shaking hands and Andres hadn't written a word. He hadn't noticed his father was selling anything until he'd already sold it.

"Well? What did you write?" his father asked.

"I thought you were just making small talk and asking questions. I didn't realize that was a pitch."

"Exactly," Rolando said. "The best negotiators don't let on that they're negotiating."

Sometimes, Elena's father, Saul, came into the office, and the men discussed the final layout of the day's paper; Saul took care of editorial while Rolando arranged the ad pages, each providing input for the other. One day Rolando suggested it was time they add more pages. Andres, just a few days into summer vacation, remembered a problem he'd worked on in math class about how many oranges should be squeezed into a glass of orange juice if they wanted to sell it for a set price. The teacher had explained to his class of bewildered students that it was an exercise in keeping costs down to maintain profit. Squeeze more than a certain amount of oranges into a glass, and you'd either have to increase the price or lose money on the sale.

"Can you print that many pages, Father? Won't it be too expensive?"

"People always need information," his father said. "Their curiosity is a bottomless well."

And so it was.

Rolando kept getting advertisers, Saul kept getting readers, and, year by year, the business expanded. It was an unspoken expectation that if the men were business partners and the women were best friends, of course the children would marry.

And they nearly did. When they were young enough to bathe together, their love seemed natural and innocent. Over time, kids started to tease them for holding hands as they walked toward the school playground. The girls called Elena a tomboy and the boys called Andres a *maricón*. By the time they were teenagers, the insults had evolved along with their hormones. They called her a slut and him a prude for refusing to admit they were doing it.

Despite all the troubles their friendship caused them, Andres and Elena would rather be together than apart.

"Doesn't it bother you? All the things they say?" Elena asked one day as they walked home from high school.

He shrugged it off. "They're nothing but horny teenagers taking their frustrations out on a relationship they're too immature to understand. I bet you they've had about as much sexual experience as Sister Mary Anne. Next time they try to tell you anything, just imagine them dressed in a nun's habit."

This made Elena laugh so hard she had to stop in the middle of the sidewalk and lean on an ice-cream cart for support. He loved making her laugh; it was what he lived for back then.

His parents, especially his mother, loved Elena. Andres was an only child and he suspected Lorena saw her as a surrogate daughter, an outlet for a tenderness she couldn't express with her son. They shared a secret language; he often caught Lorena winking at Elena, pinching her chin, or patting her on the shoulder before she left the room. He and Elena were putting together a puzzle one afternoon when she suddenly blurted out, "Your mother is the only adult who doesn't make me feel like a child."

"Really?"

"Yes. She talks to me like we're both women. She asks for my advice. Did you know I helped her pick out your birthday present?"

For his seventeenth, Lorena gave Andres a leather briefcase that was identical to his father's, and a leather-bound notebook custom engraved with the words *Make it your own*. It'd seemed so like his mother to push him to follow his father's path. But now that he thought about it, the notebook and engraving had Elena's unmistakable touch.

"That's not surprising. You two are always plotting things behind my back."

Elena laughed and shoved him with her shoulder. She reached over him, plucking a puzzle piece that looked like a small animal with its limbs outstretched, and slipped it into a spot he'd been trying to fill for the past half hour.

"How'd you do that?" he asked. He'd picked so many other pieces that looked identical.

She shrugged, scanning the table for more. "Sometimes you see one and you just know it'll fit."

When Andres looks back, he can't understand how their simple relationship turned so complicated. If they hadn't followed exactly in their fathers' footsteps, if Andres hadn't gone to one college for business and Elena to another for journalism, they might have followed through on their childish fantasies. Maybe Andres would have stuck to the plan if he'd never experienced the rush of the unexpected.

But then one day, when he went to pick up Elena after class, surprise, surprise—there stood Marabela. He didn't even wait for Elena to introduce them; something about her energy, the way she spoke with her entire body, gave Andres an uneasy feeling—and it wasn't entirely unpleasant. Elena leaned in for a kiss on the cheek and placed her hand on his shoulder, their movements so steady and natural as they came together. In that moment, he felt Marabela's presence throbbing at the edge of his mind, a weight pressing against his thoughts. It was intense and exhilarating and uncomfortable in a way he'd never realized he wanted.

❖ ❖ ❖

The call to the consultant is quick. In just a few words the man asks Andres who referred him, when he last heard from the kidnappers, and where Andres lives so he can arrange to meet him at his home.

"Right now?" Andres says.

"Do you have time to waste?"

Andres doesn't say anything. Everything feels like it's happening so fast but adding up to an eternity. He tries not to think of how much worse it is for Marabela.

"I'll be there in half an hour and you can tell me the details then. As it is, we shouldn't be holding up the phone line this long," Guillermo says.

While he waits, Andres organizes some papers scattered across his desk. The kids are still at school and the maids in their room, probably folding the laundry they hung to dry last night. He hopes Guillermo won't arrive at the house too quickly; he needs time to calm the nerves riled up after speaking to his mother. It shouldn't have come as a surprise that she'd been so cold to him, even under the circumstances. Andres shut his parents out of his life years ago, for good reason. What would Marabela think if she knew he finally caved and called Lorena?

Back when the wounds of their estrangement were still fresh, he'd tell Marabela, *Me hacen falta. I miss them*, or, really, *I lack them*, as if a piece of him was gone in their absence. Marabela would nod and try to comfort him, but she could never fully understand. Her whole life she'd been separated from family. Her father died when she was a teenager and her mother, overcome with grief or happiness — "Who could tell with her?" she once told him — gave up on their life together, moved to Bolivia with her lover, and left Marabela with her uncle and his wife. Family had never been a constant in her life; it was a way to define eras that had come and gone. On the rare occasion that she looked back at her childhood, Marabela didn't reminisce for long. That part of her life was over.

The first birthday Andres's mother and father missed was Cynthia's third. He'd hoped they would call, or send a card, or even show up at the house uninvited. He'd spent the afternoon with his eye on the doorway, hoping that the sea of red and yellow balloons would part and from behind them would emerge his parents, smiling. As if Marabela hadn't gone behind his father's back at the newspaper; as if he'd never fired her, and they'd never said the kinds of things to one another that can't be forgiven or forgotten.

"Maybe I should call them," he'd told Marabela. He was grabbing a drink in the kitchen while she arranged tiny trio sandwiches on a tray. She held them with two fingers, moving them around and stepping back to look at them, like one would a bunch of flowers.

"Do whatever you want, dear," she'd said, her attention still focused on trimming a few more crusts.

Andres knew better. He'd heard that phrase from his mother enough times to realize that she and Marabela were more alike than they'd ever admit. Just the thought of them being in a room together, stretching him thin with their silence, was enough to change his mind.

The years after that — the missed birthdays and quiet Christmases — became easier. The Jimenezes were a hardheaded family, after all. Time only multiplied their stubbornness. Even faced with her own husband's death four years ago, Lorena stood ankle-deep in her grudges. When she called Andres to tell him his father was in the hospital, she acted as if they'd only spoken yesterday. Clearly, their feud was still fresh in her mind. "Bring the kids. He'd love to see the three of you," she said. Andres waited for her to correct herself, to add Marabela's name to the request. She said, "You should know he's in a delicate place. I wouldn't want anything upsetting him."

So he went alone, hoping his mother was exaggerating his father's condition. He didn't take the kids because he didn't think it'd be fair to expose them to a death they wouldn't be able to make sense of. Marabela took it better than he'd expected, respectfully keeping her distance even at Rolando's funeral. She waited in the car while Andres buried his father. Watching the dirt hit the casket while Lorena gripped his arm with her gloved hand, Andres decided enough is enough. No more time wasted on a picture published six years ago. He gave himself and his mother time to mourn, then tried to make amends, but Rolando's death seemed only to have hardened her.

"Is she ready to apologize for what she did to him? What she did to this family?"

He knew then his mother's resentfulness ran deeper than the photo, to Elena and broken promises and a place neither he nor Marabela could follow.

The distance came as second nature this time. Lorena made it so hard to swim against her. Andres was tired and let the undercurrent of her pain push him further and further away.

❖ ❖ ❖

The buzz from the front gate startles him. Andres pushes the blinds apart with two fingers and watches as the man approaches his house. He's surprised that Guillermo appears at least ten years older than him. His dark hair is tinged with gray, and his skin is tanned gold with light undertones. His build is average—not lean or thick—but when he shakes Andres's hand Guillermo squeezes just hard enough to flex the muscles in his forearm.

They take a seat in Andres's office upstairs.

"Let me just start by telling you how sorry I am that you're in need of my services," Guillermo says. "I won't pretend to know exactly what you're going through, but I have worked with enough families to understand that there are few things more difficult than this. If we are to work together, I need you to know that I'm not insensitive to your feelings, and that the best way I can ease them is to do my job, which means being honest and direct with you." He studies Andres's face, as if assessing how to proceed.

"I would welcome that," Andres says.

He has the kind of voice that seems to suck all the air out of the room. Every time Guillermo opens his mouth to speak, he takes in a quick deep breath. It gives added weight to his words. "For everyone involved, this is essentially a business transaction. Our goal is to negotiate in such a way that your wife returns safely. If you start by offering everything you have, you'll have nowhere to go from there if they refuse, and the kidnappers are more likely to hurt her if they believe you're not cooperating."

Andres nods, taking it all in. "I hate that I have to ask this, but your payment . . ." He stretches out his words, hoping Guillermo will jump in.

"Of course. It's five hundred dollars a day, plus expenses. I'm sure you may have heard of consultants who charge a percentage of what they save the client in ransom negotiations, but I'm not one of them. I feel that presents a conflict of interest. Your wife's safety is my top priority, and I'd rather we go into this agreement in as concrete terms as possible. If, after we've discussed how this all will work, we both agree to move forward, I'll require an up-front payment to cover the month."

"A month?" He'd never considered it might take that long, but the thought of it charges at him.

"Nobody wants it to take that long, but I've seen it take weeks or even months. I believe in preparing for the worst in order to get the best outcome," Guillermo says. He lowers his voice, his words slow and emphatic. "It's important for your wife and your family's safety that you know what will happen, what is likely to happen, and what we're trying to keep from happening."

"I understand," Andres says.

None of what follows is easy for him to hear, but Andres listens and takes notes intently. Before they can start negotiating he must set a minimum, maximum, and optimum ransom amount. He's relieved to hear Guillermo say that the kidnappers' initial demand isn't an option—the first goal is to move them off it because no true negotiation can start until they've done so. Less is more, he says. The second the kidnappers start thinking he's easy money, Marabela and the family will be in more danger. It's important to make it a little hard for them to get paid.

"They have two things working for them: time and the threat of violence. You can't allow them to manipulate you with that. Remember, this is a business. It doesn't make sense for them to kill their one commodity."

Andres feels his legs going numb. He gets up and takes a few steps across the room, standing straight as he tries to take deeper breaths. "Has it ever ended like that?"

Guillermo doesn't respond immediately. "It's rare. It's the kind of thing that, if it were to happen, it would've already been decided from the start. It wouldn't be anyone's fault but theirs. It's important you understand that, but it's even more important that we move on to what we can do to help your wife."

"Of course," Andres says. He appreciates the change of subject.

"Do you know where she might have been when she was taken?" Guillermo asks.

Andres tries to picture how it all happened. The elevator is in the heart of his company's building, and Marabela usually takes the stairs by the rear entrance, teasing that it is only four floors up and that the button in the elevator marked PH for "Penthouse" is a joke. They could've taken her from the back parking lot, or ambushed her in the stairwell, where the carpeted steps would've dampened the commotion. He imagines Marabela fought them hard. She is always at her strongest when challenged.

"I'm not sure," he says. "She could have been near my building downtown."

"What about her car? Have you gone to check if it's there?"

In all his anxiety, the thought has never occurred to him, a fact so embarrassing it renders Andres speechless and he has to sit back down. Guillermo reads his face and nods forgivingly.

"We'll look for it in a couple of hours. You can't expect to think of everything in these situations," he says. "When did you last speak with her?"

"It was close to rush hour. Thursday. She left to pick up some papers at my office shortly after we spoke," he says. He wonders if she could have been followed, pictures it in his mind: a rusty car, with the front bumper decaying like Swiss cheese, and a passenger window that doesn't roll all the way down.

"Do you think they've hurt her?" Guillermo asks.

"She said they hadn't, but she sounded scared."

"It's a kidnapping, señor. She should be scared. Remember that these people's currency is threats. They'll trade them for as much as they can get."

Andres shifts in his seat, and the leather underneath him squeaks as he moves. The more he tries not to think of what they could do to her, the more he imagines all the ways she could be suffering. It's like trying not to blink in a rainstorm.

"I don't have the money," he admits. He tells Guillermo, finally, of his foolishness, of the botched ransom drop that's left him hopeless and helpless. He admits that he's not even confident he'll be able to come up with the money for Guillermo's fee. Andres is nearly breathless when he finishes; he's on the verge of crying. Afraid to see the look on Guillermo's face, he presses his fists to his forehead and leans back in his chair.

"You can come up with it. We can still make this work," Guillermo says reassuringly. "I know it's difficult, but I've seen clients come up with more in worse situations." He indicates their surroundings with one hand. The office, though simply decorated, hints at prestige and elegance. It is a room that hardly anyone but Andres enters, not even Marabela, who ordered the furniture according to his tastes but didn't go so far as to arrange it once it arrived. Andres's framed business diplomas hang on the walls along with pictures of his first printing machines. In a well-lit corner of the room, a roll of colorful canned food labels—the first major order his company ever received—sits in a glass display case alongside copies of a medical brochure, a bulky store catalog, a stack of a popular women's magazine, and strips of an elegant wine label, replicated over and over. On its own, each printed item is unimpressive, but in bulk and in perfect duplication, the colors are stunning, the crisp lines showing off the attention to detail he has become known for.

When his company was still in its infancy, Andres took enormous pride in the glossy finish of each roll of paper, how the ink never left a dry, chalky residue on his fingertips, unlike the black ink of the dailies. Understandably, at first his father wasn't happy with his decision; he hated the thought of Andres working with sensationalist tabloids, even if he was only printing them. Andres had thought Marabela of all people—with her photographer's eye and appreciation for quality images—would understand his enthusiasm, but she found the printing process rather impersonal. She'd tease him when he bragged about the latest new and improved machine.

"It's great for what it is," she'd say. "It's massive and commercial. But art is printed one image at a time, slowly and patiently. Not rushed out of a line at thirty feet per second."

"Forty-five," he'd correct her, and keep flipping through lists of prices and specs into the early morning while Marabela fell asleep on the couch, her feet pushing against his thighs. This was when they lived in a one-bedroom apartment, and the living area doubled as Andres's home office. Marabela hated going to bed without him; she'd try to stay up while he worked but usually fell asleep at his side. Foolishly, Andres looked forward to the days when they could buy a house and a bigger office closer to downtown for company headquarters. Now, with so much space for spreading out and being so far apart, he misses the cramped closeness of their youth.

Andres started out with only one press and a four-person crew; in eighteen years, he's expanded the company and created hundreds of jobs for honest, hardworking people. He houses his twelve printing machines in a factory three times the size of his original operation. He employs press operators in teams of six or seven to prepare and stock the paper feeds. There are another sixty-eight employees in the administrative office downtown, where Andres oversees accounts and holds meetings with potential clients. It's been six months since he turned down the last offer to buy out the company, his third such offer in the past five years from larger, international companies hoping to expand to Peru. He's always thought of the investors as crazy, describing the transaction like it's nothing more than a math problem. To Andres, the company is more like a child who needs guidance and nurturing, one who always needs its father no matter how old it gets. He knows he could never let it go.

"I'll figure something out," he says, excusing himself to make a quick phone call. He tries to collect whatever strength is left in him to dial his mother's number and ask for the money again. She doesn't refuse him, but she does negotiate. She'll pay only Guillermo's fee, and it'll be a loan, she adds. "Take your time paying it back. We'll have many years ahead of us, I hope."

Hope is useless, he thinks as he hangs up.

With the matter of his fee taken care of, Guillermo agrees to start working so long as he receives payment the next day. He doesn't waste time with paperwork or formalities.

"Did they say when they'd call back?"

"No. Just that they would," Andres says.

"We'll have to get them to give us windows for when they'll call next time. In the meantime, we'll be using every minute between now and then to prepare," Guillermo says.

"Of course. You're right." Andres remembers he had one more question. "My mother mentioned that you helped the Duarez family when Elena was kidnapped. Have you kept in touch with her since she came home?"

Guillermo stops his note-taking and looks confused for a moment. He gathers his papers and straightens them out with a loud tap against the desk. "It's probably best that you ask the family. I'm not at liberty to discuss my clients' personal matters. You understand."

"Of course," Andres says.

"Good."

Guillermo explains that the best way to ensure a loved one's safe return is to expect that everything will go wrong. He repeats this again and again during his thirty-minute briefing. He explains that they'll need a room to use as their base of operations and a dedicated phone line to record all calls. Andres assumes they'll take care of everything from his office, but Guillermo points to the large window behind Andres's desk and dismisses the suggestion. "This won't do," he says.

In spite of himself, even in these extreme circumstances, Andres is offended. He still clings to the illusion of being in charge, even though whatever power he's fooled himself into thinking he has vanished the second he heard the kidnapper's voice on the phone.

"What's in here?" Guillermo asks from a few steps down the hall. He places his hand on the thin white door to Marabela's darkroom that practically blends into the walls. Normally, people walk by it and assume it's a closet. Even Andres, who knows it's much more than that, has gotten used to pretending there's nothing on the other side. For a moment he's impressed by Guillermo's intuition, but this is quickly replaced by a childlike panic, as if he's trespassing into a forbidden space.

"We can't go in there. It's off-limits," he says.

Guillermo gives him a dubious look. "Andres. We need a space that won't be compromised. It doesn't need to be big, just enough for a small desk and a couple of chairs. Windowless and guarded would be best, for obvious reasons." He repeats his question. "What's in here?"

"It's Marabela's darkroom. I'll have to get a key for it," he says, and calls down to Consuelo.

When she brings the key upstairs, he can see the hesitation in her eyes as she hands it to him. As he opens the door and lets the light in, Andres feels like he's stepping into a place that was never meant for him.

After Marabela gave birth to Ignacio, everyone expected she'd stop taking photographs for Rolando's newspaper, but it was only a matter of months before she was back at the office, camera in hand, looking over her editor's shoulder in hopes that he'd assign her a good story. Her job got more dangerous with each passing year. When the military government began converting private farms into agricultural cooperatives, Marabela was there to photograph the protests. She ventured onto the streets even as they were seething with tear gas meant to dissuade thousands of striking workers. It was as if she was incapable of feeling fear as long as she saw it through the lens of a camera. Andres tried hinting that she should stay home, but Marabela refused to quit, arguing that their country needed brave journalists who wouldn't run from the truth or cower to a corrupt press now more than ever.

Everything had been so uncertain back then. In the papers, he'd read about the guerrilla insurgent groups festering in the southern Andes—how they were gathering support and arming peasants in the most impoverished regions of Ayacucho—and he'd become terrified of Marabela ending up behind the camera, on the other side of those images. There were men whose faces had been bludgeoned with machetes, their wounds half covered by handkerchiefs, and women who knelt next to corpses of loved ones, weeping. Sometimes Marabela would hold up the paper, read the image credit, and shake her head as she tossed it away in disgust. "I should've been there," she'd say.

He couldn't understand it at the time, but he also couldn't bear the thought of her wandering through the *pueblos jóvenes* growing along the edges of the city. As the Shining Path began to establish its presence in the shantytowns, she'd photograph evidence of its influence graffitied on the walls of shacks, messages of uprisings by the people and boycotts of elections. Over the years the group started targeting its acts closer to the city. By the time Cynthia was born, Andres feared Marabela would venture out farther as soon as she could leave Consuelo with the baby, chasing the kind of stories that never ended well. Every day there was another bomb, another fire, first in the electrical transmission towers that left the entire city in the dark, then near the government palace and shopping malls.

"This was my gift to her for our tenth anniversary," Andres says, volunteering the information to fill the uncomfortable silence.

Guillermo takes a look around, turning his entire body as if the room were much bigger than it is. "It's a tremendous gift for a photographer. She must have loved it," he says.

"Yes," Andres says, but he is not so proud of it now. He'd thought he could meet her halfway with the gift of the darkroom, but Marabela had recognized it for what it was: a compromise. So he rarely asked to enter, rarely even bothered knocking on the door.

"I'll arrange it so that no one would even know I was here," Guillermo says. Andres closes the door behind them and the two men are enveloped in darkness. Andres hears a switch and a deep red light fills the room, startling him.

"This kind of light is safe," Guillermo says.

"Are you sure?"

"My father was a photographer. You didn't think she fumbled around in here in the dark, do you?"

"I hadn't really thought of it. It's private. I haven't set foot in here in years."

Even so, he recognizes the room's scent. The chemicals smell like Marabela's fingertips, harsh and piercing; all that's missing is the added essence of her skin, the subtle mixture of her lilac-infused soaps and lotions. He's never felt so uneasy yet so comforted by a place, even one where he's not welcome. Marabela is everywhere here, in the still-hanging images of Cynthia playing with a street vendor's hat, in the test strips of gray and black that litter the garbage, each meticulously cut to the same exact size. She's even left a pair of slippers he's never seen her wear. The darkroom reveals pieces of her he recognizes and pieces of her he didn't know were there.

Guillermo clears his throat and scratches his neck, looking away from him. Andres feels his pulse pound at the thought of rearranging the room for their efforts. What would Marabela do if she knew her safest space was being exposed to such horrors? After all they went through to put the darkroom together, it pains him to see it dismantled.

"Keeping a private darkroom is no easy feat," he says. "The chemicals are expensive and hard to come by, and that contraption"—he points at what looks like a giant magnifying glass, vaguely remembering how Marabela explained that it shoots light through the negatives, burning an image onto the resin-coated paper—"I had to have it imported from the US because Marabela insisted it was the best."

"Very impressive," Guillermo says.

"Everything in here is fragile. We shouldn't even be in here, let alone touch anything," Andres says.

"I understand. I'll be careful setting up. Don't forget, this isn't permanent. We're doing this for Marabela's own good, so she'll be back here as soon as possible. I'm sure she'd appreciate that."

Andres shakes his head. "You don't know my wife. She sometimes has difficulties seeing the bigger picture."

"And she's a photographer?" Guillermo says. Andres catches his smile, a gentle jab. He should be offended but his first instinct is to laugh, and it feels good, this tiny allowance.

"So, where do we start?" he says.

"First, all this equipment needs to be put away. I'll need your help," Guillermo says.

They take trays of liquids and pour them down the drain of the small sink. Pictures get tucked away into a drawer, and Guillermo checks the area to make sure there are no unexposed films or papers that need to be shielded from the light. In the eerie glow of the red light, they work in silence, and when they're done the room is just another poorly lit windowless office with a view to nowhere.

❖ ❖ ❖

Downstairs in the kitchen, Guillermo makes a list of items he'll need: a cordless telephone, a duplication device to make copies of every recording, and headphones with a ten-foot wire, so he can listen in on conversations but stay out of sight if necessary. He adds notepads, extra pens, and a map, and suggests Andres send for one of the copy machines from his office. When they're done assembling this unlikely shopping list—a task not unlike Marabela's handling of the kids' school supplies, Andres realizes now—they send Consuelo to pick up the electronics and Carla to the office supply store. While they're gone, Guillermo asks how long the maids have been working with the family.

"Consuelo's been with us more than seventeen years, and Carla just a year, but she's Consuelo's niece. They can be trusted," Andres says, surprised that he's suddenly feeling defensive of the women.

"Even so, it's best that only you have a key to the darkroom. No one should enter but you and I." Guillermo continues giving Andres basic instructions as they work. He feels like he's back in school, taking an introductory course where the teacher goes over the syllabus first. "They'll make you wait," Guillermo says. "Fear and anticipation are their most powerful weapons. Remember that each time you speak. The most important thing is consistency. Each time they call, they should talk only to you. They should call only your second business line, not the home one—"

"It's not suspicious if I ask them to call a different number?"

"It's common practice by now. They shouldn't be surprised unless they're amateurs. Just tell them you can't risk missing their call if other people are calling the main line during the day."

"Of course," Andres says.

"We have to be able to notice when they do something out of the norm. We can't do that until we've established what the norm is. So we'll be monitoring everything—every call, every sound in the background, even expressions that they're fond of using, and the times of day they call. I need you to be alert." At this, Guillermo snaps his fingers. "You need to establish a rapport with these men. They can't just see you as a source of income and an enemy."

"I'm supposed to befriend them?"

"You're supposed to convince them not to do anything drastic. And the only way to do that is to let them think they're better off getting what they can and moving on."

"To someone else?"

"I didn't mean it like that. It's just that you'll have to negotiate—"

"Without letting them realize I'm negotiating?"

"Something like that."

By now Guillermo looks annoyed by Andres's constant interruptions. He's a man of few words and he seems to have exhausted his quota, so they work in silence for the next half hour. Consuelo returns from shopping, having gone to three different stores. She offers to help but Guillermo thanks her and guides her gently away from the door, explaining that the best thing she can do is help maintain as much normalcy in the house as possible.

"The kids will be home from school soon," Andres adds. "They'll want a snack." This is something he's learned in just the few days he's been staying home. "Maybe prepare some fresh *chicha*." They usually buy the purple corn drink bottled from the store, but made fresh it fills the house with the sweet aroma of cloves and the boiled pineapple rinds mixed in.

"I wouldn't mind a glass, either," Guillermo says, smiling at Consuelo as she leaves.

They're in the midst of connecting the wire to the telephone, stretching it across the hallway between Ignacio's room and the bathroom, when the kids come home. Andres can hear Cynthia talking to Carla in the kitchen, but Ignacio's steps are fast approaching up the stairs, as if he's in a hurry to lock himself in his room. Guillermo stands in the middle of the hall with the wire in his hand while Andres tries to roll up the cord as fast as he can, inching toward him, the wire limp as a jump rope between the two of them.

"What's going on?" Ignacio says. Andres follows his son's eyes as they travel from him, to the wire, to Guillermo. He can tell he's trying to connect the pieces himself but he's missing a key element. Andres hands his end of the wire to Guillermo, who gives him a nod, just small enough so that Ignacio doesn't catch it.

"Let's go to your room."

Ignacio clutches the straps of his backpack, tightening and loosening them so the bag bounces up and down against his body. He tosses it onto his bed as soon as they walk in, and Andres moves it to the edge of the bed as he takes a seat.

"Do you want to sit down?" he asks.

"Do I need to?"

Andres leans over, rests his elbows against his knees, and locks his fingers together. He could almost be praying, except he's looking right at his son, trying to think of the words that will make this information bearable. The air in the room is stagnant and warm. Ignacio flips on the fan and pulls out a rolling chair from under his desk. He takes a seat and pushes himself against the wall, away from his father.

The fan spins overhead, picking up speed slowly. A glimmer of light catches Andres's eye by the nightstand. Hanging from Ignacio's lamp and swaying side to side is a silver pendant on a fine, short chain. He's not close enough to see the engraved figure, but Andres recognizes the small oval shape: Saint Anthony, patron of lost articles. A gift Marabela gave their son when he was four and had left his favorite toy truck at the beach. She and Ignacio went back five days in a row to search for it in the sand. Even weeks later, Andres would catch Ignacio looking for the truck, digging holes and abandoning them for a new spot to unearth.

"The man outside. His name is Guillermo," he finally says. "He helps people, families, when a loved one is kidnapped and being held for ransom."

Ignacio breathes in sharply. The tension builds in his neck and jaw, in a corner of his face Andres never noticed until now. He sees his son's Adam's apple jolt as he tries to swallow his anger, and he's almost convinced by his calm, staunch demeanor until he looks Ignacio in the eyes. Andres knows better than to try to comfort him immediately. His stare is unblinking and expectant, withholding any reaction until he's heard the news explicitly.

"I received a call a couple of mornings ago about your mom . . . She's being . . . held. Guillermo is here to help us bring her home."

The boy blinks—just once—and his face goes slack. His eyes dart back and forth between his father and the door, behind which they can still hear Guillermo setting up the lines. He presses his lips together and nods, as if he's having a conversation in his head.

"How long is he here?" he asks.

"Until we get your mom back," Andres says slowly.

"How long will that take?"

He shakes his head and opens his hands. "I don't know. As soon as we can."

"And all they want is money? Is it a lot?"

Andres is tempted to correct him, to tell him that's not *all* they want. What they want is his life's work. They want every day, every thought, every waking effort of his last eighteen years. Instead, he nods.

Ignacio walks across the room and opens his bedroom door. "What's so complicated about that? We pay and she comes back. It's that simple."

"I'm afraid it's not."

"It is that simple. What do we need him for? I can help. Just tell me what to do."

"Don't—don't you worry about Guillermo," Andres says. "You don't understand how this works. We need him to—"

"No, you need him. To make yourself feel capable. To feel like you're protecting her or helping her when all you've been doing is sitting around the house doing nothing. You lied to me. You made me think she'd just left like the . . ." But he can't finish.

In the silence, Andres begins to understand all the things his son can't help but know. He walks over to him, placing his hand on Ignacio's stooped shoulder. "I'm sorry. I just wanted to protect you and Cynthia from all this. I'm trying everything I possibly can."

Ignacio steps away and stands taller, almost matching his father's eyes. "If that were true, she'd be home already."

The arrogance, from his own son, is almost too much to take. "You don't know what you're talking about." He reminds himself to breathe now, in for one second, out for another. He closes his eyes for just an instant longer than a blink, but when he opens them Ignacio's arms are crossed and he holds his head tilted in such a way that makes Andres want to slap it straight.

"I don't have time for this. Guillermo and I have work to do."

"Tell me when they call. Let me talk to her! Let me talk to them."

"That's enough, Ignacio!" He's almost screaming now, and he has to take a moment to slow his thoughts down. "I just mean, I'll handle this. I don't want you getting involved."

"But that's not fair."

"None of this is fair. Just, please. Eat something. Keep Cynthia company. Make sure she's okay, and if she asks, tell her your mom's traveling. That she misses her. *Punto.*" He pulls his son close and doesn't even care that it's such a battle. Ignacio's arms are stiff as they wrap around him, but they are here and warm and solid, and for now that is all that matters.

❖ ❖ ❖

After sunset, Andres and Guillermo go searching for Marabela's car. They have only an hour or two before the curfew kicks in, and already the streets are quieter and citizens hide in their homes like mice. From the passenger seat Andres gives Guillermo directions to his office. He'd started to feel light-headed as they left and had to ask Guillermo to drive. Now he pushes down the window, hoping for the comfort of a breeze against his face, but in an instant Guillermo swerves into the next lane, inches away from a *micro* stuffed with passengers hanging on to an overhead bar for balance. Despite getting tossed side to side, Andres knows he can't complain; driving less aggressively would only get them in an accident. Guillermo, like all of Peru, drives *a la defensiva*.

The whole country is in a constant state of defense, even the president, who only two months ago had a military tank—thirty-five hundred pounds of nerves and steel—charge the steps of Congress to declare that it, along with the constitution and the judiciary, had been suspended. That evening President Fujimori addressed the nation on television and made it sound like this was the only way to protect the country from the growing threats of terrorism and a worsening economy. Congress was at a political deadlock, and this was only temporary, Fujimori assured. Meanwhile, armed guards kept senators and congressmen out of the government palace, their stares and bodies rigid as they held their rifles across their bodies, pointed at the sky.

Andres thinks the tank was a bit much, but then again, how else do you abolish two armies of terrorist rebel groups if not with a firm hand? The time for subtleties has long passed—the tank is just another radical gesture in the wake of random bombs, fires, and blackouts that have taunted the city as of late, loading even the quietest moments with fear as everyone secretly wonders where and when the next will strike.

Still, it seems to Andres that the presidential coup, the *Fujigolpe* as it's being called, has garnered little protest from the people. They embrace it, even, with loud sighs of relief that finally someone is fighting for them. The last president left the economy in such chaos that even his promise for a new electric train was abandoned, its giant unfinished pieces still scattered throughout the city. Such poverty made people desperate; it bred social uprising and created an environment where guerrilla groups have plenty of desperate citizens to prey on.

In the last elections, Fujimori seemed to come out of nowhere. Who would possibly relate to a Peruvian son of Japanese immigrants, an engineer who had more academic and television experience than he did in government? They called him *El Chino*, perhaps derogatively at first, but eventually affectionately. Everyone, even Andres, thought the other candidate would win; he was a famous novelist, rich in ideas. But at the last moment, Andres, too, had voted for *El*

Chino. Marabela took the election results the hardest. She loved Mario Vargas Llosa's words, thoughts, and aspirations. She believed he could be the one to bridge her dreams and the tangible, and now the gap, the contrast, is too much for her.

They approach downtown and Andres tells Guillermo to make his next left so they can enter his building's parking lot from the back. Traffic lights glow against the nearly empty streets, but he feels the darkness winning. He finds he's more afraid of what he can't see than what's right in front of him. Is this supposed to be progress? Is this supposed to make them feel safer?

The questions land in Andres's thoughts, then flutter away like dragonflies on a pond. His fears strike somewhere closer to him, closer than any assassination attempt or detonated *micro* could ever reach. They always go straight to the uncertainty surrounding Marabela, the all-too-familiar terror of knowing he is one misspoken word away from losing her.

"Is this it?" Guillermo asks as the car slows down behind a pale yellow building. Parking downtown is always scarce; Andres's employees find it where they can while he and the senior executives go around the back, to a narrow alley that runs behind the office and has just enough room for five or six cars. This is where they hide their vehicles, where the wives park quietly if they'll just be in and out. The entry is wide enough for two cars to pass, side by side, at a careful speed.

He nods. "If she made it here that day, she would have parked here."

"Anyone could block this entry. They could have pulled in diagonally," Guillermo says as they drive through. He sounds aggravated, like any idiot should know this. He stops abruptly behind a lone navy-blue BMW.

"*Mira eso,*" Andres says, as if he doesn't believe it, as if he won't until someone else confirms he sees it, too.

The car is perfectly parked and seemingly undisturbed. There are no scratches on the surface, no tires slashed, none of Marabela's belongings scattered along the pavement. Andres had expected to find it with the doors wide open, ransacked. He gets out of the car for a closer look and Guillermo follows.

"It's unlocked," Guillermo says, opening the driver's-side door.

"What does that mean?"

"Maybe she got out of the car but she didn't have time to lock it."

He almost asks why but then the implication hits him. "They took her the second she got out of the car?" He's starting to wish he didn't have so many questions. He's no longer sure he can handle the answers.

"It's possible," Guillermo says, but he doesn't look at Andres. He circles the car, gets down on his knees and checks underneath it. Andres mirrors him on the other side.

"What are we looking for?"

"Nothing," Guillermo says. "There's nothing under here."

Andres tries to think like him, following Guillermo's logic. "If she was attacked here, wouldn't she have dropped her purse, her keys . . . anything?"

"A lot of times they'll check the wallet to be sure they got the right person. There's a chance they just took it with them."

"So she was taken here," Andres says.

"Nothing's certain."

"No. Just that she never would've been here if I hadn't asked her to come by."

"You shouldn't blame yourself," says Guillermo, his tone distant as his eyes circle around the car. "It's not as if they came here expecting you. I doubt that was the case. These are well-planned crimes. They rarely settle for a target they never intended to take."

"Why not choose me, then? Why Marabela?"

Guillermo stands and for a moment Andres thinks the man is clapping his hands together, mocking him in this moment of desperation. He gets up and realizes his own hands are covered in dirt and gravel, so he mimics Guillermo and brushes his palms together. He waits to see what Guillermo will do next. It's become too exhausting to doubt him every step of the way, and he starts to get the sense that everything will be fine so long as he trusts what the man tells him.

"Don't ever rely on logic in the minds of these criminals. It'll deceive you when you're least expecting it," Guillermo says. He reaches for the passenger door and Andres does the same on the driver's side. The khaki leather seats are stiff and unwelcoming as he struggles to slide into the driver's seat and fit his legs beneath the steering wheel. Even in Marabela's absence, there's no room left for Andres in her place. Her scent, having won the battle against the new-car smell that's faded in less than a year, overwhelms him.

"Do you want me to drive it to the house?" Guillermo asks.

The car will only invite more questions from Cynthia. What of her mother's car without her mother?

"No. It'll have to stay here," Andres says. "I'll just tell Edith that Marabela's car broke down and we haven't had a chance to get it fixed."

To anyone who asks at the office, he hasn't been feeling well and would rather work from home in case he's contagious. To neighbors who ask why they haven't seen much of his wife, he keeps it simple with the same story about the charity gala road trip he'd told his children. To the women like the one from the charity committee who call wondering why Marabela hasn't come to their meetings, he keeps his tale vague, his voice somber as he tells them about a family emergency in the United States, making it uncomfortable for them to ask more questions. He's sure eventually his circles of friends will collide and they'll find their concerned whispers of gossip don't add up, but that's the least of his worries.

There are so many lies now he's beginning to doubt his own truths.

DAY 7

"Well, how did it go?" his mother asks, as if she's asking about a party or a first date. Even though it's been years since she's visited Andres's house, Lorena quickly makes herself at home, unloading bags full of meals her cooks have made, telling Consuelo and Carla where they should be stored and how long they'll need to be heated.

Andres knows his mother would rather not fuss over their reunion, so he takes her in quietly. Seeing how much she's aged saddens him more than he'd anticipated. For years he assumed an eventual reconciliation would mean starting where they left off, but it's clear now that time did not stop for their sake. Lorena's hair is an ambiguous grayish blond, depending on how the light hits, and her frame is wider than Andres remembers. He always imagined his mother would be the type to stave off old age with cosmetic work, but the wrinkles along her eyes and forehead are rather becoming. They suit her, like armor scuffed in battle.

He's surprised at how relieved he is to see Lorena; her presence wrings the last drops of energy from his body. Last night he slept no more than two hours, but even then, his thoughts kept him on the precipice of consciousness. His mother's restless energy makes Andres feel useless by comparison, and he is tempted to leave her alone in the living room while the maids bring her a *café con leche*.

"Sit," she says, tapping the couch next to her, as if the house belongs to her. "What else is left for you to do right now?"

"What I need to do and what I can do are two very different things," Andres says, taking a seat. He needs to go to the office and set up meetings with clients and investors. He needs to go over the year's reports with his financial advisers and get a better idea of what he can ask for the company, if it comes to that. More than anything, he needs to pretend that everything is fine—nothing out of the ordinary. If word got out about Marabela's kidnapping, the buyers would smell his desperation and offer him the bare minimum for his business.

The more Andres tries to think of a solution, the more he feels like he's being asked to knock down a building without making a sound.

"I just keep thinking about what they're doing to her. I can't stop imagining the worst. And then when I do, I feel guilty, like if just by thinking these things I'll make them happen, and it'll be my fault."

"Sweetheart. Don't be ridiculous. No one is that powerful. Just be happy you don't know, and fill your thoughts with ways to get her out of there. And how are the kids? Are they here?"

"They'll be home from school soon. They're . . . adjusting. Ignacio already knows what's happened, but we agreed there's no reason for Cynthia to find out. She's not blind, though. She sees things changing around her and she asks questions and she has no idea what she's adjusting to."

This morning he introduced Guillermo to Cynthia, explaining that they're working together on a big project. The child didn't waste a second and asked if that was what they've been working on in her mom's room.

"Did she give you permission to go in there?" she asked.

"It was her suggestion. She told us we may as well use it while she's out of town," Guillermo said. "Now, do you mind if I tag along while Jorge takes you to school? I have some things to pick up at my office nearby." In truth, Guillermo wanted to accompany Jorge in order to study the routes he typically takes. He's told Andres the family needs to become more vigilant about security. From now on, Ignacio will walk to Cynthia's school in the afternoons, where they'll wait together for Jorge to pick them up. He's advised them to never take the same routes twice, never give the impression of a routine. He wants them to be unpredictable, quick and alert as flies.

"Ignacio doesn't like Guillermo telling him what to do." Andres reaches across his mother's lap and grabs a pack of cigarettes from a small side table. "Sorry," he says, offering her one. "And why should he? The man is full of contradictions. First, Guillermo tells me no one can find out, everything needs to go on as usual. Then he's giving the maids and the driver instructions—"

"He's very good at what he does, Andres. You can't afford to doubt him." Despite turning down the cigarette he offered, now Lorena pulls one out of the pack. Her long white-tipped fingernails look like they'll puncture the paper or catch fire as she lights up. She inhales with one hand, then uses the other to push the smoke away as she exhales.

Andres lets out a long, thin cloud of smoke. It's been nearly ten years since he enjoyed a cigarette with his mother. In the early years of his marriage, they spoke candidly only over cigarettes, because Marabela hated the smell and would often find an excuse to leave the room whenever they lit up.

"How can you be so sure of him?"

"I've seen him do his job before. I was there every evening with Elena's mother after they took her."

"I wish they'd told me. I would've tried to help."

"Are you running around asking old friends and exes to help you?" She doesn't wait for Andres to answer, knowing he won't. "So you see why they didn't bother, then."

It's strange to hear his mother describe him as just an old friend and an ex when he's always felt he and Elena were more than that. They were family, not by blood but by history, and he had just as much a right to know about her well-being as his mother did. The problem—and what kills him, what adds to the heavy sorrow he's been carrying around for years—is that he simply failed to ask.

"How is she doing?" he says, knowing that this won't count. His mother shakes her head and takes a slow sip of her coffee. Outside, the garage door rumbles open, and soon Guillermo will walk in with more supplies, more armor, for the darkroom. A part of Andres is relieved, thankful for the distraction.

"She was held for five weeks, you know—short, compared to most kidnappings, at least from what I hear. God only knows what it felt like. She could never talk about it when she got out, and then these last couple of years she just got so paranoid . . . *la pobre*," Lorena says. "She's at a private psychiatric facility now. Her parents checked her in just three weeks ago. With all the blackouts and explosions lately . . . who can blame her for feeling unsafe? It was all they could do to keep her from hurting herself."

Andres doesn't want to believe her. His mother can't be talking about Elena, who was never afraid of anyone. She was the one who insisted they sneak out of the house the first time they got grounded, the one who'd call out a waiter on his terrible service or befriend a cop for directions to the nearest bar. He puts out his cigarette and tries to think of something to say until he realizes his mother hasn't been looking at him. She's staring off into space, transported by thoughts and memories Andres doesn't want to imagine. When Guillermo calls for him, he straightens his shirt and leaves the room.

❖ ❖ ❖

"You have to expect that they'll call at any minute, and you can't afford to miss it when they do," says Guillermo. He's emptying white plastic bags of batteries and blank cassette tapes, letting them land with a thud against Andres's wooden desk, which is so large it takes up almost all the space in the darkroom. The chair Andres normally sits on would be ideal for Guillermo's body, but Andres is uncomfortable offering it to someone under his employ. Guillermo takes the smaller foldout chair that they brought upstairs from the kitchen, and Andres sinks into a leather seat across from him.

"Tell me again what happened on the first call. You're not forgetting anything, right?"

They go over it one more time—the curtness, the way the phone seemed like it was being passed among several people before Marabela's voice came on, the demand (not even a hint of a question) for a ransom that Andres knew would ruin him. At this, Guillermo asks him for the third time today if he responded yes or no.

"I was too shocked to say anything. I kept asking about Marabela, telling them not to hurt her."

"Good, good. It's too early for absolutes. They need to think you're cooperating as best you can, but that you're limited financially. Convince them that you're trying and willing, but that there's only so much you can do."

Andres nods, trying to convince himself that this is true. He's not sure he could live with himself if he didn't do everything within his power to get his wife back.

Guillermo puts his elbows on the desk with his hands together as if he's praying. Sometimes he reminds Andres of his teachers in *primaria*. To get a student's attention, they'd simply stop talking and stare him down until the poor kid realized he was being put on the spot. Realizing that Guillermo has gone quiet, Andres looks up from the piece of lint he's been squashing with his foot, only to find the man looking him in the eyes, waiting for their gazes to match up.

"I need to warn you, this isn't going to be a short and sweet transaction. Even if you had the money and loads more to spare, it's not in your best interest to pay up right away. If you make it easy for them, you become quick money, like an ATM they'll keep coming back to until it's empty. They need to think this is as far as you can go, that once Marabela's free and you've paid the ransom, it won't make sense to try the same trick with another family member. With every phone call we'll need to set goals—try to get them to show you proof of life, give you more time, agree not to hurt her, negotiate a lower price. You'll need to have counterarguments ready for anything they try to pull. Nothing quick and easy. We drive the price down and make them work for it so they don't think about hitting you up again."

"Are you really asking me to drag this out?"

"I'm asking you to realize that you'll need a strategy. This isn't just about Marabela's safety; it's about the safety of your family. Think about the way you do business. A client who can barely afford to pay you, who doesn't make it easy for you to get your money, is that a client you'll be in a hurry to work with again?"

"No, of course not."

"Okay. So you need to be that client. Make them think you're trying your best to cooperate, but when everything's over, this is all they'll be getting out of the Jimenez family."

When Guillermo puts it that way, Andres can give himself permission to think like a negotiator without feeling guilty. Marabela wouldn't want him to put the kids in danger, but perhaps none of that would matter to her in the state she's in. He imagines her alone in the dark, tied to a water pipe in someone's dank basement, with nothing but a mattress and a toilet nearby. She has nothing to do but wait—for him, for her captors, for answers.

He sets down his pen and brings his hand to his face, stretching the skin in all directions. He can barely stand to look at how they've transformed the darkroom. "You know what Marabela loved most about this room? She said that in the dark, time slows down. She always kept it quiet, no music or singing to distract her as the pictures developed. She loved the waiting."

They don't talk much after that. Guillermo is good at knowing when to talk and when to listen, and perhaps he senses that words won't help Andres's mental state.

In the kind of darkness where Marabela is being held, he imagines that each second seeps into her, multiplying her fear exponentially as they pass. Every day that she stays there means another day he hasn't paid, and that's what scares Andres the most—after all these years, Marabela will finally have proof that she was right about him all along.

✦ ✦ ✦

When Andres was eighteen, it was easy for him to think he wasn't betraying Elena. They'd never made any promises. He was too young to know that there's a difference between promises you say and promises you live every day. It was almost as if, in the comfortable silences they'd developed over the years, Elena had hidden her expectations, tucked them away in safe little spaces where he was sure to find them when the time was right. Maybe somewhere in the back of his mind he knew he'd have to acknowledge them, but Andres simply got derailed.

They had never become official. They had never slept together, had barely moved past holding hands to kissing and groping, which felt very familiar—and, Andres had to admit, not nearly as exciting as he had imagined. He didn't mind waiting for Elena because when he tried, he couldn't actually imagine himself wrapped between her legs and entering her. He loved her so completely and purely that it felt sinful to desire her. Not knowing any better, he took this as a sign that they just weren't ready.

When he met Marabela, Andres experienced for the first time what it was like to feel insecure around a woman. She barely looked at him; she shook his hand and kissed his cheek and picked up the conversation he had interrupted right where it left off. The tips of her hair swayed gently with the wind as they walked, the rest of it held in place by two braids that stretched from her temples to the back of her head, where she'd tied them together with string. Nothing about Marabela seemed proper, or calculated, or staged for appearances. Andres was instantly aware of Marabela's impression of him: privileged, with his khaki pants, leather belt, and crisp linen shirt. He tried slouching a little as they walked around the campus toward his car.

The girls had just gotten out of class, where they'd been discussing the power of the media, something about the vicious cycle of bias and elitism. Elena thought their professor was being too idealistic by assuming we could ever get close to the truth without bringing our own experiences to it.

Marabela put her hand on Elena's shoulder and shook her gently. "Think about it. What experiences are publishers bringing into the dialogue, what interests? If the press has always been controlled by the same wealthy families of the past century and a half, what reason do they have to promote progress?"

"Not all publishers are like that," Andres said. "Nobody handed our fathers their company. They created it."

"Well, that's true," Marabela said. "Your fathers are different. I admire them more than most publishers, even if I've been a little disillusioned with them lately."

"What's that supposed to mean?" Elena said.

"You haven't noticed?" Marabela's tone was casual, but still sharp with criticism. "They do great work but . . . those celebrity news and society pages? They're obviously advertising magnets and they're taking up space that should be devoted to real news."

"The stories are there because the readers are. We don't create the demand," Andres said, repeating his father's words.

"No, but do they really need to be so blown up? A bunch of dressed-up housewives hold a gala for charity and they make headlines? *Por favor*," Marabela said, rolling her eyes. "If I'm ever sent to shoot one of those . . . I think I'd want to shoot myself, you know?"

"People like seeing themselves in the paper," Andres said. "I don't see what's so wrong with that."

"Of course you would say that," Marabela said. "All I'm saying is, if your fathers are only interested in business, there are many other industries where it's easier to pursue money without compromising truth."

Andres could hear the insult behind her words, but it was hard to be offended when her tone was so nonthreatening, as if she were pointing out a dirty spot in a clean kitchen, suggesting that someone mop it up.

They had several encounters like this, in which Marabela dominated the conversation and Andres struggled to gain her approval.

Agreeing with her was about as useless as disagreeing with her, because she either looked down on him for being so easily convinced or respected him for having his own opinion, but never in the moments he predicted. She had a way of making him want to change who he was.

He'd always admired Elena's sense of duty, but Marabela was free of familial obligations. She often joked that she had the perfect family because they'd taught her to live moment to moment and depend on no one but herself. These were foreign concepts to Andres. He'd always had a plan, a place waiting for him in the Jimenez-Duarez partnership.

❖ ❖ ❖

They were waiting for Elena after class one day when Marabela asked Andres what he planned on doing with his father's newspaper when he took over.

"What do you mean?" he said. It seemed like a rhetorical question. When he took over his father's company, wouldn't it make sense to keep doing whatever had worked for the newspaper for the last forty years?

"What will you do with it? Wouldn't you want to do something different and create your own legacy?" Andres felt like she was sizing him up. Maybe she wasn't as apathetic toward him as he'd assumed.

"I don't know. Sometimes I think it'd be better if I didn't follow in his footsteps at all. It'd be nice to do something on my own. To start something that isn't already completed."

In truth, Andres had never thought of this—the words just came out, sparking a glint in Marabela's eyes and the hint of an approving smile. He knew by then that he'd finally said something right, and as he took the time to think about his idea, he realized it was exhilarating. For the next few weeks, this was all he could think about: the possibility of a life unlike any he'd ever imagined. He loved the unpredictability of it, loved the empowerment that came with knowing that all he needed to create change was to give himself permission. No one—not his mother, his father, or even Elena—could inflict their expectations on him if he simply ignored them.

And that's just what he did. Little by little he stopped visiting Elena at school and started calling Marabela for dates. Now that he knew whom she wanted—a man who stood for something, most of all himself—he found new confidence. Mimicking her desires, he became brave and generous, the type of person who listens to everyone but sticks to his own convictions.

❖ ❖ ❖

He's never noticed how much time needs to be filled, how many moments in between moments spring upon him, when one spends the day at home. Perhaps this is what Marabela meant when she'd say being around for the big moments wasn't enough. He misses the mundane with her, the nothing's-out-of-the-ordinary that they haven't shared in months.

Late in the afternoon Guillermo leaves to grab a bite, running into Lorena in the living room on his way out. They hug like old friends who don't remember each other's name, eager and reminiscent but struggling to define their relationship. Andres imagines it must be odd to become fond of a person and yet hope you'll never see him again in your lifetime.

"We were just about to have lunch outside. Why don't you join us?" Lorena says. Without Andres having to ask, she had the girls make chicken sandwiches and set the table in the backyard. The change of scenery is a nice touch. Lately he's been eating his meals alone at the dining room table, staring at Marabela's empty chair.

Guillermo insists that he was hoping to go for a walk and wishes them a good meal. The sandwiches taste as if his mother made them. Something in the way the bits of celery are cut, or how the chicken is shredded into smaller pieces, reminds Andres of home. He pictures his mother looking over Consuelo's and Carla's shoulders and finally stepping in to demonstrate how it's really done.

"Thanks for this," he says when he's nearly finished.

"I assumed it's still your favorite."

"You assumed right."

She sits back in her chair, her sandwich half eaten, and sips from a glass of wine. "I remember how fickle your taste in food used to be when you were younger. But we all get set in our ways as we age."

They linger at the table even after the plates have been picked up and their drinks refilled. He doesn't know if it's Guillermo's absence or the couple of beers he's had, but for this short meal Andres feels tranquil, or, at least, something close to it.

"The kids are home from school," he tells her when he senses a heightened energy coming from the kitchen.

Lorena straightens out her blouse and gives Andres a light nod to show she's ready. Something like timidness seems to spread across her face. There was a time when Andres thought his mother's spirit was impenetrable; suddenly he's not so sure.

"Will they remember me?" Lorena says.

He smiles and raises his eyebrows in their direction. "Why don't you ask them?"

Ignacio and Cynthia are in a good mood today, if the hurried sounds of their footsteps are to be trusted. They seek out their father, passing through the kitchen and the dining room before catching him waving to them through the sliding glass door.

"Look who's here," Andres says when they step outside. They stand one in front of the other, Ignacio's hands resting on each of Cynthia's shoulders. Lorena pushes her chair back and stands up, catching herself just before moving toward them.

"Where are your manners? Say hi to your grandmother," Andres says.

Cynthia springs forward and leaves her brother's side. She embraces Lorena without hesitation, as if she's rehearsed this or seen it in movies so many times, the yearning comes naturally. Rather than join them, Ignacio waits. He leans into her for a quick kiss on the cheek.

"You're here," he says. "What made you—"

"Time, sweetheart. Too much time." She deflects his question with the same air of casualness Andres rehearsed for years. The kids learned quickly not to ask after their grandparents, and though Andres knows they deserve better, he hopes the lesson still stands.

His mother pinches Ignacio's chin lightly with two fingers, careful not to let her touch overstay its welcome. "I always knew you'd grow up to look like your grandfather. I just didn't expect it to be so soon."

Andres contemplates his son, trying to find the resemblance. The boy is a living replica of Marabela. His mother's eyes must be playing tricks on her. Clearly, she sees what she wants to see.

❖   ❖   ❖

The phone finally rings at a quarter to midnight, and Andres picks up almost instantly so it doesn't wake the children. This doesn't give him much time to prepare or even take a calming breath. He clears his throat before speaking, giving Guillermo an extra second as he scrambles to record the conversation.

"*¿Aló?*"

"*Buenas noches,*" the man says with feigned politeness. "I hope you have better news than the last time we spoke. What do you have for me?"

Andres looks down at a card he's written and rehearsed so many times its corners are curling. "Yes, last time was an atrocity, for both of us. Trust me when I tell you it's not something I'll let happen again. I've given this a lot of thought and I want this to go as smoothly as possible. I'm willing to cooperate if you'll do the same."

"Enough with the games and speeches. Where are you with my money?"

My money. My money. Andres squeezes the card between his fingers until it hurts. He thinks of Marabela and the closeness of her face on Sunday mornings, the smile that became his world.

"I'm working on it. But the sooner I can go about my everyday business instead of waiting for the phone to ring, the sooner I can get it." He's careful not to say *waiting for your call.* They'd agreed that could come off as antagonistic. "Let's agree to make this simpler for everyone."

"Go on."

"I have a separate phone line in my house. Call there instead so I always know it's you." He gives the man the number, not knowing if his silence means he's writing it down or ignoring him. He waits for any reaction but eventually continues. "If you tell me when to expect your next call, I can make sure to be home and make better use of my time otherwise."

Again, no yes or no. Guillermo signals for him to keep talking.

"So I'll always know it's you, and not some frauds pretending to be you to get the money, you'll have to use a code name. And I'll need to talk to Marabela first. I need to know she's alive and safe. I won't discuss anything more until I hear her voice." He finally stops and takes a moment to breathe, his heart pounding in his chest. "This is in everybody's best interest. Do we have an agreement?"

The man explodes into laughter, as if he thinks this is all very cute. As if he knows Andres is powerless, and he's only entertaining the thought out of boredom.

"You wised up fast, *viejo. Está bien.* But I choose the code name. I don't want to end up with something silly like double O seven. I'll be Hades."

"Hades," Andres says. "I'd like to speak with my wife now."

It takes a few long minutes, but finally Marabela answers with a quick *aló* and curiosity in her tone, as if she isn't sure whom to expect on the other line. "They're telling me to tell you not to play games. That they'll know if you're lying."

"Have they hurt you? Have they touched you?" Andres asks.

"It's nothing I haven't been through before." She's about to say something more when they take the phone away.

"That's enough. Time for some of my rules. From now on you'll talk to her through me. You'll ask me a question only she would know the answer to and I'll ask her about it myself."

Guillermo had told him this could happen. He'd told him they'd have to choose their battles, and he knows this is not one worth pursuing.

"Now, back to business," Hades says.

"I don't know how you came up with the number you did. You must have me mistaken for somebody else. But look, I can still come up with some of it. I'm looking through my accounts and I—"

"You're lying, Señor Jimenez." The words come out like a song.

"I'm not. This isn't a game to me; it's my wife's life. Trust me, if I could I would hand it over, but this is all I can do right now. I've put the car up for sale and I'm taking another loan out on the house for so-called renovations. It's going to take a little more time, but I can have forty thousand soon." He cringes as he says the number. Hanging on the wall in front of him is a chart depicting the minimum he and Guillermo agreed to offer and a steep slope as it creeps up to the most he can possibly give. He knows it's low, but it has to be. Today's goal is to lower the captors' demands and expectations.

Hades scoffs. "You'll have to do better than that. Make it three-quarters of a million and we'll reconsider. I'll give you two days to think about it."

They hang up and Guillermo plays the tape back, first once in its entirety, then again on and off as he adds his own commentary.

"It's not much, but he lowered the price. That's something." He keeps his hand on the tape player as he stares at the wall, listening. "Hades. What does he think, that he's being clever choosing the god who took Persephone as his captive into the underworld? That bastard's not the only one who knows his Greek mythology."

It's the first time Andres has seen Guillermo so flustered, so discomposed. He can't help but smile and play along.

"Not at all a narcissist. It's not like he sees himself as a god or anything." He flicks his wrist as he leans back in his chair and lets out a half laugh, thankful for the levity.

"It's the most powerless people who get obsessed with power," Guillermo says.

Just like that, the moment is gone, having done its job without overstaying its welcome.

They get back to the tape. This time, Guillermo stops it right after Marabela speaks.

"There." He points at the tape player, as if the words are etched in the airwaves. "What does she mean there?"

It's nothing I haven't been through before.

"She means she can take it," Andres says, and he feels a familiar fury turning his limbs stiff as stones. The first time Marabela told him about her uncle's beatings, he'd wished he could've been there to set the coward straight. The worst part was that she could never predict when they were coming; they were fueled by nothing more than rage. When hiding and fighting back didn't help, Marabela said she learned how to leave her own body. She redefined what pain meant in her mind, and in this way she created an ocean between him and how he could hurt her.

Andres wonders sometimes if this is how Marabela manages to be so distant with him, but for once he is thankful that she can remove herself from almost any situation.

"She sounds like a very strong woman," Guillermo says.

Andres closes his eyes and nods.

"You did good, Andres. You handled yourself well. And now we know we have two days to prepare for the next call. We'll make the most of it."

DAY 8

He leaves early in the morning, hours before Guillermo arrives, feeling like he's trying to run away from a problem that can't be outrun. It's quiet and dewy on the road. The sun has barely started to rise and, without its brightness, the stretches of farmland look as dull as the American sitcoms Andres used to watch on his parents' first color television. He speeds down a lonely two-way road, and every once in a while he turns his head to watch the rows of corn pass him by. For a moment he's mesmerized by them—that straight tunnel of light through a crowded field that becomes the next row, and the next row, and the next as he speeds by. They appear identical when in fact they're like the frames of a strip of film; no one would know they were moving save for the flicker, when things have shifted from one frame to the next.

The facility where they've tucked Elena away is twenty-five miles outside the city. He doesn't know what to expect from it, but he's grateful it's not one of the state-run mental hospitals. There are only three in all of Lima, and he's heard they're run-down and over-crowded, the kind of places where people don't forget their problems but rather go to be forgotten. He assumes this private rehab clinic—Comienzos Pacificos, they call it, Peaceful Beginnings—is for people with enough money to pay for both quality and privacy.

It must be convenient to think she's safe there, so far from the source of her trauma. No one knows he's going to see her, and he's not even sure if the staff will let him come in, but he has to try. In the passenger seat sits a bunch of flowers, the plastic wrap crinkling from the wind. He bought them off the side of the road from an old woman who smiled so wide he saw the bottom row of her teeth.

Andres rolls up the window and takes his frustration out on the accelerator, arriving at the facility sooner than he expected. The building is a boxy, utilitarian structure with neat rows of windows covered by ornate metal bars and a navy-blue awning hovering over the main entrance door. A stone-covered sidewalk winds through a lush, manicured yard with palm trees scattered about, and to the side there is a gated area with several white benches and what looks like a basketball court without any hoops. The court is framed by two gazebos that have small, round tables underneath them.

He enters through a wooden door accented with several square panels of glass, its polish almost shinier than the windows. Everything creaks as he walks inside—the hinges, the doorknob, even the heels of his shoes against the linoleum—and he gets the sense he's in a vacuum, a sterile place where sounds and scents are cast out as quickly as they're detected. The walls are covered with posters depicting happy scenes of family picnics and children running into their parents' arms at the beach. Except for a couple of small tables full of magazines and old newspapers, the lobby is arranged very much like a church; an aisle cuts through the center of rows of chairs, leading up to a large reception station shaped like a semicircle and pushed completely against the wall. To the left is a long window to a living area that Andres assumes is where patients gather. There are several plants, tables, and couches, and a large television set hanging from a tall corner of the room.

Andres approaches the reception area, but the woman enclosed in it is so busy scribbling notes in a manila folder that she barely looks at him. He lets his keys tap against the desk as he rests his hand on it. She looks at him, smiles, but doesn't speak.

"I'm here to see Elena Duarez. I'm her cousin." He lies, hoping that the blood relation will make a difference.

"Visiting hours aren't until eight," the woman says.

"Please. I just want to check in on her. I won't bother anyone. Besides, I know she's never been one to sleep in," he says, tilting his head toward the door as he smiles.

The woman nods and exhales, as if she's just grateful to be understood. For now the building is still; the only real sounds are the light rattles of the vending machines in an alcove adjacent to the guest area and the steady steps of staff members preparing for whatever commotion the day may bring. Of course the receptionist would want to preserve the peace for as long as possible. She taps her pen against the desk, considering his request, then stops, decided.

"Fine. But only because she's one of the quiet ones," the woman says. Her tone softens as she adds, "It's hard to tell the difference between her good days and her bad days."

She gets up and lets herself out of the enclosure through a small door that blends into the furniture. With small, hurried steps, she walks completely around the desk, passing Andres and signaling for him to follow.

"This way," she says.

They pass by a cluster of folded chairs leaning against a wall before turning into an arched threshold that leads to a long, narrow hallway. Not a single door is open, and Andres is tempted to look through the square windows as they pass, but the receptionist walks too fast for him to catch sight of anything. He's mesmerized by the lightness in her steps and finds his own legs inadequate as he tries to control his heavy strides.

They stop at room 382. The woman rises up on her toes and looks through the window. Satisfied, she lets Andres take a look.

The first thing he notices is the tiles, four-by-four-inch squares that repeat themselves across the entire upper half of the walls, separated by a thin line of bleach-white grout. These tiles look shiny and cold, the type you'd see in a bathroom. In the center of the room is a small bed that sits on an accordion-looking frame; the metal, painted beige, can probably be cranked to rise and lower like a construction crane. Finally Andres's eyes wander to the corner, to a plush brown armchair where a woman sits, curled into her gown. Elena looks surprisingly at peace; the stiff linen covering her body seems to float over it, barely touching her arms and legs. Her skin is freckled and pale, and her nearly blond hair is longer than he's ever seen it.

Even in this unlikely and foreign setting, Elena still looks like she did when they were teenagers and Andres used to read to her from his favorite books. They'd made a deal back then that they would take turns—reading the first chapter of a book they loved as a way to convince the other to read the rest. He always knew when Elena was enjoying it because she'd bring her knees to her chest and rest her head on them, her eyes staring past Andres to whatever world he was creating in her mind. Sometimes she'd pull on the bottoms of her pant legs and wiggle her toes—a dead giveaway that she was excited to find out what happened next. Andres would stop, smile at her, and she'd urge him to keep going.

Two things occur to him too late. One: That the flowers were a stupid idea for a gift (a book would've been much more thoughtful). Two: Will she even want to see him? Will she want him to see her like this?

"Try not to sneak up on her. Knock as loud as you can, and if that still doesn't get a reaction from her, make noises as you get closer," the lady from the front desk tells him as she twists the doorknob open. This turns out to be easy—the cellophane from the flowers announces his presence before Andres does. He feels like one of those annoying people at a movie theater, trying to open a candy wrapper. As he walks closer, he imagines every possible scenario when she sees him, from her breaking down and crying to her yelling at him to leave. He can't decide which would be worse.

She turns and looks at him, her eyes lazy and distant as if she's not really seeing him, but then the spark of recognition sends a spasm through her body and she sits up and pulls her gown closer to her neck. He can tell she's embarrassed, that she wishes she could hide. She tucks her hair behind her ears and runs her fingers through her splintered strands, all the while looking behind Andres as if to make sure no one else is coming.

"What ... what are you doing here?" Her voice is a cracked whisper.

"I wanted to . . . I had to see you. It's just me. No one else came along."

With her arms still crossed over her chest and her legs folded underneath her, Elena turns away from him and brings her fingers to her lips. They're dry with small spots of blood from the cracking, and dark circles sink into the skin beneath her eyes. Her movements are small, sporadic, but somehow still graceful and calculated. If Andres didn't know any better, he'd think Elena was acting a part in a movie, the introspective heroine who sits quietly in the corner of the room, her obvious sadness only adding to her beauty, as if she understands something about life that no one else can know.

He studies her and is surprised by the smallest details he never knew he remembered until now. Her face is a map of nuances only he knows where to find: a scar, just where her hairline meets the tip of her ear, from the summer she got hit by a rock kicked up by a truck as they crossed the highway toward the beach. The slight dimple beneath her lower lip and her chin, which disappears when she smiles and gives her away when she's forcing it. Even her long neck exposes a mark left over from the time they both got chicken pox when they were seven. After so many years of not seeing her, Andres finds it hard to look away. Theirs is a history time cannot erase. He could stare at her for hours and find the stories of their past written all over her body.

He clears his throat but all the things he'd planned to say are gone. "How are you feeling?" A foolish start, he realizes, and continues. "I'm sorry. It's hard to know where to begin. I heard you were here and I had to see you. I didn't give it much more thought than that."

With this, she seems to remember who she once was, and her fragility melts away. "*Para variar*. Sounds like nothing's changed. You didn't give plenty of things much thought."

He shakes his head side to side. The words are a painful relief.

"Why are you smiling?" she says, more curious than annoyed.

"Because you're still you."

She looks at him then, her eyes narrowing, and he meets her gaze. He can't believe how comforting it is to find her again.

"I'm sorry, but . . . I missed you. You're my best friend even if you no longer consider me yours. Even if too many years have passed." He's nearly breathless, having spoken so quickly without thinking. When she still hasn't answered he begins counting his breaths as they slow back down.

But she seems unaffected. He begins to doubt she even heard him. "Ele?"

"I stopped hurting for you a long time ago. You can't miss what you've let go of." She speaks in a gentle whisper, but her voice strikes him with such force that he plops onto the bed behind him, his hand on his chest.

"I deserve that."

"You do." As usual, Elena never misses a chance to assert she's right.

They sit in silence for five, maybe ten minutes. When he looks at her, he knows she's aware of his stare because every once in a while she changes positions, as if he were an artist deciding which angle best to draw her from. He wonders how long he'll have to suffer her silent punishment, and finally decides this was a mistake. What if his being here is the most painful thing of all?

He leans toward her, stops short of kissing her on the forehead, and whispers, "I'm sorry. I'll go now." As he gathers his jacket and sets aside the flowers, he feels a loose grip around his wrist.

"Don't. Just wait. Please." He can see now that every muscle in her face is fighting not to cry. "It's too hard and I'm so tired."

"What is?"

Elena takes a deep breath and looks to the ceiling. "Hating you. Missing you. You make everything so damn difficult," she says, pretending to laugh through her tears. He kneels at the edge of her chair, resting his hand on her ankle. She sits up and embraces him so completely it's like her whole body has been lifted onto him. She's practically weightless and it feels so natural that they just rock slowly side to side in silence.

When they finally pull apart, her eyes wander to the flowers he brought.

"*Para ti,*" he says.

She takes them and sniffs them one by one — first the yellow daisies, then the pink alstroemerias, which look like miniature lilies with freckles sprinkled along their centers. On the table next to Elena's bed sits an empty ceramic vase, and the two of them unwrap the flowers and arrange them together. It reminds him of how they used to do puzzles together, finding the perfect place for each piece.

"I'll get some water for them before I go," Andres says. "And I'll come back with more before a single petal has wilted."

On the drive home, as Andres pulls into the garage, as he sits at the dining room table waiting for Consuelo to bring him his breakfast, he thinks of Elena and everything she's been through. He wonders if her pain is unique or if it's like a set of mirrors that face each other, trapping their subjects so that their images multiply, each less vivid than the next.

4

WHEN ANDRES WALKS into the darkroom, he can tell
somebody's been there who shouldn't have. Even though
nothing looks like it's been touched — the stacks of papers on the desk are still in the same order, the cable is still wrapped
around his headphones in tight spirals —

Andres's chair gives it away. It's facing the office door, as if someone leaped straight from the desk to the exit, and Andres is not the
type to leave in such a hurry. He takes a closer look at the headphones, which sit on top of the cassette player containing the tape
from last night's call. The tip of the cable is folded into itself, as if
someone wanted to tie a knot but stopped himself.

He crosses the hallway and walks into Ignacio's room without
knocking. The boy starts to protest from his bed, where he's lying
faceup, reading a magazine that he's holding with his arms stretched
toward the ceiling. His shoes are still on and his feet dangle awkwardly off the side of the bed. Andres imagines his son dashing from
the darkroom and jumping onto the bed, trying his best to act casual,
as if he's been lying there, looking terribly uncomfortable, all morning. He doesn't appreciate the charade.

He tries to stay calm, but then he thinks of the tape and last
night's conversation, and how easy it must be for Ignacio to judge

him. "What were you doing in the darkroom? What's the one thing I asked you not to do?"

"What are you talking about?"

"You should be very careful right now. Think about what you're about to say next, because it had better not be a lie." He opens Ignacio's armoire, where he keeps his television and Super Nintendo, and takes out a remote control. He sets it on the bed next to the headphones, with both tips of the cables facing up, tucked into themselves. It's obvious that Ignacio tied them both, obvious that he knows there's no longer a point in denying anything. At first he says nothing; his breathing quickens as he sits up to take a closer look. He rubs both eyes with one hand and stretches his fingers to his temples. When he finally looks at Andres, his eyes are full of accusation.

"How could you tell them you need more time when they're hurting her? Every hour that passes she's in danger, and you're just sitting around having breakfast as if nothing has changed," Ignacio says.

"Did I ask for your opinion? You think you understand the situation enough to give me advice? It's not as simple as you think. There are hundreds of factors that you don't know the first thing about—"

"Then tell me! Let me help. Let me log the tapes and stick stupid stickers on them with the dates in permanent marker. Or something. Anything, Dad. I want to help."

"I can't. I can't let you do that." He knows he can't drag his son into this. "I don't want you anywhere near those tapes. I don't want you playing with them, I don't want you thinking about them, and I certainly don't want you listening to them. Understand?"

"She's my mother."

"Exactly. She'd want me to protect you from this. It's too much for a boy."

"I'm not—"

"I'm not discussing this anymore. I have too many important things to worry about right now." Andres picks up the headphones and starts unraveling them, staring down his son as he does this. "Don't you dare pick the lock again," he says on his way out. As he steps into the hallway, Guillermo's silhouette startles him.

"Would it kill you to make some noise when you come in?!"

They haven't even been in the darkroom for five minutes before Consuelo knocks on the door to tell them that Andres's mother is waiting for him downstairs with a visitor. He waves her away, annoyed that her gaze shifts back and forth between Guillermo and Andres as she speaks, implying that she requires both their permission to interrupt their meeting. Guillermo may have better control of the situation—he may be the only one in this house with any semblance of calm nerves—but Andres is still the one in charge. Ignoring Consuelo and his mother, Andres continues discussing the next steps with Guillermo. They've agreed that if they told Hades they were selling the car and taking out a loan, they will have to do just that. There's no sense in risking him finding out otherwise. No one, especially a criminal who thinks he is a god, would be willing to negotiate with a man he can't trust.

"Then of course there's the issue of a backup negotiator, in case for some reason you're ever unavailable," Guillermo says.

"Can't that just be you?"

"I don't recommend it. If they know you've hired someone like me, they'll assume you have a lot of money. It'll only make negotiations more difficult. Which is why you need a backup . . ." Guillermo's voice, deep and heavy as it is, is no match for Lorena's downstairs. Even though he can't decipher her words, Andres understands her tone, much like a song's bass when the volume is turned down low. He knows she's throwing a passive-aggressive insult his way. The more he tries to ignore her, the more he finds himself filling in the blanks of her fragmented sentences. Every few words he hears another person's voice, soft and steady and almost familiar. He can't place it, and he knows he won't be able to concentrate until he does. Andres excuses himself and heads downstairs.

"Oh, good. Mr. Graves was just saying that this must be a bad time for you, but I assured him that you were expecting him and looking forward to revisiting his offer."

In an instant it hits him, but he can't believe his mother would be so devious. Yesterday, while they shared an afternoon cigarette, Lorena had brought up the possibility of him selling his company. He said he hadn't given it much thought since turning down an offer from Eugenio Graves months ago; they'd been barely a few signatures shy of finalizing the deal, with all the paperwork and inspections completed, before Andres changed his mind. But everything was different now. He feared if it came to that, he'd reconsider.

"I'll see what I can do," Lorena said, and Andres had brushed it off, apparently underestimating his mother's connections. He'd forgotten her tendency to keep promises even before she's made them.

Now Mr. Graves, Andres's biggest competitor for the last eight years, rises from the white couch that's just for guests and extends his right hand. It takes a moment for Andres to extend his own hand in return; his mind is so preoccupied with thoughts of ransom negotiations and bank loans that the shock of seeing Graves in his home barely registers. In that small delay, the tension in the room multiplies. Though they've always been cordial, today Graves's smile is more like a smirk, and he squeezes Andres's hand harder than usual, as if trying to make a point.

"Please, sit down," Andres says, gesturing toward a chair next to the couch. Half the chair's legs rest on the living room carpet while the other half rest on the tile, and Andres is pleasantly surprised to see that the chair wobbles as Graves takes his seat. "Excuse us," he says, guiding his mother into the kitchen.

"Why is he here? Why would you pick a time like this to bring him into my house?" He tries to whisper, but the words hiss out of him. At the stove, Consuelo and Carla pretend not to hear anything, but their slowed movements give them away.

"We discussed this. Better to talk to him now and know your options than to wait until the last moment when you're desperate. A time like this is exactly when you need a man like him. You should be thanking me. Do you know how many of your father's old contacts I had to call to get him here? You're lucky he even agreed. Now you don't have to go to the office and pretend like you're not in talks to sell the company."

"You told him? Do you realize what can happen if he knows how desperate I am? He can offer me practically nothing and I'd have to take it!"

Lorena waves her hand across her face, as if tossing his words aside. "I'm insulted you would think that after forty-five years of being married to a man like your father, I wouldn't know how to negotiate. Who do you think your father came to for advice at the end of the day? You think he did it all on his own? Of course not, and neither should you. I know that's hard for you to believe, seeing as how Marabela's never once supported this company of yours, but I don't agree with letting someone you love carry a burden like this on his own."

"Mother, I didn't mean it like that."

"I told him that you've turned down several offers since last time. That much is true, isn't it? I told him you're stubborn, and you work too hard, and that you think nothing's worth selling the company only because you haven't gotten the right offer yet. He thinks he and I have teamed up to convince you to finally let it go."

"That much is true, isn't it?" Andres says, mocking his mother's tone.

"I'm just trying to help, Andres."

"I know, I know. Thank you. But I'm not thinking about selling the company. It hasn't gotten to that point yet."

"Good. Just keep that up and see if we can drive up the price," she says, her eyes wide with excitement. "Think of this as a backup plan for your backup plan. Now, don't make him wait any longer."

On their way out, Lorena tells Consuelo to bring refreshments to the living room. "A whisky for the men," she says, and just like that she's back to a version of herself Andres recognizes—a main character disguised in a supporting role.

They dance around the topic of business for several minutes, at first talking about the traffic that only seems to worsen and about each other's children, who are all growing so fast. Mr. Graves mentions that he isn't originally from Peru; his company sent him from Mexico to expand their presence in South America nearly a decade ago.

This isn't news to Andres, but Lorena seems very interested in his transition. "Do you feel you can ever completely adjust? Being in a new country?"

"Well, it's all so relative. Nothing will ever replace my home country, but Mexico City is changing so quickly that even when I visit there are places I no longer recognize. I'm starting to think the only way to go back home is to invent a time machine." He laughs, leaning forward to rest his elbows against his thighs. He looks uncomfortable on the chair, fidgeting to find a better position. Andres tries to contain his smile.

"And you travel to Mexico City often? To visit family?" Lorena says.

"I do. Though I'm afraid it's more often for business than pleasure."

"I can only imagine, with the way Primatec is prospering." She smiles at Andres as she says this, but he can only marvel at her finesse, wondering how many steps ahead she choreographed this conversation. He knows she would just love it if he'd cut in, but he'd rather listen and let the two of them take the lead.

"It's true," Graves says. "Our main focus now is on expansion."

"That's wonderful," Lorena says, making a big fuss out of reaching behind Andres for her purse. She passes around her pack of cigarettes and lets Graves offer her a light. "You'll have to forgive my son's silence. When he told me he'd reconsider your offer, he said he's not saying yes but he's not saying no. I didn't realize this meant he wouldn't say anything at all." Her laughter is so strong and guttural it startles Andres.

"I've always thought listening is just as important as talking."

"You're so right, dear." Lorena pinches his chin, her cigarette dangling in front of his lips.

"Good then. I'm glad to hear you're open to the conversation," Graves says. "Since I'm sure much has changed since the last time we spoke, I'd like to reevaluate where things stand with your company so we can come up with a number that's more in line with the present situation."

"Of course. Andres, you mentioned you've already had Edith set aside some of the paperwork, right?"

The ones Marabela meant to pick up, he thinks, but he nods and has to clear his throat before he can speak. "I'll arrange to have those and others next time we meet."

They chat for several minutes more but nothing they say registers. When they've said good-bye to Graves and he's halfway to the gate, Lorena closes the door and claps her hands together, bringing them pressed to her lips.

"I think that went well." She places a hand on his shoulder and kisses him on the cheek. "Remember, nothing's happened yet. We're just talking right now."

He sighs, exhausted from it all. That's precisely the problem.

❖ ❖ ❖

Andres and Marabela's secret had a short life span: it could only sustain itself and their passion for so long. When he looks back at their beginnings, Andres tries to bury his suspicions that Marabela was more enthralled by the idea of their relationship than the reality.

They kept to themselves that first summer. He successfully avoided his family and Elena's, but hiding from their shared holiday traditions was nearly impossible. As they'd done for nearly twenty years, the Duarezes and Jimenezes got together for New Year's at the Club de Regatas. They had two adjacent bungalows facing the ocean, where the rooms that Andres and Elena slept in shared a thin wall. As children, when their parents were asleep, they'd communicate through a system they'd devised of light taps against the wall with their knuckles. It was mostly simple words like *yes, no, good night*, and *are you awake*, but the rush of it came from the language's secrecy, that it belonged to only them.

Andres was unpacking his suitcase in his room the night before New Year's Eve when he heard Marabela's laughter next door. It was high-pitched and short, almost engine-like. Impossible to mistake.

He rushed to the Duarezes' bungalow and found the two women settling into Elena's room. It had a set of bunk beds with plaid-patterned blankets and sky-blue sheets folded over them. Elena's clothes were stacked in neat piles on the bottom bunk, waiting to be arranged in the closet; Marabela was climbing to the top. They looked so young and happy, like sisters.

"It's about time we invited her, don't you think?" Elena asked. "It wouldn't be fair to keep this beach all to ourselves." The club was one of the most exclusive in the country; since the late 1800s, only men had been allowed to join. Everyone else was either a family member or a guest, and although Andres had fantasized about bringing Marabela here himself, it would've been impossible to escape speculation from other members.

As the days passed Andres and Marabela discovered it was easier to ignore each other than it was to feign casual acquaintance. When they sat down at the balcony for meals, Andres chose the chair farthest from Marabela. He served her drink last even when her cup was closest within reach from the bar. At the beach, he laid his towel next to Elena's, barely looking in her direction if Marabela happened to fall within the same line of sight.

On the third day, Elena announced that she was going for a swim. Andres and Marabela watched her from the shore, eyes squinting, heads fixed straight ahead, and discussed when to tell her about their relationship.

"It'll make the rest of the week awkward if we do it now," Andres said.

"This isn't awkward enough already? I can't imagine it being any worse," Marabela said. "You're not the one who's sharing a bedroom with her. She keeps asking me what I think of you. I feel so guilty. She should've never invited me here. I don't deserve it."

"What'd you tell her?"

"About what?"

"When she asked about me."

Marabela's scorn quickly gave way to a smile. She paused, playing with her thoughts. "I said you seem like a good guy. I don't know. I try to keep it vague. I can't remember what I am and am not supposed to know about you. She thinks the only time we've spent together is when it's been us three."

Up ahead, they watched as the waves seemed to swallow Elena and spit her out. Each time, she stood up stronger, welcoming more. Keeping her back toward the horizon, she'd lengthen her body in anticipation of the ocean's punch. It came upon her so fast it thrust her hair over her head. When she'd come up for air she'd only laugh, adjust her top, and wait for more.

"It's got a lot of fight in it today," she said when she came back. "I think I need a drink." She signaled to a young man dressed in white linens and brown loafers, then ordered two pisco sours and a fresh pineapple juice.

"Which room, señorita?" he asked.

"Mine's Duarez," Elena said before Andres could speak. "The two of them are together. Under Jimenez." She pointed at them with one finger, left it suspended in the air as she rested her elbow against the wooden chair. The anger in her eyes quickly faded into sadness under the heat of the sun.

"Don't act so surprised—it's hardly a secret. And I gave you every possible chance to tell me."

He hadn't realized it until then, but she had. In the most mundane way, in the moments when the rush of party preparations and meals together seemed to pause for breath, Elena had commented on how happy Andres looked, how good a friend Marabela was. Her bitterness revealed itself draped in kindness, carefully crafted and hardened by pain.

"We didn't know how—" Andres said.

"It was my idea," Marabela interrupted. "I didn't want to say anything until I knew it was worth it."

Elena remained calm, gentle, like she was tired from a fight she'd never even started. "So you were trying him out to see if you wanted to keep him? If not, I could have him as planned?"

It was the first time Elena had spoken about their relationship in such certain terms. She was claiming it and relinquishing it all at once.

"Ele, please. We just didn't want to hurt you. I was trying to think of the right time. I thought we'd go to dinner, talk things through . . ." Andres said.

"Break it to me gently," she said, finishing his sentence for him. "You really flatter yourself. And you underestimate me. I can't believe you'd think I'm that fragile."

"So you're okay with this?" Andres said.

She shrugged and brought her sunglasses from her forehead over her eyes. "What does it matter now?"

"It matters to me."

He waited for Elena to respond, but she only lounged back and fell asleep with her feet buried in the sand. Andres relaxed and allowed himself to do the same, assuming her silence was a truce, but when he woke and walked Marabela back to their room, Elena had already left, her bedsheets tucked tight under the mattress, smooth as a fake smile.

DAY 9

The end of the week comes, carrying the worst kind of anticipation. He can't stay away from work any longer without arousing suspicions, so today Andres will go back to his routine even though everything is different. Jorge drives him to work, taking a new route. This is just a quick trip in and out of the office, to keep his employees from asking too many questions, but secretly Andres wishes he could stay there forever and forget any other obligation.

In the elevator, he feels his nerves grow tense with every passing floor. When the doors slide open, he gets the sensation he's been dropped into a chaotic yet structured operation. It's the reason why he chose this building, but in this moment he regrets it. Stepping out of the elevator makes him feel like a lonesome ant, out of place where everyone else is busy. The company headquarters are in a large, high-ceilinged room filled with wooden desks arranged like dominoes, buttressing one another in random, unified order. Windows line the entire upper half of the walls, too high up for workers to gaze out at the busy streets, but perfect for letting in lots of sunlight, which makes the space feel larger than it is. Andres's office, along with the other top executives', is in a private room along the perimeter. It is impossible for him to arrive unnoticed.

It's as busy a day as any, but Andres feels as if he's watching his employees shuffle papers around and make phone calls through a one-way mirror. Occasionally, they look up as he walks by, and a few nod or say hello, but it doesn't feel like anyone can really see him. They're all worried about work and he's trying to find a way to save his wife, their jobs, and their families. No matter how hard he tries, Andres has never been able to look at his employees without seeing their families. It is a burden and a responsibility that he can't—and won't—take lightly.

He walks along the outside of the domino desks instead of cutting through the middle like he usually does. He passes fewer people this way.

There's Jacqui Saez by the fax machine, who recently took two days off because she had family in town for her daughter's christening. Rodrigo Marquez is typing at his computer and talking on the phone at the same time. Andres knows he has five sisters. He passes Donna, Rebecca, and Ada, all secretaries who bond over their jobs and have children who go to the same school as Cynthia. It's not unheard of for them to take turns carpooling, and they've asked Andres several times to let them know if he ever needs a ride for Cynthia. He tilts his head and smiles at each of them as he nears his office, afraid that if he says hello, his voice might crack and give him away.

"Good morning," Edith says, carrying a mug of coffee in one hand and a manila file in the other. "Before I forget, these are the papers your wife meant to pick up the other day. You said they were urgent so I wanted to bring them to you first thing."

"Of course. Thank you," Andres says, placing the file in his suitcase before he forgets. His mother and Graves will be expecting to see the reports the next time they meet, but for now he can't stand to look at them. These papers were meant to be a lesson in enterprise for his son; now they'll be just scrutinized so a stranger can name his price.

He closes the door, takes off his shoes, and sits with his legs crossed and with his back against the couch across from his desk. The everyday sounds of his busy office are dampened, and he's left to his own helplessness, unsure what to do next. Edith always places the day's paper and his coffee on the table next to the couch, and Andres rarely takes the time to ingest either. But ever since Marabela was taken, he can't help but look through newspapers for information on kidnappings.

With his back curled like a faucet over today's *El Tribunal*, Andres scans the stories. The letters blur together as he runs over the lines with a covered pen, a habit he picked up from reading contracts quickly but carefully, ready to make changes at any moment. Today's news is not some document that can be edited, but still Andres clings to his small rituals.

When he recognizes a name on page five, he's almost afraid to keep reading. The thirteen-year-old son of Edgar Villanueva was stolen from his own home two nights ago. He had been sleeping in his bedroom while his parents were still at work. Police think the kidnappers watched the house for weeks, learning the patterns of their life, the times that people came and left, the times that the maids opened the gates to check the mail and take out the trash. In the perfect moment, one man gagged the maid and took her back into the house. Three others went into the bedroom, covered the boy's head and tied his hands. They pushed him into the back of their truck and drove off, so fast that they left the smell of burned rubber in the air.

Andres imagines it was similar for Marabela. They were quick. They covered her face and tossed her against the hard metal bars of a truck. They cared if she was alive, but barely.

Andres imagines the agony is similar for Villanueva. Instantly, he feels a kinship with Edgar, one he never could have imagined feeling when Andres met Villanueva and his wife six months ago at a mutual friend's wedding. They'd all sat at the same table and Andres had made sure to be polite and approachable but otherwise assumed that would be the extent of their acquaintance. His wife was a petite woman with blond hair and freckles, who spoke with a Spanish lisp and a hint of suspense in her voice, as if she were always on the verge of telling a joke. She'd kept her arm wrapped around Edgar the entire time, gently scratching the back of his hand with her fingernails. Andres found he didn't like looking at them for too long. They were a mirror image of the couple he and Marabela used to be.

"They were nice," Marabela said afterward, as they walked to their car. "I invited them over for dinner next week."

"Why?"

"You didn't like them?"

He just shrugged his shoulders. "They seemed a bit fake."

"They seemed happy."

"Too happy."

"Only you could turn that into a bad thing," she said. She began searching through her purse for something he knew she wouldn't find; it was her way of avoiding eye contact when she was annoyed.

"It just didn't seem real," Andres said.

"And what? Is it hard for you to believe a married couple could be happy?"

"You know I didn't mean it like that."

"I don't know what you meant," she said as she climbed into their car. "Look on the bright side; it'll be good for you to get to know each other. For business." But she was bitter when she said it, and they didn't speak the rest of the ride home.

The article has a picture of the boy in his school uniform, and a picture of his politician father sitting in what Andres assumes is their home, with his face buried in his hands. He pleads for no one to hurt his son in the pages of the very newspaper Andres's father used to own. Edgar doesn't bother threatening anyone. He just talks about how money isn't an issue, and that the captors will get whatever they want as long as they get his boy home safely.

Andres is afraid for him, and then jealous, and then disgusted that this kind of jealousy can even exist. The fact that Edgar has gone public tells him that these kidnappers are nothing like Marabela's; Edgar can go to the police, can go to the press, because his son's captors are part of a revolution they want to publicize. Their crime is all politics, not business. Targeting a politician's son is a way for the terrorist organizations to reassert their power, in case anyone's forgotten. In some twisted way, Edgar has a freedom Andres can only hope for; he has no secrets and therefore everyone's support.

There is even a radio station for families like Edgar's to send messages to their loved ones. Sometimes Andres imagines himself waiting in line for five, six hours, as some of the families do, all for the chance to broadcast a few words and hope that they find their way to Marabela. But he can't bring himself to defy Hades's demands for secrecy and silence.

Instead, he's been listening to the radio late at night before bed, with the volume turned so low that if he breathes too hard he can't hear it.

We love you. We are always thinking of you. We will never give up until you're back with your family, where you belong.

Their grief has a voice, when all Andres can cling to is quiet desperation.

He decides he needs to leave the office and gives Edith an excuse about being needed at home, but as he makes his way back to the car he realizes it's the last place he wants to go. It's still early, and he could use some time to clear his head.

He stops at the bronze statue of the city's founder in the center of the plaza while passersby swirl around. Nobody seems to notice him, though he must look out of place: a lost man in a three-piece suit, clutching his briefcase like a child with a plastic lunch box, wandering around with no real place to go. He turns toward the breeze so he can feel the wind in his hair. The flower beds surrounding the statue give it an artificial touch, their brightness too intense to be real. He's always walked by them in a hurry, and he regrets that only now, when his mind is incapable of appreciating their beauty, does he have time to stand and look at them.

On every street corner, men in bright vests make a business out of exchanging tourists' foreign money for their own. They've stuffed their pockets so full of cash and coins it looks like they're carrying rocks. Andres wonders how they keep from being robbed; it's no secret that cash is their trade. Since the exchange rate changes constantly, no one ever knows what they'll get. Tourists approach the men, ask, "How much for fifty?" and the men type numbers into their handheld calculators, holding the screens up to their customers' faces. The tourists always look so impressed. *So much for so little?* they seem to say. It is the greatest illusion of all.

The locals know better, though. Their currency is ever changing. First there was the inti, named after the ancient Incan sun god, then the sol, Spanish for "sun." Now the nuevo sol promises something new. The government says it is stronger, but still no one trusts it will be worth tomorrow what it's worth today. The people can't easily forget their shock when their money plummeted not even two years ago, and they realized that even a million amounted to very little. How was it possible to have a million of anything and nearly nothing all at once?

The truth is, Andres stopped counting his wealth in soles long ago. With inflation the way it's been, counting cash is like counting grains of sand as the tide comes in.

"*Señor, cuatro soles,*" a little boy says to him. "I'll polish your shoes. Sit down right here, señor. *Cuatro soles.*" The boy pulls a brush and black shoe polish from a wooden box, then places it on the floor and sits on it. He taps the side of it three times, signaling for Andres to sit.

Andres knows he could get his shoes polished for less about a block away, but he sits down on the green bench because he has nothing better to do, or nothing better that he'd like to do, or simply because he's tired and he hasn't the energy to argue.

The boy can't be older than four, but he rubs the brown leather shoes with a strength that makes Andres rock back and forth. The sensation is not unlike the feeling of hurtling down an unpaved highway. Every five strokes or so, the boy tosses the brush so it spins and circles in the air, then taps his box twice before catching it. It's a little show that might help him get a few cents of extra change, but Andres is too busy staring at a crack in the sidewalk to notice.

A flash of yellow cloth catches Andres's eye across the street, a woman with a pale dress caught in the wind, walking at a slow pace, as if admiring the grimy buildings along the plaza. He realizes with a start that it's Marabela—unmistakably—the wavy dark brown hair that bounces as she walks, the way she swings her arms side to side, nonchalantly. Andres jumps up and begins running toward her, brushing the little boy off his wooden box. In the distance, he hears the boy shouting after him, demanding payment, but the voice fades as Andres picks up speed. Marabela turns at the corner of the street, still about a block ahead of Andres. Even though he runs faster, he can't catch up to her in time. It's like a strange scene out of a horror film, where the villain advances at a steady pace while his victim dashes through the woods. Andres pushes people out of his way, bumps their shoulders, and almost trips over a woman's basket of fruit on the edge of the sidewalk, but none of it matters, just that he reaches Marabela before she disappears from his life for a third time.

Finally she stops at a phone booth about forty feet ahead of him. In an instant Andres jumps to several different conclusions, from the best (she's escaped and she's trying to call home) to the worst (she set this whole thing up and now she's walking around in a brand-new dress). He knew she was capable of leaving him, but putting the family through so much pain just for money and the satisfaction of destroying his company is a new low. He supposes she always had it in her—the seeds were there, in the form of jokes and sarcasm.

Andres swings open the door of the phone booth, out of breath. She just stands there, her eyes wide open and afraid of the stranger in front of her. The woman in the phone booth cannot possibly be the same one he followed. She has a sharper nose than Marabela's and tired wrinkles around her eyes.

He apologizes but slams the phone booth shut. The woman jumps, and he tries not to look back at her so he won't have to see her judging him, losing his grip on what he wants so badly to be real.

When Andres wanders back to the plaza, he finds the shoe polish boy rooting through his briefcase.

"Here," he says, taking eight soles out of his pocket, doubling the amount he owes. Andres knows he shouldn't be tossing extra money around, even if it's just a few bucks, but it's what Marabela would have done. She always used to say, "What's a little change for us? Nothing. For them, it's everything." The boy's smile tells Andres she was right, and soon he runs off with his box and brushes in tow, leaving the briefcase open and ransacked on the sidewalk.

It's an exhausting effort for Andres to pick up the papers and pens. Each time he bends over, his pant legs lift over his ankles, revealing the beige socks he put on this morning without bothering to check whether they matched. He can feel his slacks slipping past his waist. In just a few days, he's lost not only his sanity but also quite a bit of weight.

His thoughts turn to his dry throat and a sudden urge for a drink, something strong that would sting on the way down. About a block away, there's a bar he frequents after work, and now his body wanders over without him giving it much thought. Instead of walls, the bar has a large mirror that extends from one corner of the room to the other, and Andres can see his addled reflection as he places an order. The bartender quickly fills up a glass and Andres slouches over it, a warm fire that he wants to keep to himself.

But his quiet moment is quickly interrupted by a familiar voice: "Andres!" He turns to find Nico Valdez, the head of a company Andres works with frequently, holding a drink as he walks through the dense crowd.

A smile spreads across Andres's face. He's always liked Nico. In the fourteen years they've worked together, their companies have grown at similar rates. They've talked at this bar many times before, venting about lazy employees and difficult business partners, sharing tricks for how to beat traffic in the mornings. They've been to each other's house for dinner, though less in recent months, when his and Marabela's problems became nearly impossible to conceal. They shake hands and pat each other's back.

"*Hola, hermano,*" Andres says, relieved to see a familiar face but nervous that this is as far as his lies about Marabela will go. Surely Nico's heard from his wife that Marabela's disappeared from her social circles. Surely someone has already talked.

"How are you? How are the wife and kids?" Nico asks.

"They're great. Just fine, thanks." The lie is instinctual; he can't remember the last time he didn't feel the need to put his guard up.

Nico doesn't seem to be paying attention. He's got his eyes on the bar, contemplating his order. "A certain kind of day requires a certain kind of drink," he says, slapping his palm against the bar. "What are you having?"

Andres tilts his glass at him. Whisky. Straight.

"Oof! That bad, huh?" Nico laughs, not realizing the truth in his joke, or perhaps not caring to uncover it. "Two glasses of that, a nice nap in the backseat while Jorge drives you home . . . tell him to take the long way and go around the block a couple of times, and you'll be set."

Andres takes another sip and waits for the next question to come, tries to think of how he'll answer it. The captors said no cops, utter secrecy, but how would they know if Andres told one trusted friend? He can't be expected to carry the burden of this secret on his own. It'd be so nice to finally unload, to have someone listen to his side of the story.

"So tell me, how long do you think before *El Chino* starts showing up to everything in a tank?" Nico says.

Andres takes a sip of his drink, already tired of hearing and reading about the *Fujigolpe*. He knows there's little he can say to keep Nico from declaring his opinions in dramatic fashion as usual, so he decides to fuel the flames. "Personally, I think it's about time. At least someone's doing something."

"*Hermano*, really? He suspended the goddamned constitution! This is going to change everything. Watch, years from now when these *terroristas de mierda* have been locked up for decades and no one remembers their names or what they did, then the people will start complaining about democracy and everything they willingly gave up when they were too afraid to stand up for it. Remember, I said it first. Anyone who gets rid of freedom in the name of freedom is no better than the terrorists."

"But they'll be locked up. Isn't that the point?" Andres takes a couple more sips of his drink and gets up. This casual encounter isn't providing the relief he hoped it would. He can tell Nico is disappointed in him but doesn't want to end the conversation on a sour note.

"Don't forget—tell Jorge, twice around the block and you'll be rested like a baby."

"Right. Nice to catch up, Nico."

"You didn't finish your drink," he says.

Andres shakes his head and waves. On his way back to the car, he passes the phone booth where he encountered Marabela's look-alike. It's empty now, and the receiver dangles from its metal rope. He contemplates picking it up, wonders whom he could possibly call. His childhood friends haven't been in touch in years, having distanced themselves after he and Marabela married. He tried to convince himself that it was because these friends were jealous of his happiness, but now he can admit that Marabela might have made them uncomfortable with her habit of turning even the most casual conversations into an opportunity to lecture about racial divides between the classes or the short-term collective memory of citizens who continue to support militarization. He would do anything to hear one of her impassioned diatribes right now.

Of course, their current circle of friends—Paula and Juan from when Marabela worked at *El Tribunal*, and Mari and Tomas, who co-chair a literacy program Marabela volunteers at once a week—adore her. They know her too well to believe she would disappear for days without telling them, and when Andres gives them his rehearsed excuse each time they call, he gets the sense they're not fooled. He suspects they've agreed to take turns calling, one every other day. They no longer ask where she is, just if she's all right and if anything's changed. He wants to tell Paula more than anything.

"*¿Como va todo?*" she'll say.

Things are not going all right, he wants to answer. Nothing is going, everything is at a standstill, and sometimes he fears what will kill them in the end is the waiting.

He knows Paula's concern is genuine. She's the kind of person who listens to everything you do and don't say, and it's exactly this quality that makes her a great friend and an even better reporter. But Andres knows Marabela's friends are not the right people to tell. Confide in one, confide in all of them, she used to say, and even she admitted this wasn't always a good thing. Even if he wanted to tell them the truth, Andres isn't comfortable enough to reveal such vulnerabilities. He doesn't feel the same confidence with the friends he's met in adulthood as he did with the ones from his youth; their relationships are tinged with formality. There are lines he can't cross, gray areas he can't explore.

In the bar with Nico, maybe he could have complained about the distance he's felt from Marabela, but he'd never admit that he first noticed because of the sex. She stopped initiating nearly a year ago, and on the rare occasion that Andres coaxed her into intimacy, it felt like she expected him to do all the work, like it was a privilege he had to earn. By the time she left him four months ago, he'd stopped trying. The anticipation of her rejection smothered any sexual urge he had. Instead of mourning this aspect of their relationship, Marabela had seemed relieved.

Andres walks to the end of the block where he usually meets Jorge and waits for the car to pull up. As he climbs into the backseat, he chuckles at the absurdity of Nico's advice.

"God, what a day. I ran into Nico and he said I should have you take the long way home so I can sleep back here. Like a baby in a carriage. Ridiculous, right?"

"Señor?" Jorge looks through the rearview mirror at Andres, puzzled by the question. Andres shrugs sheepishly.

"My mother never had a carriage quite like this. There's really no comparison," Jorge says. Even though Andres can't see his mouth in the mirror, he catches the driver's smile in his eyes. As they drive home, he drifts in and out of sleep, his head bobbing up and down, side to side.

"Same time tomorrow?" Jorge asks when they get home. It's a rhetorical question but a necessary one, his voice just loud enough to wake Andres from his nap.

"Thank you," he says, grateful to be spared the embarrassment of having to acknowledge that he was dozing in the middle of the afternoon, half drunk, while his wife's whereabouts are unknown.

He tries his best not to make much noise as he drags his feet up to their bedroom. Once there, Andres closes his eyes to think, but all he hears is the *click click* of the alarm on his nightstand. It's a fancy digital clock he bought a year ago when Marabela started sleeping in. She used to be first to wake in the house, naturally and without any sort of clock, ready to start the day. On weekday mornings she'd walk over to Andres's side of the bed and kiss him on his forehead, cheeks, eyelids, and mouth, because she thought people should be woken gently if they were to be pulled from sleep at all. He looks at the clock's large letters and silver face, wondering how he could have been so blind to Marabela's unhappiness. He could've asked what was making her so tired, why she'd lost her eagerness to face each day.

Instead, he'd bought an alarm, an ornate, cold metal clock that he now remembers cost twelve dollars. The wooden nightstand it sits on is an antique; he could probably get two hundred for it. He starts doing the math in his head, calculating prices and converting them to dollars. His black leather dress shoes, the books he said he'd read but never got around to, the magical eyeglass cleaning kit he let an old woman convince him he needed, his collection of Mozart and Beethoven cassette tapes aligned in their cardboard package, the audio set and its two brown speakers with silver mesh—everything that surrounds him has a price tag. He lies back on his bed and tries to tally it all up in his head, but there are too many numbers to keep track of. The money he has. The money they want. The amount he can get for the company and the number of employees who will lose their jobs if he sells it. The number of days Marabela has been gone and the years it might take her to recover.

If it were as simple as multiplying or dividing and carrying the remainders, he'd be satisfied. But these figures all blend together, losing their meaning, and his eyelids dim the lights in his mind until he falls into a deep sleep.

❖ ❖ ❖

He wakes up to the sound of Cynthia's footsteps running down the hall, followed by heavier steps that make his heart race until he realizes they belong to Guillermo. The two of them are laughing, and Guillermo is out of breath as he chases her downstairs to the living room, shouting, "I got your arm!" and "Your elbow!" and "Your knee!" each time he catches her.

It's nice to hear laughter again. Andres stretches and descends the stairs unnoticed.

Cynthia seems to have worn out Guillermo, who is now catching his breath on the couch. He reaches over to the coffee table where he left several documents and starts sorting them into a neater pile.

"What is all this, anyway?" Cynthia asks.

"Just a whole bunch of work stuff," Guillermo says. He quickly scoops up the pile and taps it against the wooden surface to straighten out the edges. He keeps the writing faced away from her.

"It's about my mom, isn't it?" She looks so sad and dejected. Andres, who wasn't purposely eavesdropping until now, freezes in his steps at the edge of the stairs.

"Why do you say that?" Guillermo asks. He doesn't talk to her like most adults speak to children. His voice is casual, his tone genuinely interested. He acts like her question is nothing out of the ordinary.

"It has to do with her being gone, doesn't it? I'm not blind; I know how these things go. My friends whose parents are divorced say they each had lawyers to help them. Is that why you're here all the time, and she's not?" The way she looks at him, it's like she's begging to be proven wrong. Andres wishes it were so simple. From where he's standing he can't see Guillermo's face, but all the usual stiffness seems to slip out of him.

"I'm not a lawyer, *chiquitita*. I'm sorry if somehow I made you think that's why I'm here."

She doesn't respond—even if she didn't believe him, Andres knows his daughter is too polite to say so. Yet he's afraid of what she'll ask next, so he takes a few steps back up the stairs and dashes down noisily, hoping the distraction will be enough to change the subject.

"What's all this running around I just heard?" he asks, struggling to sound cheerful.

They both turn, and the relief in Guillermo's face is palpable. Cynthia, no longer in the mood for games, shrugs her shoulders but manages an unenthusiastic smile.

Andres takes a seat on the couch across from Guillermo and wraps his arm around his daughter, pulling her close to him as he sorts through the day's mail.

"*Tremenda*, isn't she? I'm surprised you kept up with her as long as you did," he teases. It's nice to pretend this is a normal situation. The proud father, rubbing his daughter's belly, bragging about her to the security consultant.

Guillermo happily plays along. "I have three nieces. I'd forgotten how much energy they have at this age. Nothing like a child to make an old man feel older."

"Careful. I'm not too far behind you," Andres says.

They laugh and thankfully Cynthia joins them. Andres looks

down at the papers in his hand and stops to clear his throat. At the top is a small, square envelope, unlabeled except for his name in black capital letters in the very center. With one look, the men decide it's time to head upstairs. Andres taps Cynthia on the behind and suggests she go check if Consuelo needs any help with dinner.

In the darkroom they take their usual seats across from each other, Andres feeling like they're carrying a bomb they have to isolate from the rest of the household. When he finally opens the envelope, it takes several seconds for the image to register. He has a hard time believing this is real, that the guns pointed at each side of Marabela's head are not toys made of plastic, the grenades hanging from her neck not just heavy, flashy jewels. He holds the tiny image in his hand and remembers what Marabela used to tell him about the paradox of photography: it is an art meant for the viewer, not the subject. It captures a stolen moment, shows it to the world so it's always remembered, while the subject who actually lived it would probably rather forget.

Marabela's cheekbones are sharp instead of round, her face black and blue, and her shoulders droop toward the floor. In her hands she holds a copy of *El Tribunal* with today's headlines. Marabela clutches it across her chest like a shield, as if words and images will protect her. Everything Andres has lost, everything left for him to lose, stares back at him.

The woman in the picture is not his wife but a remnant of her, a desperate body cast away in some dark corner. It's hard for him to believe that such a drastic transformation could take place in only a few days. The look in her eyes is terrifying, as if the person behind the camera just sprang upon her from behind a wall.

He flicks the photo at Guillermo, who takes a quick look and says, "We knew this might happen. They're just trying to manipulate you."

"Let them. So long as they don't touch her I don't care what they do to me. They can twist me into little knots for all I care."

"That's not going to help the situation. If they're going to hurt her, they're going to hurt her. You have to remember that they're the bad guys here, not you. None of this is your fault."

But it is. Andres can't bring himself to say it, but he knows it's true. There is so much he could've done differently. If he hadn't asked her to pick up the papers, or if he hadn't chosen the location he did for his office, if he hadn't opened his business in the first place, none of this would have happened.

The phone rings. It shatters his thoughts.

Before the first ring is even finished, Guillermo has leaped out of his chair and placed the headphones over his ears. It is almost as if he's programmed for this—a man on autopilot, on a mission to calculate his enemy's every move—while Andres needs a moment to collect himself.

He clears the desk and answers, asking first for the speaker's identity and then for Marabela's proof of life.

"She's not in the mood to talk today," Hades says.

"What does that mean? What have you done to her?"

"Relax," he says, like this is a joke, like he's only hidden some small belonging. "She's here but you'll have to talk to her through me."

Guillermo snaps his fingers and points at Andres's desk. Where there used to be a calendar, Andres now has a list of questions, and he looks to them for comfort because they are proof that despite everything that's happened, there are still some things in this world shared only by him and Marabela.

"Ask her about the flower vendor and the cabdriver. What were their names?"

Andres waits and tries to listen for a trace of Marabela's voice in the background. It's been years since either one of them has mentioned the witnesses at their wedding. The ceremony was spontaneous, like everything Marabela did. They were hiking in Machu Picchu one July and got caught up in the energy of the place, the mysticism. Maybe it was the elevation, the lack of oxygen in the air, or the way the city, hidden away from the world for centuries, seemed so impenetrable. Here was proof that some things could live on forever. As they stood at the Inti Punku, the Gateway of the Sun, Marabela had said, simply, "We should get married." For witnesses, they chose the cabdriver who took them to the chapel and the flower vendor who sold them Marabela's bouquet.

Andres wants to laugh now at the naïveté of their first years together, but it's more depressing than it is funny. Their love had been so selfish, blind to the suffering of those around them. When they'd returned to Lima, they'd learned that the military had seized control of the city's major newspapers—it was only a matter of time before they'd take over Rolando's. Yet Andres still expected his father to celebrate the marriage, to be happy that his son had even more incentive to start his own company, now that Rolando could no longer guarantee that he'd have a legacy left to pass on.

In the days that followed their wedding, Andres wondered if his father might disown him. Instead, he offered Marabela a job as a photographer.

"I know you'd be miserable working for a state-run paper, but they haven't come for ours yet. We'll hold down the fort together," he told her. It was a peace offering, a way for the paper to stay in the family, even if it wasn't the family he'd chosen. Marabela accepted, and Andres took it as a silent blessing, a sign that his father had finally embraced his new bride.

Hades's voice interrupts Andres's thoughts: "Iyarina and Maiqui."

"Okay," he says, relieved to hear the right answer to his question, but also feeling like he's sullied one of their most precious memories.

"You're welcome. We didn't have to do that, you know. We've already sent you the proof you need," Hades says.

"Please, I'm doing everything I can. I can have seventy thousand for you. Just don't hurt her."

"For seventy thousand? I can't promise you anything."

"If I could get more money for her to be safe, don't you think I would do it?"

"I think you don't realize yet what either one of us is capable of."

"That's not—that's not true."

"You think this is just another business deal, and you're so used to being in control that you can't help but try to negotiate."

"I may be used to business going a certain way. But we both know there is more at stake here. This is the mother of my children. Are you . . . are you a father?" Andres asks, hoping to appeal to the man's emotions, as Guillermo had suggested.

"That's none of your business."

"All I'm saying is that, if you are, you know I'm not playing around. I'm doing everything I can. Once we get the loans from the bank I'll have seventy and—"

"You expect me to agree to less than a tenth of our original agreement?"

Andres looks up at Guillermo, who's waving and pointing for him to read one of the many cue cards he's pinned to the walls.

"We never had an original agreement. I never agreed to it," he says, his words slow and punctuated. "I never agreed because it was an impossible number. The money you were asking for doesn't exist. There's nothing I can do to make that happen. It's a fake number. This one I'm offering is real. You can't think of it as lost money because . . . it never could have happened."

He stops then, unsure where these words came from, and takes a moment to breathe as Guillermo gives him an approving thumbs-up.

"It won't work. We'll call you tomorrow with what will."

The line goes dead, but Andres still feels his heart beating, and it's like he's been running for miles, wishing for a moment's rest, only to realize his body wants to keep going without him.

He releases a long heavy breath and puts his head in his hands. The list of questions he prepared for Marabela's proof of life stares back from underneath his elbow. He draws a thick blue line over the flower vendor and cabdriver. It was a risky question to ask, but he had to know if she'd held on to this. Intertwined with his fear is a thread of doubt he can't stop pulling, the one that screams he's already lost her, she's already moved on.

And yet, she remembered.

"That's a beautiful name," Marabela had told the flower vendor as Andres counted out the coins for her bouquet. "Where is it from?"

The woman smiled and told her it was Quechua, the language of the Incas. "*Iyarina* means 'never forgets.'"

5

DAY 10

WHEN HE VISITS Elena for the second time, Andres takes a book and two sets of flowers, anticipating that Betty, the lady at the front desk, might need some extra convincing. The bouquet of pink roses and white ranunculus filled out with baby's breath is a big hit. Betty hurries around the desk to receive them and thanks him. She unlocks the door and tells him that since he probably knows his way to Elena's room, she'll be off getting a vase.

The facility seems busier this morning. Nurses and doctors rush past him carrying small metal trays and syringes. Others push carts with plastic cups filled with pills, the wheels creaking as they move. The practitioners take quiet steps, but the medicine trays keep giving them away. Andres catches a few moans and screams in the second it takes a nurse to open and close the door to her patient's room. It occurs to him today is the first time he's seeing this place for what it truly is. During his last visit in the off-hours, he let himself believe it was nothing out of the ordinary, just a friend stopping by to check in on another at the hospital. Except here, the patients are sick from loneliness or despair, and their wounds don't always heal. He feels like he can't trust what he sees—perfectly healthy people with invisible demons. As he nears Elena's room, he picks up speed and enters without so much as a knock, feeling like a kid looking for a place to hide.

But one scream has followed him inside. Before he can even close the door, Elena ducks underneath her bed and covers her face.

"It's okay, it's just me!" He sees her peek through the empty space beneath the bed, and she looks at once relieved and agitated.

"You scared me," she says, standing up.

"Shit, I'm sorry, are you okay?"

She stands with one hand in the air as if it's wet, and when he reaches her side he sees she's scratched her thigh against the bed's metal frame. Her blood—so bright it looks like it could catch fire—sticks to her fingertips and has stained her thin white gown.

"I'll get a nurse to bring you some bandages," Andres says.

"It's not a big deal. Just . . . knock next time." She looks around the room, hands still suspended, for something to clean her wound.

"But the blood." He feels like he has to do something. "Just push down on it, put some pressure . . . I'll be right back."

Now he is like the nurses and doctors, trying to mute his steps as he runs through the hall and back to the kitchen where Betty is clipping the stems of her roses.

"What happened?"

"It's just a scratch, nothing to worry about. Can you help me bandage it up?"

They hurry back to her room and Andres sits in the corner armchair, nibbling his nails and trying not to stare as Betty pulls Elena's gown up to her stomach, exposing her thighs and her yellow string-bikini panties. After she's bandaged up, Elena runs her fingers over the gauze, gently tracing its path around her inner thigh. She stretches her leg out and points her toes, as if making sure everything still works. She takes her time covering herself back up, and when he sees her head rise, he quickly looks away, hoping he was quick enough to dodge her glance in his direction. He feels ashamed he didn't look away sooner.

Betty, still kneeling on the floor, tucks her gauze and tape into a plastic box and leans into Elena, rubbing her knee. She eyes Andres suspiciously and turns back to her patient.

"Everything okay in here?"

"I'm fine, Betty." Elena cuts her off and turns to face Andres, tucking her hair behind her ear. He nearly apologizes again for scaring her, but she looks so upset by the situation that he thinks it best to ignore it.

"Let's go for a walk. We can do that, right?" He looks at Elena but catches Betty nodding behind her.

"Whatever," Elena says. "It's all the same to me."

It's early enough that the heat hasn't settled in yet, and when they stand in the shade it's so refreshing it's almost chilly. Elena looks away from him, scratching at the bandage underneath her gown. "Don't you have to be at work or something?"

"Do you want me to leave?" Andres asks.

She tilts her weight from one foot to the other, bobbing from side to side as she crosses her arms. "What do you suggest we do?" she finally asks.

"I just thought we'd talk. Catch up on lost time."

At this, she chuckles. "Lost time is gone forever. Nobody ever catches up."

Andres tries to stay cheerful, keep smiling, but this is not the same Elena from a few days ago. "Well, then we start over. Or we start from where we left off."

"Where did we leave off?" she asks, though they both know the answer. There's no point in avoiding it now.

"With a conversation we never had. That weekend at the beach, you told me you were fine with Marabela and me, but then you left without saying a word."

"You could've asked me about it."

"You could've protested. You had every right. I kept waiting for a fight from you."

"Someone who doesn't want to be with you is not worth fighting for." She says this with so much conviction it's like she's rehearsed it, repeated it, many times before.

He'd never thought of it like that. He looks away and wonders what takes more courage: asking someone to stay or accepting that they shouldn't need convincing. "You're right, I see that now," he says.

For a moment, Elena looks like she wants to say something, but then her cheeks relax and her eyes soften. "You've gotten better at apologizing. I like that." She takes his hand and squeezes it at his side, a gesture so quick he almost doesn't notice it.

They decide to walk around a bit, squinting and smiling at each other as the sun catches and melts away the tension. Andres studies the small wrinkles around Elena's eyes, the way her skin looks thinner and almost translucent, revealing the pain that her face tries to hide. He wonders if it's an aftereffect of her kidnapping or her time here at the facility, and if he should prepare for Marabela to look the same if—when—she comes home. There is so much he wants to ask Elena; he wishes she could lead him through her experience and say it all works out in the end, but he's afraid of where his questions will take her.

"How do you like it here?" he asks.

She shrugs and twists the ends of her gown. "It's nice. My parents say it's the cleanest, quietest rehab center in the country, so I guess I can't complain."

"Have they visited often?"

"Just three times so far. They've come every Friday since I've been here. Maybe they need the weekend to recover from seeing me."

"Or . . . maybe they look forward to visiting you so much, it gets them through a busy week."

She gives a low, forced laugh—out of gratitude or disbelief, he can't tell.

"How is your father, anyway? I don't remember the last time I saw him."

"At your father's funeral, I think," Elena says.

"Of course." He feels so foolish. If he'd thought about it for half a second rather than trying to fill the silence, he would've remembered the funeral. Elena's father had tried to say a few words in Rolando's honor, but words had failed him. The men had been friends and business partners for longer than they'd known their own wives. The image of Saul's hands, how they shook as he reached for a handkerchief to clear the sweat from his face, is one that still comes back to Andres in the most unexpected moments.

"But he's still writing," Elena adds, quickly changing the subject. "Everyone here knows to bring me the paper early in the morning. I think his pieces on the last elections and the *Fujigolpe* were his best yet."

"They were very well argued. I imagined your mother beaming with pride as I read them."

"Well, she is his biggest fan."

"Yours, too, as I recall."

"Yes. So you can imagine how hard this has all been on her."

He puts his arm around her shoulders, and she takes a few quick steps forward until their legs are synched up—two pairs of right legs followed by two pairs of left. "Don't worry about that right now. You know she'd want you focusing on yourself. On feeling better. Does it help? Being here?"

A long silence passes as Elena looks around, and her eyes stay on the horizon when she finally speaks. "I think so. I mean, it's nice to not be the craziest person in the house for once. Here, everyone leaves me in peace. Being home just felt like I could never be alone. Everyone always kept an eye on me, like I was a bomb waiting to explode."

"Were you?"

"Maybe. I am full of surprises lately."

"That's always been one of your best qualities."

"You say that now," she says, rubbing his hand and smiling long-ingly. "Because you remember who I used to be before. These are different types of surprises."

"You can still be that person. You still are that person, even if you don't see her. I can see her."

"Because you bring it out in me," she says. "Not every day is like this, you know. It's not all walks around the yard."

"You can leave anytime you want. Right?"

She nods. "My parents found this place, but I checked in voluntarily. I needed to get away."

He looks around and finds it an odd choice of words. The grounds may be vast, but they're still locked behind gates at the edges. "How long do you plan on staying?"

She shrugs as if the question is unimportant. "However long it takes till I feel safe out there again."

He doesn't understand. "How will you know unless you leave?"

"It's not that simple. I just want to take it slow. Did you know today's the first time I've been outside?" She looks up at the sky and wraps her arm around his. "Everyone else has a schedule. They have times when they come out and play cards or throw a ball around. I've just never felt like it. I prefer being left alone. Usually."

They make their way to one of the gazebos and sit across from each other, holding hands over the table.

"I don't like the thought of you being left alone," Andres says.

She takes her hands away and crosses her arms. "Well, see, that's over now. You don't have to worry about it anymore."

"But I do."

"I'm safe here."

"That's not what I mean. I know you're safe, but you're not free. You shouldn't have to sacrifice one for the other."

"My freedom isn't like your freedom. It doesn't exist in the same form. What good is discovering new places if all I can think about is how unknown it feels, how threatening every stranger looks? Sometimes, I can't even remember what my kidnappers' faces look like, and I end up seeing them in everyone who looks unfamiliar. And then other times, all I have to do is fall asleep, and there they are."

"I know it's hard, but with time—"

"Time is torture, Andres. People say time heals all wounds, but it's because they don't know what it's like for time to have created those wounds. I still go there sometimes. It's like a dark place inside of me that never leaves. I know that might sound crazy, but, well—" She shrugs and gestures at her surroundings. She's always been the type to joke her way out of discomfort, and Andres laughs. *Just this once*, he thinks. *I'll give her this one.*

Elena covers her mouth with both hands and gasps. "I can't believe I haven't even asked you about the kids. And Marabela. Tell me, how is everyone doing?"

He smiles, knowing he can't possibly tell her the truth and risk bringing her more of the fear she's trying so hard to outrun. "They're fine. We're all fine," he says.

She seems satisfied with this and turns her attention to his jacket pocket, its bulk giving away where Andres hid the book. "What did you bring this time?"

"It's nothing. It's silly."

"Tell me. I won't laugh, I promise."

It's the last book Elena read to him when they were young, maybe six months before they started college, but suddenly it feels terribly inappropriate for the situation. He knows Elena won't let this go, so he pulls out his copy of *Pride and Prejudice* and runs his fingers along its spine. The book is so old parts of the cover are peeling, despite his best efforts to hold it together with tape. Quickly, before she can look at it too long, he slips it back into his pocket.

"I finished it many times. I know how much you loved it."

"I see that," Elena says. "Maybe you can read it to me this time."

A breeze kicks in, so he gives Elena his jacket. The first thing she does is reach for the book.

"Go on. Please?" she says.

He takes a long look at her and she urges him on with a smile. So he starts. "It is a truth universally acknowledged, that a single man in possession of a good fortune, must be in want of a wife . . ."

✤   ✤   ✤

Night comes after an uneventful day. At dinnertime, Andres decides it's as good a time as any to resume some semblance of a routine. He tells Consuelo the family will be dining together, not in fragments like the past several nights. All seems to go well until Carla sets a plate where Marabela would normally sit. When Andres and the kids take their seats, the emptiness stares back at them.

He calls into the kitchen, where Carla and Consuelo have sat down to eat with Guillermo, who arrived a few hours ago in anticipation of tonight's call. "Carla! It's just going to be the three of us eating tonight," he says.

The poor girl apologizes at least six times in the few seconds it takes to pick up the place mat, silverware, and plate and take them back into the kitchen.

Ignacio slouches over his soup and keeps his voice down as he turns to his father. "We don't have to pretend she's dead, you know."

"Not right now," Andres says, keeping an eye on Cynthia. His daughter may be young but she's more perceptive than he expected. All day she's been asking for her mother, asking when she'll be back, where she is, asking for specific answers like *Tomorrow?* Or *Monday?* Or *Will she be home for dinner?*

Without her mother, Cynthia wanders around the house listlessly, trying to find ways to entertain herself. Seeing her today only made Andres angrier with Marabela. It's not her fault that she's gone, but he couldn't help thinking of the time when it was her decision to disappear. He realizes he's never forgiven her for that absence. Marabela made a choice to go, knowing that the kids would miss her as they do now. She left without so much as an explanation, leaving Andres to make excuses for her.

In some ways this kidnapping is not all that different from Marabela's sojourn four months ago, and when the similarities overlap, Andres can't help but feel like he's back there again. He blames her and then he blames himself. He waits for a call that he knows may never come.

"You okay, little one?" Andres asks. "You haven't taken a single bite."

Cynthia rests her head on the table and closes her eyes. Her arms and face are warm, and when Andres feels her wrist for her heartbeat, checking like Marabela always did for a pulse quickened by fever, it pushes against his fingers so fast it seems it might burst. He shouts for Consuelo to bring the thermometer and a blanket. The yellow mercury rises, stopping at 104°F. It leaves him motionless, struggling with what to do next, but Consuelo is quick to act. She gathers her purse and a bag stuffed with Cynthia's nightgown and favorite dolls. She hands it to Andres and tells him they need to go to the hospital.

"But the phone—"

"I can take her," Ignacio says.

"No. You stay here. In case of anything," Andres says.

"I'll help him through it. You go," Guillermo says. "Is she going to be okay?"

"I don't know. It could be dangerous for her to have a fever this high." Though he knows it's nearly impossible, he thinks back to last year's cholera outbreak, how the entire country panicked, afraid to drink the water or eat any seafood. He turns to give Ignacio a kiss on the forehead. "I'll call you once we know more, or if we have to stay overnight. Listen to everything Guillermo tells you, got it?" Andres hands his son the keys to his mother's darkroom. "I'll call you as soon as we get there," he says over his shoulder. He fumbles with Cynthia's buckle in the backseat until Consuelo offers to do it. They start backing out of the garage but stop as Ignacio bangs on the window.

"Are you sure they'll call tonight?"

Through the windshield and in the review mirror, all Andres can see are the house and Cynthia, one superimposed over the other. He can't find the words to answer his son; it feels like he's being forced to choose between two immeasurable risks. Seconds pass, until finally Andres says the only thing that comes to him:

"Pray that they don't."

"Okay. I'll take care of it," Ignacio says. Guillermo stands behind and casts a worried glance over Andres's shoulder to Cynthia in the backseat.

"Write down everything. Tell them you need to speak to your mother first. Tell them we need more time, but we're getting closer. Then call me, as soon as you hang up. Got it?"

Ignacio nods, his lips moving as if he's repeating his father's words and trying to commit them to memory. When Andres reaches the end of the driveway and straightens the car onto the street, he can still see his son at the top of the driveway, waving and nodding and shrinking as the distance stretches out between them.

DAY 11

The nurse at the hospital is a short, round woman with tired eyes and a lively voice. Andres sits on a plastic chair next to Cynthia's bed and watches the woman's deliberate movements. Without saying a word, the nurse hooks her up to a boxy contraption, slips a thermometer into Cynthia's mouth, studies it, and pushes a few green and gray buttons.

"What's that for?" Andres asks.

The nurse holds up one finger but still says nothing. Andres scowls. The stethoscope around her neck hangs over part of her name tag, leaving only the letters "Mar" exposed.

"Maria."

"Marta," she says.

"Is my daughter going to be all right?" Though she's asleep now, Cynthia vomited in the hospital parking lot as soon as they arrived. Only when the doctors asked did she admit she hasn't been able to keep her food down since she got home from school.

"Her fever has barely gone down a degree. We'll have to monitor it and make sure she stays hydrated. But don't worry, she's in good hands."

Marta walks out of the room, leaving the door open and letting the light in. Cynthia is in such deep sleep that she won't be bothered.

Andres wonders what Marabela would do if she were here now. She liked to braid Cynthia's hair while she slept in the afternoons, into tiny ropes that unraveled at the ends, because Cynthia's hair is so thin. When Cynthia sleeps, she's usually so still that it looks like the life has gone out of her. Sometimes, Andres feels the urge to check and make sure she's breathing.

Now, she stirs in her sleep, and every once in a while a moan escapes from her throat. Andres doesn't know whether to wake her or let her sleep through the pain.

"Your coffee, señor." Consuelo stands at the doorway holding two cups in her hands, the vapor floating out of them.

"Thank you."

"How is she?" Consuelo whispers.

"They don't know yet."

She nods and takes a seat against the wall behind Andres.

"I don't know why this is taking so long," he says, looking at his watch. It's already a quarter to two. He feels exhausted but wide awake, the worst kind of contradiction. His body begs for rest while his mind refuses to relinquish even a moment of alertness. When he closes his eyes, the world fades away except for the sound of Cynthia's labored breathing. With her hand in his, he feels the muscles in her fingers spasm as small jolts of sleep rush through her. There's almost a rhythm to it—two quick flicks of the wrist, followed by a tap of the finger—and he tries to let the predictability of it soothe him.

Then a grasp. She squeezes his hand and opens her eyes so quickly, it's like she's been scared awake.

"*Papi?*" Her eyelids rise and fall.

"I'm here, *hijita*. How are you feeling?"

"Is Mom here yet?"

"What?"

She looks around the room, which is barely lit by a warm yellow bulb in the back corner and a sharp ray of white light coming in through the half-open door to the hall. Cynthia searches between the light and the darkness but finds nothing. "Why is she still not here?" Her voice cracks and tears fall down her temples to her ears. "Tell her to come back. I want her to come back!"

Andres doesn't know what to say. Her cries are his cries when he goes to bed at night and when he wakes. He has no answers for any of them. "I know, I know. Shh . . . it's okay. It'll all be okay. Just go back to sleep. Please." He begs her to stop.

"Why won't she come back?" She cries so hard her body shakes and her eyes squeeze shut, but somehow the tears still come. Andres sways her in his arms until her questions turn to deep whimpers, then to moans, then to silence and a weary sleep. Behind him, he hears Consuelo sniffle, trying to keep quiet as she blows her nose.

"Is there anything I can do, señor?"

"No. Thank you. All we can do now is wait."

"Cynthia is a strong girl. She'll be all right, you'll see."

He forces a smile and sits back down on the chair next to Cynthia's bed, facing away from Consuelo. They've never spent this much time together, but now he understands why Marabela confides in her so much. Anything she says has a quiet certitude about it, as if she could hold a mirror to all truths. He knows she's not just talking about Cynthia, and he fears that if he turns to see the sadness in her face, he won't be able to contain his own.

"I hope you're right."

"That's the most important part. You have to have hope. *Esperanza.*"

Andres nods and reaches for Cynthia's hand, careful not to pull on her IV. He remembers how his father once ripped the IV from his wrist and announced that he was tired of waiting. He never mentioned for what, but everybody knew. Still, Andres sat for days at his bedside, just as he's sitting now with Cynthia, and talked to the doctors daily, searching their words for any glimmer of hope. All they could tell him was that they needed to wait. *Esperar.*

Andres doesn't understand how one word ever gave birth to the other. There is no hope left in waiting.

❖ ❖ ❖

Cynthia's fever breaks around four A.M., and they wait for the curfew to rise, as the muted predawn light augurs the sunrise. When they arrive home, Andres expects to find Ignacio still sleeping in his bedroom, but the boy is sitting in the darkroom with his head on the desk. He wears the headphones that connect to the tape player, and the cable stretches across the room like an empty clothesline. The play button is pushed down, and even from the entrance Andres can see the cassette turning, the thin brown film winding slowly around and around. He takes three large steps across the room and pushes the stop button, and only then does Ignacio notice his father is home. He slips off the headphones and lets them dangle around his neck.

"How is she?"

"Cynthia will be fine. She just needs lots of rest now. So do you."

He pushes the eject button on the cassette player but Ignacio bolts up in protest.

"Put it back!" His eyes are red and swollen. It's five o'clock in the morning and Andres wouldn't be surprised if his son spent the entire night listening to the tapes.

"What are you doing? Where's Guillermo?"

"He went home hours ago."

"And you stayed here all this time?"

He doesn't answer. He only turns away, looking defeated.

"I knew I shouldn't have let you do this. I just wanted you to be ready to take the call. Did they call?" Andres asks.

Ignacio slouches so low that it looks like he might fall off Andres's chair. He wipes his face with his sleeve and pushes himself up. Each movement seems like a huge effort, like he's aged sixty years in just one night. With one hand, he yanks the headphone cable until it snaps off the tape player. He stretches his body over the table and rewinds the tape. After several seconds, he presses play.

The two of them stand in the room, fingertips resting on the desk, and listen.

Hello?

Who the hell is this?

This is Ignacio. I'm Andres's son. He can't talk tonight.

Is this a joke?

No—he had an emergency. He'll be back tomorrow, but he left me in charge. I—I need to talk to my mother. Please.

He's not the one who decides who's in charge. This isn't his office, where his secretary takes a message and he gets to call back at his earliest convenience. If he thinks he can get away with ignoring me . . .

He's not ignoring you! He had to take my sister to the emergency room and he told me to pick up if you called. He says he just needs a couple more days.

Here I was, about to cooperate, and he blows me off. That's not a proper way to do business. I'm a little insulted. Tell him he'll need those extra days

*because the price isn't moving. Tell him that's what he gets for making me
waste my time considering his bullshit.*

*No, he didn't—he didn't plan this. You have to believe me! It was just
an emergency. Please, let me speak to my mom.*

*She can't come to the phone right now. She's having an emergency, too.
You understand, don't you?*

No, wait! You can't do that! We're doing everything we can!

*I don't make deals with intermediaries. You're the little secretary, you
give him this message, all right? Tell him everybody's going to pay for this.*

Ignacio jumps across the desk to stop the tape. Nothing is audible
at that point; it's just a lot of begging and crying, and it's hard to tell
which side of the line the sounds are coming from—if it's Marabela
pleading in the background or if it's Ignacio being tortured by the
helplessness of the situation. Andres is relieved when the boy shuts it
off. He knows there's nothing more to hear, nothing more that will
help them. He covers his mouth and feels his own stubble scratch his
fingertips. There are no words that will help the situation, nothing
he can say that will erase his son's voice begging for his mother's life.
He wishes he could unhear it for both of them.

Only now does he get a chance to look around. All the tapes they've
made are scattered around his desk, separated from their cases.

"Did you listen to all of these?" The boy nods. "I didn't give you
the keys so you could listen to them."

"I wanted to be prepared."

"Did you feel prepared?"

He shakes his head.

"Have you just been playing them all night?"

Ignacio nods, his lips pressed tightly together. Andres walks
around to his side of the desk and puts his arms around his son.

"You did good," he whispers, though he knows there's no such
thing. "Nobody is ever prepared for this sort of thing."

"I have to know what they did. I have to know what they did to
her." He steps away from his father and rewinds the tape, just a cou-

ple of seconds this time. The screams and the begging fill the room again, and Ignacio kneels so that his ears are closer to the tape player. "Right there!" He pauses, rewinds again. "Is that her? Does it sound like a weapon?"

He's about to press play again when Andres stops him. The boy slaps his hand, and Andres has to pull him away, but he won't stop resisting and pretty soon Ignacio is hitting him; they're rolling on the ground and pushing each other's face away, trying to reach for the tape player to see who can make the sounds come back, who can silence it, first. Finally Andres rolls over on top of him and holds him down.

"Stop! Whatever's happened has happened. Nothing you do will change it," he says. He watches as the words sink in, watches as his son, who so desperately wants to be a man, cries like a child for his mother.

❖   ❖   ❖

He thinks of the few conversations he's had with Marabela lately. Some he replays on the cassette, but the one that scares him the most is only recorded in his mind.

Hola, Andres.

¿Dónde estás?

You know I can't tell you that.

When will you be back?

I don't know yet.

And the kids? What do I tell them when they ask me where their mother is?

I just need some time. To think.

Don't do this, Mari.

Don't beg, Andres, and don't try to play the victim, either. I know what you and your father did, after what happened with my picture. Did you really think I'd never figure it out?

Is that what this is all about?

You went behind my back. All these years, knowing you didn't support my work, that's one thing. But to find out you jeopardized everything I—

We were protecting you! I was only thinking of you and the kids. Don't pretend I'm the bad guy when you're the one who got everything you wanted. All day long you do nothing but hide away in the darkroom . . .

You left me with nothing else. And that's what you always wanted, isn't it? To have me safely tucked away inside. It all makes sense now.

Mi amor, please. Come home and we'll work this out. We need you. You can't just leave.

Or else what? This shouldn't come as a surprise, when you really think about it.

Andres has tried to think about it, from every possible angle, but still he hasn't found a way to fix things. He can't go back far enough or dig deep enough to understand where they started to fall apart.

He thinks back to the conversation and remembers the familiar silence on the other end of the line, the gentle click, the monotone beep that went on and on and on. Three days after they spoke she came home. Said she couldn't leave the kids. She ordered a foldout bed from the furniture store across town, had it delivered while the kids were at school, and tucked it away in the closet. They agreed it'd be temporary, until they could work their problems out, but the promise stayed as hidden as their separation. Every night, Andres would pull out the bed and fall asleep with Marabela lying too far from his side. In the morning, he'd wake up and expect her to be gone again. Now, every morning, he wakes up and she is.

❖ ❖ ❖

In the morning Lorena comes over with more groceries: chicken, vegetables, and noodles so Consuelo can make soup; a pink blanket, a stuffed toy rabbit, and a digital thermometer for Cynthia. Andres tries to tell her it's unnecessary—they have their own thermometer—but Lorena insists hers is better.

"The digital reading is more accurate. And what little girl doesn't like new things for her room? Is she sleeping now? When can I see her?"

They tiptoe up the stairs and stop at Cynthia's door, quietly stepping inside once it's clear she's in a deep enough sleep. He puts his hand on her head and practically engulfs it with his palm. It's still warm, and he fights a sudden urge to curl up next to her, his little furnace, and let her energy soothe him.

"What did the doctor say?" Andres's mother asks.

He points to a bottle on her dresser. "One tablespoon every four hours. And lots of fluids."

"What time did you start?"

"Two."

Cynthia was so tired, she hadn't even protested when the doctors put the spoon in her mouth. She'd closed her eyes, leaned into her father, and swallowed.

Lorena looks at her watch. It is almost ten o'clock. Andres tugs at the child's shoulder and she yawns herself awake, suddenly remembering the body aches and the dewy sweat on her skin. She looks exhausted and in pain, but despite breathing with her mouth open, still manages to reject the medicine that Andres tries spooning in.

"Let me try," Lorena says. "Shh . . . this will make you feel better." She fills a glass of water from her nightstand and holds it close to the spoon, ready to switch one for the other. Lorena puts the spoon in Cynthia's mouth and lifts it quickly toward the ceiling, and Cynthia looks up and tilts her head back, like a fish caught in a hook. As soon as she's swallowed, Lorena puts the glass of water to her lips and pours the liquid down her throat, gently closing her jaw. Cynthia is too stunned to protest.

"Look how easy that was. Look how easy it is to be a healthy, good little girl. Are you hungry?"

Cynthia nods and Lorena extends her hand. They make their way past Andres and head downstairs to the kitchen. He watches as Cynthia takes her time with each step, leaning into her grandmother for balance.

DAY 12

He wakes at five knowing his sleep won't return. When he tries to close his eyes, he feels like he's entering a prison, and he's afraid to stay there long. He grabs a pair of pants and a shirt in the dark, unsure if they go together but completely unconcerned either way. He cringes as he turns on the engine in the garage. It's amazing how a sound he normally doesn't notice can seem deafening at such a quiet hour. It follows him as he pulls away from the house.

By the time he reaches the end of his block, the music from his tape player has ended, and Andres doesn't bother flipping the cassette over because he feels the need to be quiet, inconspicuous. Driving so slowly reminds him of when he used to sneak into the house late as a teenager—the door always creaked, but he'd crack it open little by little in the hopes that it would make a difference.

He contemplates driving through the stop sign he's approaching like cabdrivers do during the day, speeding right through and honking their horns twice to warn oncoming traffic.

Up ahead a man and a woman lean over a rusted car with the hood popped, poking at the engine like it's a dead animal that might come back to life. The woman smokes a cigarette while the man rolls up his sleeves. His hands are black and oily.

Andres slows down at the sign but doesn't come to a full stop. He looks straight ahead, ignoring the man nodding in his direction.

"You know anything about cars?" he yells through his window.

Andres hits the gas and watches the man and woman in his rearview mirror. Both have their hands in the air, making vulgar gestures in his direction. In a few seconds their silhouettes are swallowed by the darkness.

He turns the corner into another neighborhood where none of the houses seem to match. A boxy gray-and-red brick fort with wooden panels over its window presses against a home made of white painted cinder blocks. Black bars cover the front doors, and those who can't afford a proper gate have built cement walls with shards of broken glass sunken along the top. The street is poorly lit, with three of its lights out. A brownish basketball skitters onto the street, its momentum dying with each bounce. It stops in the middle of the road, maybe ten yards from Andres's car, and he lets the car idle, wonders if he should get out and push the ball aside or if someone will be coming for it soon. To his left, he hears skin slapping against the pavement, tiny feet running toward him. Here is a little boy, no older than nine, playing in the darkest hours of the morning and diving in front of a moving car to save his basketball. Andres stops and watches the boy, who is now practically tiptoeing to his ball as he keeps his eyes on the stranger behind the wheel. When he reaches the ball he snatches it, pauses for a second, and takes off. As Andres drives away, he tries to shake the image of the little boy's eyes. He recognized his own fear in them, and now that he knows what it looks like he sees it everywhere—in the man who pumps gas across the street, in the teenage girls who stumble down the sidewalk, in the transvestite prostitute who steps forward and back, indecisive, at the intersection while Andres prays for the light to turn green. It is a fear that he can't get away from, and seeing it in others doesn't make him feel any safer.

He makes it to the institution in his best time yet, barely under a half hour. Walking into the lobby is like listening to a giant seashell; the building gives off a heavy silence, but he's comforted by its vastness.

"You must be crazy to be coming by so early," Betty says when he reaches the sign-in window. "You know these are emergency hours only."

"It is an emergency," Andres says. He tries to keep his voice to a whisper, tries to go for a joke. "I may go crazy if I don't see her right now."

Betty just rolls her eyes. "I can't have you disturbing the patients."

"I'm not disturbing anyone. It helps her to see me."

"Yes, but not when she's sleeping."

"But she's an early riser. She won't be sleeping right now."

Betty hesitates. "We have rules here, and visiting hours. We can't change the rules for everyone."

"Betty . . . please. I need to see her." It's clear the begging is getting him nowhere, but he can't imagine leaving and facing this day without seeing Elena. He sets both hands on the reception desk, practically reaching for Betty's, and looks her straight in the eyes so she can't look away. "Please. I'm trying to help her recover, but the truth is, seeing her helps me, too. Elena's the only person I can talk to. She's the only one who understands what I—what my wife—is going through right now. You understand?"

Betty leans back in her chair and cups her hands together in her lap. "I'm sorry. I know this must be hard but—"

"Betty. I wasn't actually joking when I said I may go crazy . . . Please."

She looks over her shoulder at the hallway. "Fine. But only if she's already awake."

Andres breathes a sigh of relief. He knows Elena will be sitting in her chair as usual, waiting for the sun to rise. When they reach her room and peek through the window, he sees her just as he imagined, and the predictability soothes him. "Thank you," he whispers to Betty, and then, in a voice that's barely any louder to Elena, "Hey. Got room for me?"

He sits on an arm of her chair with his arm stretched over its back. Outside Elena's window, the moon and the sun are visible in the sky, both so dim their light cancels each other out. The two old friends sit in silence. Finally, Elena rubs Andres's arm and asks how he's doing.

He shrugs, eyes on the window. "Just thinking."

"Obviously. About?"

"Can I ask you something?" He pauses in between words to close his eyes and rub his eyelids, stretching the thin skin toward the bridge of his nose. He feels Elena's hands, warm and light against his face, gently covering his to make him stop. It'd be so easy just to purse his lips together and kiss them. Instead he takes her hands between both of his, like he's praying, and lowers them away. He's here for truth, not comfort, and he knows he won't find one where there's the other.

"After you got home, what made you decide to leave again and come here? I know you said you didn't feel safe and that you were afraid, but what about being with your family? How did you choose?"

"I didn't really feel like I had much of a choice. It was just a matter of one emotion winning over the other. The fear was too powerful, I guess. Or maybe I'm too weak."

"Don't say that. I didn't mean to imply that."

"I know this is going to sound horrible, but part of me stopped trusting my family. Or at least, I stopped trusting in their ability to keep me safe. If they could only do so much to get me out, then how could they keep me from being taken again? Sometimes I'd think it would've been different if I had a partner to come home to, someone who could be strong enough for both of us. But my parents, they're not so young anymore, and I can't ask them to take care of me forever. At least here, I can try to heal on my own time. I know I'm no good to anyone until I do."

"That's not true. You're good for me."

She smiles. "That's sweet of you to say."

"Are you sure you're healing?" He hesitates to say what he's about to, but he feels it can't be avoided anymore. "How do you know you're not just hiding?"

For an instant, he sees the look in her eyes harden, the slightest hint of her raising her defenses. "I'm fine here. I'm safe."

"But those aren't the same things."

"What is this really about, Andres?"

He gets the urge to light a cigarette. Andres pats down his coat, his pants, to see if he has any in his pockets, but no luck. He stands up and sits on Elena's bed, slouching to rest his arm on the footboard. "Marabela left me a few months ago, and then she came back. And now she's gone again, and I'm trying everything I can to bring her back, but every day that passes, I can't help but imagine that she'll never feel at home with me again. Not the way she used to. I don't want to bring her back to a place where she feels as trapped as she is now."

"What makes you think she wants to come home again?"

"Didn't you?"

"I was in a completely different situation."

"That's the thing. It's not that different. This time, she didn't leave. Marabela was taken."

Elena stares at Andres. She covers her mouth, closes her eyes, and takes a deep breath. The air comes out slowly, in hysterical whimpers that build momentum until they start to get out of control. Her cries are quiet but violent. Andres gets down on his knees next to her chair, just like on the first day he came here.

"It's okay. Shh . . . it's okay. She's going to be fine. I'm—I'm trying everything I can."

"It's all my fault. It's my fault they took her. It's my fault."

"*Tranquila, linda.* It's not your fault."

"You really don't understand. You don't understand at all. It's my fault they took her."

"How is that even possible? It doesn't make sense. Maybe we should go for a walk again."

She thrusts herself deeper into her chair, practically standing on the cushion. "You're not listening to me! I gave them a list. I gave them names. Names in exchange for my life. That's how they said it. I told them no, but they kicked me until I spoke, and by that time I couldn't, and they gave me a piece of paper and a pencil and they left me in the dark to think about it. And I couldn't move. Or think. Or write. When they came back they said if I didn't give them the names, it would only get worse every night. But I couldn't imagine it getting worse, so I didn't give them anything. And then the fourth night—"

"Elena, stop. I—"

"—and the fourth night they came and took my clothes," she says. "They did everything and anything to me. They were trying to tear me into pieces. I gave them everything, Andres. I gave them all the names. They wanted the easiest targets. The richest ones. And Marabela was so easy and I just wanted them to stop. They said it's common, that everyone makes a list. I didn't think they'd actually take her. I just wanted them to stop."

He sits, frozen, on his feet, which have fallen asleep by now. The numbness spreads to his legs and soon he thinks it'll be in his core, and he won't have to deal with any of this because he could just as easily retreat the way Elena has, curled into a ball in the corner of a bare room. And yet he knows that he'll never be able to do this. He is not the victim here.

He wants to reassure her. But the words that come out of his mouth aren't the ones he expects.

"They came for her . . . because of you?"

She nods, feeble, pathetic.

"What—what did you tell them? Was it just a name? Or was it our address, where our children sleep at night?"

Elena brings her knees closer to her chest, turns her body into a fort. "It was just a name. It was one of many. I never thought they'd—"

"Why not mine instead? Did you ever think of that?"

"I wasn't thinking clearly."

He says nothing because he's incapable of putting himself there, of imagining what it must have been like.

Elena spits her words at him. "I don't expect you to understand. You think what you're going through is torture because it's the worst thing that's ever happened to you."

"I never said I was the victim," Andres says. He feels like he's shrinking, like the world could swallow him whole.

She follows his gaze, holds it steadily. "You can't imagine what's on the other side of that phone," she says, and he knows she's right. He's tried to so many times.

"I can't . . . I don't want to hear it," he says. His whole body is so tired now he lets it fall back against the wall. He stares at his legs, stretched across the floor, and wishes he could find the strength to stand up and leave.

"Have you been listening when they call? Really listening?"

"Just . . . please stop."

"You get to hang up at the end of it. That's a luxury I didn't have."

"Please, Ele . . . please don't," and he feels this moment carving itself into their reality, a massive hole they'll never bridge. She finally grows quiet.

Outside, the halls are starting to fill with the sounds of a regular morning. Elena doesn't move but her eyes shift to different parts of the room each time she blinks: first the door, then the bed, the courtyard, finally him.

"I should have done more," she says. "I should've held on a little longer."

"They would've never stopped."

She shakes her head, side to side as if she's got a bee stuck in her hair and she's trying to push it away. "They didn't."

"They didn't what?"

"Stop."

"I'm sorry. You don't have to talk about it if you don't want to."

She wipes her eyes and smiles again, and he realizes her smile isn't from happiness but submission. "You don't understand. What I meant was, they didn't stop. Ever. Even after I gave them the names, they had their way with me. I should have just kept quiet."

Already, Andres has forgiven her. Already, he knows he has to leave. He knows he can't just leave her like this, but he also can't stay. He holds Elena until her body stops shaking and the sun has risen, and when the room starts getting warm she looks up at him and says, "You should go to her. As soon as you can. Go."

"You're a good friend," he tells her. "Don't ever think otherwise."

❖ ❖ ❖

On his way home, it occurs to him that Elena's connection to the kidnapping is a lead. They can follow it, they can find out who these people are and where they keep their hostages, and they can try to rescue Marabela so she doesn't have to stay there another minute more. They can talk to Elena, help her remember details that'll give them clues. Although remembering will be painful, her guilt will heal knowing that she made things right again.

Back at his office, he tells Guillermo everything. He's expecting the man to jump out of his chair, gather more supplies and perhaps even weapons, but Guillermo barely reacts. He focuses on some notes, and Andres wishes he could shake him by the shoulders.

"It's actually not that simple," Guillermo finally says. The words seem to hurt coming out of him.

"What more do we need? They're the same people who kidnapped Elena. She can lead us to them."

"That's not how these things work. The ones who took Elena, they're just minions. None of these guys stay in the same place for long. The whole system's a monster—it'll cut its own legs off for survival anytime it gets in a tight spot. It moves somewhere more comfortable and grows a new set. The men who took Elena are probably in prison or already working for someone new. The man in charge, at the top, is too smart to stay in the same place with the same people for very long."

"You can't be sure."

"Andres. It's been two years since they took her. Two years."

But Andres can't accept this. He needs a plan to hold on to, something that he can do besides wait. He's haunted by the possibility that Marabela might endure what Elena went through, only to emerge a shell of her former self.

"We'll go to the cops. We'll see if Elena's kidnappers were ever captured," Andres says.

"No cops. You know that already."

"Then what the hell am I supposed to do?"

"You're already doing everything you can. It'll take some time, especially after the last call. He wasn't happy not to find you on the other line. He said they won't move off three-quarters of a million. But we can still make this work. We can still talk the price down."

But nothing Guillermo says can help anymore. Andres looks at the chart of their offers again, plagued by the thought that he hasn't done enough. So far he's only tried the minimum and optimum price; the maximum still stands far below the current ransom, which is marked on the chart by a thick red X.

"I want to raise it. Make this go faster."

"You know how important it is for them not to get everything they ask. Besides, you said so yourself, you don't have that kind of money."

"No, but I can get closer to it." He takes a marker and draws a new dot on the chart, farther away from his last offer and much closer to the ransom.

Guillermo shakes his head. "It's your choice, but I don't recommend it."

"I'm tired of waiting. I'm tired of feeling inadequate. This is it." Although he wasn't completely sure until he said it out loud, Andres knows now there's no going back. With every important decision he's made in his life, he's had the luxury of time and a safe estimate of the outcome. This decision he's just making because he has to, because there comes a time when doing anything is better than the alternative.

Andres calls his mother and tells her he's ready to talk to Mr. Graves, but he won't negotiate anything outside his home. Everything has to be done within the safety of these walls, if even that exists. They agree to talk over dinner, and Lorena makes arrangements with Consuelo for each aspect of the meal.

"The children will eat earlier. This is a very serious meeting, you see." Andres can't help but notice a tinge of excitement in her voice. Is she happy that he'll have nothing now? He thinks this and immediately regrets it. He'll have Marabela back, and that should be enough.

Except he still doesn't know how long she'll stay this time. And if she does stay, he'll never know if she's staying out of fear or from a genuine desire to be with him.

DAY 13

It's a bleak, quiet Tuesday night. Andres has asked Guillermo to take the children to the movies and without them the house feels abandoned, too peaceful for his own comfort. Andres dresses in a dark suit—the same one he wore to the wedding of one of his colleague's daughters last month—and tries to imagine Marabela at his side. She would be happy to learn he's selling the company. When the first offers from Graves came in last year, they made love like they hadn't since their twenties. Every night that Andres considered it, Marabela came to bed rejuvenated. Maybe she imagined he would change once he'd let go of his life's work. She always said it tied him down, that it was a burden he carried with him everywhere, even in his sleep. She'd talk about all the free time he'd have, how this would be a new beginning, but the truth was he couldn't fathom starting something else. His company was not something he could set aside and be done with.

When is one finished with love, or a friendship, or a child? When he tried explaining this to her, Marabela again grew distant.

By the time she left, it took Andres almost an entire day to notice; he'd gotten so used to rarely speaking with her, rarely getting a call from her to check in.

When Graves arrives for dinner, they talk about the new board members he'll bring in, many from the United States and parts of Europe, to advise him on how to best grow the company once his and Andres's businesses are merged. He talks about it like it's a done deal, like they've signed the papers and there are no hard feelings. Even worse, he talks about his people like they're not people at all. They are their titles, not their names. They are their job descriptions, not their hobbies or accomplishments.

"Your advisers are willing to move here? With their families?" Andres asks.

"Why wouldn't they be?"

Andres has been noticing trends in the papers. The new money lies in US imports—top executives of banks or tobacco companies or soft drink corporations. "You don't worry for their safety?"

"We insure them, Andres. You know how it is."

Of course, he wants to say. Of course he knows this all too late.

"And what about my employees? Most of them have been with the company for ten years or more."

"We'll keep as many of them as we can so long as there are no re-dundancies. No point in having two people doing one person's job, just because one was there first." Graves laughs as if the alternative is the most absurd thing he's ever heard. Loyalty means nothing to him; the thought makes Andres lose his appetite. This is why he swore never to do business with him, years ago, when even Marabela was smitten by his charm and his ultrasupportive wife.

As if reading his mind, Graves wipes his mouth and asks, "How is Marabela? I was hoping to see her tonight."

"She's visiting friends in Florida," Andres says. He has become more comfortable with this lie. In Florida, he imagines, people drive any car they want and wear the most extravagant clothes without worrying about attracting danger like a magnet.

They are only on their second course and already Andres is tired of the pleasantries and small talk. He starts growing curt, speaking in monosyllables and answering questions with a yes or a no, fully aware that his mother is probably burning from embarrassment. She's kept quiet most of dinner, but now she starts dominating the conversation, telling a story about her husband back in the day, how he spent a summer in London watching the Olympics with friends.

"He was fascinated by the runners, how their legs could go so fast that when the race was over they'd just collapse. My husband's business partner, Saul, preferred watching the swim meets, so they'd argue about which was better: land or water. Never were two business partners more opposite than they were," Lorena says.

"There is as much beauty in teamwork as there is in competition," Graves says. But there is no sincerity in his voice, and Andres realizes they are more alike than he'd like to think. He wants to buy his company not just because it's good business, but because he wants to be the last one standing. He wants all the pieces to himself.

"You know, you don't have to say things you don't mean just to humor my mother," he says.

"Excuse me?"

"It just seems a silly thing for you to say. You love being the only one in charge. And you'll love it even more with less competition, right?"

The silence speaks volumes. Lorena looks like she wants to protest, but keeps quiet in the end, and Graves only chuckles like he's been caught enjoying himself in the naughtiest kind of way.

"Let's just get this over with," Andres says.

They skip dessert and go straight to the paperwork. Andres recognizes most of it from the last time they played this game, only now there's no backing out at the last moment. After he's signed away his company and confirmed the transfer of funds, Andres lets his mother escort Graves to the door.

"I don't see why you felt the need to burn a bridge," she tells him once Graves is gone. "You're starting over now. You'll need connections."

It occurs to him that maybe he won't.

"Maybe it's time I found some new bridges to cross," he says, surprised at the relief that overcomes him, the realization that his only responsibilities in this world have been stripped down to the basics. Right now, he is a man in charge of taking care of his family, nothing else. For one delusional moment it makes him smile.

❖ ❖ ❖

Andres finds Carla and Consuelo in their room, which he hasn't entered since he first moved into this house nearly twenty years ago and Marabela decided this would become the maids' quarters. He has a vague recollection of how it looked back then: small, but with a refreshing amount of light coming in through the window. Perhaps a quarter the size of his room, tucked behind the hallway leading out to the garage, the maids' room is another place he passes every day without noticing. He is beginning to realize his house is full of hidden spaces he can't claim as his own.

Andres taps on the door with one knuckle.

"*Pase*," Consuelo says from the other side. He finds them both sitting on their beds with the television turned to the news. Carla is filling out a newspaper crossword puzzle while Consuelo sews a button onto a pair of navy pants, part of Ignacio's school uniform. She finishes pushing the needle through the fabric before looking up, surprised to find Andres in the room.

"Oh!" she says, handing the task off to Carla while she stands up and clears a chair for him. Then, as if she has to explain herself, she adds, "Ignacio popped a button."

Andres takes a seat on an old wicker chair he recognizes from their first apartment. He had no idea Marabela kept it, but right away he remembers how it would sink and creak under his weight, this artifact from their past life.

Consuelo tightens her robe while Carla tucks her bare feet under the covers. It's the first time he's ever seen them out of uniform, and it makes him feel like a guest in his own home, like he should've called ahead or made an appointment.

Consuelo, perhaps sensing his discomfort, breaks the silence. "How are you, señor? I'm afraid we've all been so worried about *la señora* and the children that we haven't asked how you're doing. It must be such a difficult time for you." Her voice is gentle, but he hears wisdom in her calm tone.

"Yes, thank you. I—" Andres isn't sure how to respond. "I worry that I've failed her," he says, surprised by his sudden urge to tell her everything, as he imagines Marabela did at the end of her day. "I keep thinking I must have done something to cause all this."

"Señor. What good do those thoughts do us? Focus on doing the best for Marabela now. Pray for her and have faith that the Lord will give you the strength to get through."

"It's just that they've taken so much from us. Not just her, which is practically everything. But even the little things that I never thought I cared about. There's this bakery that Jorge used to drive past every morning on the way to my office. I'd roll down the window as we got close just to take in the scent of their bread, and now even that doesn't feel safe. And the way Cynthia gets so excited every time the doorbell rings, insisting on opening the door herself. Do you think we'll ever let her do that again?" He shakes his head and rubs his palms against his knees, grasping at the soft fabric of his slacks. "None of these moments belong to us anymore. I'm plagued by the sensation that they know my whole life, that they can take it all away."

Andres looks up at Consuelo, who listens so attentively that he feels his only job is to keep talking. In his nervousness he'd almost forgotten why he came here in the first place.

"Jorge won't be driving me to work anymore. I've had to sell my company, so I told him yesterday that I wouldn't be needing his services. He didn't seem surprised—I think he might have been expecting it. He said that he and his wife have been praying for Marabela every night. I've never met his wife, have you?"

"Emma. She's a schoolteacher. She taught my nephew how to read a few years ago. Very patient, that woman," Consuelo says, shaking her head and smiling.

"That's good, I guess. I could barely look at Jorge because I kept thinking of how he'd have to come home at night and tell her he lost his job."

Consuelo tenses a little, but she quickly sits up straight and dusts off the small pieces of thread from her lap. "Jorge understood the situation, señor. He was very sad to say good-bye to us, but he doesn't blame you. He knows you didn't make this decision willingly."

"It's not really a decision then, is it? Not mine, anyway. It's like someone else is making all these decisions for me, someone I've never even met." At this, Andres leans forward, clasps his hands together, and looks Consuelo in the eyes. "He leaves me no choice."

She takes a deep breath and nods, but her head stays tilted toward the floor. The skin around her neck seems to double, creating a soft new layer for her chin to rest on. "I understand," she says.

"It's not that I don't want you to stay. Believe me, I wish you could be here when Marabela returns."

Carla, perhaps just realizing that this conversation now applies to her, looks up from her button. "You mean we have to leave?"

The disappointment in her voice shames him. If Marabela knew what he was doing right now, she would hate him for it.

"I'm very sorry. I no longer have the means right now to keep you."

"We can stay and help until we find other work," Consuelo says.

"Thank you, but I don't know how long it'll be until she's home. I have to wait for them to call to arrange everything, and then who knows how many days will pass . . . I'm very sorry," Andres says again. "I know this is not what Marabela would have wanted."

"You're doing the best you can, señor." Consuelo reaches over and places her hand over his for such a brief moment it's almost a tap. He thanks her, but it's clear they're only comforting each other out of obligation. They've never been close.

"Will you call when she returns? We'd like to know that she's home safe."

"Of course," Andres says. "I'm sure she'll be happy to see you both. She's always spoken so highly of you, like you're a part of this family."

"And the children?"

"My mother will be helping me watch out for them. Guillermo is staying, too."

"She is strong, señor. She will come back and she will fight for everything she loves."

"Yes, thank you." He says good night and tucks the wicker chair under a small writing desk that rests against the wall. On his way out he leaves an envelope of cash on top of the television set. "For what we owe you," he says. They say nothing as he goes.

6

THE KIDNAPPERS HAVEN'T called in three days, the longest they've cut off communication. In that time, Andres has imagined Marabela dead, beaten, raped, escaped, left in the desert to die. Nothing can compare to this kind of anticipation, not even the dread of Monday, when he knows he'll have to tell his employees, his friends and colleagues, that their livelihoods are no longer in his hands.

The lack of control has become familiar, though its constant presence doesn't make it any easier to deal with. All day, he sits in the darkroom and waits. He eats all his meals at the desk and avoids eye contact with Ignacio when he walks the few steps it takes to get to the kids' restroom instead of using his own, which is in his bedroom farther down the hall. He tries not to look at the clock, even plays games to test how long he can go without a quick glance.

He thinks, *If more than five minutes have passed before I look again, Marabela won't die. If more than ten have passed, she won't ever leave me again.* This bargaining helps him focus on other things, anything other than the phone that doesn't ring.

He hears the sound of Guillermo's footsteps coming up the stairs

and is surprised when they turn out to be Ignacio's. When did the
boy start throwing his weight around as if it were a weapon?

"These are for you." His son hands him a manila envelope with
Edith's handwriting in the top right corner. *Para Señor Jimenez*, it
says in thick black marker. It's stuffed with so many documents it
looks like it could tear at the edges. Andres takes it and quickly sets
it aside, but Ignacio keeps his eyes on it.

"Don't you want to know what's inside?" he asks.

"Don't you?" Andres invites his son to sit down across from
him. He doesn't have to look inside the envelope because he already
knows it's just filled with unread mail from the office, papers scattered across his desk, and cards from his Rolodex—numbers, names,
and addresses of people he may never speak to again. This morning,
knowing he couldn't leave the house and unsure he could bear to face
the people at the office anyway, he asked Lorena to stop by and have
Edith clean out his desk.

"Did you help your grandmother unload the boxes from her car?"

The boy nods. "Me and Guillermo did. We left them downstairs
in the living room. She asked me to bring you the envelope, though."

He can't understand why Ignacio is so curious about it. Maybe he
imagines it's stuffed with cash for his mother's ransom. "That's everything I have left of the company. You can look through it if you'd
like. I'm sorry I won't be taking you along to more meetings anytime
soon." He tries to smile, raising one side of his mouth. "I'm sure you
won't mind."

"It wasn't all that bad. It was fun seeing you in action," Ignacio
says, but Andres knows he's just trying to make him feel better. "I
know it wasn't easy giving up the company."

This sudden acknowledgment of his sacrifice is unexpected. Andres feels undeserving of the admiration and wishes it could be the
other way around: father consoling son.

"So what now?" Ignacio asks.

He knows Ignacio's not referring to the company, but Andres's mind still turns to all the employees he left behind without even a good-bye. One day, when this is all over, he hopes he'll have the chance to redeem himself in their eyes. For now, he can't add to his suffering and dwell on it. "We wait for the call," he says.

So they do. Ignacio makes himself comfortable in the chair across from his father. Guillermo comes in half an hour later and takes the chair by the door. They go over every detail so many times he loses count.

"They need to know you've done everything you can. This is your final offer, and they can either take it or get nothing," Guillermo says. "If they suspect they can get more from you, they will try."

Andres feels his stomach grow heavy at the thought. There's so little left of him; what more could they possibly ask? What would he do then? All around him, rows of yellow cue cards hang from a string where Marabela's pictures used to be. Each says the same thing with different words.

> *This is all I have.*
> *I've sold the company, the car, taken money out on the house.*
> *I have nothing more.*
> *You have the wrong impression of me.*
> *This is as far as I can possibly go.*

One phrase that was never written but keeps reverberating in his mind:

> *This will ruin me.*

He wishes he could crumple the thought.

The cards are reassuring, though; they solidify what he has been trying to convince himself of since the beginning. There is nothing more he can do. He catches Ignacio's eye across the desk and suddenly regrets inviting him into the room. If things don't end well, he'll have failed everyone he's ever loved. Whether or not his son would ever forgive him, Andres knows he'd never forgive himself.

Behind him, the clock ticks and tocks. Moments linger between each second. Time fills with emptiness and anticipation. He remembers Marabela wishing during their honeymoon that they could stop time, wondering which moments they'd stretch.

It was a rhetorical question, and now experience has answered it for him.

Time can never stand still, but some moments stay with a person forever.

The phone rings. He feels the sound etching a scar into his memory.

A second time. An eternity squeezed into a second.

A third ring.

Guillermo points at him like a stage director.

"Hello? Who is this?" Andres hears his own voice as if from miles away.

Hades confirms his identity and asks for a question.

Andres shakes his head. "No questions today. I need to speak with her."

"We agreed on this already. Is this how you do business? By going back on your word?"

There is no way to win that argument, and the looks on Guillermo's and Ignacio's faces confirm it. Andres skims his list of questions and tries to choose one that won't upset her. "At what time was Ignacio born?"

He watches his son sit up, suddenly more alert. They hear a knock on the other end, like someone banged the receiver against a hard surface, and then a painful silence.

"Three hours after eternity," Hades says, laughing at a joke that was only meant to be shared between husband and wife. Andres doubts he'll ever be able to hear those words again without thinking of Hades.

"Are you ready to make a deal, Señor Jimenez?"

"Tell me when and where and I'll be there with a quarter of a million."

"We agreed on one million."

Andres looks to Guillermo for reassurance. "I never said I could get that. This is all I have. I've sold everything for it. I swear to you, there is nothing left. I have the money in cash, ready for you. Today, if you want."

"I'll decide the time."

Hearing this, Guillermo pumps his fist in the air, miming victory, but Andres isn't ready to celebrate. He needs to hear the words, wants to know that this will be over soon. He listens for the words and relief that can come only from Hades. How cruel that the man who torments him is the only one who can save him.

"Fine. Pay attention. This is exactly how it's going to happen."

Andres writes everything down. His hands are shaking, his handwriting is illegible, and he can see the tape recording each of Hades's words, but still the simple act comforts him. As drops of sweat fall to the paper in place of tears, blurring the instructions, Andres starts to feel the familiar rush of a closed negotiation coming back to him. The finality of it reassures him. For the first time he sees an end to this, and for once he lets himself believe it because it is written in black and white, his only language of truth.

✤ ✤ ✤

It is the first time Andres has noticed how many worlds exist between his neighborhood and his mother's. The ride from one safe place to another is not a simple one; they are never driving in a straight line for long. When they finally hit the last stretch of road, it is narrow and steep, and the journey weighs down on them as the car climbs up a hill toward Lorena's home.

In the backseat sits Ignacio with his arm wrapped around his sister. She is too weak and tired to fully realize what is going on, but Ignacio is alert, shooting sharp whispers at his father.

"Let me go with you," he says for the fifth time since they started packing clothes.

Andres looks in the rearview mirror. He tries to be patient and reason with his son. "I need you to be with your sister and your grandma now."

"If they wanted to get us they would have already. How is Grandma supposed to protect us?"

"That's not the point. Think of it this way: now you're the man in the house, right?" This reasoning seems to satisfy Ignacio. He keeps quiet the rest of the way.

Andres approaches a roundabout and turns the circle into the street leading up to his mother's house. It's like going through a revolving door—just a few degrees is all it takes for the world to change. Here, the trees are trimmed and the gates are manned by guards. Dressed in a khaki uniform with a navy hat, the guard asks for Andres's name and calls his mother's home to let her know she has guests. Within seconds the gate is opening on its own, so slowly it looks like it's hesitating.

Andres hasn't been to his mother's home in six years, but this isn't the time to get reacquainted. Lorena puts her arms around Cynthia and shows the children to their bedrooms. They walk through the house apprehensively, their heads tilted up at the oil paintings of saints, their hands barely brushing the brass railing as they climb the stairs. Cynthia is too young to remember any of it, but he wonders if Ignacio can piece his surroundings with bits of memory. If he does, he doesn't mention it, and Andres knows this isn't the right time to ask. He kisses them each good night and asks Lorena for a glass of water. He sips quietly, standing next to the refrigerator.

"What time do you leave tomorrow?"

"Six in the morning."

"Where are you meeting?"

"Somewhere in the desert. They gave me directions. Sounds far."

"You're leaving extra early?"

He nods. She looks torn, like she just swallowed something sour.

"What is it?" he asks, making his way to the door.

"Nothing. Just go. Be careful."

"Mother."

"I just don't want to see you get your hopes shattered twice. What if she leaves you again?"

He shrugs. "I guess that's her choice."

They say good-bye and Lorena draws the sign of the cross on his forehead with her thumb, begging him to take care. "Get some rest," she says, but he knows he'll only lie in bed tonight, waiting wide-eyed for this all to be over.

7

H E WAKES AROUND dawn and waits for Guillermo to arrive. The streets are quiet, even for an early Saturday morning. The few cars on the road speed past and are gone. Andres feels like the whole world is watching him, like the city has been staged for this, and any wrong move will swiftly decide his fate.

He drives through the center of town and gets on the highway, passing the usual exits he'd take to get to work or go to friends' houses, and continues to the edge of the city. The roads start to narrow and disintegrate. The ride turns almost violent as he speeds over cracks and holes. Every few minutes he glances at his passenger seat, at the black duffel bag stuffed so fat with money that he wonders if the zipper will give. Its contents are neatly stacked piles of American money, the green and beige dull compared to Peru's bright orange and blue and purple bills, adorned with the faces of people working in fields, picking crops under a sun they used to worship.

The contents of the duffel bag represent the fruits of eighteen years of hard work. Eighteen years of having doors slammed in his face and feeling the eyes of everyone around him digging into his back, silently hoping that he was setting himself up for failure. In the beginning, his father saw Andres's company as a betrayal, but it hadn't bothered Andres because he'd had Marabela's support, a faith he could fall back on when his own failed. By the time the company started thriving, he was spending so many hours away from home that Marabela's enthusiasm for it began to dim, and he was left to forge ahead while she tended to her photographs in the dark.

Up until now, Andres has had financial stability, food on the table, and, most important, the security of knowing that he would have it there the next day, and the day after that. Now he is driving toward the sun, on a potholed road that will soon turn to dust, unsure of what the next hour will bring.

He checks his rearview mirror, paranoid that he's being followed. Guillermo warned him that the kidnappers are likely to test that he's alone before giving him the directions to the drop-off point. He told him not to deviate from their instructions, not even if there's a back road that will be faster or if traffic gets too hectic. Andres had begged Guillermo to come with him, in case there was a way they could rescue Marabela without giving in to the captors.

"Without giving them your money?" Guillermo asked, incredulous.

Andres felt ashamed for even mentioning it. "I was just thinking, in case something happens, and things get dangerous."

"This isn't like the movies. They already told you she won't be there. Your only choice is to drop off the money and wait for them to send her home. Remember, it's a trade-off," Guillermo said.

One life for another, he'd thought.

"All that's left now is for you to do your part," Guillermo said. He shook his hand then, and they patted each other on the back and held it in a stiff embrace. "Go with God."

Andres feels the road deteriorating underneath him, the ride rougher until it is all dirt and sand, leaving a plume of fog in his wake. In the rearview mirror, he can hardly see the city behind him.

❖ ❖ ❖

He arrives at his first destination at a quarter to seven. All Hades told him is that he was to arrive at a billboard for an ambulance service off the side of the highway and find a set of instructions.

"You like puzzles, don't you?" Hades had teased. "Just be quick about it. I don't have all day."

Andres parks his car next to a pole that towers over him. He starts at the bottom of the billboard, knees bent, and walks his hands to the top, the metal scorching his skin with each quick tap. There, almost out of his reach, is a piece of duct tape, wrapped multiple times around the pole. Picking at it does nothing; he goes back to his car for a knife Guillermo packed for him. When he tears it, it releases a small plastic bag with a note inside.

Take the next exit thirteen kilometers east, it says. *Come alone. We'll know if you don't.*

He rushes back to his car, looking in all directions for any sign of someone watching him. He drives faster, but his car protests. It takes every bit of self-control Andres has to slow down; it's like walking out of a burning building when his instincts are telling him to run.

Every once in a while, a car will fly by in the opposite direction, and Andres wonders if it's one of the kidnappers, checking to make sure he's not being followed. After he's driven fifteen minutes without seeing anyone, he realizes his steering wheel is soaked in sweat. Andres rummages through the backseat with one hand for a bottle of water. Placing it between his legs, he unscrews the lid and is about to drink when the car phone rings. Even though Guillermo has called twice already to check in, the sound continues to startle him.

"How are things going?" he asks.

"*Todavía no hay nada*," Andres says.

Still.

Nothing.

Maybe there won't be anything. Maybe this is just it, maybe that was it, and the last time he saw Marabela he didn't say a word to her, didn't tell her how the rhythm of her breathing helped him fall asleep all those nights when he got home after she'd already gone to bed, didn't tell her that Cynthia did this pensive thing with her eyebrows the other day and she looked just like her mother, didn't tell her how much he's loved her all these years.

Sometimes he wishes Marabela had just left him four months ago and never come back. Maybe then she wouldn't be out in this lonely desert, carrying around so much uncertainty and pain and fear. Then he could at least imagine her in some other city, living another life where she might be happy. He keeps his eyes on the road, his ears ringing with the voice of the man who has been with Marabela all this time, putting his hands on her, striking her, slowly wearing her down one day at a time.

✤ ✤ ✤

Hours have passed and Andres has collected only two additional notes, each more detailed than the last. He's starting to feel like he's just going in circles and headed nowhere. He holds up a small piece of lined yellow paper to the steering wheel and struggles to read the instructions as it shakes in his hand. When he merges off the road onto a highway, he realizes that his destination is somewhere in the forgotten, destitute districts sprawled miles ahead of him.

"Not here," he says into the emptiness.

He takes his foot off the accelerator as the *pueblos jóvenes* get closer. The dwellings scattered along the sides of the desert dunes have a loose sense of order to them — shacks in every color from mint green to cracked white to faded blue cluster together in off-kilter rows. From afar, from where he's used to seeing them somewhere in the background of his existence, they almost look like a colorful tapestry blanketing the bluffs. As he approaches he begins to see the threads of dirt and sand that run through them. Everything is covered in a dull brown layer, like years' worth of dust.

Andres drives past a dilapidated billboard advertising ice cream and makes his first left, leaving the last of the ragged asphalt behind him. He slows his pace, and the ground crunches and cracks beneath his tires as he drives over stones and debris. He double-checks that his car doors are locked. This neighborhood is exactly the kind of place Andres has spent his whole life avoiding, while Marabela spent years venturing into its depths, chronicling the struggles of the city's poor. Most of them are migrants from the countryside who came to the capital in search of a better life and found it had no room for them. Instead, they built their homes out of the city's discarded materials, creating settlements without running water and electricity.

He tries not to look at his surroundings, but he's sure he's being watched, and he can't shake the thought that he's walking into a trap, that it's only a matter of seconds before swarms of people raid his car. Why else would the kidnappers lead him here? And how could he be so stupid as to follow their directions so blindly? He wants to turn his car around and leave this nightmare in the past, but he has to keep going.

He drives a few hundred yards before seeing his destination: a house with a wooden ladder resting next to the front door. It's the last one on this block, and next to it, a wall is painted white with red letters that say VIVA EL PUEBLO PERU. P.C.P. The wall seems to go nowhere; it's as if someone started building it and ran out of bricks. But everywhere around him, the walls speak. Some shout messages of allegiance to the Peruvian Communist Party. Some echo cries for Cambio 90, Fujimori's promise of change when he ran two years ago. All seem to fall on deaf ears.

His instructions are to wait by this home—for how long, or for what, he doesn't know. Andres can't bring himself to put the car in park. He leaves his foot on the brake, pressing so hard that his leg muscles begin to shake from nerves and exertion. From what little he can see through the house's small window, which is partially covered by a bedsheet, no one appears to be inside. He keeps focused on the door, then checks his rearview mirror, then the side ones, his eyes darting everywhere at once. Everything is still and too quiet.

Something about this stop seems final—not just a way station along a highway but a place where people actually live. Andres has this daydream playing out in his mind, of encountering the kidnappers and handing them the bag of money. At the last second he swings it at their heads, knocking them unconscious. He imagines two of them, a boss and his willing apprentice, falling to the ground like a pair of dominoes. In this fantasy, Marabela is waiting for him in a van just a few yards away. She looks healthy and happy.

Boom! A knock against his window nearly shatters him. Terrified, he turns to see a small fist pounding against the glass. The hand opens and waves at him side to side. Andres follows the arm and sees it's a little boy. He can tell by the way the boy's face searches the space in front of him that he can't see through the tinted glass. Andres's first instinct is to shoo him away, but he's afraid to roll down the window. He puts the car in reverse and is about to pull away when he hears the boy's muffled voice.

"*Le tengo un mensaje, señor.*"

He stops and turns to get a good look at the boy, who repeats himself.

"I have a message for you, sir."

Slowly, he rolls down the window just enough for the boy's hand to shoot through and drop a note inside. He's gone before Andres can catch it in his lap.

Put everything in the bag inside the house, then leave exactly the way you came.

Dread washes over him. So this is how it all ends—the nightmare or his life. He puts the car in park and picks up the duffel bag. The weight of his life's work digs into his shoulder as he walks toward the house.

The door, when he knocks on it, turns out to be open. It budges just a bit and he pushes it the rest of the way slowly. The inside of the shack is little more than a narrow, long space, and the floor is just more dirt, as if someone simply put a roof over the earth and called it shelter. It's completely empty except for a navy-blue bag against the wall.

Andres stands over the bag, hesitating. He'd always imagined that when this moment came he'd be eager to be done with it. Now he fears he's just repeating the same mistake he made at the bus stop and handing his hopes over to a thief. He has to remind himself that this time is different. This time, he has Guillermo's guidance. Even Hades, in his own twisted way, tried to reassure him that things would work out so long as he did as he was told.

After you've made the drop, it'll take time for us to pick it up and make sure all the money is there. You will go home and wait. You are not the only one expecting this to go smoothly.

He moves quickly, emptying his bag and transferring his money into the kidnappers'. Andres makes sure each bundle of ten thousand dollars is lined up evenly with the next. There are twenty-five bundles total, so he makes five rows of five. He remembers how his mother used to pay the maids in cash when he was a child, always counting the money right in front of them so they wouldn't be in the awkward position of having to count it themselves in front of her. He knows this is a situation beyond the bounds of trust, but still he lines up the edges of the bills so they make tight, sturdy packages, hoping that his precision will make a difference.

He zips up the bag, pushing it back against the wall like he found it. Before leaving, he feels the cash through the canvas one more time. It's just paper, he reminds himself. It adds up to nothing more than a number.

❖ ❖ ❖

Andres rushes home with the foolish anticipation that Marabela will already be there, waiting for him. Even though he knows that logistically this is close to impossible, his hope takes on a life of its own. Every second that he's in traffic, every car that cuts him off just inches shy of his side-view mirror, serves only to convince him that life will be different once she's back. When he pictures her in his arms, any fear or darkness gets cast away by his love for her. He can practically relive it now, as pure as the first time he held her. He swerves from lane to lane, passing cars and honking at those that try to cross him. For a moment he forgets everything except for a truth that hasn't happened yet. Marabela's rescue will be their rescue. Her survival will be theirs to share. Nothing will matter except for that.

But when he finally arrives at the house, it's empty. Without the kids, the maids, and the driver going about their normal routines, the space feels like a museum. He feels disoriented, like he's just woken up from a dream. The only person here to greet him is Guillermo.

"How did it go?"

"I . . . I don't know. I guess we'll have to wait and find out." He paces around, hesitating to touch anything for fear of changing it. The thought of Marabela coming home to yet another foreign space is more than he can handle.

They make their way to the kitchen table, each of them hugging a warm cup of coffee with the palms of their hands. The coffee is a prop, something to keep them occupied. It's the first time they've sat together, face-to-face, outside their normal headquarters in the darkroom. They've silently agreed that they have no business going there anymore, as if waiting there would be a form of surrender. The phone stretches out from the darkroom to the foot of the stairs, its extra-long cord winding through the hall like a bomb fuse in an old cartoon. The men have taken their places at the most inconspicuous spot in the house, where Consuelo and Carla used to eat dinner. From here, with the kitchen door held open by a clay pot of herbs, Andres can see the living room and the front entrance to the house. He can see the hallway that leads to the garage door, and behind him, through a window in the wall, the dining room and the glass door that opens up to his backyard. He will be able to witness Marabela's arrival from any angle.

"Maybe I shouldn't have sent the kids away."

"Maybe. But we don't know what condition she'll arrive in. It could be hard on the kids to see her like that," Guillermo says.

Andres tries to focus on his cup of coffee, but his capacity for waiting, even for it to cool down a bit, is gone. He burns his tongue on the first few sips and doesn't even feel the rest. "How will she get here? They're not just going to drop her off."

"It varies. I've had clients tell me they were sent home in a taxi. Others have been left to fend for themselves on the side of the road. A few walked to the nearest phone and called home; one man walked the whole way."

"For how long?"

"A few miles. He said his body just remembered the way. The human body's capable of more than you'd expect," Guillermo says.

But Andres doesn't know what to expect. They've arranged for Marabela to see a doctor tomorrow, so that they can attend to her needs right away. Guillermo explains that he's worked with this doctor for years, that the man is discreet and experienced with crisis situations.

"How much experience?" Andres asks.

"Some would say too much. It's unfortunate that our jobs are necessary. In a better world, no one would ever have to hire me, or see the doctor under these circumstances."

"And if that was the case, you'd be out of a job. Then what would you do?" Andres takes another sip, wishing for a stronger drink.

Even though he meant the question as a joke, Guillermo answers it without hesitation. "What I used to do. I was a cop before I got into this, twenty-six years ago. I never set out to work in kidnappings, but we started getting more and more of them. At first, we even solved a few. We helped the families make the drop, and when the victims were safe we investigated to find the captors. There were even rescue missions when the opportunity seemed right. Those were rare, though, but gratifying."

"You don't do those anymore?"

He shakes his head. "If it were up to me, I'd still be fighting on that side. But eventually I couldn't tell which side we were on."

"What do you mean?" Andres asks.

Guillermo sets his cup of coffee down, turning it in circles like it's a dial he's trying to adjust. Neither of them is used to talking about anything other than business, and clearly Guillermo isn't eager to start.

"*Dale, pues.* How else do you expect we'll pass the time?" Andres says. He knows he has a point Guillermo can't argue with.

"The cops are supposed to be the good guys. No one believes that anymore, and I can't blame them. I made the same mistake and I worked years with these guys. On our last rescue, I went in with my captain. The space was too small to send in a larger group, and it was just me and him on the inside, a few other men on the perimeter, guarding the exits. We basically walked into a trap. We were expecting a small operation and one hostage, but we found a room with seven, eight captors and several hostages in a room. Lots of cash, too. Piles of it." He scoffs at the memory of it. "They could've killed us, but they wanted to make a deal. Let them go, and they'd release the hostages and we keep some of the money. I wasn't in a position to speak or negotiate—I was supposed to do whatever my captain ordered. He agreed to the offer so fast, you could tell he'd done this before. So the captors took some of the cash, gave most of it to my captain, plus a little extra so we could say we recouped it as part of the raid. We came out looking like heroes, and those imbeciles got away. They probably kidnapped twice as many people after that, trying to get back the money they lost."

"Anything to stay in business, huh?"

Guillermo grabs an apple and a knife from the counter next to the refrigerator. His movements are precise as he peels the apple, forming a long green spiral ribbon. His eyes don't move from the knife as he talks. "To them, it's just an investment in their future growth, the cost of doing business. If you think about it, it's the perfect business model. Who is willing to gamble their loved one's life just to break the cycle of supply and demand?"

"Then why do you keep working in it?" Andres asks. Guillermo bites into the fruit and looks up at the ceiling as he chews, as if he might find the answer there. Andres can't tell if he's stalling for time, or if he's just taking his time to swallow.

Finally Guillermo gestures to the empty space around them with his knife. "Working with the families is the one place you won't find corruption. It's the one place people value life in a way that can't be counted with money."

"So what will you do after this? Wait for the next one?"

Guillermo shakes his head, looking, for the first time since Andres has met him, exhausted and uncertain. "I think this is it for me."

"You're quitting?"

"Retiring, Andres. There's a difference. Maybe I'll turn my attention somewhere I'm actually needed. Like a garden or a wood shop or . . . I don't know. I haven't had a chance to give it much thought."

Somehow, Andres can't picture Guillermo on his knees with his hands in the dirt. "A nice, quiet life. I can see why a man in your profession would miss that."

"Quiet is just a lack of noise. What I really miss is the trust. Working in kidnappings makes you cynical. You don't take anything for what it is. You're always looking for hidden motives and traps."

"That's what makes you good at what you do, though."

He chuckles to himself. "It's what makes me bad at living my life."

Andres sits back in his chair and lets out a long breath. He's just now realizing that for all the plans and wishes he made for Marabela to come home, he'd never bothered to picture life beyond that. Everything has been defined by this crisis, and he's not sure he's capable of handling it without Guillermo. He tries to think of ways to ask him to stay, at least until life feels safe again, when they hear a scratching sound coming from the backyard. Without hesitating, Andres leaps up from his chair and runs outside, but the lawn is empty, and the sound is coming from the opposite side of the thick stucco wall that divides his property from his neighbor's. To look over the wall, he needs a ladder or something tall to stand on. He takes a stool from the patio. It wobbles as he steps onto it, and Guillermo rushes over to hold it steady with both hands.

The scratching continues. Each second that passes it gets more intense and desperate. Andres tries to hurry, but he has to be careful not to cut himself on the barbed wire along the top of the wall. He pulls himself up and looks down. It's just the neighbor's dog, trying to escape. The dog starts barking at him, his whole body shaking.

Disappointed, Guillermo and Andres go back to the kitchen and wait again. After an hour, Andres makes his way to the living room and Guillermo to the dining room. Both are restless. Guillermo starts reading yesterday's newspaper, stretching its pages across the table. All Andres can do is sit on the couch and pick at the stitches in the cushions. He stares at the ceiling, chasing the translucent shapes that float, like amoebas and worms, across his sight. Every few minutes, he hears a car approaching the house, and each time he sits up and looks out the window only to see it pass by.

He's just about to go back to the kitchen for another cup of coffee he doesn't plan on drinking when he hears the faint click of the metal gate. Ever since he dropped the children off at his mother's, the gate has remained unlocked. He'd rather risk intruders than lock Marabela out. The gate swings open with a high pitch. Andres runs out the door.

Seeing her, his hope gets flung around inside him, unsure whether to be grateful or deflated. Her steps carry their usual rhythm but lack strength. She wears a silk blouse and a pair of dark pleated pants — the same outfit she was wearing the last morning he saw her — but the clothing has aged like she has. The fabric hangs loose like a bunched-up curtain as she stumbles down the pavement. Andres runs to meet her, helps her walk down the path. When their bodies touch she flinches.

"It's just me, Mari," he says.

For a moment, she looks at him with terror and confusion, her eyes squinting under the dull sky. Then he sees the recognition sinking in and relief spreads across her face from her forehead to her neck; it gives out and her head falls forward, shaking side to side in disbelief. Andres tries holding her, whispering and repeating, "You're home, you're here, it's all over," but his words fall weak and far beyond her reach. She's somewhere else. Her body came home before her senses did. With one arm wrapped around her waist and the other stretched out so she can press down on it, they walk down the long pavement to their home. It is one in the afternoon, and already the sun has slipped past the clouds, turning everything gray. He sees Guillermo watching them through the window, but by the time they enter, they're alone.

"Mari . . ." All he can seem to say is her name, all he can seem to do is marvel at her—her hands that he holds in his, her eyes so flooded with tears, he can barely look into them, and the very stiffness of every muscle in her body. It is both the most beautiful thing and the most terrifying thing he's ever seen. Her pain is so self-contained, it makes her brittle against his touch. Every inch of her is hard as bones, but when she leans into him, her elbows pierce at his side and her body feels like it could crumble.

Inside, Andres leads her to the couch, the same one she asked him over and over again never to sit on, so that she can rest. He puts his hand on her shoulder and stares at her. It is an awkward moment, full of pain intensified by a longing to hold her, coupled with a certainty that this is the exact wrong thing to do. He'd imagined this moment as a happy one, a celebration of survival. How foolish, he realizes, to think they ever shared two sides of the same experience.

They sit next to each other like strangers, fully aware of the significance of this reunion but hesitant to intrude on each other's space. Finally Andres puts his hand behind Marabela's head and pulls her close. She doesn't resist but she doesn't contribute in any way to the forward momentum of her head onto his shoulder. Her movements are stilted, like images in a flip-book. Even when she's breathing on his neck, he doesn't yet feel her weight rest against him.

"You're home now," he tells her. "It's over. You're safe here."

A gust of warm breath explodes against his neck, and as she nods and begins shaking violently, digging herself into him, Andres feels her tears burn against his skin, and he is happy to receive them, happy to feel their moisture sink into his clothes—until he realizes what he missed most about her is that she once needed him, and now she needs him in a way he never wanted.

PART TWO

Days 17 and On

8

————

I T'S AS IF the house has aged without her—still recognizable, but different. It smells slightly of lemon—maybe from a new cleaning product the girls tried in her absence. Everything looks smaller and farther away, as if items recede from her at the very moment she's stepping toward them. The house is just a space, full of furniture and things that used to be hers, but she doesn't feel like she belongs to them or to the life they hint at.

There was a time when this home was her domain. Sometimes she felt proud of it, sometimes she felt tied to it, but whether it was a burden or a blessing, it was hers to keep. She'd known better than anyone what this house needed; lately it'd become one of the few aspects of her life she could control. There is no corner, no ridge along the steps or crack along the wall, that she doesn't know like her own body. The house may never have been the sanctuary she'd always dreamed of, but at least it carried no surprises. It was comfortable. Now all that has changed.

After a few glances around the living room, Marabela feels like curling into bed and sleeping the past few weeks away. In the dark room where she was kept, she used to lament that time was being stolen from her, but she no longer wants that time back. She'd happily let it go on without her if it meant she could be spared these strange, disconcerting moments. Andres holds her in an embrace she can't get out of. When she cries, his grip becomes tighter—a vicious cycle of misunderstanding.

"We kept everything the same for you," he finally says.

He starts to say something else about what it was like when they'd have dinner without her, but Marabela hardly hears him. "The kids. Where are they? Are they safe?" Her voice is dry and hoarse, harsh against the inside of her throat.

"The kids will be here soon. They're with my mother. I wanted the house to be calm and quiet for you."

Marabela sits up. Her hair sticks to the moisture on her face, the tendrils light as spiderwebs. She pushes them aside and ends up scratching her cheek. It burns, and when she pats the skin with her fingertips she can already feel it reddening, rising.

"When will they be here?" She feels impatient for their warm bodies. Even the thought of Lorena bringing them home, filling in for her in her absence, gets buried beneath this longing.

"They're already on their way. They won't be more than twenty minutes. You must be hungry," Andres says, covering her with a blanket. "I brought some soup for you, and some *causa*."

Soft food for this soft body, Marabela thinks, but she only shakes off his offer with a thin smile. "I'd rather wait for them." She stands up and tries to walk to the window, but her whole body begs for rest. The sudden rush of adrenaline from just a few moments ago has died down, and her eyelids feel like they might fall to the ground, taking her head with them.

"You should rest. I'll let you know as soon as they're here," Andres says.

They don't bother trying to climb the stairs together. She lays back down on the couch, and the home she so longed for starts to fade from her vision, taken over by a darkness she thought she'd escaped.

❖ ❖ ❖

When she wakes up she hears whispers coming from the kitchen. The door is open, and she scoots up the couch to get a better look inside. All she sees is half of a man—a leg, an elbow, and a neck, too thick and strong to belong to Andres. Marabela walks slowly to the kitchen, careful to keep her steps light. Even though she knows she's free, trying to be invisible is a hard habit to break. Instinctively, she guards this little liberty of being able to stand and move as she pleases, hoping that no one will notice and try to take it away from her. When she reaches the threshold, she has to lean on it for balance.

The two men don't notice her at first.

"I'm sorry," the stranger says. "But this isn't how I normally work. I'm happy to recommend colleagues to you, people with years of experience. I'm no bodyguard, Andres. What you hired me for and what you're asking me to do now are two very different things."

"I know that, I just . . . I trust you. The kids already trust you. They're finally getting used to you and I'd hate to bring in someone else for them to adjust to, right when we're trying to get life back to normal. Please, it wouldn't be permanent."

The man puts his hands on his hips and shakes his head. "If it were for anyone else but Señora Jimenez . . ." Marabela takes a step back, confused as to what she could possibly have to do with this man. "I'll stay, but only to finish the month. I've been as flexible as I possibly can in this agreement."

"I understand. We are both businessmen, after all." Andres says this with a melancholy Marabela has never seen in him before. They shake hands and slap each other's back in a tight hug. The man, perhaps sensing Marabela staring at them, suddenly turns around. She stands frozen outside the kitchen, shocked at his intensity. Andres urges her to come inside, looking almost proud to introduce them.

"Marabela, this is Guillermo. I hired him to protect us. He helped me through every step of this . . . process."

Guillermo holds his hand out and Marabela shakes it lightly, feeling the cracks in his dry skin. His touch sends a vibration through her entire body, makes her head twitch as she tries to shake off the touch of yet another stranger, but it stays with her, and for a moment it is the only thing she knows. Then she hears footsteps coming from outside the front door. They are quick and light, the happiest sound she has heard in seventeen days. The kids.

"They're here?" she asks.

Andres jumps into action and smiles, raising his eyebrows just like he used to when he would pretend Ignacio's spoon was a train. He takes Marabela by the elbow and helps her make her way toward the door, but his stride is too slow for her. Marabela ends up rushing out of his arms, swinging the door open with the force of a gust of wind. Just the sight of Cynthia and Ignacio rushing toward her almost knocks her over. The children engulf her, hugging both her and each other at once. Her own body is so thin it gets lost inside their arms, and she lets her hands clutch at the soft hair on their heads, their sturdy backs, their faces that have a way of dissolving the rest of the world when she stares into them.

Ignacio leans into her neck and whispers at her through his tears. "I missed you so much."

"Cynthia, Ignacio, my little everythings," she says. She finds there aren't many words more beautiful than their names, and she keeps repeating them just to hear the syllables and see their faces in the same moment. She rests her head over their shoulders and catches sight of Guillermo leaning into the window of a black Mercedes at the end of the driveway. No doubt it's Lorena, trying to leave without being noticed, but Marabela's thoughts quickly turn back to the kids. They walk into the house, unwilling to let go of one another like contestants in a three-legged race. Cynthia laughs at their clumsiness as they almost fall onto the couch together. Andres lunges toward them, his voice suddenly stern and full of caution. "Gently. Your mother is very tired."

She smiles and waves off his words, annoyed at the interruption. "Andres, it's fine, really." But now that they're inside and have taken a moment to calm down, the frailty in her voice is hard to ignore. "Come here," she says to Cynthia, patting her lap. Cynthia slides on top of her and wraps her arms around her mother's shoulders like she would a porcelain doll. She kisses her cheek, her lips barely touching the skin. She looks confused, trying to figure out if she should smile or pout, be happy or angry. The moment is precious but fragile.

"Where did you go?" Cynthia finally asks.

Marabela looks down at the floor, afraid to look her daughter in the eyes, afraid that even through her smile she will see the tears, the pain — and know. "I had to go away for a little bit. But I missed you. So much. Did you miss me?"

Cynthia nods, still pouting. "But where did you go?" she repeats.

Marabela forces a laugh to hide a sob. "It's supposed to be a secret," she whispers. "But if you're good, I'll tell you someday, okay?"

Cynthia's face brightens a little. She's always liked secrets. "Did you bring me anything?"

"Can't you see she had a rough trip?" The way Ignacio says this, with a smile meant to diffuse the truth, confirms to Marabela that he knows everything. Only Cynthia was spared the horror.

She plays along, of course. Ignacio's maturity takes her by surprise; his transformation makes her sad and proud. This isn't how her son was supposed to learn about love and selflessness. It came at too high a price.

He sits on top of the coffee table across from her and holds his mother's hand. He has a content look on his face, and his eyes are glassy, holding back so many things she knows he can't say. "How are you feeling? Are you okay?"

A laugh escapes her, from deep inside a place she didn't know could hold laughter anymore. "Seeing you both, I know I will be." She stretches her arm toward his knee and covers it with her hand.

After a few moments of silence Cynthia turns to her mother with an exaggerated tilt of the head.

"So, no presents?" she says, but Marabela knows her daughter is only trying to ease the moment.

"You'll get it when you're older," Ignacio says. "Why don't you get the bags we brought from Grandma's and start unloading them. I'll help you in a minute." Cynthia gives her mom one last squeeze and starts toward the garage. Ignacio helps Marabela up in one smooth movement that rises into an embrace. Like always, he towers over her, and her neck bends back at an awkward angle, pressed against his shoulder. She almost can't breathe, but it doesn't matter. Here is her son, and at least for this instant the world feels safe again.

He kisses her, over and over on the forehead, then takes a deep breath. She can tell he wants to say something, wants to figure out the right words in a situation like this. But his first words are an apology. Marabela doesn't understand.

"I'm so sorry," he keeps saying, as if just by looking at her he can see everything she's been through. He has a sad, eager look on his face, and she's reminded of how cavalier he would be as a little boy, slipping into the role of the little gentleman just as easily as policeman or firefighter. He'd always walk ahead of her to open doors and offer to take her bags even when they were his size. He's always wanted to relieve her of burdens, and she has tried hard not to lay them on him.

"None of this is your fault," she tells him. "Blaming yourself won't make it any easier to deal with. Understand?"

Ignacio blinks back tears and nods. As they walk across the room, she can feel her body breaking down, aching and tightening with anticipation. It's all starting to feel real now. Home. After everything. Somehow she had imagined this would be different, that when she came back she would leave behind everything she went through. The weight of it bears down on her. Suddenly she is only aware of how weak she feels. Her knees buckle underneath her and she places her hand on a side table for balance. Andres rushes to her side.

"I need a shower," she says. She feels heavy from the dirt that has caked onto her skin over the past seventeen days. It cracks as she moves, like glue holding her together. Andres leads her up the stairs, follows her through their bedroom and stops.

"Do you want me to—?"

"No," she says, too quickly. "Thank you. I'll be fine."

"I'll be right outside if you need anything," Andres says, shutting the door gently behind her. For a moment she stands still, hypersensitive to everything around her. Through the thin walls she can hear Andres breathing. She follows the sound of his steps, muffled by the carpet but still pronounced enough that she can picture him pacing back and forth, guarding her in the same way her captors had on the other side of the door.

Aside from a small window over the shower, there is barely any ventilation in the bathroom. Marabela strips with the care of a nurse unraveling a bandage, and her skin sticks to the silk of her blouse in parts where she bled and started to heal. The scabs, newly exposed, burn bright red. Her pants fall quickly to the floor, bunched around her ankles. It is only once she's completely bare that Marabela realizes she hasn't turned on the light. She flips the switch and tenses at the sight of a small figure moving in the corner. For an instant, she doesn't realize it's her own reflection.

Marabela has not seen herself in a mirror in weeks. It was one thing to look down at her legs, arms, and stomach, but it's another experience altogether to have some perspective on herself. She sees her face for the first time, not knowing she'd look so different. Of course she'd seen the bruises on her wrists, her chipped and dirty nails; and she'd known from the way her shoulders hurt when she sat against the wall that she was missing the cushion of a normal amount of flesh.

Now, Marabela realizes that her arms and legs look like candlesticks that have been left too close to a fire. Her body looks like it simply melted away.

She turns her back to the mirror and looks over her shoulder. If she hugs herself, she can see ribs protruding through her skin. She taps them like they're keys of a piano, her fingers stepping gently over the deep gaps between each bone. She has never felt so small, so shrunken into herself, while at the same time heavy with everything her body has held on to. It tells a story she never wants to hear again.

The events of the past two and a half weeks are written on her skin in shades of yellow, green, blue, and black, each hinting at the chronology of her days in captivity. The first day, the men focused on her face. They wanted to hurt the most visible parts of her, the ones that would be noticed most easily and mourned. They should have known that what would hit her the hardest was not the weight of the biggest man's fists or the steel of his boot against her cheeks when she fell to the floor. What made her collapse into herself was the sight of the grenades they hung around her neck and the guns they pointed at her face the day they photographed her.

"Yes, they're real," a younger man said as he looked into her eyes and grinned. In that moment she knew there was no hiding; even her thoughts were within earshot. They took pictures of her and she remembers thinking how cruel it was, to have the camera used as a weapon against her. She'd tried to look away but it was unnecessary. By then her eyes had swollen so much that holding them open was painful, like pushing down on a bruise. The flash permeated her lids.

The marks on her cheekbones have almost healed by now; they look like the hints of green on a slice of old cheese. The scabs on her right shoulder have hardened. The last time she got to speak to Andres on the phone, after the men claimed that he wasn't going to pay and no one was coming for her, she'd lost her will to move. They'd dragged her over the threshold, insisting that they didn't have to, that she should be grateful they were letting her speak with anyone, and thrust her into a wall of exposed cinder blocks. Her shoulders scraped against the cement, shaving off her skin as her body fell to the floor. She doesn't remember what Andres said to her on the phone that day, but she remembers how the fresh wound stung.

Marabela steps into the shower, marveling at its smooth, cold surface. She lets the water fill up to her ankles. When the water warms, she crouches down, naked, so she can scoop her hands under the stream. She takes the handfuls of water and rubs them against her body, watching as the dirt gets pulled toward the drain.

She remembers her first summer married to Andres, how they spent the day after Christmas at the beach, fighting with the ocean as it pulled them in. When they finally came home, they realized how much the sun had toasted their skin. Within days, they'd started to peel. They drew a cold bath one night and sat with their legs crossed, removing thin layers of dead skin from each other's shoulders and back.

"How long do you think it takes till we grow back new skin?" he asked.

Marabela shrugged. "Who can know for sure? I read we shed and grow it back all the time."

"Like snakes?" Andres said, an exaggerated excitement in his voice.

"Exactly," she said, laughing and rolling her eyes. She liked the idea of them constantly changing in and out of their skins, shedding old layers to make way for new ones.

Now, as she runs her fingers over these new cracks and scrapes, she considers how long her body will take to heal. She wishes she could hurry the process along. Marabela picks at a scab by her hipbone (her captors were fond of throwing her onto the floor) and peels away several others on her palm (she tried, but failed, to fall hands first). She rubs at the dirt on her ankles, toes, and heels, and it flakes away like pieces of an old eraser. If she scrubs hard enough, it all falls away, so she rubs harder, first with her fingertips, then with her jagged nails, until she's drawing new blood from old wounds and crying out in pain, cries she can't hear anymore, until finally the door bursts open, as it always does. She stops and looks up and there is Andres, watching in horror.

"How long till it grows back?" she asks. "Do you remember?"

❖ ❖ ❖

Andres and the kids are afraid to speak while she's asleep. Together, they make dinner in near silence—a simple chicken soup with a ham sandwich—setting the table with so much care that the plates and silverware hardly make a sound as they are placed on the table.

Andres and the kids work in an assembly-line fashion: Cynthia sets the place mats and folds the napkins into triangles; Ignacio presses the forks and knives down, diffusing the clinking of the metals; and Andres lays the plates in the center. It's a soothing routine; Andres understands now why Consuelo often hummed as she worked, why she and Carla gossiped as they folded laundry or dried the dishes. The mind memorizes the movements to free up the brain. It's a dance that needs musical accompaniment. But not today.

When they're done, Ignacio clears his throat, standing behind the chair at the foot of the table, the only one with arms at the side, like a throne. He gives a quick, violent nod in the direction of Marabela's room.

"Are you going to wake her?" he whispers.

Andres shakes his head multiple times and wrinkles his face at the absurdity of it. Why would he do that? They'll wait until she is ready. He indicates this with a stiff hand in the air. He pulls out a chair, lifting it half an inch off the ground, and lets his body slide down its back. Ignacio follows his lead and takes a seat, his arms stretched over the chair as if held by puppet strings.

"What now?" he says.

They've waited so long for Marabela to come back, it's hard not

to remain in a state of perpetual anticipation. Andres can't stop trying to predict what she'll need before she needs it, can't stop thinking of answers to questions she's sure to ask. At times he feels he'll
never be able to do enough for her, then worries his attempts will
only smother her. How long till he is not afraid to touch Marabela,
or ask how she's doing for fear she'll actually answer? How long till
the sight of her no longer hurts?

"Tomorrow I'll take her to the doctor," he tells Ignacio once Cynthia leaves the dining room to get her drink. "Her health is the most
important thing right now."

From behind them, a voice breaks in. "What if she doesn't want to
go?" In all his efforts to keep quiet, Andres forgot to listen, and he's
surprised that Marabela managed to get through the living room and
into the dining room without a sound.

Andres rises to help Marabela to her chair, but she makes a point
of doing it herself.

"It's just a simple checkup. Just to make sure everything's—"

"I'm fine. You can take my word for it." As proof, she leans over
the table and reaches for a sandwich, but quickly pulls back her arm
when her sleeve starts riding up, exposing a greenish patch of skin
around her wrist. She looks first to Ignacio and then to Cynthia, who
stands with two glasses of Inka Cola, trying to gauge if her bruise has
been noticed.

Andres frowns. "Guillermo suggested this would be best. He says
this doctor is excellent and very experienced."

"What does he know? I don't even know the man. And I'm not
comfortable having him here. What is he still doing here anyway?"

"*Mi amor*," Andres says. Now he feels like he's rehearsing lines in a
play. "Maybe we should talk about this later. We don't want it to ruin
your appetite."

Dinner is quiet and cautious. Andres watches Marabela as she
eats, how her eyes travel the house; he wonders what he sees and
what she doesn't see, what she thinks is missing. The children keep

an eye on them, and every once in a while Cynthia tests the tension in the room. She peels the crust off her sandwich and rolls it into a ball, biting into it like an apple.

"Want some?" She giggles as she offers it to her brother, who just smiles and rolls his eyes.

"Don't play with your food, sweetie," Marabela says. Andres is surprised by how easily she slips back into her role. It gives him hope.

She takes small bites of her sandwich and wipes her mouth with the napkin resting on her lap. When she's done, she holds her empty plate with both hands and lets her gaze wander to the kitchen. "So, where are the girls?" she asks. He's never understood why she calls them "the girls" when Consuelo is an old woman and Carla is a teenager.

He's thought of many ways to break the news to her since she arrived, but at the last moment he decides on the straightforward approach: "I sent them home."

"For the day or for good?"

He stops his spoon midway. "Why do you ask?" Without thinking, he resorts to his business instincts to field the question.

"Their room is cleared out. I checked on my way into the kitchen. Except for the bed, of course. Guillermo seems to have made himself very comfortable."

❖　❖　❖

On her way up from the dining room, Marabela notices the door to the darkroom cracked open; light is sneaking through it. The sight is so foreign to her, she might as well be seeing toxic sludge ooze out of the room. She tries to remember what she last shot, before all of this, but the experience of that life appears before her like a desire, not as a coherent memory.

Marabela remembers a roll of film she'd just finished developing, a series of pictures of hands and feet along the street. Several weeks ago, as she reached into her pocket for a few centimos to buy a paper fan, she accidentally snapped a picture of a little girl's shoes. At first, Marabela had been upset—each exposure is precious, not to be wasted—until she saw the film against the light, how the tiny image of two feet, awkwardly tilted at the toes, revealed a story she hadn't realized was there. This little girl's shoes were open-toed, but her feet barely poked through. They had yet to grow into the shoes, but for now they could hide from the sun that was so hot it could burn her skin. From then on Marabela developed an interest in shooting hands and feet. In these extremities, she looked for clues into a person's life. On the feet, a person's entire existence bears down, grounds them and carries them through life. In the hands, she can see everything they've touched, reached for, accomplished. The rest of the body can be shielded, but hands and feet can tell no lies. Marabela began snapping them everywhere she went.

She had a nonchalant way of shooting that put people at ease. People trusted her, even with the scrutinizing eye of her lens. Every once in a while, when she got a truly breathtaking image, she'd frame it and gift it to the subject.

She wonders if that film is even here anymore. She approaches the room with the same caution as someone returning to her home, knowing full well it's been robbed.

"Hello?" she says when she hears a rustled footstep.

Inside Guillermo is standing with his hands crossed over his chest, staring at a wall of cards and maps where there used to be images.

"What the hell are you doing in here?" she says.

"Andres didn't tell you?" He reaches for a stack of papers and sorts through them on a desk where her tub of chemicals used to sit. He is unapologetic. He goes about his business like a man who's been interrupted by a secretary or a coworker.

"Tell me? No. He failed to mention a lot of things. Like why you're still here and not the people who could really be of use."

"I'm sorry you feel that way, señora. I know this is an adjustment for you."

"You don't know shit."

"I'm sorry. I was just saying, in my experience with these things—"

"I don't care about your experience." She hates that he wants to lump her together, label her a victim and file her away into a drawer along with all his other cases, as if they each aren't unique.

"We thought this would be the safest place to conduct our efforts. I'll clear out now that my services are no longer necessary."

She walks past him to the enlarger and twists the knob that focuses film negatives in and out.

"I can't believe you turned on the lights," she says. The room looks different to her, all its faults exposed. In the dark it'd been a sanctuary, a quiet, still place where life took its time showing her its true colors. Seeing it like this is like seeing the lights turned on at a favorite nightclub.

"I'll put it back the way it was," Guillermo says reassuringly.

She laughs because even she can't remember exactly what that looked like. "What does it matter? It won't be the same."

He sets down his papers and walks right toward her, his eyes never leaving hers. He comes close enough to hold her against the wall with his body. Her breath gets suspended in her lungs, heavy and still as he reaches behind her. "*Permiso*," he says. And turns the light off.

The darkness brings panic for a moment, but she can hear him moving through the space—not clumsily like a person stumbling through the dark, but with the confidence of a blind man who's memorized a room. Within seconds he's turned on the safelight, and his skin takes on a warm hue, his features softened by a reddish glow that casts shadows across his face.

"I'd never seen a darkroom as organized as yours. It's a work of art." He pauses, perhaps waiting for her to thank him. When she doesn't, he continues quickly. "Almost everything had already been exposed, so the light wouldn't have damaged it, but I put it all away regardless. It didn't feel right to bring the photos out into the light without the photographer seeing them first."

For the first time Marabela notices there's a small chest of drawers from Andres's office in the room. It's sealed shut with duct tape along the cracks to block out the light. Guillermo rips the tapes off the top drawer, revealing a tray full of photographs, testing strips, overexposed and underexposed images that she might've thrown out in a few days had she returned. They've all been guarded with care.

"My father used to be a photographer, señora. He rarely let me in. He said the darkroom was his escape."

In another life she might have thanked him, but now her sense of defense is a stronger impulse than being polite. "And knowing this, you still came and took over this one." It's not so much a question as it is an accusation. She doesn't expect him to answer.

He unseals the next drawer to reveal a single blank sheet. "This one was under the enlarger. I didn't know if it'd been exposed or not, and I was tempted to drop it into the chemicals to see what it was."

"How dare you . . ."

"I didn't. It waits for you, whenever you're ready." He shuts the drawer, reseals the chest, and turns the light back on.

"I'll have it back for you exactly the way it was by tomorrow," he says.

When he leaves, she's grateful that he's left the light on. She's not sure she's ready to be left alone in the dark.

❖　❖　❖

That night, Marabela stays up, listening to Andres's deep breathing and wishing that she hadn't taken such a long nap in the afternoon. Every once in a while he stirs and the foldout bed creaks, but eventually quiet settles over the house. The peace mocks her; she feels alone in the world, as if she doesn't really exist. She wanders the halls, peeking into Ignacio's and Cynthia's rooms. Tucked tightly into their beds, they look calm, and likely soothed by the knowledge of her presence. She's glad that her return has brought them tranquillity; she only wishes she could find it as well.

She sits on the couch in the upstairs living room and gazes at the white walls, now gray against the darkness. Everything around her looks like the color has been leached out of it. Outside, the occasional car drives by, the sound of its engine humming like a cold breeze. She thinks of what could be happening beyond the walls of her home. Somewhere, someone is feeling fear like the one she has lived through in the past few weeks. She gets up and goes to the window, stares at the houses lined up and down her street. Even in a well-off neighborhood like hers, the homes suffocate one another. One building starts where another ends. There is no space between them for privacy, no land available to waste.

It is hours past curfew, but occasionally an old man or a teenager walks quietly down the sidewalk, unable to resist the night. Marabela scoots down the couch toward the window, noticing for the first time how fragile the glass is. With a small pebble thrown just so in the air, someone could crack the surface. With a determined brick, it could all explode, sending shards of glass piercing into her skin. Marabela imagines the clear, glimmering pieces swimming in small rivers of blood along her skin, and she thinks that perhaps it's not worth the risk to watch the world through the window when her house is full of perfectly good rooms that don't reveal her to the world beyond. She tiptoes back to her bedroom and double-checks that the windows are locked and the blinds are sealed tight.

In time she falls into a sleep so light, she still feels aware of her surroundings—the heavy silence, the cool air outside, the suffocating anticipation of daylight. To avoid consciousness she tries to sleep for as long as possible, and surprisingly her body welcomes it, knowing what her mind has yet to comprehend: she is safe now, she is far away from those fears.

When Marabela wakes the next morning, she doesn't recognize

anything. Someone stands at the doorway, a small silhouette creeping toward her, speaking to her in words that she doesn't understand. Marabela sits up on the bed, pushing her body against the headboard with her legs. When she finally gains focus, she recognizes her own fear in the figure standing before her: it's Cynthia, come looking for her mother.

"*Hijita*," she says, letting her panicked motions melt away into a casual stretch in the hopes that Cynthia doesn't catch on. "What a beautiful sight to wake up to. Is that a new dress?" The question is unnecessary; Marabela knows every button and thread that belongs to her little girl. Seeing her dressed in this light green linen sundress that ties in bows at the top of Cynthia's shoulders, Marabela is reminded how much life has been taken away from her.

Straightening out her skirt, Cynthia nods and says, "Grandma gave it to me after I got better."

"Oh?" The thought of Lorena being here in her absence, easily gliding into her place, is becoming harder to suppress. "You were sick?" Marabela pulls Cynthia close to her so she can feel the warmth of her skin. The child eyes her with caution.

"Mm-hmm. Were you sick, too? Is that why you had to go away?" She imitates her mother, placing her small hand on Marabela's cheek. At last, Cynthia starts to cry.

Marabela braces herself. "It's okay. Let it out. Mama's here," she reassures, pushing back her own tears.

❖   ❖   ❖

She goes looking for Andres and finds him in the dining room, looking busy with papers scattered across the polished wood. Marabela sits on a leather chair in the corner of the room with a blanket hugging her shoulders. The chair sinks gently underneath her weight.

"How did you sleep?" Andres asks. He stands up and sits next to her on the arm of the chair.

She nods. "Good enough."

Slowly, he puts his arms around her and rests his head on top of hers. She can tell he is tense, taking care not to let his body push down on her, but her whole body is tender and everywhere he touches, no matter how gently, aches. Her shoulder throbs under the warmth of his palm. The more she tries to push it out of her mind, the more the feeling intensifies.

"Andres . . ." She shifts away from him. "*No puedo*."

"I'm so sorry," he says, backing off completely. He jumps off the chair and kneels next to her. His eyes look everywhere except her face. "God, I'm so sorry. I can't imagine what you must be going through, what you went through. What can I do? Just . . . just tell me what I have to do to make things better for you and I'll do it."

Marabela begins to shake her head. She is unaccustomed to asking anything of him, but then she remembers. "I'm not comfortable with that man being in our home."

"Guillermo?"

"*Me da algo*. I can't explain it. But it makes me feel weird, having a complete stranger in here all day, watching everything we do."

"He's here for your protection," Andres says. He shifts his tone to a gentle whisper, as if he's talking to Cynthia. "He's been with us for almost three weeks now."

"I know how long it's been. But he's still a stranger to me."

Andres covers his nose and mouth with his hands, like he always does when he's trying to find a way to win an argument. "Guillermo has experience with these kinds of things. It was because of him that we were able to get you out of there." His words come slowly, cautiously. When Marabela still won't look at him he continues. "I want him to stay with us for a while, to protect us in case things . . . change."

"Isn't that your job?" Marabela says, and leaves.

❖ ❖ ❖

In the afternoon Andres insists on taking Marabela to the doctor but she refuses to leave the house. "Let them come here," she says.

"But we need X-rays, Mari. To see if you've suffered any internal damage." She cringes at the softness of his voice. Every time he speaks it's like he's trying to massage the words into her skull. "And you need nutrients to get healthy again. Come on, we'll be in and out."

She takes up the entire backseat of the car, stretched out and covered in a blanket with her eyes closed. They arrive sooner than she expected. When she gets out of the car she doesn't recognize the building. They've gone underground to a parking lot full of scratched-up cement columns and tight spaces; there isn't even an elevator to take them to the ground floor.

"I don't understand why we can't go to Dr. Urriega," Marabela says.

"I wasn't sure you'd want to see him under the circumstances, and I didn't want to take you to just anyone. We can trust this guy."

"Right," she says, doubtful. She can't argue about Dr. Urriega, though. He is perhaps too close within their circle, having studied with Andres's uncle. He regularly attends Marabela's charity functions, and she doesn't like the idea of him carrying the thought of her kidnapping in the back of his mind.

As they pass through the narrow hallways, Marabela glances through the open doors of other businesses. There's a travel agency—empty except for a young woman making photocopies, gazing at a poster of Hawaii as the machine drones on—and an accountant who's left his door and windows open to let a breeze in, his papers scattering everywhere as a result. Toward the end of the hall she passes a waiting room packed with men and women in business attire filling out forms. A fan points to the center of the room, flipping the pages of magazines spread over a large table.

They enter a small room filled with white plastic folding chairs lined up against a yellow wall. Marabela stands in the center of the room as Andres announces them to the receptionist behind the glass.

They're called in right away. The young nurse mispronounces their last name, but she asks no questions and hands Marabela a paper gown. She's told to undress and directed toward the X-ray room, which is cold and made colder still by the metal surface on which she has to lie down. The bed shakes as an X-ray technician stands over her and shoves giant squares of film into the slots underneath her.

"Now don't move. And hold your breath," he says before disappearing.

The machine sounds like an elevator taking off. They take several more X-rays, all in different areas—her head, her chest, her hips, her knees. Never once does the man look her in the eyes.

Back in the examining room, Andres sits on a round leather chair with wheels on it, shifting side to side on its rotating axis.

"That's the doctor's chair," Marabela whispers.

He gets up and sits on a wooden stool next to the bed. It's so short that Andres's knees jut out as he places them on the stool's steps. He puts both hands on the seat between his legs and starts tapping against its surface with his fingers.

"Are you nervous?" Marabela asks.

"I'm sorry. I suppose I'm not helping the situation much." He stops tapping his fingers and locks his hands together, resting them on his lap.

"It's okay. I'd just like to get this over with and go home."

"I've always known you were strong, Mari, but this . . . that you can be so calm—" His voice catches. "I hope you know you can talk to me. Whenever you're ready."

What good would it do to tell him? Marabela thinks of how many times a day she prepared for death when their footsteps approached, of how the food, which she assumed was caked in the same dirt and filth that she was, made her gag as soon as it touched her throat. Her body would visibly shake anytime her captor came into the room, and he'd only laugh as he touched and taunted her, warning that tomorrow, his boss would be gone for the day. How could talking about these things possibly help?

"I know, Andres. Thank you. But for now let's just focus on what's in front of us. One thing at a time."

"Right, of course. The doctor should be here any minute."

They listen for the heavy footsteps, the click of the doorknob, and when it finally comes they both sit up straight in anticipation. The doctor looks down at the blank chart before him and smiles. "A new patient," he says, but when he looks up the enthusiasm fades, and Marabela smiles feebly, out of the habit of being courteous.

Andres stands up to shake hands with the doctor, and the two begin talking about her case in voices so deep it's hard to understand them. She is used to the men in her life doing this by now; instead of whispering, they take the bass in their voices so low, it's like listening to a radio with the speakers blown out. She catches few words. *Secuestro. Three weeks. Be sure . . . that's she's okay.*

The doctor nods and scribbles notes on her chart. He examines her methodically, looking at her body, but not at her; at her eyes, but not into them; at her bruises, but not at the pain.

There is no indication of anything in her X-rays, he tells her. "The damage seems to be mostly superficial. Are you in any pain at all? Any injuries you're concerned about?"

Instinctively, she crosses her arms and rubs her shoulder, careful not to push down too hard. "No, Doctor, nothing major."

Andres exhales and put his hands on his hips upon hearing this, but Marabela only nods. "So then we can go?" he asks.

"I'd like to speak with my patient alone, if you don't mind." For the first time the doctor directs his words at Marabela. She nods at Andres, who looks hurt, or offended, or something that Marabela isn't interested in deciphering. When he leaves the room, the doctor stays quiet. She already knows what's coming.

He scoots his chair toward her and puts the chart behind him.

"I want you to know that I've seen countless patients who, like you, were kidnapped. I understand that each experience is different, but the women, unfortunately, almost always share one thing in common. Please know that you don't have to hide anything from me." He takes a breath, gives her time to anticipate the question. "Were you violated sexually?"

She likes that he doesn't sugarcoat it. There's no euphemism, no hand placed gently on her knees.

"No, Doctor. At least there was that." The words leave a metallic taste in her mouth, a displaced sense of relief. Of all the days that never came, she is grateful only for that one.

9

───

HER FIRST FEW days back, Marabela sleeps well into the early afternoon. When she finally wakes in time for breakfast on Saturday, she is surprised by how much she misses the bustle in the kitchen. With Consuelo and Carla around, life moved at a faster pace, in tandem with her needs. Now Andres struggles to take over their duties, and Marabela simply waits.

"Let me help you," she offers when she hears a pot clank against the kitchen sink, a small hiss escaping Andres's lips as he shakes his hand in pain.

"I'm fine! Just relax," he shouts.

Marabela smiles and opens her eyes wide at Cynthia. "*Imagínalo.* Your father playing house."

"It doesn't look as fun when he does it," Cynthia says.

"He's just not used to it, that's all. We have to give him time. Right, Ignacio?" She turns to her son, who sits scowling, low in his chair.

"It's not funny. At least he's trying."

"And what is that supposed to mean?"

"Nothing. I'm going to help him." He swings his arms with purpose as he walks away, and Marabela suppresses a laugh. Her son has grown so fast these past weeks that she's the only one who seems to notice his lack of coordination. Perhaps his mind hasn't caught up with his body yet. It's endearing, actually. It reminds her of a younger Andres from their college years. He was never clumsy, just the opposite. His movements were full of intention, always so self-aware. She'd never had a man try so hard for her affection.

The rumbling sounds of plates being pushed and the dull clanks of wooden spoons burst out from the kitchen. Marabela can smell fried pork being reheated in the microwave.

Cynthia reaches for a bread knife in the center of the table, but Marabela pushes it away just as her fingers tap the handle.

"Let me do that for you. You could hurt yourself."

Cynthia sits up taller, chin raised high, looking offended. "I know how to handle a knife, Mom. Guillermo says I'm more coordinated than his niece. And she's twelve."

Marabela looks over her shoulder, wondering where Guillermo is hiding. Until now, she'd almost forgotten about him, and she's surprised to be reminded of him by her daughter. "Wow. That *is* impressive. What else does he say?"

"He says I pick the best spots to hide."

"You play hide-and-seek?"

"Mm-hmm."

"What else does he say?"

"He says that being scared is normal."

"It is."

"But being strong when you're scared is brave."

"That's also true. That's very true."

For a moment the house is quiet and then Andres and Ignacio come through the door, their arms full with trays of plates and hot dishes.

It's been so long since she's been excited about a meal. Marabela had gotten used to fearing everything they bought her, not because it was bad food—usually leftovers of whatever they'd just eaten, like *pollo a la brasa*, *chifa*, and insipid oatmeal in the mornings—but because anything they touched was tainted with threats. She has to remind herself that this meal with her family is nourishment that will help all of them heal.

"Thank you, dear," she says as she helps him set a tray of pork and a bowl of sliced red onions, drenched in oil, vinegar, salt, and *aji* so they're nice and soggy, in the center of the table.

She keeps her eyes on the plate, but she can feel the heavy pauses from both sides of her as Andres and Ignacio marvel at her use of the word *dear*. She knows it's not like her, but on a whim she decided to try it.

Marabela tries to recall the last time they had breakfast together, alone as four, and she's shocked to realize she can't pinpoint a time before several months ago. Now, they talk about silly things like the weather, make jokes at how pretty the men would look in aprons and mittens, fill Marabela in on the latest gossip about celebrity marriages and breakups in the news. When she asks what everyone has planned for the day, Ignacio and Andres look at her with blank expressions, as if they're just now realizing they have permission to do something besides attend to her. But Cynthia doesn't disappoint.

"I want to rearrange my room."

"Yeah?" Marabela says. "*¿Cómo?*"

"I was thinking if I move my bed against the wall and push the dresser into the corner, I'd have more room."

"Room for what?" Ignacio asks. He seems genuinely interested, but Cynthia's not used to him taking her seriously.

"Stuff. I don't see why I have to tell you."

"I think it sounds like a good idea. I can help move the furniture if you want," Marabela says. A few times since she's come home, she's caught Cynthia dancing in the hallways with her headphones on when she thought no one was looking. Judging by the way she kicks her legs in the air and jumps off the ground with her arms held in a V shape, ending with one knee on the ground and a very dramatic tossing back of the hair, it makes sense that Cynthia would want more space and a little privacy.

"I'll help, too," Andres adds. "Maybe it'll give me some ideas for ways to freshen up our own room."

"You'll have enough room in there to train the Selección Peruana," Ignacio says.

Marabela takes a bite out of her fried sweet potato to suppress a giggle. She doesn't like encouraging the kids to pick on each other, but the thought of Cynthia coaching the national soccer team in her bedroom is irresistible.

Apparently Andres agrees. "It's not a bad idea, so long as you don't mind the smell of dirty socks."

Cynthia shakes her head and scrunches her nose. "Eww! Gross!"

"You can certainly teach them a move or two," Marabela says.

Cynthia's eyes light up; suddenly, she's in on the joke. "And anytime they lose, I'll make them clean my room!"

By the time they're done with breakfast, Marabela's throat is hoarse from all the laughing—Ignacio and Andres seem to have an endless supply of jokes, and they take turns with their fake stories, each one taking longer than the last.

The family lingers at the table. "Thank you for breakfast," Marabela says. "It's nice to be together like this. By the way, Andres, I've been meaning to ask—how long did you tell the company you'd be gone?"

Andres's smile quickly fades. Ignacio starts picking up the dishes, as if her words were a signal to clear the table.

"It's not important," he says.

"What do you mean?"

He runs his hand through his hair. He's not looking at her when he answers. "I'm not going back. I sold the company."

"Well . . . wow. I never thought . . . What will we do now?"

"It's a fresh start, *mi amor*. We'll work it out."

Left alone at the table, Marabela turns to Cynthia, but the child has snuck away amid all the cleanup and commotion. She calls out to her. "I didn't say we were playing yet," she teases.

Cynthia crawls out of a cabinet in the living room, the same place they'd normally keep things like old photo albums and tablecloths. Marabela takes a mental measurement of the space and decides she would not fit there. There are only a few windows in the house she's decided she could squeeze through if she were suddenly trapped and had to escape. It's not something she calculates intentionally, just a habit she's picked up. Everywhere she goes, she finds she needs an exit strategy.

✤ ✤ ✤

By the beginning of the second week, the novelty of having Andres at home starts to wear off, replaced by an odd sense of intrusion. He fusses over Marabela like a paranoid mother: Is she cold? Hungry? Tired? Andres is always ready to bring her a blanket or a snack, but his attention only reminds her of how much help she needs.

When Andres mentions that he'll have to start looking for work soon, Marabela is both relieved and apprehensive. Lately she's been caught between craving her own space and not wanting to be left alone, and she doesn't know which yearning will win out in the end.

She hasn't asked about the sale since the morning he mentioned it because what else is left for her to know? The company is gone and that's that. Marabela always thought Andres should have sold the company long ago, when his family life depended on the sale in less literal but equally urgent ways. Now she's too tired to resurrect the argument.

During the day when the children are at school, Marabela spends most of her time in the garden. The walls in the house suffocate her, but she doesn't dare step beyond them into the streets. Instead she sends Guillermo to the market to buy flower seeds—any he can find, as long as they are colorful and plentiful. By ten o'clock in the morning she's on her knees with her fingers in the cold, dark soil, planting the seeds in little holes she digs with her own hands, covering them gently and humming as she goes on to the next. Guillermo sits on the patio, drinking *chicha* quietly but for the deep *ching ching* of his ice cubes. When he leaves to pick up the kids from school, Marabela eats her lunch on the patio. She nibbles on light pieces of ceviche and kernels of *choclo* until the kids come home.

Little by little the sun puts life back into her. Most of her bruises have faded, and when she strips to shower at the end of the day she can see the traces of scars along her shoulders and legs are growing fainter. She tries to eat more and more each day, and has begun setting small goals for herself to measure her recovery. Four steps up the stairs without using the railing is progress; five is cause for a private smile. She's not sure if the exercise is helping, but she's tired of staying still. When Andres suggests she rest while he makes dinner, she paces back and forth along the hallway upstairs, passing her bedroom, his office, the children's rooms, and, finally, her darkroom. She longs to go inside but the thought of such tight quarters keeps her moving past it.

❖ ❖ ❖

It's strange, but Marabela resents Guillermo's unobtrusiveness, how he's constantly there but tries to hide his presence. When she walks into a room, he pretends to ignore her, avoids looking directly at her, even though they know it is his sole purpose to look after her. As soon as she turns away, she feels his gaze shift in her direction.

This morning she is not in the mood for it. Marabela turns around swiftly and bellows out, "Good morning!" more loudly than she expected to. Only she is caught off guard by her voice; Guillermo simply smiles and nods hello back, his lips tight.

"Do you need any help?" he asks, taking a few steps toward her.

She estimates that he is a foot taller than she is, but the crick in her neck the closer he gets tells her otherwise. Marabela shakes her head no as she rummages through the drawers, slamming them shut each time her search proves fruitless. She knows she could easily tell him what she's looking for, but she's tired of feeling helpless. Knowing that Guillermo is watching and waiting, she exaggerates her motions, moving abruptly from one end of the kitchen to the next. In her periphery she watches him follow her with his eyes.

"There you are," she says. Consuelo's meat-cutting scissors are sharper than any knife atop the counter. They're tucked away, hidden from little hands.

Marabela pulls them out slowly. She snaps the scissors open and shut, runs her thumb across the blades to test their sharpness. When she's satisfied, she wraps her palms around the pointy end and makes her way upstairs.

"Señora?" Guillermo says as she reaches the staircase.

She hadn't realized he'd followed her down the hall.

"What?"

"Do you need any help?" It's the same question he asked earlier, but now his tone has changed. Guillermo points at the scissors.

Confused, she starts to wave him off. The realization hits her just as they lock eyes. "Oh! No. It's just for a skirt I'm taking in," she says. "All my clothes float on me lately."

"I know a great tailor," he says.

"You know all sorts of people, don't you?"

"Señora?"

"Nothing. I'm sorry. Never mind. I was just saying you seem to be very resourceful."

He smiles. "That's a nice way of putting it."

"It's meant to be a compliment. If you knew me, you'd know—"

"I understand. Thank you."

They stand in silence, face-to-face since Marabela is a couple of steps up. She wishes he'd turn around first but knows it's not in his nature. "Thank you for the offer, but I'd rather do the sewing myself. It's a welcome distraction."

"Of course. If you need anything at all . . ."

"I know," she says, surprised to find herself feeling grateful for his warmth. "I know."

❖ ❖ ❖

Cynthia has started referring to herself in the third person. "She wants an ice cream," she says when the man with a D'Onofrio cart passes in front of the house. Or "Can she have a Doña Pepa?" if she wants something sweet before dinner.

One day Guillermo brings her home from school as Marabela is wiping the soil stains from her knees. Cynthia drags him out to the garden by the arm and tugs on her mother's gardening apron, smiling a gap-filled smile. "Do you want to play a game she just learned?"

Despite the odd phrasing, Marabela realizes she's discovering a new part of her daughter, witnessing a new growth. It doesn't matter that Cynthia speaks as if she is talking about someone else; her usual shyness around adults other than her parents seems to have melted away.

Marabela falls back on the grass and takes Cynthia with her. "*A ver, ¿cómo va?*"

It's a simple game Guillermo taught her on the way home. Standing next to her, Cynthia leads Marabela across the yard, making sure that both are using the same legs. She sings a chant to keep a rhythm, but with Cynthia's small legs, it isn't long before they're both off track.

"Now you have to move back!" she shouts. "Four steps!" She giggles like a child. Like herself.

It takes them countless tries to get across the yard, and eventually Cynthia insists that Guillermo join them. He hesitates at first, but it's clear to Marabela that the man has trouble saying no to her daughter. Cynthia stands in the middle, holding both their hands with her arms up as if she were swinging from a tree. They take three steps before they have to move back again, and as they do, Guillermo and Marabela lift her into the air, her legs dangling like ribbons in the wind.

"Again, again!" she says.

When they're done, Marabela's entire body is sore. Her stomach aches from laughter and her arms feel cold and stiff from lifting Cynthia too many times to count. She rubs her worn thighs and smiles at the pain.

❖   ❖   ❖

There's an hour in the day, after dinner's done and the kitchen's been cleaned up and the kids are about to shower, when everyone retreats upstairs and all the lights on the first floor of the house are dimmed. That flip of the last switch is a moment Andres cherishes, a sigh of relief at another day's accomplishments. As he double-checks the locks in the house, he can hear the quiet footsteps of his family overhead, the tucking away of worries and tasks that can be attended to tomorrow. Briefly, he lets himself fade into the shadows of his home, feeling untethered and content.

No one notices when Andres uses these few minutes to make a phone call. He dials the facility by memory, counting the long, low buzzes on the other line. The staff never lets him talk to Elena—the patients don't have phones in their rooms and it is against the rules to disturb them for a simple phone call—but Betty gives him updates in quick whispers. *She's fine, she went for a walk today*, she told him last week. *She didn't have much of an appetite*—a few days ago. Tonight Betty tells him that Elena didn't wake till late in the afternoon, but that she received the flowers he sent and went promptly back to bed.

"I'll be by to visit soon. It's just been hard to get away lately. I wouldn't feel right leaving." He doesn't know why he tells Betty this, as if she'll relay the message. When they hang up, he calls his mother and asks her to check on Elena for him. She agrees to go first thing the next morning.

Andres climbs the stairs and is quietly making his way to the bedroom when a thin shadow in his office catches his eye. The door is slightly ajar, so he leans into the threshold to peek through and finds Marabela, haunting the room like a ghost. Her gaze floats over the hardwood surface, empty and weightless. It strikes him that she has become so utterly unnoticeable. There was a time when she could walk into a room and the chatter went down a decibel, as if everyone had stopped to hold their breath. Now no one would notice her; they wouldn't even notice the absence of her.

He's hardly been in his office since Marabela's return. Last week Guillermo took all the contents of the darkroom and emptied them back into these quarters, and Andres hasn't felt up to the task of sifting through them. A stack of cue cards sits next to his phone. The list of questions—some of them crossed off because he changed his mind about asking them, others checked off because he did ask—are faceup on his desk. The tapes, the recorder, and all the cables they had to run are tangled in a small mountain at the very center. Marabela stands behind his desk, arms crossed over her chest, and reads the papers, pausing only to flip each sheet with two stiff fingers, as if the paper is toxic and she's afraid it might rub off.

Andres can't decide if he should interrupt her or let her have this moment. If she's ever wondered what he went through while she was gone, what kinds of decisions he was faced with, this is her chance to understand. He knows it's selfish of him. He knows he could never compare his experience with her own, but this was all he had.

Her hands meander over to the tapes, the ones Ignacio carefully labeled with the date, time, and a circled number designating their order. When her fingers glide over the play button, Andres steps through the threshold.

"Please don't. You don't want to hear it, Mari. Maybe it's better to just put it behind you."

She startles a little; he sees it in the way her neck looks like a tree for a moment, tendons stiff as roots, and then relaxes as she pulls her sweater close.

"It's just a morbid curiosity. I could always tell when he was talking to you. I could never understand the words, of course. But no one else spoke like he did," she says, with a hint of admiration. "It made me wonder—how does one negotiate a life for money? You wouldn't think there'd be much negotiating at all. Just a man who hands over whatever is necessary."

"I wish it had been that easy." He takes a step closer to her and places his hand on her shoulder. She doesn't welcome it but doesn't push away. The indifference hurts the most.

"I guess it seems simple. Someone puts a price on something and you want it, so you pay. It's not the kind of thing I imagined you'd overthink," she says.

He tries to remember how Guillermo explained it to him, in those days that seem like months ago. "But there had to be a strategy. For the long term. So they wouldn't keep coming back, like we're some ATM machine that can be easily replenished."

"They said you were better at protecting your money than your wife."

"And you believed that?"

"I know what they were trying to do, but there are very few things to hold on to in a place like that. Enough time passes and you start believing the lies."

"Mari, I swear. I did the best I could. They thought we were millionaires. I don't know where they got their numbers. Even if I'd wanted to, I simply didn't have it."

She points to the stack of cue cards, at the top one facing up. "You did everything you had to do, flawlessly. It's a good thing you had plenty of time to rehearse your lines."

He tries to argue, but she's already gone, vanished from the room noiselessly. The air feels thinner, the space emptier. Everywhere she goes, she seems to take something with her. She is a void that can never be filled.

10

ORE THAN ANYTHING, she enjoys sitting outside on the backyard patio. The space is larger than the entire first floor, and although it's enclosed by three thick cement walls, Marabela no longer feels trapped when she looks up at the sky. In the two weeks since she's been back, the weather has started to turn cold, but she doesn't mind the chill against her skin. She is fresh out of the shower, moist and dewy from a lilac-scented lotion she found underneath her sink, and when the wind touches her body she feels the breeze wrapping itself around her rather than passing her by. When she closes her eyes she feels light again.

Her friends have been calling, every few days as Andres explained they did in her absence. She's let him assure them she's home and safe and resting, but she hasn't felt ready to speak to them yet. Initially she didn't want them to see her in the state she was in, but as the days have passed, Marabela feels the need to protect this moment in her life. It's an odd kind of blessing, to be able to dedicate time to yourself so completely. It's also fragile; amid moments of simplicity, she still gets flashes of terror.

And yet this morning, when Andres suggested she invite friends over as a way to settle back into her life, Marabela surprised herself by agreeing. She requested that Consuelo and Carla visit, causing Andres to give her a brief, questioning look before he made the call. She had to resist the urge to tell him that these women had always been there for the most normal parts of her day. Their absence has been like a bruise that refuses to heal. Marabela has yet to discuss how much Andres paid for her ransom, or what sacrifices he had to make, but from the looks of the house—the way the dust has accumulated on the light switches, the stickiness of the handles on the kitchen cabinets—it's clear that her confidantes were the first to go. Marabela knows she shouldn't resent Andres for their absence, but she simply can't help it. He never could understand the level of trust she had with Consuelo and Carla; to him, they were expendable.

"I sent Guillermo to pick them up," he tells her, clearly uncomfortable as he sits down across from her. He crosses his leg in a wide ninety-degree angle, then closes them as if to command less space. He rests both arms on the chair, then only one as he leans his chin on his fist.

It seems wasteful to her, to have a bodyguard doing a driver's job when his salary alone could probably cover the costs of two maids, even ones who, at Marabela's insistence, were paid more generously than most.

"Are you thirsty?" she asks. It is really her way of telling him that she is.

He brings out glasses of store-bought lemonade that is far too sweet, but Marabela doesn't complain. She relishes drinking something other than the lukewarm water she survived on in captivity, now preferring Coke and teas drowned in honey. She laughs at Andres's face, the way his mouth puckers with each sip.

They hear the garage open, the door creak, and a cacophony of footsteps and plastic bags being brought into the kitchen. Someone gasps behind her, and from that one small sound she recognizes Consuelo. She stands to hug her, and Carla joins them, embracing Marabela's back.

"*Gracias a Dios*," Consuelo says, over and over again. "I prayed for you every day and every night. I just knew He'd watch over you and return you home safely!"

Carla holds Marabela's hand and mumbles that she missed her. Without realizing it, by standing so close to one another and speaking in hushed voices, they've shut Andres out of the conversation. When they finally sit down, he offers Consuelo his chair, even though there is an empty one right next to him. Nobody protests when he excuses himself.

Marabela is in awe of how Consuelo and Carla look. They are fresh faced and radiant, the only people she's been reunited with who are consumed by happiness at her return. Her family always seems so hesitant, no doubt wondering exactly what she's been through.

"I'm so happy you're both here. Home doesn't feel the same without you."

"It will in time," Consuelo says. "I made you some chicken and rice the way you like it, a little mushy." She holds up a clear container tainted green from the cilantro the rice was cooked in.

"You didn't have to do that. Thank you." She turns to Carla. "You look happy."

"Because you're back, señora."

Marabela has tried for months to get Carla to call her by her first name. *Señora* makes her feel old; it puts her on a pedestal she has done nothing to earn. Consuelo at least calls her *Doña*, but over the years the word became an endearment, a nickname only she can use.

"How are the children?" Consuelo asks.

"They're fine. They're a little afraid, I think. I don't know if it's because they worry they'll lose me again, or that we're no longer safe."

"Cynthia never understood the situation. We never told her exactly what happened," Consuelo says. "I think Ignacio just wished he could have done something to bring you home sooner."

"I don't think that frustration has left him. If anything, it's probably intensified," Marabela says.

"Youth doesn't always make one ignorant. Some simply struggle with the knowledge of the pieces they're missing."

"How much does he know?"

"I don't know details, of course. But it seemed to me that Señor Jimenez tried to keep him out of it. He and Guillermo were always locked up in your room upstairs, but I think your son snuck in there a few times. The last couple of days they were in there together."

"Was he home a lot? My husband?"

Carla glances at Consuelo.

"He didn't go to the office much," says Carla, looking at her hands. "His mother brought him papers and things—"

"Yes, I heard Lorena was here," Marabela says. She would be surprised that Andres still hasn't mentioned it, except he's barely mentioned anything to her about what happened while she was away. Intent as he is on planning for their new future, he doesn't seem to realize that Marabela needs to catch up on all the things she's missed.

"Moments like these make old feuds seem irrelevant, don't they, Doña?"

"Of course," she says, only she doesn't really believe it. She thinks of the moments she experienced—nothing like the ones everyone else did. Her moments constantly promised to be her last. Time was cruel to her; it stretched for weeks that felt like months, but still nothing changed. During her first days in captivity, when it still felt so unreal, neither the darkness nor the voices upstairs could destroy her hopes and prayers. But the human soul adapts all too quickly, no matter how unexpected the circumstances. The days repeated like a tape stuck on replay, until there was nothing left to look forward to. Eventually the only thing she could be sure of was that she would die, on a day just like the previous one, in a dark room with her arm tied to a bike rack that'd been wedged into the cement floor. The only uncertainty, and thus the real torture, was the question of when.

She reaches across the table to hold Consuelo's hand. Their callused fingers rub against one another like an old toothbrush scraping the bottom of a pot.

"Who else has come to visit?" Consuelo asks.

"No one. You're the first."

Both Consuelo and Carla look surprised, even a little flattered. "You are very loved, señora. So many people called asking for you." She tells Marabela how friends and acquaintances called, how Andres had told them she'd gone to the United States for a family emergency.

"Yes, he told me about that. It seems a little absurd, though. I doubt anyone believed him. I don't have a single relative over there."

"He said it was a distant second cousin, maybe third or fourth. Some uncle's cousin's sister-in-law who you'd never met before."

"Who would believe that?"

Consuelo shrugs. "He told them what they needed to know. Señora Paula and Señora Mari called a lot at first, and Señor Tomas and Señor Juan, too. After a while they only called every few days."

Marabela shakes her head. "It's just all so ridiculous. All these lies."

She and Consuelo are still holding hands, and she feels the woman's grip tighten, gently, for a small moment. "He was desperate, señora. I don't think I've ever seen him look as lost as he did while you were gone. He questioned every decision he made—Lord knows how many times—and even after he made it, he seemed full of doubt."

As usual, Consuelo humbles her. Marabela wishes she could have a fraction of the woman's sense of compassion. She lets out a long breath and tries to relax her defenses. "I didn't mean to be insensitive. I'm sorry."

Andres returns to the patio to offer everyone a drink, and at this the women blush, eyes on the floor and backs held firmly against their chairs as they shake their heads no. Carla tucks her hair behind her ear as she thanks him anyway, and the sun catches on a small diamond hanging just above her jawline from a delicate gold chain. The earrings are simple but elegant, giving Carla's plain appearance an added flair.

"You look beautiful in those earrings, Carla. They suit you," says Marabela.

Andres glances at the girl and suddenly he's very focused. His lips part and he squints at her; Marabela can see a rush of realization coming over his face. "Where did you get those earrings?"

Carla doesn't answer. Maybe she doesn't realize he's talking to her.

"Carla. He's asking you a question," Consuelo says.

"Those earrings were my grandmother's," Andres blurts out.

"Andres!" Marabela doesn't like his accusing tone, but he holds up his hands to stop her.

"If you would've taken them from our home, that's one thing. I wouldn't care at this point. Take anything you want as long as my family's safe. But—" He coughs, a weak attempt at covering up the quiver in his voice. "I gave those earrings to someone. I put them in a bag, along with our entire life's savings, in exchange for my wife. I gave them to a man who saw an opportunity to take advantage of another man who couldn't think clearly. And only a few people even knew Marabela had been taken when I delivered my first ransom. So those aren't just any earrings. Tell me where you got them, before I assume the worst."

Carla is so stunned, her lips tremble as she tries to form words, but none comes. She fidgets with the earrings, caresses them softly between two fingers. She stares at the floor, her eyes darting from side to side, as if she's arguing with herself and sorting through a pile of thoughts to find one she can agree with.

"It's impossible. He wouldn't—"

Consuelo jumps out of her chair and kneels next to her niece, holding her hands. "Just tell us, Carla. Tell the truth."

"Javi. He gave them to me a couple of weeks ago. He said he'd been saving up for them," she says. With every word, the conviction leaks from her voice.

Andres curses her. He leans half his body through the glass door and calls upstairs for Guillermo. Marabela covers her mouth in disbelief but quickly catches herself and puts her arms around Carla and Consuelo, who are holding each other's hands. While they wait, Andres paces the patio.

"And you'd told him, hadn't you? About Marabela's kidnapping? You didn't waste much time opening your mouth."

"Andres. *Cálmate*," Marabela says.

"I said tell no one! Did you think it was a joke? Some gossip to bring home at the end of the day?"

"I'm sorry! I was upset and worried and he asked me what was wrong . . ."

"And then he used you. He used you to destroy us. Marabela could have been killed!"

"That's enough, Andres." Hearing him say the words out loud only cements the fears Marabela's been trying to shed, and she feels them sinking deeper into her the more he seems to lose control.

"*¿Que paso?*" Guillermo runs out to them with a confused look on his face. Marabela rolls her eyes. If they were being attacked, they'd all be dead in the time it took him to make his way downstairs.

"Carla's boyfriend is the impostor who took the first ransom," Andres says, with so much indignation in his voice Marabela worries it will rot his teeth.

Guillermo raises his eyebrows and shakes his head at her. "Carla. Who is this boy you've been keeping company with?"

Her whole face is running with tears. "He's not a bad person. I can't even believe he would do this."

"He never told you what he was up to?"

"No! I wouldn't keep that from you. I would never put señora in danger."

"So you'll help us now?" Guillermo's language is gentle in a way that Andres's could never be.

"What do you mean? Help how?"

"Just information. We need to know more about him. Is he dangerous?"

"No."

"Are you saying that because it's true or because you hope it is?"

"He's never done anything like this. He doesn't steal. He doesn't hurt people."

"How long have you known him?"

"Five months."

"Does he own any weapons?"

"Not that I know of."

"What about his friends? What are they like?"

"I don't know. I don't see them very much. I've only met two of them and they're just quiet. They try to act tough, you know? I never bought into it."

Andres cuts in, right to the point. "But you know where he lives, right?"

Carla closes her eyes, takes a deep breath, and nods.

"Good. Then you'll take us there. Today."

❖ ❖ ❖

It takes some convincing. Though Carla agrees to give them directions, Guillermo doesn't think it's worth the risk to go. Too dangerous, he says. Too many unknowns.

Andres is in no mood to heed his warnings anymore. "What do you think I hired you for? You're supposed to help protect this family."

"That's exactly what I'm doing. You won't know what you're walking into."

For once, Marabela's on Guillermo's side. She doesn't want Andres taking Carla back to her boyfriend's neighborhood to start trouble, so she stands in front of the girl, her arms held out protectively. "It's crazy, Andres. Just let it go."

But he can't, and neither can Carla. She's so consumed by guilt, she steps out of Marabela's shadow and stands next to Andres. It's clear they'll go with or without Guillermo, a fact that leaves him no choice. The three of them make their way to the garage as Marabela and Consuelo beg them not to. Marabela puts her hands on the half-open driver's-side window, tries slapping her palm against the hood of the car as they pull away. From inside the car, the sound is but a weak thud, completely unthreatening.

In the backseat, Carla tries to stifle her crying. They drive twenty-five minutes in complete silence, except for Guillermo occasionally asking Carla for directions from the passenger seat; a right turn here, a left turn there, a good ten minutes on the highway until they get off in a completely different side of town, where the streets are full of potholes and the houses are cement colored with tiny, trash-strewn yards. Andres speeds up the car so that they won't have to stop at any red lights.

"I don't know what you think we'll get out of this," Guillermo says in a deep monotone.

"We're just talking to him, getting information," Andres says.

Guillermo raises his eyebrows but says nothing.

"Take a right," Carla says. "It's here." She sounds disappointed to see her boyfriend's house, as if the whole ride over she'd hoped that it'd be gone when they arrived. Andres doesn't pull into the driveway but parks along the curb. The door slams into the sidewalk as he opens it, and for a moment it's caught there—metal scraping against the grain, a dull clamor. He catches up to Guillermo, who's walking across the yard with his arm flung over Carla's shoulders, as if he's an old friend and wants her to tell him a secret.

"*Tu amiguito.* What's his name again?"

"Javier," she says.

"You're not scared of him, are you?" She shakes her head. "You're scared of losing him." She nods.

Guillermo stops in the middle of the yard and bends down so he's at eye level with her. "A boy who starts with the filthy business of robbing honest people and other thieves in one go . . . he's already on his way to a place you don't want to follow."

She won't look at him, her fingers and eyes occupied with a loose thread along the hem of her blouse. Andres feels the tendons in his neck tense; he looks away.

Guillermo clears his throat and they both turn back to him. "Or do you? You're better than that, *chiquitita*."

Carla adjusts her blouse and straightens her back. Andres gets the unsettling feeling that this is no longer about him or his money, and since he's only here to reclaim what's his, he begins to feel cheap.

Carla knocks on the door, louder than they were expecting. They all jump back at the sound. The boy who opens the door smiles at her for an instant, until he realizes she's brought company.

"What's this?" he says.

In their rush, Andres didn't realize that Carla has taken the earrings off. She holds them in her hand, rubbing the tiny diamonds with her thumb as if for comfort. When she opens her palm to show him, her fingers stretch out slowly. They shake along with her voice.

"Did you think I wouldn't find out?"

The boy's face is expressionless. He shrugs and looks at all three of them. "I don't know what you're talking about," he says, the lie slipping like water from his lips.

"Just give everything back. They won't call the cops or get you in trouble. They just want everything back." Each word Carla says sounds more like a plea than the last. "You don't—don't you realize they could have killed her? You could've had her blood on your hands, and you used me to get it."

"What do you care? They just had it lying around. It's easy for them. Don't you see? It's right under your nose every day."

Guillermo takes a step toward the door, and the boy backs up. "Javier, right? Look, we can make this very simple right now. Just give back the money and the jewelry and we'll go."

Javier seems to consider this. He still has one hand on the doorknob and the other pressed against the threshold, his body guarding the entrance to his home. Andres watches as Javier braces himself and then launches his body out of there, as if he were a rubber band stretching and releasing. He bolts to the side of the yard, trying to put as much distance as he can between himself and Guillermo, but the man is like a goalie, anticipating this very move. Guillermo catches him and flips him over so Javier's back is pressed against his chest.

"You had to make this difficult, didn't you?"

He squirms and his voice rises. "I don't have it! I swear. It's all gone."

But Andres can't, won't, believe him. This can't be where everything ends, where his hopes get washed away by some *cojudo*. He runs into the house with Guillermo's voice chasing after him, telling him to stop and slow down, be careful. Carla is shouting and crying, worried about her boyfriend's arm getting pulled from its socket and about Andres going into the house alone. She calls his name and Javier's in the same breath. He yells back, "*Cállate!*"

The house is dark inside—little more than one room with a couch covered in blankets and an old television balancing on a cinder block on the opposite wall. Clothes, cassette tapes, and old paper plates cover the floor, and several half-empty cardboard boxes are stacked together in the corner, sinking into themselves under the weight of pots, pans, and cans of food.

"He lives like an animal," Andres mumbles to himself. First he checks the couch, lifting it from the side, then flipping over the cushions, but finds nothing. He slaps his hands together, trying to shake off the dust. As he rummages through the room—kicking aside the boxes, gathering old newspapers off the table—he gets that sticky feeling he usually gets at gas stations. Behind him, Guillermo enters the room with Javier in tow.

"*Puta madre*. What the hell's wrong with you? You can't just throw my shit around. Be careful with that!"

The boy has some nerve, but Andres ignores his request. "What did you do with it? Did you buy some *coca* with the money for my wife's life? Throw a party for your piece-of-shit friends? Did you sell the rest of the jewelry for more money? Or did you give it all to Carla? Doesn't seem like such a smart idea now, does it, giving the earrings to a girl who works for the family you robbed?"

"*Tranquilo*, Andres. He's not clever enough to hide it anyplace good. Check the kitchen," Guillermo says. He studies the boy, whose eyes dart to the other end of the house, which holds a refrigerator no taller than a small child. "The refrigerator. Check the freezer." Javier looks down at his shoes. "It's probably in an old ice-cream box. Something stupid like that."

Guillermo laughs and Andres plays along, though he's never seen this side of him before. It's a part they're playing, he realizes, extreme versions of themselves that feel more like caricatures. Intimidation works best when there's no humanity left for the victim to appeal to.

Andres walks to the refrigerator slowly, taking his time to torment the boy with each step. "I bet you thought that much money would take up more space, didn't you?" The little door resists him, then opens with a swoosh of cold air that floats in front of his face, thick and white. In the center of the freezer sits a yellow cylindrical plastic container, the same kind that Consuelo uses to put away leftover soup after dinner. He shakes it, but it has an unfamiliar heaviness to it, and when he pops open the lid he sees the green stacks of money, curled into each other like guinea pigs trying to keep warm. He picks them out of the container and there, at the very bottom, finds the two blue sapphire earrings. His grandfather's watch is gone, as is Marabela's diamond bracelet, but otherwise several chains, pendants, and rings are tangled into one giant piece. Somehow he manages to pick the earrings apart from the rest of them. They feel like tiny chunks of ice between his fingers.

"Is it all there?" Carla asks. She's been so quiet Andres had forgotten she was with them.

"It's enough," he answers, clutching the earrings in the palm of his hand, unsure where to put them. All the pockets on his person are too loose, and though he hates putting them back in the container, it's the only place he knows where they won't fall out. He covers them with the stacks of money, which he doesn't feel the need to count. Most of it is still there. The boy didn't even have enough imagination to know what to do with such a large amount. He kept it hidden somewhere so he could take from it in small pieces. In this way, Andres figures, he is no better than Marabela's captors.

He studies the boy's face. Javier has dark black eyes and innocent, reddened cheeks, but it is still the only face Andres can give to his anger, to his torment, to Marabela's misery. He rushes out of the kitchen, taking four long steps toward the boy, bringing his fist through the air too quickly to give him any warning.

He can still feel the sting against his knuckles after they're back on his side of town, the crushing of skin and bone against each other, the warm splash of blood. It is all he can think about when they pull up to his house, and he has to force himself to let it go, like a suitcase molded to his grip, before he lets himself inside.

❖ ❖ ❖

Back at the house he finds Marabela sleeping on the couch, her head resting on Consuelo's lap while the woman runs her fingers through her dark, thick tendrils. Marabela's breath is steady but emphatic, like a quiet snore. Andres doesn't want to wake her because in the days that she's been home, she's looked so vulnerable as she sleeps, something Andres is still not entirely used to. In the twenty years he's known her, he's seen Marabela look defensive and distant, but never vulnerable. He doesn't know why he needs to see her like this, but he stands over her and tries to ignore the look on Consuelo's face that asks, *Can I help you?* as if he is intruding on a private moment. And maybe he is. Maybe she will never be this way for him because this kind of frailty requires trust.

Since she's been home, Andres has hoped that Marabela would invite him back into bed, but she makes sure to place his pillow on the foldout while he brushes his teeth at night. To give herself to him so fully, to let him lie next to her while she surrenders her senses — that would be the ultimate intimacy.

Consuelo just looks at him, not even trying to shush him with a finger pressed against her lips. She is no longer his maid, but he suspects their old roles still apply. If that's the case, why does he feel so powerless? He waits for her to speak first, and when she doesn't he grows impatient and whispers, "How long has she been asleep?"

She raises three fingers and makes a circle with her thumb and forefinger: thirty minutes. Andres lets out an exasperated breath and Marabela stirs awake.

"What happened? Where's Carla?"

"She's fine. She got rid of a good-for-nothing boyfriend today," Andres says.

"So he did do it?" There's disappointment in her voice, as if she'd been hoping none of this was true.

Carla steps in front of Andres and sits on the floor next to her. "I'm so sorry, señora. I had no idea. To think I put you in danger after everything you've done for us . . . I'll never forgive myself."

"You'll never have to because none of this is your fault," Marabela says.

He wonders: if it's not Carla's fault, then whose is it? Andres steps back, feeling like he's fading into the background, while Carla recounts the events of the day with his wife. The excitement in her voice angers him. This was his victory, his story to tell. He tries to read Marabela's face when Carla gets to the part about them recovering most of the ransom, but she looks neither surprised nor relieved. The way she's listening to Carla, looking in her direction but not at her, reminds him of when Marabela watches television just to pass the time.

Outside, the garage door rumbles open and Guillermo calls to the ladies from the kitchen. "It's getting late. I should take you home."

"Yes. Good night," Andres says, almost too quickly.

When they're gone, he sits next to Marabela on the couch. She tucks her feet away from him and asks him to turn on the lamp at his side. The sun has started to set, and though the house is not dark yet, it will soon sneak up on them gradually.

"I thought you would be happier that I got the money and the jewelry back," he says.

"I'm not unhappy. I'm just . . . disappointed that you and Carla had to go through that."

"It's my own damn fault. I should've known better. It was too quick, too easy. I was stupid to fall for it." Andres shakes his head, rubbing his thighs with his palms to wipe off their sweat.

She puts her hand on top of his and he holds still. "You only believed him because you wanted it to be true. You can't blame yourself."

Hearing Marabela say this, after wanting it so long, brings surprisingly little relief. Just because she says the words doesn't make them true; he knows that.

"I'll make things right, Mari. I know things weren't right with us before. We can move forward. Start over. I believe that."

She considers this. Her eyes shift to the yellow container on the table in front of them. "Would you be saying this if you hadn't recovered the money?"

He hadn't thought of it like that. He'd only thought about getting the ransom back, not so much for the money but because he'd needed to reclaim something, take back at least a part of what was taken from him. Now he's not so sure it was enough. He feels unsettled and un-satisfied. The money will let them keep the kids in their schools, maybe get them out of having to sell the house, but alone it won't be enough to save them. It'll only buy them time, and what will they do when their time has run out?

"Show me. Show me the life you want instead, and I'll do what I can to give it to you," he says.

She only nods and covers her face with her hand, letting her fin-gers stretch from her cheeks to her forehead and, finally, over her hair. Because she hasn't said no, Andres takes this as a yes. They will start over. There is life after the kidnapping, and they will go search-ing for it together.

11

———

MARABELA IS TRYING. Not in a way that anyone would notice, like holding Andres's hand at the dinner table (she never did that, even when they were happy) or starting a conversation with him spontaneously. But in her own way she is making an effort to cover up the flaws in their relationship. Yesterday Andres made lunch, and instead of complaining that he overseasoned the meat, Marabela asked for another scoop of rice, which was bland and could use a little spice. She didn't tell him to stop looking at her when he'd finished his meal and had nothing better to do as she caught up. At night, while he washes up before bed, Marabela fluffs his pillow. She's not ready to let him into bed with her (some nights she wishes he would sleep in another room altogether), but making sure he's comfortable seems like the kind of thing good wives do. She thinks she at least deserves credit for trying to play the part.

She's not entirely convinced that a new start will solve things, but she's willing to entertain the idea. It feels like an attempt to erase the past and she's not sure how far back would be enough. Should they pretend she was never kidnapped? That she never tried to leave Andres? That ordeal was only a few months ago, but her reasons spanned further than that. When did she start doubting that she loved him? Somewhere along the way she realized that they were supposed to make a life together, and his had soared while Marabela felt she'd been left to wilt in the darkroom. She hated her own resentment of his success. He'd once been such a gentleman, so concerned with her happiness and well-being that he'd do almost anything to please her. Now, though the effort is still there, his ability to listen is gone. For their anniversary when he got her the darkroom, he was excited about Marabela staying home, yet not nearly as concerned with how she felt about her profession turning into a hobby. Still, she'd thought it cavalier that he'd turned her inability to find a job into an opportunity to indulge her passion for photography. He was always going out of his way for her . . . how could she have known he'd take it too far?

It got to be too much. She just needed to get away from him, decide what came next for her. But in the four days she was gone, Marabela realized she cared too much about him to hurt him. Maybe that was the problem, she'd thought the day she returned. They both cared too much, and it drove them to betray each other in ways they'd never imagined.

Marabela studies herself in the mirror as she waits for the water to warm, knowing that she'll never again take this kind of small moment for granted. There was no running water available to her in captivity; what little water she got, she drank. It was always too warm, as if it'd been left in the sun for hours. Every once in a while, she'd use the last drops to rinse her hands of dirt and her own filth—she had little more than a roll of paper and an odd box with a hole in it to relieve herself. In those moments she'd learned that the deepest form of humiliation isn't experienced in the eyes of others, but in the lonely desperation of oneself.

She tries concentrating on the shiny faucet knobs, the careful art of adjusting them just so. Control of the water temperature is a luxury; the bathroom, with its privacy, is a gift. Even when she closes her eyes, she can see the whiteness of the sunlight puncturing her eyelids, unable to block it out completely. She is thankful she will never be in such darkness again, but still her thoughts sneak back there sometimes, seeking the truths she got close to in silence. In a cold, dark room that she thought she'd never leave, she let herself be honest. She saw herself and her life for everything it'd become, and it was terrifying to find that kind of liberation in captivity.

Of course, she thought a lot about her children. She daydreamed about helping Cynthia with her homework in the afternoons. She longed for her drives with Ignacio (those quiet stretches of road on the way to the movies or a friend's house), because even though she usually does most of the talking, every once in a while he says just the right few words to let her know he's been listening.

But those were happy, easy thoughts, and her mind was like a child that needed a puzzle to pass the time. She and Andres were more than a puzzle; they were a giant knot that grew more complex at each tug. Always, at the end of the day, she turned to this.

Sometimes she tried convincing herself that there was one moment, one action, that destroyed their marriage. It was easier to blame Andres when she let herself feel the pain and anger brought by his actions, but even then, she knew it was anchored by years of truths and lies they couldn't face. In the months before her kidnapping, Marabela didn't just wake up one morning and think she wanted to leave; she simply realized the time had finally arrived. Their marriage didn't change from night to day; there were sunrises, and sunsets, and times when the sky was neither dark nor light, when the dawns and the dusks became indistinguishable from the constant fog they tried to ignore.

Being back a second time poses some familiar challenges. It's like they're living two separate lives under one roof. They've stood on the same ground without noticing a shift gradually pulling them apart. Now when Marabela rests her head at night, she tries to forget how small she feels when she looks at the ocean that swallowed them. She knows she won't survive without hope in her life, so she holds her breath and gets ready to swim.

❖ ❖ ❖

It doesn't help that she no longer feels beautiful. Marabela has never thought of herself as vain, but beauty was a constant in her life, something she took for granted. When she can stand to look long enough in the mirror, she pulls at the skin on her face, surprised by how uneven it looks. She runs her fingers over her eyebrows, which are slowly reclaiming their natural shape, one uninvited hair at a time.

"These eyebrows need to be tamed," she jokes on a morning she's feeling surprisingly chipper. "That's two—plural, for now. If I'm not careful they'll grow into one."

"You'll still be beautiful," Andres says.

"I bet Diego Rivera said that to Frida Kahlo and lived to regret it," she says.

Andres laughs before going downstairs to prepare breakfast. Once in her robe, Marabela takes a pair of tweezers to the children's bathroom. The light is better here, and if she leaves the door open, it shines in through the windows in the hallway. Bending over the counter with her elbow resting against it, she starts plucking her brows. It stings more than she remembers. Her eyes water; lone tears fall down her cheeks.

She's almost done shaping her right eyebrow into a perfect arch when she catches Guillermo's reflection in the mirror as he walks down the hall. It's a small moment. If either of them had blinked, they would've missed it. But their eyes meet in the reflection. They see each other; then they look away. And then he's walked on, out of the frame, and it seems that he's picked up the pace a little, from one step to the next. It's like they've seen something they weren't supposed to.

Marabela wipes her right eyebrow with a tissue and starts on the left, pulling harder this time, relishing the tiny shocks of pain. Underneath her the floor reverberates with the steady rhythm of Andres making his way up the stairs. In an instant he's at the bathroom door, his cheek and hand pressed against the threshold. He looks so eager and young.

"Did you want one piece of toast or two?" he asks.

She can't help but smile. It'd be nice to join him in this innocence, to anticipate the start of a new day. How many years did she long for this simple kind of attention from him? Rather than dwell on the price they paid for this moment, she decides to embrace it.

"Maybe two," she says, setting down her tweezers and tightening her robe. "Maybe later."

For a moment Andres looks confused, but then Marabela takes his hand and walks him to their bedroom. She closes the door behind them and right away sees his breath catch. She can't tell if he's nervous or excited, then realizes she doesn't know what she is, either. As she sits, Marabela pulls down on his hand. She lowers him to the edge of the bed, next to her. Still he keeps his distance.

"It's okay," she says, following his eyes to the window over their bed. The sunlight fills the room, but instead of closing the blinds she lies down. Holding on to his hand, she pulls Andres's arm over her as if his body were a blanket.

He starts with small caresses along her arms and down to her hips, like he used to when they were young and still discovering each other's body. She lets him chase the skin of her belly with his lips as it moves up and away from him with each quick breath. Exposed and cold, she revels in the warmth of his body against hers. Their love is quiet, maybe even desperate because of this, and it takes every inch of her by surprise. It's been so long, it's like embracing a stranger. She pulls at his hair, which feels finer than she remembers, and he silences his moans into the pillow beneath her, his breath warm and moist. He quickly forgets how careful he's been with her, folding her legs over one side of her body, twisting her limbs to create new forms of entanglement, gripping at her hips for leverage. He moves as if trying to find something they've both been missing. Neither of them holds back.

When they're done Marabela relaxes and slips into a new kind of ecstasy. Her body is finally free of tension and her mind free of thoughts. For moments she forgets herself, forgets where she's been, forgets even the body lying next to her, sharing her bliss.

❖   ❖   ❖

Today will be the first time she's left the house in the sixteen days since she went to see the doctor. Andres doesn't put it like that; he suggested an outing rather nonchalantly, a quick trip to the market to pick up some fresh produce for dinner. But Marabela recognizes this as a maiden voyage. She's testing the world again, and she's terrified of what might happen if it fails her. Andres looks so excited, humming as he pulls on his shoes with his plastic tortoiseshell shoehorn. It's a pleasure to him—just another day. Marabela doesn't want to ruin his good mood.

They leave as soon as Guillermo comes back from dropping the kids off at school, and Andres opens the driver's-side door, announcing that he wants to take the wheel. Guillermo looks uncomfortable, not sure where he should sit if he's not driving. Taking the backseat would make it appear he's a guest, while taking the passenger seat would be presumptuous.

"I'll go in the back," Marabela says.

"It's a beautiful day," Andres says as they pull out of the driveway. The streets of their neighborhood have that midmorning emptiness; everyone is either at work or at school, and whoever else is out and about seems to be on a casual stroll. She envies these people the most because there is nothing casual about her life right now: her purpose today is simply not to die, not to panic, not to be taken.

"Isn't it?" Andres says when Marabela doesn't answer.

"Mm-hmm." It was just as sunny the day she was kidnapped. She remembers when she felt the man push her against the wall at Andres's office, how she'd been thinking she'd need a sweater soon, anticipating colder days ahead.

As they pass familiar sights like the park in the center of town, bright with freshly planted flowers, or the multicolored tents strewn across the market up ahead, Marabela sighs at how much it's all changed. The outward features are the same, but she's seeing it with different eyes. She sits back in her seat, pulling a shade over her window, dreading the moment when the car stops and she'll have to step outside.

❖ ❖ ❖

"I'll drop you both off here while I find parking," Andres says, stopping on a busy curb where people quickly start honking if a car stays motionless too long. This gives Guillermo and Marabela little time to protest. They jump out of the car as if it's on fire, and Andres idles away, relieved to have this one moment to himself.

He meanders through the crowded parking lot and passes a couple of empty spots before realizing he missed them. His mind is simply elsewhere. Part of him feels like a teenager again, expecting the world to be different after sex, but the other part knows better. This morning was only a small step. It's why Andres suggested they go to the market. He needs to keep pushing, needs to nudge things forward now that there's a little momentum.

Recovering the first ransom has brought surprisingly very little relief. Ignacio keeps asking when he'll hire Consuelo and Carla back. Cynthia wonders why her mother no longer takes her to the park in the afternoon. It's like they're waiting for the day when someone flips a switch and things are back to normal, but Andres can't seem to find the switch.

He has tried being everything Consuelo and Carla were to Marabela, so she doesn't have to lift a finger while she recovers. These are not easy tasks—he is learning and fumbling through them as he goes. He has tried being a mother to Cynthia and a sympathetic ear to Ignacio, but all they have to do is glance in the direction of their parents' bedroom, where Marabela spends most of her time, to know that his children are not fooled by imitations.

This morning was a sign that Marabela is ready to step outside of her comfort zone. After they made love he decided to seize her good mood, show her what life can be like with a little effort. It is a desperate attempt to get something out of her—a reaction, a smile, a tear—anything to tell him she's willing to try living again. Because if she never leaves the house again, how is that freedom?

On Monday Andres will do something he's never had to do before: he'll begin searching for a job, for someone who will employ him. He tries to push the thought out of his mind and focus on the challenge at hand. Several yards ahead, a car backs out of a spot, and Andres flicks on his turn signal with an air of triumph. As he inches closer to it, the phone rings, startling him. He had almost forgotten about it altogether.

"Hello?"

"Oh, thank heavens I caught you," Lorena says in one quick breath. Her voice makes him feel like he's swallowed a rock.

"What is it? Did something happen to the kids at school? Are they all right?"

"I'm sure they're fine. It's Elena, dear. She tried to take her own life last night."

Andres's foot slams on the brake, bringing his idling car to a jolt. He's in the middle of the road, unable to move, and already a car coming in the other direction has taken the spot he'd been eyeing.

"How could this happen? Weren't they watching her? Wasn't that the whole point of her being there?"

"I don't know details, Andres. What's important is that she didn't manage it. But she's not well."

"I'll be right there."

"I'll see you there, then. And hurry. She needs you," Lorena says, with a softness in her voice that Andres hasn't heard in years.

He races through the parking lot, barely slowing down for the speed bumps along the way, cringing as the underbelly of the car slams into the gravel. Ignoring all the cars that are honking at him and the drivers who shout for him to move, Andres leaves the car by the entrance and makes his way into the market.

For a weekday, it's busier than usual, and as he passes make-shift tents with wooden figurines and pirated cassette tapes, Andres searches for Marabela's yellow scarf. The noises of the market—the vendors calling out to him, the patrons cursing at him to watch where he's going—all of it falls away when he spots her. Marabela stands behind a mountain of kiwis, massaging them with two fingers before dropping a few into her bag. A few feet behind her, Andres catches Guillermo's silhouette, discreet as a shadow.

Andres calls to her, and when she looks up they lock eyes. Her eyebrows lift swiftly and settle back down in a moment of recognition. Suddenly, the apathy behind her eyes is gone; she can tell something is wrong, and he can recognize for once the part of her that hurts when he does, and finally, here, in this unlikely place, he starts to remember how it feels to know everything will be all right.

He feels the vibration in his feet first, then the explosion in the distance. It sounds like the world is crumbling into thousands of little pieces. It happens so fast he doesn't think, but his body moves toward Marabela, wanting to shield her from whatever is behind him, even as his eyes clench shut. It is only when he opens them that he realizes she's no longer there. Through the rush of people running, through the sudden panic, he sees her, clutching Guillermo.

The only thing worse than the explosion is the silence that follows. It's like the moment at the end of a play, when the audience is holding its breath, waiting for the curtain to drop so it can burst into applause. Except this anticipation lingers, thick with fear. All around him, people are ducked, low to the ground, covering their heads or their loved ones with their bodies. Andres finds himself alone under the white-and-blue-checkered apron that hangs from the kiwi table. Slowly, like children after a game, people start to emerge from their hiding places.

He hears a man say, "It came from over there," as he points into the distance by the overpass.

A woman behind one stand shakes her head, tapping her boxes of produce, carefully arranged in clusters of five tomatoes. "Another car bomb, I suppose. Bless the souls of whoever got caught in its path." She makes the sign of the cross and goes back to her work, making sure all tomatoes are accounted for.

He hears sirens somewhere far away.

Andres isn't ready to stand up. He crawls to where he spotted Marabela last. Loose pieces of gravel and dust scrape against the palms of his hands, and he lifts his knees off the ground, letting his weight fall to his feet as he makes his way past several fruit stands, looking like a bear on the prowl. He almost misses her, but her yellow scarf catches his eye. Except for the silk fabric waving like fire in the wind, Marabela is concealed by Guillermo's body. Her hands stick to his back, pale and stiff, reminding Andres of two pieces of meat frozen together. Even from several feet he can see that she's shaking. A stranger might think she was having a seizure.

When he reaches her he lets his body fall to the floor, exhausted. "Mari! Are you hurt? Are you all right?"

She's on him so fast it takes him several seconds to realize she's not embracing him, but hitting him. Her punches are desperate but weak, fueled by fear.

"It's *your* fault! How could you make me come out like this? You knew I wasn't ready!"

His first instinct is to defend himself, but not with words. Instead, Andres finds himself curled into the ground, arms up, shielding his face. He waits for the impact of her frail fists but then he hears Guillermo's voice—a whisper, really. His arms are wrapped over Marabela's, reaching around her from behind, and his lips are so close to her ears that Andres can't hear what he's saying. Fierce, quick breaths pump out of her, slowly giving way to a steady, quiet pace. After Guillermo helps her up, he extends his hand to Andres, who turns away.

"Let's go home," Andres says, feeling like everything he's ever known has been shattered in the explosion.

❖ ❖ ❖

When they get back to the car, Guillermo jumps into the backseat with Marabela, like it's not even a question to be discussed. Andres heads to the driver's seat.

"Come on, come on, come on," Marabela mumbles, over and over like they're still running from danger. Every second it takes him to find his keys, grasp the right one for the ignition in his trembling hands, and turn on the engine is a second too long. A part of her wants to reach over the front seat and yell at him, hit him all over again, but the other part, the rational part, wins out. She lets her body sink into the seat until her head is ducked beneath the window. Guillermo sits beside her, one hand on the seat in front of him, the other arm stretched over the back, as if just by holding on he is anchoring both of them in place. His head turns in every direction as they pull away. His eyes are everywhere.

"Make a left here," he tells Andres. "We'll double back to avoid the traffic jam on the highway. It's safer."

Andres obeys wordlessly.

From where she's sitting, Marabela can feel the vibration of the engine stirring through her chest, can feel every bump in the road like it's a mountain. It reminds her of being transported to an unknown destination, hands tied behind her back, face digging into the dusty carpets as she tried to rub off the blindfold in hopes of seeing where they were headed. She wants to sit up but her body won't let her. It's as if her brain is trying to send a signal that her legs are rejecting. This little alcove in the car is both her sanctuary and her prison, and she can't will herself to get out of it.

"You can come up now," Guillermo says.

She shakes her head no.

"It's really okay."

Eyes shut now. Still, no go.

With her head practically underneath Andres's seat, she can hear him mumbling to himself.

"This can't . . . this can't be happening," he says.

"What is it?" she yells. "What now?" She is not completely surprised at the possibility that things have gotten worse. They always do.

"Nothing. I just . . . there's something urgent that I need to take care of as soon as we get home. I'm going to drop off you and Guillermo."

"This isn't urgent enough for you?" she says.

"I'm sorry I can't stay, Mari. I know you need me right now—"

"What is it? Is it the kids? Are they all right?" They're so far from the schools that the thought hadn't entered her mind, but seeing Andres like this erases her sense of logic. "Call the schools. Call the schools right now!" She finally gets up, reaching for the phone in the partition between the two front seats. Her sudden movement startles Andres, and the car swerves into the next lane, tossing her back and to the side. It takes all the strength Marabela has to fight against the momentum and reach again for the phone.

"I have to know that they're okay."

"Will you please control her!" Andres barks at Guillermo. "I can't drive like this."

Guillermo lowers her arm back to her side. "They're fine, señora. The explosion wasn't anywhere near them."

"I can't live like this anymore. I can't. Andres is hiding something. I knew it before the explosion and I know it even more now."

Her voice is so loud, it hurts coming out of her. "I deserve to know. If something has happened—"

He slams the brakes at a red light and turns to her, his hand grasping the back of the passenger seat. "It's Elena. She tried to kill herself last night. She's not well, Mari."

"*Elena?* Why would she do that?"

"It's complicated." Andres sighs.

"How would you know? Have you been seeing her again?"

"Yes, but it's a long story. I'll tell you after I see her. Please, just let me concentrate on the road right now."

"All I'm asking for is an explanation. This doesn't make sense. Why would she . . . ?" Marabela lets her voice trail off.

They drive the rest of the way in silence, both knowing that the conversation isn't over, but acknowledging that it's not one they want to have in the car. Guillermo is not the problem—he is so quick to turn invisible. But the conversation they are about to have is one they've put off for years. It's like an old weapon they've hidden in the depths of their drawers, hoping that they'd never have to dig it up and dust it off. Now it requires all their caution and attention.

They wait until they've pulled into the garage and Guillermo helps Marabela out of the backseat. Andres still has the car running, still sits behind the wheel. Understanding that time is against them, Marabela gets back into the car, sitting in the front this time while Guillermo enters the house.

"Tell me everything. Quickly."

His hands and eyes on the wheel, Andres chooses his words slowly. "Maybe it's easier if I start with how I hired Guillermo. He was recommended to me by my mother because she was familiar with his work. He helped recover Elena when she was kidnapped a couple of years ago."

Andres gives Marabela a concerned glance, but she just nods at him to continue. He turns away.

"When she came home, it was too much for her. She was scared to leave the house, and even then, she didn't feel safe. Saul was worried she'd hurt herself so they took her to an institution where she'd be supervised and have some time to deal with her pain. I visited her there while you were gone. I couldn't keep pretending after all she'd been through. I couldn't stand the idea of her being alone, with us never making amends. And there was only so much I could do, Mari, while I waited for the calls and the negotiations. Maybe in a way I thought if Elena was okay, you would be, too."

She doesn't know what to say. Her voice, when it comes out, is feeble and shaky. "Is that why you wanted me to leave the house? So you could pretend I'm okay?"

He shrugs, looking ashamed at the very idea. She clears her throat, refusing to fall apart all over again. "Okay then. Let's go. What are we waiting for?"

Marabela readjusts herself so she's sitting in the center of the seat and reaches over her shoulder for the seat belt.

"Mari. It's not a good idea for you to go."

"She was just as much my friend as she was yours."

"She's too delicate right now. It'll be too much for her."

"Then I'll wait outside. I don't care if she doesn't see me or I don't see her, but I want to be there. It's the least I can do."

At this, Andres doesn't try to argue. He pulls out of the driveway slowly and then, once they've straightened out on the road, drives like he's chasing the sun.

12

THE FACILITY IS busier than ever, bustling with patients who wander the halls, dragging their feet across the linoleum, and nurses who speak to them in exasperated tones. The space is so full of life and yet all Andres can think about is death. If Elena slips away today, if she succeeds in a mistake she never would've made had it not been for him, Andres will never forgive himself. He thinks back to the last time he left her nearly three weeks ago. He'd basically revealed that her worst fear had come true and naively assumed she was strong enough to pull herself together. He curses under his breath.

The guilt spreads over him.

He walks down the corridor, feeling torn by the distance growing between him and Marabela, whom he left in the waiting room, and the distance that's shrinking between him and Elena. Andres follows two steps behind the doctor who is leading him to Elena's room. He wishes the man would pick up the pace, and he considers telling him that he can find his own way, but he changes his mind when he realizes he would betray the morning nurse by revealing his earlier visits.

"How did she do it?" he asks.

The doctor flips through a chart as they walk, perhaps out of habit or to avoid looking at Andres. He never stops at one page long enough to read anything. "We found pieces of a ceramic vase. Frankly, I'm surprised how deep she managed to cut herself. They weren't very sharp," he adds defensively.

"Thank God someone found her in time."

"Our patients are constantly supervised. They're never out of our sight for long."

"Long enough," Andres says.

"*¿Perdón?*"

"Has she had many visitors?"

The doctor nods distractedly. "Her family was here earlier." He opens the door for Andres. "She's been in and out all morning. Try not to upset her."

Before he sees Elena, Andres hears the mechanical beep of her heart. As he turns the long corner of the hall in her room, a white figure under a flurry of sheets moves and rustles. She calls his name out before they even see each other.

"How did you know it was me, *linda*?"

"I recognize your footsteps." She gives him that sad smile. She looks like she hasn't slept or eaten in weeks. Her face sinks into her skull, and even the slightest turn of the head seems like an exhausting effort. She is almost unrecognizable except for the softness in her eyes.

"Do you want some water?"

She shakes her head and reaches for his hand, pulling it down in her direction so he'll take a seat. "You must be so disappointed in me."

"Never."

"I heard my mother tell my father I was selfish for doing this. That suicide is a coward's way out. They thought I was asleep."

"That's just anger and fear talking. The anger will fade—it's just a reaction."

"And the fear?"

He doesn't have an answer for that, so he holds her hand, careful not to tug at the IV pressing into the back of her hand, the blue veins poking out of a white bandage like rivers and deltas. "I should've never told you about Marabela. I got you all worried for nothing. She's home and safe now." Andres knows Lorena told her this weeks ago, but he feels the need to repeat it, as if it would bear more weight now coming from him.

Something that is not quite a smile spreads across Elena's face. It is more like a stretch of the mouth and skin, her lips pressing together and her eyelids wrinkling shut as she nods her head in gratitude, tears crawling across her temple to her pillow. Her breath and her heart monitor accelerate, and Andres stands up to call a nurse but she pulls him back down. "Does she know that it was me? Does she hate me?"

"She doesn't know and she never will. And Marabela could never hate you. Not in a thousand lifetimes."

"If she ever found out—"

"She won't."

"She would hate me. I would. I do," she whispers, the words shaky but resolute. He has never heard her speak like this, and he starts to wonder if the Elena he once knew is gone, if there is really power or experience strong enough to erase a person completely.

"Do you remember when we were ten and I ran your leg over with my bike? You were trying to sunbathe in the backyard and I thought I could jump over you while you slept."

She gives a short, courteous laugh.

"You said you wanted to be angry with me, but you couldn't stay that way for long, because you knew I never meant to hurt you. You said me feeling bad about it was punishment enough for the both of us."

"It's not the same thing, Andres. We were children . . ."

"And these people you were dealing with are criminals. They made choices for you that you never had."

"That's not true. I could've let them—"

"Could've let them what?"

"Kill me."

"Please don't talk like that. I didn't come here to upset you even more."

"There's no one else I can talk to about it. Not even the doctors, or the therapists, even though it's their job. They think I'm just another number they can plug into a formula."

He sighs, not because he's tired, but because he's bracing himself for what's to come. "I'm here if you need to talk. You know I'll always listen."

She sits up and rests her hands on her lap. He realizes that this is something she needs to psyche herself up for, like a runner who stretches before a race, or a speaker who gathers his thoughts before going onstage. Her face glistens with sweat even though the room is perfectly cool. He can almost smell it on her, how close she came to death. Andres rubs her arm, lets his hands travel up to her shoulders, her neck, her face. He's like a child who needs to touch, squeeze, feel, that something is real before he can let himself believe it. He leans forward and kisses Elena's forehead.

She closes her eyes and takes a deep breath.

"Here's how it happened for me, though you never asked and maybe that's why I want to tell you so badly. Everyone else has been a morbid spectator. But they can't handle the real story. They want to relive it with the safety on — with the knowledge that it'll all work out in the end. I refuse to be their source of catharsis.

"I was driving home from a friend's house, trying to make it back to my parents' before dinner. She'd lent me some patterns for my sewing, because I had an old fabric I'd been wanting to use for years, and in my boredom I'd decided to take up a hobby. It was gray, with pale green leaves and purple berries. The fabric, I mean. Not the day. It was gorgeous out that day. Funny how that works sometimes, isn't it?

"That afternoon I'd picked up my sewing machine from the shop and stopped by her house for the patterns. I always took back roads to avoid the traffic. I suppose they expected that. There were two cars, though I didn't know it at the time. The one in front stopped so suddenly I crashed into him. He ran out of the car, shouting about a cat he was trying to avoid, and when I got out to check the damage, he pointed at the bumper and said, 'See? See?' When I leaned in to look, his hand was on the back of my neck." She moves her hand up, grabbing the spot. "This is how much reason fails us sometimes: for maybe half a second, I thought he'd tripped and lost his balance. I thought he'd grabbed me for help, and that I was falling with him. My head slammed against the hood of the car. It was so warm. Nothing really struck me until I tried to recover my balance and couldn't even lift my head. The man was holding me down.

"He said, 'Scream and it'll be your last. No one will help you.' He was so confident. I actually thought that maybe people had seen him do this before, in this very spot, and they'd heard the screams and just walked right by, pretending not to see.

"The car behind me, its tires hadn't screeched at all, while the sound of mine could have woken up the whole neighborhood. I only noticed that later, looking back, and I realized it should have been a warning sign that the accident was planned."

Elena reaches for Andres, and he realizes that he's been so afraid to move that his whole body hurts. His face feels like it's made of plaster. He takes a deep breath and squeezes her hand, just once, silently reassuring her to go on.

"So the man in the second car gets out and helps the guy who's holding my head on the hood of the car. I can see him grabbing my purse and looking for my wallet. Then they trade, handing me off, and now I'm in the backseat of a four-door car, shoved down on the floor. I threw up the second I got in there. As the driver's friend covered my head with a sack, he said, 'Better hold it in this time, or you'll be floating in your own vomit.'

"That's when I started counting. I thought I could gauge how far we were going, but I lost track around twenty-five hundred.

"I swear, I've never had my heart beat so fast for so long before.

By the time we arrived wherever they took me, I was close to passing out. They carried me out of the car like a cardboard package."

Andres wants to tell her that she doesn't have to go on, but she looks so determined.

"Then it was nighttime, and I didn't see daylight again for five weeks. The first night, they just left me alone, and I worried about the silliest things. I worried that my parents would think I was mad at them because I never showed at their house for dinner. Or that someone would take my sewing machine from my car and I'd have to take it back to get fixed again. I think my mind was rejecting the truth. Of course I was scared, but it wasn't the same kind of fear I felt once they came back the next morning. That was . . . unimaginable.

"There were three men. At least, I only saw three men. Sometimes I thought I heard other voices but I couldn't be sure if my mind was playing tricks on me. The first time they beat me, they ripped my clothes. I think they did it so they could show my bruises in the pictures. They had one of those instant cameras. I didn't eat for days, until they said they'd beat me even harder if I didn't. They had this one guy—a short, skinny young guy—bringing me food, and he'd beg me to eat, beg me to not make them hurt me again. You know what's crazy? In that misery you cling to any semblance of kindness. Something that would normally make you spit in a person's face gets magnified into a kind act. I trusted this guy, so I ate. After a week or two and beatings two or three times a day, they brought the pencil and paper, asked for names. I know I told you this part already. I just . . . it's not that I didn't believe them. It's that I didn't believe God could ever betray me so much. And you know I've never been that religious but . . . I thought, *This doesn't happen to people like me.*

"And then that short, skinny young guy was the first to take his turn with me. Even after I gave them a dozen names. I couldn't believe I ever saw any trace of kindness in him. I felt like the world's biggest fool.

"When I got back, I asked about Marabela as much as I could

without people wondering what I was up to. I asked after all the people whose names I gave up. I know you'll say I should've warned you, and I don't know why I didn't.

"I know I'll never make it right. God, I wish I could. I try to tell myself Marabela is stronger than I am; but I thought I was stronger than this, too, and look what happened. She's safe and she's home but I know that's not enough. What if she ends up like me, Andres? What if she just—"

"She won't. And you're going to get better. Is that—is that why you did this? Because of Marabela?"

But she's too exhausted to answer. Elena's head falls back on the pillow. He sees her mouth move, but no words come out. He holds a straw to her lips. Her mouth curls as she sips and her eyes stay on his face, unblinking. Even at her most vulnerable, Elena is beautiful, like a statue sculpted tenderly from stone.

Finally, she shakes her head, full of sympathy. "I didn't do it because of Marabela."

"Then why?"

"It was the memories. Seeing you again. Realizing what I missed. There's so much I'll never get back."

"Don't think like that. There's still so much ahead," Andres says. His eyes are starting to water.

But Elena only shakes her head again. "I thought I'd rather be nothing than be so alone."

There's nothing he can say that would be right. "There has to be something more," he says, more to himself than to Elena.

Now she's the one who comforts him; she brings him back to this moment with her touch. "Do you know how they say your life flashes before your eyes when you're about to die?"

There's a tinge of excitement in her voice. He nods, defeated.

"That's not how it happens. You get one moment, relived. It's not a moment that sums things up. It's the one when you felt most alive. It's cruel, if you think about it. 'Here's one last taste of what you'll

never again have.' It's small, too. It's one you never thought you'd remember, but then you can't imagine letting it go."

She brings her hand to his chin, tilts his face up so he'll look
at her.

"Mine was of us," she says. "It was that time we were seventeen,
and we were walking back to the bungalow at the club. It was night
and the wind blew away my scarf and we ran after it, past the gazebos and the pool lights, into the ocean. I was scared, and cold, and
amazed. Nothing had happened to me yet, but anything could've.
And if you suspend that moment, stretch it out just as we were, waiting . . . that's what it was like when I was dying."

❖　❖　❖

The room where Marabela waits with Lorena sitting across from
her, both trying their best to pretend this isn't an extraordinarily
uncomfortable situation, is unlike any hospital waiting room she's
ever been in. There are tables piled high with magazines that nobody
reaches for. The television is on but the volume is turned so low that
all Marabela catches is an accusation here and there, shouted by an
angry soap opera actor. Rows of thinly cushioned metal chairs are arranged one after the other, all facing a large window that overlooks a
living area for the patients.

Marabela stands up from her chair to get a closer look through
the glass. It's lined with thin metal wires that form small Xs across
the entire surface, like a very delicate fence. On the other side, the
people don't look the way she expected they would. They're not in
wheelchairs, or wearing robes, or talking to themselves. They wear
scrubs like the nurses do, except theirs are white, but even in uniform
each finds a way to stand out. The middle-aged man who sits by the
window with a deck of cards wears his pants rolled halfway up his
calves. A woman, maybe ten years older than Marabela, turned her
shirt into a tank top by tucking the sleeves under her bra straps. She

tiptoes across the lounge, stopping every few tables to whisper something in another patient's ear. Nobody pays attention.

She hears Lorena give a deep, loud sigh behind her. "It makes you wonder if they were crazy before they got here or if being here drove them to it." She makes no effort to keep her voice down. Marabela considers shushing her mother-in-law, but realizes there's no one around to hear them.

"That's cruel," she says, thankful that despite never getting along with her mother-in-law, they were at least always honest with each other. It's strangely refreshing. When Marabela and Andres arrived at the hospital, there was little time for reintroduction. Andres gave his mother a quick kiss and asked if he could see Elena on his own. The two women took their seats, each facing the other, but neither looking straight ahead. Finally Lorena uncrossed her legs and said, "You look well, Marabela."

"Thank you."

Now Lorena joins Marabela by the window. "I don't say it to be cruel. But if it were me, I would hope my family would respect my madness enough not to put it on display. Better to hide it at home."

Feeling Lorena's eyes on her, Marabela crosses her arms and keeps her gaze on the other side of the glass. She wishes she were wearing a sweater, because suddenly she feels exposed. "Is that what you think I'm doing? Hiding? Did Andres say something?"

"You know he would never betray your privacy like that. But, if you were . . . nobody would blame you."

"And you?"

"I said nobody would blame you."

"It's not the same thing."

"I suppose not, when you put it like that." Lorena takes a deep breath and shakes her head. "I wouldn't blame you. I would . . . I would feel very sorry for you."

"That's worse," Marabela scoffs.

"Who can help it? In my old age I've learned two things: One, nothing is ever as it seems. And two, people are much more empathetic than we realize. Even a bitter two-faced witch like me."

Marabela winces at the mention of a name she called Lorena years ago.

"People will feel for you what they think you feel for yourself. It's that simple. Look at poor Elena."

Marabela tilts her head and closes one eye, focusing on the wire mesh in front of her. She can't stop wondering which side of the glass she belongs on.

13

ANDRES GETS HOME early in the morning, just as the curfew is lifted. He stayed with Elena after Lorena offered him her car, saying that it was important for him to be with her and that she would get a ride home with Marabela. In their hushed corner of the waiting room, where people kept their voices low and braced themselves to see damaged loved ones, Marabela hadn't felt right protesting. What if she, too, needed Andres's support and attention? Was is not important for him to be at his wife's side?

Marabela hears the click of the lock in the front door and her husband tiptoeing through his own home like a bandit. When he comes into the room, she is lying on her side of the bed, facing the door, her eyelids fluttering even though they're shut. She hears the closet creak and knows his back is to her, so she opens her eyes. She watches her husband undress with disinterest. His body has changed so much over the years. His muscles look softer and less defined, as if they've grown tired of holding him together. Andres takes off his pants and loses his balance, grasping at the bed to avoid falling. It shakes her, but she only twitches and turns around in a sleepy, clumsy motion to sell the lie that she's not awake. She feels the sheets next to her being pulled over, the cold air brushing against her legs, and then the weight of his body, climbing into bed.

"What are you doing?" Marabela sits up, holding the covers

against her skin. Her sudden movement makes Andres jump back and hit his foot against the closet door. He holds his heel in one hand, grimacing from the pain.

"I thought you were asleep."

"I heard you coming in."

"Oh. I just thought you'd be more comfortable if you weren't alone." He sits on the edge of the bed.

Marabela still hasn't moved. "You don't have to do that. I've been fine when you slept on your own bed." She tries not to look at the hurt expression on his face.

"I thought we'd moved past this."

"Past what?" She hates it when he does that. He speaks about it like it's forbidden, like it's a superstition, or a curse.

"Don't be difficult, Mari. I'm just trying to get things back to how they used to be."

She lies back on the bed, diagonally. "How they used to be was that you slept on your bed, and I slept on mine. Don't try cuddling with me all of a sudden just because you feel guilty."

He gets up and fluffs his pillow. Even in the silence, she can feel him gathering his thoughts.

"I hoped you wouldn't wake up when I got home," he says, his voice resigned.

"Why?"

"I don't know. I guess I hoped I wouldn't have to face you. I wake up early every morning and take a walk, and I actually miss going to work, getting stuck in traffic, because it means I don't have to see you like this."

He looks disappointed when she doesn't respond, realizing he has no choice but to continue. "So I walk around, and I ask myself if it was my fault, and I play back the events of the day you were taken, and I wonder what I could have done differently if I was there, and nothing is ever good enough. I try to make myself feel better by focusing on the happy ending: you're safe now, you're home. But it's like you're not really here."

Tears build up in Marabela eyes, burn, then fall on the pillow. "You left me there longer than you had to," she says. "I *knew* you wouldn't want to part with your money, even if it meant getting me back."

"That's not fair. Listen to what you're saying, Mari. What man would want to be put in that position? What, did you expect me to be happy about it? To give up so easily like I had no other options? No, but I did it. I did what I had to do."

"Then what took you so long?" She stands up, pacing the room, shouting even though everyone in the house is sleeping. She has to take a moment to control herself to keep from waking the kids. "Did you need some time to build up the courage? Did you think those extra days you needed would pass as quickly for me as they did for you?"

When Andres starts to cry, his tears are too late. She hates that this is who she's become.

"Tell me how to fix it, Mari. I'll do it, I swear, I don't care what it is."

"You keep saying that. You talk like you won't hesitate to do what you have to do. I wish I trusted that were true."

"I just did what I was told. It was the best I could do. I know this is hard for you to believe, but not one second of this was easy for me. We all suffered with you."

Marabela climbs back into bed and turns away from him, pulling the covers over her shoulder as if she's trying to flip the page of their conversation. "Yes, I'm sure that's why you decided to go back to Elena. That must have been such a difficult decision for you."

He looks down and nods, a sad understanding finally sinking in at the mention of Elena's name. She's a wound that has never quite healed with them, freshly reopened. It is pointless now to try covering up the pain.

14

———

THE SUN ISN'T even a faded ink stain on the edge of the horizon when Andres wakes up Monday morning. He sits up and taps his feet blindly against the carpet, searching for his shoes. It's going to be a long day, so he takes a quick shower and begins sifting through the closet for something to wear. The sound of metal against wood slices the morning's silence as he pushes hangers from one side of the rod to the other.

"Andres . . . the noise," Marabela says, mumbling into her pillow.

For a moment Andres forgets that he is in a hurry and stares at her. He remembers when they were first married, when they would make a large pot of hot chocolate and bring it with them to bed in their one-bedroom apartment. It was in the days before they had maids, and the tiny quarters were all they could afford, but what did square footage matter when they spent their days trying to push out the space between their bodies? After they were done, with the sunlight casting bars of shadows on the white sheets, they lay there talking about the future.

A familiar guilt creeps into him as he ties his shoes. Had he stolen Marabela's dreams, betrayed her even before she was kidnapped?

Marabela lies in bed with her eyes clenched shut, forehead tense, annoyed that she's been woken.

"What time will you be home?" she says.

"Late." He grabs some papers scattered on the floor and places them in his briefcase.

In the car, he scans the radio for a signal, a newscast, a song, anything to help drown out the silence. Nothing is clear today, least of all his past or his future. When he finally catches a song on an oldies station, it reminds him of Marabela, not because they ever listened to it together, but because she is like that song: one he was infatuated with to the point that he could never get the tune out of his head. He'd memorized every word, not realizing that his tastes would evolve and one day he'd forget how to sing along.

He changes the station and his thoughts turn to Elena — a song he never knew he remembered. He wishes he could go back to the hospital and tell her this, because she's the only one who'd understand. But he has work to do, a job to find, and an unkind world to play along with.

As he makes his first stop at an old client's building, the phone rings.

"You have impeccable timing lately, Mother."

"Are you done looking yet?"

"You know I haven't even started."

"Then you'll have time to come by the house."

"I really don't."

"It's important, Andres. I need to talk to you before you make another terrible decision."

He fights the urge to ask what the previous ones were, but decides that would open a door he'd rather remained shut. Besides, he's tired of arguing, and even more exhausted at the thought of begging old clients and business associates for job leads.

"Have breakfast ready for me?" he asks, surprised by the whining that slips through his voice. As much as he hates to admit it, since Consuelo and Carla have been gone, he's missed having a hot meal prepared for him, the table set when he gets home, as if by magic.

Andres longs for the comfort of his childhood home and the dining room with its burnt-orange walls and rustic wooden furnishings. It was the only place in the house that never felt formal. Sometimes after dinner with the Duarezes, he and Elena would pretend to go camping underneath the table while their parents played cards. In the world he and Elena created under the tablecloth, the adults provided much-needed sound effects. Their laughter, interspersed with long moments of quiet suspense, was the thunder in their forest. The women's whispers were the rain. When the men lit up their cigars and the room filled with smoke, the children pretended they were burning firewood, rubbing their hands and shoulders together for warmth.

Andres drives through the gate, pulls up to the house, and rings the doorbell. The maid who answers the door must be new; he doesn't recognize her, but she greets him by name, and he realizes she's probably polished silver frames containing his picture.

The stillness of the house, which he once described to Marabela as cold and unwelcoming, now feels peaceful. Lorena takes his face in both hands and kisses him on each cheek. The motion doesn't come naturally, but the effort is there, and for now that's all that counts.

They sit perpendicular to each other, she at the head of the table and Andres to her left, while the maid brings eggs, toast, and a pot of freshly brewed coffee with milk. Andres looks down at his plate and laughs.

"You still have these plates," he says, surprised that his mother didn't replace his favorite wooden set with delicate china as soon as he moved out.

"They remind me of a set I used to have for my dolls when I was a child. And one should always have unbreakable dinner plates in case of rowdy guests, or if you're expecting an argument. It's easier to clean up," she says, smiling as he's rarely seen her smile, with a subtle wink punctuating the lift of her cheeks.

"It's nice to see you so happy, considering the circumstances."

"I'm just trying, Andres. I know you might not believe this, but

I don't like to be the worst part of a bad situation. Grudges fade quickly when you're faced with losing the ones you love."

"I never thought I'd hear you talk about Marabela like that."

She smiles sheepishly. "I meant you, dear. And Elena. I'd never wish any harm on Marabela, but I care for her only because she's the one your heart's attached to. Although . . . I feel like that's not as true as it used to be." She sets her cup down and takes a moment to study his face, and suddenly Andres is very much aware of every muscle in his forehead, his cheeks, his lips. He holds them still and finally relaxes them, his face dropping down with a sigh.

"We've been having problems. All I wanted was to have her back, but it hasn't been enough to bring us together. She says we've changed too much."

"Well, of course you have. Look at us, even. If us sitting here talking about your marriage isn't proof enough that these last few weeks have changed everything . . . well, I don't know what is."

They both laugh under their breaths, polite and deflated.

"All you can really do—if you don't plan on staying miserable, that is—is take what little good has come out of it all, and run with it," she says.

"What little good, Mother? My company's gone, my marriage is irreparable, my best friend is finally back in my life and she tries to kill herself, and somehow I'm supposed to pick up the pieces and build a life from them. I don't think I can do it."

"So then don't." She sips the last of her coffee. "Pick up the old pieces. The ones that were waiting for you years ago."

"What are you talking about?"

"You once told me you couldn't wait for you and Elena to run your fathers' newspaper together. You had a place there. Just because you didn't take it doesn't mean it's gone."

"Dad sold his shares before he died."

"He sold the shares that would've been yours. His, he left to me."

"You already had shares."

"Exactly. He wanted me to have more. Your father always said I was the foundation for his success. He was never cheap when it came to giving people credit where it was due. In the end, he went above and beyond with me. He said he could never take care of me the way I took care of him, but me having control of the company would be a start."

A breath he didn't realize he was holding in escapes him. "Why are you telling me this now? Why not before?"

"Now you see, all the time we wasted not speaking?" She takes a small sip of her coffee. "But now it's about more than the money. It's about you finding your place again and finally being honest with yourself. And I don't think you could have done that if it hadn't been for Elena being back in your life."

Knowing this is true, but unwilling to admit it, Andres simply thanks Lorena and asks her what the next step will be. She sets down her teacup, so delicately it makes no sound against the saucer, and rests her elbow on the table, bringing her thumb to her chin. "Well, what plans do you have tomorrow?" she suggests.

"That should be fine."

"So we'll meet at the office. At this time."

He tries to imagine the newspaper's offices, realizing the only reference he has is outdated, from a time long gone with his father. Housed in an old Spanish-style building, it had arched doorways and white plaster columns, but the walls were lined with gray metal filing cabinets.

"Will I even recognize anyone?"

"Except for Saul, probably not," she says, looking down at her coffee. "Nothing's been the same since your father died. Saul's tried, but it's like the memory of Rolando is gone from the place. I think this is what he would've wanted." She places her hand on his, a sad smile stretching across her face. "He never let go of the hope that you'd come back to the paper one day. It's the only reason I was able to convince him to offer Marabela the job after you two eloped."

"That was you?"

She presses her lips together but says nothing. Andres wonders how many more secrets are sealed behind his mother's familiar smile.

"Promise me one thing," Lorena says later when she walks him to the door. "You'll help Elena pick up the pieces, too?"

"I'll try, Mother. I've already promised her, and now I promise you. I'll try twice as hard since you asked."

As he drives home, Andres takes a quick detour through the Plaza de Armas. He's not looking forward to telling Marabela about the plans he's made with his mother. At the mention of the newspaper, he's afraid she'll chastise him for going back, or, even worse, expect that he'll reinstate her as a photographer. The thought seems absurd, considering that she can barely leave the house, but Andres knows better than to underestimate Marabela. He parks the car next to a bus stop and rolls down the windows, letting the breeze wrap around him. The plaza is busy as usual, looking like a replica of when he saw it last. But today he feels distant, like he's no longer a part of it. It amazes him, how different the same places can look when a person has been through what he has.

❖ ❖ ❖

That same morning, Marabela finds herself in the last place she ever would have expected to be—and by choice. She's rattled by nerves and anticipation, unable to even focus on the congested road ahead of them.

"Do you mind if I smoke?" Guillermo asks. They've been in the car for nearly half an hour in silence, and the question strikes Marabela as ridiculous, considering it's his car they're driving.

"Of course not. Please," she says. He keeps one hand on the wheel while he pulls a pack out of his pocket and holds it out to her, offering a cigarette. She smiles and takes one for each of them so he won't have to fumble with the box as he drives. Though she's never been much of a smoker, his small offer of kindness does much to soothe her. She admires Guillermo's unconscious chivalry. In his company, Marabela feels protected but not weak, considered but not scrutinized.

Marabela hands Guillermo his lit cigarette and emulates him when he rolls down his window to let the smoke out as he dangles it outside the car. When she first stepped into his vehicle, she'd been surprised by how well kept it was. Sitting by the curb in front of her house, it'd always looked beat-up and hostile, much like her first impression of him. Now it's obvious to her that he minds the small details, and she supposes this makes sense for a man in his profession. He isn't one to overlook dust on his car panel any more than he would a threatening stranger.

"You seem to know your way pretty well," Marabela says as they get off the highway. This morning after Andres left and she informed Guillermo where she planned on going, he had only nodded with a worried look on his face. She'd taken care getting ready, unsure what to wear for the occasion, but she'd figured it'd give Guillermo time to come up with directions. Now she suspects he never really needed them. "Have you visited her before?" she asks.

Guillermo starts to nod but tilts his head to the side, as if he's changed his mind. "I went to see her once, but I didn't let her see me. It was just to check up on her."

"Why didn't you let her know you were there?"

"I doubt I would've been any comfort to her. She didn't know me. I'm just a stranger she found in her house on the day she came back from the worst experience of her life. It's not a good association to have with a person."

Marabela can't argue with him. It was only a short couple of weeks ago that she tried to make Andres send Guillermo home. "Do you usually visit your . . . clients?"

He shakes his head, scratching his jaw with his right hand, suddenly looking uncomfortable. Still, Marabela has to ask. "So why

Elena?" She tries to push aside a familiar jealousy that's creeping up on her.

"It was a personal favor for your mother-in-law. After Elena came home, Señora Jimenez was worried about her. She often called me to ask how it normally works with my clients, how long it takes them to get better."

"How long does it take?"

"There is no normal, señora. That's what I tried to tell her, but when Elena's parents sent her away, Lorena asked me to check in."

Marabela finds it odd that Guillermo would refer to Lorena in such a casual manner, but he doesn't seem to have noticed his slip of the tongue. "So you still keep in touch with my mother-in-law?"

"She's the reason I'm still here," he says with a mixture of gratitude and admiration.

"What do you mean?" Marabela remembers the first time she ever saw Guillermo, how he seemed so eager to leave.

"I'm sorry. I thought you knew."

"Knew what?"

He doesn't bother hesitating. They both know there's no point in keeping it from her now. "Señora Jimenez agreed to handle payment for my services. And to extend them, that's all."

"Oh." The word escapes her, more of a sound, really. She understands now. When she'd heard him say he was doing this as a favor for Señora Jimenez, he'd meant Lorena.

As they pull up to the hospital Marabela wonders if this was a good idea after all. It's been nearly six years since she last saw Elena, and enough has happened to change them both for a lifetime.

"Do you think she's crazy?" Marabela asks.

He considers her question carefully, as if the thought only now occurred to him. "By definition madness lacks logic. We think people are insane when they have no reason to act the way they do. But with everything she's been through, Elena's more than justified. She's not crazy; she's traumatized. I believe there's a difference."

He gets out of the car and opens the door for her, and as they walk across the parking lot dark clouds roll overhead, almost as if nature is warning them to stay away. The last time Marabela was here, she was too caught up in her own desperation to notice how isolated the building is, surrounded by little else than barren plains and nearly naked trees. It's the kind of place no one would find unless they were looking for it.

Once inside, Guillermo makes a request with the receptionist on Marabela's behalf. She rubs her moist palms against her jeans and takes a deep breath, letting it out slowly through her nose. Within seconds Guillermo is holding open the door to the hallway, where a nurse waits to show her the way.

"I'll be right here," he reassures her as she steps through.

She nods as she looks back at him, then forces herself to turn away.

When they first met, Marabela and Elena bonded over an exam they were both terrified of taking. She remembers sitting in the library, close to tears, when she recognized the same book and the same desperate expression in the young woman across from her. After venting in loud whispers, they went to a late-night café to quiz each other on the material, drinking one cup of coffee after another until they were giddy with caffeine and exhaustion.

Now, Marabela follows the nurse down the cold, dark hall, longing to go back to a time when the only things that mattered were what you wrote on a blank sheet of paper.

"Here she is," the nurse says, opening a door with a small square window.

It occurs to Marabela as she steps through that she shouldn't have come empty-handed, but within a second of taking in her surroundings she realizes a bouquet of flowers or a card would have made things awkward. She walks toward the bed, where Elena is lying on her side with her back to the door, clearly awake but not interested enough to turn her head to see who's arrived. Now faced with the task of announcing herself, Marabela has to push back tears. She walks around the bed, entering Elena's line of sight, waiting for the recognition to sink into her face. What she sees instead is horror.

"You're not really here," Elena says, more to herself than to Marabela. She shakes her head and repeats it over and over. "You're not really here. You're not really here."

"I know," Marabela says, wanting to acknowledge Elena's words but not fully understanding their meaning. "I can't believe it took me this long to come, either."

"Did Andres send you?"

"He doesn't know I'm here." She tries to get closer but Elena keeps inching away, her body practically hanging off the edge of the bed. None of this makes sense to her—she was expecting to see anger, maybe sadness.

"I didn't come to fight. We both know that talk about putting the past behind us is just talk. But I think we're bigger than that. At least, the fact that I still care about you is bigger than all that."

The room is so quiet Marabela can hear the tiny bones cracking in her fingers as she tries to do something with her hands. She opens and closes them, fighting the urge to take her friend's hands in her own. She's reminded of the days, ages ago, when Ignacio had his first fever, how she would've done anything to make his pain go away. Never in her life had she felt so helpless, until now.

Elena is crying and is so still that Marabela wonders where her mind has gone. There must be a reason she came here, but she can't think of it now. All she can think of is the last time Elena, Andres, and Marabela were in the same room together, on the night that Elena called them from Andres's parents' home and demanded they come over right away, without giving an explanation.

When they arrived, Elena was standing behind Rolando's chair, her hand resting on his shoulder with an intimacy completely beyond Marabela. The day's paper—not the families', but one of the bigger dailies—was stretched over the table before them, and Lorena sat at the very end, tapping her fingers over the pages' edges.

The front-page image was that of a woman taking cover with her child as an explosion lunged from the nearby horizon. Knowing she'd been caught, but too proud of her hard work to care, Marabela smirked.

"What's this?" Andres asked. He was the only one in the room who didn't know yet. When Marabela had sold the picture, she'd asked the editor to use a different name for the credit. Even so, word traveled fast in their industry, and despite their rivalry the paper's editors loved Elena. Marabela had been naive to think she wouldn't find out, or that Elena would waste time asking for an explanation—she brought it straight to Andres's parents the morning it was printed.

"It's terrifying, isn't it?" Lorena said, her eyes fixed on the photo. "You just never know where the threats are coming from anymore."

"What did you expect me to do?" Marabela said. "A picture like that, the chances of me being there in just that moment. It's a once-in-a-lifetime image and he refused to print it."

"It's my company. It's not your place to tell me how to run it or what to print," Rolando said.

The five of them argued for what seemed like hours, each attacking the other for being too entitled, for being too much of a coward, or for being too selfish. Andres chastised Marabela for her betrayal but defended her from the others' harsh words. Lorena called her ungrateful and sensationalist, while Elena only shook her head and asked, "What were you thinking?" Rolando was quiet until they were on their way out the door.

"I always knew you weren't good enough for this family. You've done nothing but tear us apart since you came into our lives."

For once, she was speechless, but Andres took her by surprise. "If that's how you really feel, then we won't bother coming back to try to change your mind," he said, and left.

In the car, Marabela reached for Andres's hand, but he pulled away from her and shook his head in disgust. "There are journalists getting killed out there and you'd rather spend your days among them than at home, with a family that loves you."

She could've called him on his hypocrisy, could've told him that he was never home, either, but she knew it wouldn't have mattered. He'd once fallen in love with her courageousness, and now his fear had betrayed them both. All he saw when he looked at her work was terror, but she knew her photography was more than that. The only way to find hope in these stories was to let them be told. "This is what I do, Andres. It's what I love. Don't ask me to stop just because you're afraid."

So he didn't, but he didn't have to. In the weeks that followed, Marabela failed to find work at another paper, even with the one that had printed her picture. Andres tried consoling her and even apologized for not realizing how much it all meant to her. When he promised her the darkroom, he said it was for her artistic freedom. She saw it only as a trick to lock away her passions, but years later, she learned how far he'd gone to turn the key.

It was five, maybe six months ago now. Marabela ran into the wife of *El Tribunal*'s rival publisher in the restroom of Andres's favorite restaurant. The women had always been acquaintances, but had recently crossed a line into friendship, confiding in each other their parenting frustrations, the occasional marital spat. Marabela was reapplying her lipstick when Lidia asked if she still took pictures.

"Only as a hobby," she said, squeezing a piece of facial tissue between her lips. "Why? You hiring?" Marabela meant it as a joke, but Lidia barely cracked a smile. "What's wrong?"

"You never found out, did you? Years ago, Andres told my husband he shouldn't hire you. He asked it as a personal favor, to all the big papers. I thought you should know."

It only made sense that Andres was behind it. She'd once suspected Rolando of jeopardizing her career; it was clear he'd never really wanted her on his staff. But only Andres would've wanted to keep her from working for any of the papers. She couldn't believe she'd been so blind.

Marabela tries to push the memories away. They are not the reason she came here, but every time she tries to think of something to say, it disappears beneath the baggage between her and Elena. She leans forward and whispers the only thing that feels right.

"I'm sorry, Ele." Her friend's old nickname slips past her tongue, surprising them both. Elena turns and looks her in the eyes. "It was wrong of me to step into your life like that; to take your place. I regret it. I think in the end it didn't work out as well as it could have for any of us."

Marabela tries to reach for Elena's hand, but she pulls away before they've even touched. It's not a strong motion—just a twitch, really, the kind of thing a person does when she's been startled by the pop of a balloon. There's no part of Elena's body that isn't tense with fear. Marabela wishes she could help her, but the only thing she has to give is a story she's never wanted to tell.

"I came to see you today because I realized we have more than we'd like in common now. I was kidnapped, just like you. Everything you went through . . . I know what it's like."

These words are like invisible knives stabbing into Elena, and she squirms as she starts crying out, yelling for her to stop. "No. No! You weren't there. You don't know how hard I tried. It wasn't my fault—they said they'd stop. They said they'd stop!"

Marabela's strength is no match for Elena's madness. Within seconds a nurse rushes into the room with a sedative, screaming for Marabela to help her hold Elena down, and as she kicks and flings her arms around, Marabela remembers the moments when her kidnappers first grabbed her. The thought of causing such terror to someone she once loved is too much for her. When the nurse finally injects the needle into Elena's pale skin, Marabela feels the life flowing out of her, too, every bit of fight suddenly exhausted.

❖ ❖ ❖

The driveway is empty, and Guillermo's car is missing from the curb. This surprises Andres. He can't imagine Marabela being alone in the house, but he doesn't know what would make her leave, either. When he walks in, he catches Ignacio running up the stairs, chasing after his little sister. His first reaction is to run after them, thinking they're in some sort of danger, but when he arrives at Cynthia's bedroom, they're just rolling around the floor, Cynthia laughing under Ignacio's tickling fingers.

"What's going on? Where are your mother and Guillermo?"

"They had to go out for a couple of hours," Ignacio says.

"He was supposed to watch you two."

"It's okay. We're fine."

Andres nods. "You're right." This moment feels almost normal, so long as he lets it be. "Well, I'll wait for them in my office."

He stops by the bedroom first for a change of clothes. As he unbuckles his belt and loosens his tie, Andres feels like he's coming undone; the things that used to hold him together no longer do. In his office, he finally opens the thick manila envelope that Edith sent home for him, and ends up tossing most of its contents in the trash.

It's odd to be back in this room that used to be the heart of his home. The display cases for his company souvenirs have a thin layer of dust covering the glass, so he carefully wipes them off with his sleeve. Andres is proud of what he accomplished, but it's all in the past now. He can't imagine what to expect at the paper tomorrow, but somehow it doesn't matter; he is about to do something with his life that he should have done long ago.

An hour passes before he hears the garage door open. Andres rushes to the stairs to see Marabela taking the steps two at a time, her head facing the ground. He's actually happy to see her so full of energy until they meet in the middle of the staircase.

"Where were you?"

Her eyes are bloodshot, her cheeks puffy and red. "I had to see her, Andres. I couldn't have her thinking I didn't care."

"Please don't tell me you mean Elena."

"Who else?"

He has to grip the handrail just to keep from losing his temper. "What happened?" he whispers.

She passes him and continues on to the bedroom. When they're both inside, Marabela reaches under the bed for her suitcase. Even though it's empty, she struggles with the bag's weight. Despite his horror, Andres offers to help.

She refuses. "This was all wrong from the beginning." Her voice is low and she's not looking at him, so he can't tell if she's talking to herself or to him.

"Please don't do this. Don't leave us."

She opens their closet and starts pulling out clothes, letting them pile up in the center of the suitcase. As the closet starts to empty, he sees the frame they had hung on the back wall, of the certificate of papal blessing for their marriage, and the white rosary next to it. It was meant to be a small display over the chest of drawers, but over the years an excess of shirts and sweaters obstructed the view. Marabela doesn't seem to notice it as she grabs and tosses several items onto the bed. When the pile finally tilts over, Andres bends down to pick up a pair of pants. They're his. It dawns on him that Marabela is packing for him.

"I'm not leaving," she explains. "I won't do that to the kids again. It's your turn now."

"What? No. There's no way."

"It's what you want. You may not admit it to yourself, especially now that you think I need you. But I don't. So you need to go." She waves her arm toward the window, as if he were a bird that needed to be shown the way out of a house he accidentally flew into.

But suddenly, he has no idea what he wants. He stands still and waits.

"You're free to go," she says, coaxing him. "It's something we both should have done a long time ago. I can't live like this anymore. Neither can you."

"Live like *what*?"

"We can't keep lying to each other."

"You said we'd try to start over. We agreed we'd try to pick up the pieces."

She scoffs. "What pieces? You keep acting like it's this big favor we got, the fact that my kidnapping tore us down to nothing. Can't you see what it really did? How it exposed all our weaknesses? We shouldn't *have* to start over. If we were stronger, we'd be picking up where we left off. But we have nothing left to stand on anymore. If this is what it took for us to realize this, then I refuse to ignore it. Even if you choose to."

The pants are still in his hand and he folds them several times over, setting the small package of fabric on the bed so he can smooth out the wrinkles with his palms. It helps calm him and gives him time to think.

"What about the kids? They finally have you back and now I leave?"

"It won't be the same as when I was gone. They'll know where you are; they know you'll be back to see them. We can talk to them together."

Nothing like when you left them the first time, he wants to say.

She sighs. "They'll be strong if we are."

"Do you feel strong?" It's a low blow, but she ignores the malice in his words and tries to answer the question.

"I don't know. I'm trying to be. Seeing Elena today, it made me realize I don't want to live another moment of regret, as much as it might scare me. You and I both know this is as far as we go." She sits next to him on the bed and places her hand on his knee, as if Andres were the weak one. This isn't the way things were supposed to go. It feels unnatural to have her try to comfort him when he should've been the one carrying them.

She stands up quickly and adds, "Don't worry about me. I'll figure things out on my own."

When she resumes packing, Andres reaches for her arm and nods, barely, in a silent plea for her to stop. She steps back and lets him take over. He arranges his belongings as he always does before a long trip: shoes with socks stuffed inside them to save space, pants rolled instead of folded to avoid wrinkles. When he's finished, the exhaustion of the past weeks, months, even years, finally catches up to him, and he feels he could sleep for days. Andres lifts his suitcase off the bed, but the room no longer belongs to him; it's not his place to rest here.

He gives Marabela a gentle kiss on the cheek. "Okay. We'll try this. If it's what you want. I'll call you from my mother's tomorrow. Maybe you can bring the kids over."

She offers to help him load the car and he lets her. In the garage, under the dim shadows of dusk, he sees that the muscles are slowly returning to her body, small but more defined than ever.

15

A UGUST IN THE city always brings a cold breeze at night, just enough to crack open the windows and sleep with the curtains dancing against the walls. On these quiet nights, Marabela lies in bed and imagines that life is different.

Tonight, she can see silhouettes melting into each other through the red curtains of the house behind hers. They are slow movements, and when the wind blows, the curtains lift up like fire and reveal glimpses of flesh pressing into flesh. She can't help herself: she watches the lovers' movements escalate; their gentle touches turn to desperate grasps. Their moans travel into her room, and Marabela closes her eyes, thinking of past winter nights. They were always the best nights to make love.

When it's over, she hears a light knock at the door. "Señora?"

She sits up and sees Guillermo standing outside her bedroom. She crosses her arms to cover herself, even though she is fully dressed.

"I hope this isn't a bad time. Andres hasn't called yet and I wondered if you knew when we could expect him home." His eyes travel away from her as he speaks, and she follows them, watches as they settle on the open window for just a second.

"It's fine. He's not coming home tonight. You're free to go if you'd like."

He nods and wishes her a good night. As he walks away she listens for the fading sound of his footsteps, but hears nothing. She tip-toes to her bedroom door and looks into the hall to see Guillermo unlacing his shoes and getting comfortable on the couch. When he catches her looking at him, he only pauses for a moment, then continues fluffing a green-and-yellow decorative pillow Marabela knows is far too stiff to sleep on.

"You don't have to do that," she says. "It's not just tonight that he's not coming back. I don't want you to feel like you have to keep staying."

He already has his eyes closed, his arms crossed over his chest. "Just until I'm needed, then." He leaves it at that.

Marabela starts to close the door but looks out one more time. The sight is strange to her; no one except she and Cynthia ever uses the living space upstairs, but it used to be her favorite part of the house. It gets the most sunlight through the windows that cover the entire length of a wall, and she used to dry her pictures here, images of villages and children and lives that no one paid much attention to at all.

She misses those pictures. She thinks about the ones left behind, still undeveloped, from her last roll of film. They've been waiting for her like a homeless person waits at a street corner, with a quiet longing that's difficult to ignore.

Back in her room, Marabela opens the nearly empty closet and pulls out the top drawer of her dresser, rummaging through socks and bras and underwear to uncover her camera. Andres used to say this was an odd place to keep it, but Marabela argued that she'd just as soon leave the house without her underwear as she would without her camera. She holds it in her hands and it feels heavier than she remembers, all the weight in the lens, tilting forward. The film inside is all used up, though she can't recall what she shot last. With her thumb and forefinger, Marabela turns the small knob at the top of the camera, winding the film back into its case. She feels the faint, familiar click as it turns under her thumb, and when she's sure that no exposed film is left, she pops open the camera and tips it over, letting the roll fall into her hand. It fits perfectly in her palm, blanketed by the curl of her fingers.

A roll with twenty-four exposures might contain just four or five images worth developing; if you're lucky, maybe one or two will be worth keeping. There are shots the photographer knows will be spectacular the instant she hears the click of the camera, and because of this, developing the film becomes a rushed, impatient thing, like unwrapping a gift when its contents are already known. Other images are complete surprises. Their beauty is not obvious in the moment or through the lens; it hovers beneath the fluid's surface and reveals itself slowly, like the fog of breath against a windowpane.

Marabela clutches the roll of film in her hand and wonders what moments it holds, weighing her curiosity against her fear. No other lights are on in the house, and the room will give her complete darkness if she can take it. Unlike developing a photograph, which can be done under the warm tint of the safelight, developing film to create a negative is a delicate, precious thing. It requires complete absence of light; the kind of darkness Marabela's eyes never adjust to.

She takes small, quiet steps as she crosses the hall into the darkroom, leaving the door ajar to let the moonlight in. The room is just as she left it, just as Guillermo promised it would be. From a small cabinet over the developer trays, she pulls out a stainless steel reel, a cylindrical tank the size of a small soup container, and a half gallon of developer fluid. The reel looks like two round coils set apart by a few one-inch bars in the center, and it's about as wide as her hand. She sets all three items on a small table in the corner of the room, taking a moment to commit to memory where everything is arranged.

All that's left now is the door. Marabela steps back toward it, clutching the roll in one hand and the doorknob in the other. She twists the doorknob, but doesn't pull. She lets it turn back into place and tries again. With one deep breath, she closes her eyes and gently shuts the door.

When she opens her eyes, she can't be completely sure she's done so. She blinks several times, hard enough to feel her lashes press together, but she's overcome by a disturbing sensation that her sight's been robbed, that her eyes no longer function, and the wider she opens them, the more the blackness swallows her. The dark is unforgiving. This is how it looks when she closes her eyes and remembers the kidnapping. Her breath accelerates and her heart pounds, and her fingers tremble as they feel around, wanting answers but afraid to find them.

Marabela's hand still clutches the doorknob, her only connection to a physical sense of self. She wants to turn it back and push it open with the full weight of her body, but instead, she waits. She lets the darkness and fear wash over her, and for a moment it feels like she could drown in them. Her breath quickens uncontrollably until it's all she can hear. The air rushes in and out of her, the sound of her body clenching and expanding, steady and impatient as her heart.

I'm home, she thinks. She tries to let the full meaning of the words sink in. The past can be nothing if she'll let it be, if she simply lets it slip from her fingers. But then what else would she lose with it? Life is a fluid mix of all the things she's been through, and she's not ready to throw out the good with the bad. She thinks of Ignacio and Cynthia sleeping through this night, remembers the sour sweetness of their breath when they would wake her, gasping for her milk as newborns. She thinks of the birth and death of her marriage, hopes that she'll look back one day to find the happiest memories outlived the rest. She imagines new moments unspooling before her as she pulls the strip of film from its case, small pieces of life before the kidnapping that she managed to freeze in time. They will be a gift, she thinks, proof that life existed before this. She steps away from the door and begins to feel her way through the dark.

❖ ❖ ❖

Andres waits for Elena to wake up, wonders what kind of dreams she has, if any. Every few seconds, her left hand twitches, and two of her fingers flinch as if they're being pulled by invisible strings. For the first time in years, he studies her hands: nails so short that the skin of her fingertips seems to have grown over them; cuticles with tiny beads of dried blood along the edges from her biting them. They were once smooth and graceful, with nails so long Andres teased that she could paint a mural on them.

He's been hesitant to touch Elena, but now, without thinking, he picks up her hand and starts kissing each finger. First the nails, then the knuckles. His lips make their way over her bandaged wrists, soft as air.

It was in this way that his lips first came to touch her, back when they were only teenagers. Elena had given herself a paper cut while opening a piece of Andres's mail, an acceptance letter from the university. He'd asked her to open it, thinking that whether it was good or bad news, it'd be better coming from her. Seeing the paper in her hands made it less intimidating. The moment became small and intimate; this wasn't his future or his life, it was just he and Elena, learning something new together. When she hissed from the sudden sting and brought her finger to her mouth, he pulled it away from her and kissed it. It was meant to be innocent, but the flutter of Elena's lashes—the way she nearly blinked but opened her eyes wide again, as if everything before her had disappeared from her vision for that one millisecond—gave her away and changed everything. No longer could they pretend they were just friends.

But they weren't lovers, either.

He never understood until now that being someone's lover requires longing, a painful wait that turns small moments into several eternities. Since they'd never felt the threat of losing each other, they'd never known the pleasure of needing each other. He sees now what brought him here during those early-morning drives. He finally recognizes what his concern for Elena was disguising. Not nostalgia, or guilt, or even consolation that Marabela would be all right so long as Elena was. What brought him here, stumbling, weak, and dizzy from the loss of everything he'd built his life around, was the need for orientation. Every day they've spent apart, every year he shared with Marabela, and every moment he received with his children was a gift with a hidden purpose. He needed to lose Elena to long for her.

He kisses her now, again and again, until she finally stirs. Even with her eyes still closed Elena smiles, recognizing his touch, and because he doesn't want to ask anything else of her but to listen, Andres begins to speak. "You've always been too good to me. The first time I came to see you, I was so afraid you'd be angry that I hadn't come sooner, and you welcomed me as if I'd never left."

Elena opens her eyes and smiles. The sadness he's come to recognize has started to fade. "I'd been angry for so long, but when I saw you it didn't matter. I didn't understand it at the time, but all I felt was calm. Like this was how it had to be."

"Because I had to be ready?"

"Because we both did," she says.

"I think I've always needed you."

She shrugs, her movements lazy and quiet. "Maybe we didn't know it at the time."

He remembers a game they used to play as children. "Remember *gallinita ciega*?" Elena would blindfold him, and spin and spin him until he got so dizzy it was as if the world were falling away from his feet. In this state Andres was tasked with tagging her.

"You always wanted me to spin you more," she says.

"I liked the chaos more than the search." Now, he is so tired of spinning. "I got so dizzy I could never find you. And that was the whole point of the game."

"The point was to have fun. We just had different ideas of how to do that."

Elena turns to him and Andres marvels at how she can bring him so much calm even when she's the one who's hurt.

"And now?" he says.

"I saw Marabela. She apologized."

"She's moving on, Elena. I think she's doing it for us just as much as for herself. You've helped in ways you'll never know, and she's getting stronger every day. But she wants to do it on her own. Without me. She thinks our lives have been going in different directions for some time now. After everything that's happened, I can't help but agree."

Elena takes this all in and chuckles.

"What?"

"Look at us, all shuffled together like a deck of cards, trying to pick up where we left off. It's crazy."

"We're all a little crazy," Andres says, bringing his hand to her face. When he does, she takes it and kisses his fingers, just like he did minutes ago. He smiles because he remembers what it was like to not be ready for this, to fear it. The feeling rushes back to him because it is the flip side of the same coin. Now that they're together again, he's not sure they're ready to love each other, but the longing is there, waiting for them both to uncover it.

He helps her up and kisses her on the neck, on the only small piece of skin that isn't hidden beneath her hair. She closes her eyes and tilts her head to the side, exposing herself just a little more, trusting him with the most vulnerable part of her, her pulse beating beneath his lips.

Acknowledgments

I'm never shorter on words, never more humbled, than when I think of those who helped make this book possible. If you're reading this, thank you—know that my gratitude runs deeper than pen on paper and that I'll carry it with me always.

Endless thanks to my agent, Brandi Bowles, for her tireless belief in my work. I don't know how you do all you do, but I can always trust that you will. To my editors at Amazon, Katie Salisbury, for being a source of calm reassurance along this incredible journey, and to Liz Egan, for having faith in this story and making it become a book. Your enthusiasm and support are the stuff all writers dream of. My deepest gratitude to all who contributed their talents and hard work to this book: Jenny Carrow, Nancy Tan, and Phyllis DeBlanche.

Over the years I've been lucky to have found not one but three writing groups that prove our craft is far from a lonely endeavor. Thank you to Roxanna Elden, Gariot P. Louima, Nicole Tallman, and Jackie Taylor for reading draft after draft of my work, for the honor of reading yours, and for your continued support even after I moved. To Terence Cantarella, A. J. Hug, and Nadine Seide Gonzalez: I often think of our regular meetings at MDC and it warms my heart. And finally, to Demery Bader-Saye, Everlee Cotnam, Kate Cotnam, and Barbara Sparrow, who've read and helped shape this and other books before it. Your feedback has always been invaluable, but what I treasure most is the friendship we discovered along the way.

A special thank-you to the Florida Center for the Literary Arts and the Writers' League of Texas for their incredible resources and guidance. Much gratitude also to Richard P. Wright for your time and expertise.

I'd like to thank all the teachers and mentors who've made a difference in my life. Amy Scott, you may not remember (though I'll never forget) that you once told a shy ninth grader to never, ever stop writing. To Susan O'Connor, for always reminding me that there's a story behind every story. To M. Evelina Galang, who helped nurture the first seeds of this story when I was a senior at the University of Miami, and who once told me, "If you're gonna go there, go there." To Jacqueline Sousa, who gave me my first yes in a sea of nos when I started submitting my work to magazines.

Thank you to countless Twitter friends and bloggers whose encouragement and support inspire me daily (you know who you are). We've shared e-mails, phone calls, letters, inside jokes, family pictures, meals, hardships, and triumphs. If that's not true friendship, I don't know what is.

I have a big, beautiful family that's filled my life with more love, strength, and happiness than I could ever describe. To my cousins, aunts, uncles, *nonnos, abuelitos, tíos,* and *tías*: I could write a book about the adventures and life lessons you've taught me, and I suspect in many ways, I always will be writing it. Thank you (those words fall so short) to my parents. Ceci, when I struggle to find strength—in myself, my writing, my characters—I look to you. There are pieces of you in all I do. Ramon, ever since I was little you've always had a book in your hand and words to make me smile. Thank you for inspiring my love of reading, for sharing part of our family's story with me, and, most important, for trusting me with it. To *Abuelito,* for your bravery, and *Abuelita,* for your quiet strength through it all. *Mi tío* Juan Carlos, who walked me through the *Yuyanapaq: Para Recordar* exhibit in Lima in 2003. The images and your retelling of those years will forever stay with me.

To my older sister, Ursula: I love you not just because we come from the same place, but because you're always at my side no matter where I go. Thank you for always making me feel loved, protected, and like there was nothing I couldn't do. To my precious nieces, Sofia and Olivia: your life has helped me grow. To my *primas hermanas*: Franca, because every conversation we have changes me in some way, and Flavia, for helping me see things in myself I didn't know were there.

My deepest gratitude to Nadine Ferranti, for saying hi to the new girl and being proof that neither time nor distance matters in the face of true friendship. Daniel Chor, for being the kind of friend who pushes you to be a better person but stays by your side even when you're not. Maggie and Pita (yes, you!), for the simple joy you bring to each and every day.

Thank you to my in-laws, Odalis Sylvester, Rey Sylvester, and Kathleen Sylvester, for treating me like family since day one and for your unwavering support as Eric and I dreamed the dreams of our lives.

And finally, always, Eric. Moments with you take my words away and bring them back with new meaning. Thank you for every kiss good night and every kiss good morning. It all starts and ends with you.

About the Author

Born in Lima, Peru, Natalia Sylvester came to the U.S. at age four and grew up in South Florida, where she received a B.A. in creative writing from the University of Miami. A former magazine editor, she now works as a freelance journalist and copywriter. Her work has appeared in *Latina*, *Writer's Digest*, and *The Writer* and on NBCLatino .com. She lives in Austin, Texas, with her husband and their two rescue dogs.